DON'T CROSS THE X

TINA LEPERE

For the descendants of John Pierce and Janie Herndon

No one said life was fair.
But did it have to be so cruel?

Chapter 1

June 22, 2001

Black eyes with red slits down the center stare at me. Bugs scurry out of the gray, matted hair and down the puckered, crackled face that belong to those villainous eyes. Tight, splintered lips turn up and display tawny, rotten teeth. The mouth opens, dispensing the scent of burning flesh. "Pearl, it's time—"

My eyes spring open, but my mind is empty, unoccupied by any thought of remembrance. Why is my heart beating so fast? With a trembling hand, I cover my heart until it slows to a dawdling pace. I lift my head and search for the red numbers, which reads *10:28.* "Is that all?" I drop my head back on the soft pillow and close my eyes.

Is it true your life flashes before your eyes right before you die?

What if you can't remember that life?

Tap, tap, tap.

I open my eyes.

The door opens, letting in a hint of light from the hallway into my dimly lit room. "Are you awake, Mrs. Pearl?" a soft, feminine voice I don't recognize whispers through the crack.

I heave a sigh. "Yes, come in." I brace my hands underneath myself and push up, but my elbows buckle and slide back to my sides, making my back hit the mattress. My eyelids flicker when tears swell behind them, and I wipe at them quickly with my quivering hand.

The woman with the soft voice strolls in, closing the door behind her, and goes straight to the only window in my small room. She edges open the darkening curtains, letting a trace of sunshine seep through the cracks of the blinds.

"Okay?" she asks, glancing over her shoulder.

When my eyes adjust to the faint light, I nod.

She flings the curtains the rest of the way open, filling the room with daylight. She turns around and gives me a soft smile as she walks to the light switch and flips it on, making the room come to life.

Without taking my eyes off the woman in the light pink scrubs, I feel around on the bedside table until I find the ceramic bowl. I grab my teeth, clanging them against the rim and shaking off the excess water, before popping them into place with ease.

The woman standing in front of me slowly fades away, and Mary appears. My breath gets caught in my throat, and my praying hands cover my opened mouth. "Mary, is that you?"

She laughs. "Yes, Mrs. Pearl. It's me."

I tilt my head as my eyes scan her. "You're different. Did you cut your hair?"

Her eyes light up. "Oh, Mrs. Pearl, you noticed. Yes, I did, and colored it." She runs her hands down the burgundy bob and pushes up on the ends. "Do you like it?"

"Yes," I mutter, peeking at the red flashing numbers on the clock. "It's lovely." I look away from the clock and back at her. "You're late."

"Uh-huh, it took longer than I thought. I'm sorry I'm late."

"Oh, it's all right. The big one took care of me just fine."

She lifts a brow. "You mean Debra."

I look at my hands, now knotting the blanket. "Yes, that's what I said. She brought me breakfast. Burned oatmeal." I pause, twisting my lips. "No, no—it was runny eggs and flat pancakes." I beam. "Yes, that was it."

She sighs. "I'm sure it wasn't that bad. Do you need your bed pan?"

"Yes, it was, and no, I'm fine," I grumble. God, I miss the days when I could pee on my own, or do other things that are too embarrassing to share with others. It's not fun getting old.

Her hands find her hips and she taps her foot. "What year is it?"

My eyes fix on the veins under my thin skin covering my hands as they straighten the cluster of pleats of the blanket. "Doesn't matter."

"It's 2001, Mrs. Pearl."

"Already? Time sure flies when you're having fun." I smirk.

"Mm-hmm." She rewards me with a crooked smile and walks to the closet. "Who's the president?"

I roll my eyes. "Don't care." I put my arms underneath myself and push up, but fall back for the second time. Or is it the third?

She shakes her head while pulling open the shuttered bi-fold doors. "Don't be like that, Mrs. Pearl." She claps her hands together. "Now, let's get you dressed!" she says, disappearing into the closet and emerging with a purple dress, fanning it against her body. "How's this one? I like this one."

I shrug and look away. "Sure," I mumble and push up. At last I get into a sitting position, feeling elated. Arching my stiff back, I hear *crack, crack,* and I wince. *Urgh.* My back aches all the time. Not slightly, God no, it hurts like the devil's inside me, pulling my spine apart. Some game he's playing, and by George if he isn't winning! But I guess that's an unpleasant part of getting old, one of many. When you get to be my age—well, whatever age that may be—the aches follow you from the time you wake to the time you fall asleep, and then after.

I throw the blanket off my legs and swing my feet off the side of the bed, dangling above the tile floor. I take a deep breath before I stand on rickety legs and flap my arms as I wobble.

Mary's at my side in an instant. "Oh, Mrs. Pearl, let me help you." She grabs my waist, but I fall back on the bed and take her with me.

She regains her balance and straightens. "We'll need your wheelchair, Mrs. Pearl. Your legs don't want to cooperate today, do they?" A small, sad smile creeps over her face.

"I'll just take a nap." I grab the old, worn-out red-and-white flannel shirt I like to snuggle with and lay my head back on the pillow, but she grabs my arms and pulls me back into an upright position.

"Oh, no you don't! You just woke up from your nap. We need to get you dressed for your party."

Before I can protest, she lifts the silk gown over my head, tosses it in the hamper, and replaces it with the muumuu.

"What party?"

She grabs my hairbrush from the dresser. "Your birthday party."

I look at the floor and scratch my head. "It's my birthday? Today?"

"Well, no, it's tomorrow, but it's the only day your family could come." She runs the brush through my tousled, thinning white hair.

I look back at her as my head bobs to the side with each yank of the brush. "My family?"

"Yes, your great-granddaughter, Meredith, was here last month and…"

My eyes drop to the floor as Mary's voice fades. I remember having a daughter at one time, but I don't remember her name. It's at the tip of my tongue, and it's so frustrating that I can't reach it. What *is* her name? I rub a finger along the rivers on my forehead. I had boys—two, maybe three—but I can't recall their names either. A feeling of desperate suffocation starts in the middle of my aching back, crawling forward slowly to envelop my wheezing chest.

Why can't I remember their names?

I clutch the flannel shirt tightly, frantically, and notice it's missing a few buttons and is frayed and tattered at the edges. I hold it to my nose and take a deep breath. The sweet vanilla-and-cherry scent I loved is no longer there. Where did it go?

"…that family is super rich." Mary huffs, waves the brush in the air, and drops it on the dresser. "Meredith wanted for nothing, I can tell you that," she says as she steps toward the wheelchair sitting in the corner and bends at the waist, releasing the brakes.

"What?"

She straightens, grips the handles with tight fists, and glimpses at the ceiling. "Oh, never mind," she says on an exhale before pushing the chair toward me.

"Where are we going?" I ask as she hoists me up and quickly helps me slide into the seat.

She sighs. "To your party. I just told you, remember?"

I shake my head, my face burning with frustration. "I don't want a party."

She grabs my thick glasses from the nightstand and puts them over my eyes before placing the multi-colored afghan from off the end of the bed around my legs. "It's your hundred and fifth tomorrow. You're the oldest here at the home, maybe even the whole state of South Carolina. Don't worry, it's just your family. But…" She beams, her eyes sparkle with excitement, and she bites her bottom lip. "*Live 5 News* and *The Post and Courier* want to do a news piece on you. You can be on television! Isn't that great?"

I wave her off. "Oh, I have nothing worth talking about."

"Well, you can think about it. It sounds like fun." She opens the door, pushing down on the stopper with the thick sole of her soft leather clog. "Let's go to your party." She wheels me out the door and kicks the stopper, releasing it. The door closes behind us with a soft click.

"All right, let's get this over with," I say with spite not directed at Mary. I want to get this over with—*this entire miserable life over with.*

We pass by doors with colorful drawings attached to them: big black trains with red cabooses, stick figures under blazing yellow suns, and farm animals in front of bright red barns. Most aren't even colored in the lines. They're dangling their family in front of my face like a slice of sweet, sticky pecan pie. They're taunting me. *We have family, and youuu don't!* A heated wave crashes into my heart when a pang of jealousy comes out of nowhere. It's an emotion I'm not used to, and I hate it. Others here are lucky to have a family who visits them often. My door has sat unadorned since the day I arrived, and it will be that way until I leave in the back of the coroner's van. No, I don't want the pie—they can keep it.

The aroma of turkey and gravy, macaroni and cheese, and green-bean casserole wafts through the cafeteria when we enter. A dozen round tables fill the open room, occupied by residents chatting with their relatives. It's all the same. *"How are you today, Papa? You look great, Granny! Oh, my bunions are killing me."* Blah, blah, blah.

My eyes roam amidst my bitterness, stopping on a young woman with a little girl sitting at a table near the wall of windows overlooking the backyard, staring in my direction. The woman whispers in the little girl's ear before they both stand.

This must be my family.

Mary pushes me forward, stopping at the table with a small store-bought cake that doesn't look edible enough to eat, but I'll never complain…out loud.

A flash of red catches my eye. I turn my head and see the woman's cherry nail polish melt from her fingertips. I glance around, but everyone else is greeting one another with pleasantries. I rub my eyes behind my glasses before looking back at the dripping polish and leaning in. No, it's not polish—it's blood!

It trickles from her nails, making ten tiny puddles on the floor. The sound amplifies like water dripping into a cave's pool. *Plop. Plop. Plop.* She must've chopped off her fingertips with the cake knife. But I get a glimpse of the knife blade—clean—on the table. When I look back at her nails, the blood is dry and turned back into the God-awful red polish. I shudder and rub my eyes again. They're playing tricks on me. God, I hope I'm not hallucinating, but I'm afraid that's what has happened. What kind of pills did that big woman give me this morning?

"You're shivering; let me close the vent. It's a hot one today, and they have the air cranked up." Mary slides a chair under the ceiling vent. "That's Southern heat for you."

I slouch. "No, I'm fine, Mary," I say before she has a chance to

6

step onto the chair.

"You sure? It's not a problem."

"I'm fine," I repeat. I don't want her thinking I'm going crazy on top of my forgetfulness.

"Okay." Mary looks at her watch. "Do you want your lunch?"

I shake my head and look at the white fluff in the pink cardboard box next to the *clean* knife. "No." I swallow; my throat feeling like it's coated in sand. "I'll just have cake."

I watch the woman's cherry nails land on my shoulder as she bends and kisses my cheek. "Happy birthday, Nana," she says into my ear before straightening.

"This is your great-granddaughter Meredith," Mary say.

I shoo her away with my hand. "I know, I know. I remember," I snap.

Meredith's fancy black dress, which is hanging from her scrawny body, makes it appear as if she's on her way to a funeral. By the looks of her sickly thin figure and pale complexion, I'd say it's her own.

She tosses her long, brown hair over her shoulder, showing off an enormous diamond ring, among others, and several thick gold necklaces wrapped around her tiny neck. More diamonds decorate her ears. Are they sure I'm related to this woman?

I turn to the cute, little brown-haired, blue-eyed girl, and my mind surges with perplexity. My breath hitches, and my back straightens. "Angela?"

"This is Sara—"

Oh. I slouch again.

"—your great-great-granddaughter, Nana," Meredith screeches.

"I'm not deaf," I say, cringing, and swat my ear.

Meredith pushes the timid girl closer—her flip-flops shuffle across the tile while her hand fists the skirt of her pale yellow dress.

She lets go of her dress, and I take her small hand in mine. "You remind me of someone I knew a long time ago." *Angela.* I smile, feeling rejuvenated by remembering her name. *Angela.*

She drops her eyes and grins as her pale cheeks turn the color of a pink rose and expands over her freckled nose.

"Here, let me have that." Mary takes a blue balloon that reads *HAPPY BIRTHDAY* from Sara's other hand and ties it to the arm of my wheelchair.

Sara gives me a gentle hug as if afraid I'll break. "Happy birthday, Nana," she says, her voice small and apprehensive.

"Thank you, sweetheart," I say, smiling at her when she releases me. "How old are you?"

"I'm eleven, almost twelve."

"That's a good age," I say, turning away and glancing around the room at all the unfamiliar faces involved in trivial conversations. Meredith is sitting on the sofa, alone, watching us, chewing a piece of gum with her arms folded, and rapidly bouncing her leg over her knee. I look back at Sara. "Where's your father?"

Sara's face drops as she puts her hands behind her back and twists back and forth. "He died in a car accident a long time ago."

"Oh, dear. I'm sorry," I say to her as Mary hands me a piece of cake. "Thank you, Mary.

"You're welcome," Mary says.

I pick up the plastic fork with shaky hands and shove the cake into my mouth, swallowing the dry morsel with a gulp. My taste buds don't care it's my birthday. But I don't want to hurt Meredith's feelings, so I nod my approval of the *delicious* flavor to her and eat it without complaining. She shakes her head when Mary offers her a piece.

"Are you nervous, Nana?" Sara asks.

I turn my attention back to the little girl in front of me. "No, sweetheart"—I chuckle—"I'm not nervous; I shake sometimes. It's a part of getting old. When you get to be my age, you'll do things you can't control. It's life."

"How old are you?"

I stare at her. How old am I? Mary told me earlier…

After a moment, Mary answers, "She'll be one hundred and five tomorrow." She places a hand on my shoulder. "I'll leave you to your party, Mrs. Pearl. Will you be all right?"

I pat her hand. "You go. I'll be fine."

"Okay, I'll come back and check on you later," Mary says and walks away.

Sara stands beside my wheelchair, gawking at me.

"What, sweetheart? What's on your mind?" I ask.

She scrunches her nose. "You're old."

"Sara!" Meredith shouts, and Sara jumps. "That's not nice; you can't say things like that."

I narrow my eyes at Meredith. "Why not? I am old, and I'm not ashamed of it."

"But—" Meredith starts as loud music shrieks from her direction.

I grab the chair's arms and recoil away from the sound. "Good lord, what is that awful noise?"

Meredith digs around in her huge black purse and pulls out a little silver gadget. She flips it open, silencing it. "Hold on, Scott," she speaks into it before pulling it away from her ear and standing. "I've got to take this." She turns to Sara. "Will you be okay here with Nana?"

"She'll be fine." I flick my hand at Meredith. "Go, so Sara and I can get acquainted."

Without saying another word, Meredith marches down the hall, already speaking into the small telephone. Her voice fades when she disappears, and I shake my head.

Sara's arms wrap around her midsection tightly and she drops her chin to her chest, as if she were trying to hide the enormous frown on her face.

I pull out one of the plastic folding chairs sitting around the table and pat the seat. "Come sit next to me."

She plops down, heaving a great sigh, before she picks up the fork in front of her and stabs lumps of spongy yellow and creamy white, spreading it across the paper plate.

"What's troubling you, sweetheart?"

Sara drops the fork on the plate, forgetting the cake massacre, and pulls a necklace from under her dress. She slides the object attached to the chain back and forth across her chin and narrows her eyes as she looks at the floor. "She's *always* talking to her boyfriend on her cell phone," she says and tightens her lips.

I nod at the necklace. "What do you have there?"

She stops, lifts her chin, and holds it toward me. "It was Grandma Lillian's. I never met her. My mom gave it to me." Her weary eyes glance at the empty hall before returning them back to me. "She gives me presents, but she never spends time with me. She—"

I lean forward as my eyes fix on the X-shaped diamond pendant and all the sound around me disappears. I reach for it, not able to look away, and the moment my fingers touch it, my body turns cold, pins and needles shoot down my spine, and a burning pain sears my fingertips. I quickly drop the ornament and shrink back in my chair. My unfocused eyes clear and all my forgotten memories rush back all at once like two steam trains colliding in my brain. I remember Lillian and Meredith. I remember Angela, my boys, and Pierce. I remember Hazel and her X—her godforsaken X. Hot bile threatens to come up in my throat, and I grind my teeth behind tight lips. Everything she did to me throughout the years sickens me.

I remember it all.

I take a deep breath before focusing on the amazing blue eyes glued to mine. "Your mom loves you," I say with clarity. "People today are too busy for what's truly important. Things were different when I was growing up. We were poor, we didn't have a lot." I look at the empty hallway where Meredith disappeared and flick my wrist. "It was a time before they had portable telephones. We talked to each other. We told stories." I look back at Sara. "Would you like to hear a story?"

Her back straightens. "Yes, ma'am."

"Have you heard of a witch named Hazel Sullivan?"

Her eyes bulge, almost popping out of their sockets, and she sucks in a lungful of air. "You mean a *real,* live witch, Nana?"

"Yes, dear, a *real,* live witch. She wasn't like the witches from fairy tales or movies you see today. You know, the ones with big noses, who wear the pointy black hats, and ride on brooms? No, she was none of those things. I lived next to Hazel for five years." I hold up an outstretched hand. "The first time I met her was the summer of 1919, and it was the worst summer of my life."

I shake my head and gaze at the tall glass windows overlooking the back patio. I can't believe it was so long ago.

I look back into Sara's eyes, which are dancing with attentiveness. "I wish I would've never met her, but by accident I did. That summer haunted me throughout my entire life."

Chapter 2

March 21, 1914

I don't like the brown-haired, blue-eyed girl watching me; never have. She looks too young and naïve for her seventeen years. And why does she have those specks of brown dotting the bridge of her nose? Why can't she be pretty like her sisters?

I lean forward, almost touching the mirror with my forehead, and rub the light-brown constellation with my finger, but it won't come off. I can't count the many times I've tried to rub, scratch, wipe, and scrub the little specks until my nose turned bright red, but they're stuck for good. No getting rid of them; at least I only have a handful of them.

I straighten and bite the inside of my cheek, giving the girl in the mirror one more hard glare when she touches the white ribbons holding her braids together. "It'll just have to do," I mutter. With a sigh, I walk out of the room I share with my three sisters.

Thomas and Samuel's pallet is lying in the middle of the living-room floor. I shake my head and pick up the blankets, fold them, and drop them in the corner. It's the least I can do since I'll be at the auction with Daddy while my siblings are working on the farm all day. They're already out in the field, throwing seeds in holes and covering them back up again.

I'm the lucky one.

Mama's pouring a bucket of well water into the sink, getting ready to clean the breakfast dishes, when she hears me and turns. She sets the bucket on the counter and wipes her wet hands on the flour-coated apron tied around her baby bump. "Now remember, one pig, that's it. Don't let your father buy nothin' else. You hear me?"

"Yes, ma'am."

She straightens my collar and touches my braids. "Why do you wear your hair like this? It makes you look younger than you are. With your height, you don't need any help with that."

My eyes drop to the floor and my lips chase after them. "I like it this way," I mumble and run my hands down the front of my white dress.

I only have a few dresses: a blue Sunday dress, a black work dress, and a white school dress. We're poor, so we sew our own dresses, but with four girls, buying fabric is expensive. Even though I'm the oldest, at only five feet, my sisters are taller than me. They're able to share their dresses, but I can't wear theirs. I'm stuck with the same three.

She lifts my chin. "If you make sure your father buys only one pig and nothin' else, I may have enough money to buy another piece of fabric, so you can make a new dress," she whispers, wiping dust off my shoulder.

I grin. "I sure would like a new dress."

Our heads whip toward the back door when it opens. "Ready, Pearl? Let's go git us some animals," Daddy says, and then he's gone, leaving the door open.

My grin fades, and I turn back to Mama. She raises a brow and folds her arms over her chest.

"I'll watch him. Only one pig," I say before stepping out the door, knowing good and well I can't promise that. Daddy's the man of the house, and he does what he wants.

The auction is across town, and it takes almost two hours to get there traveling by horse and wagon, but it beats working in the fields all day.

Ahoohga! A shiny black roadster with its top down screams by, kicking up dirt in its wake. I cough and wave my hand in front of my face. The woman's blond hair flies in the wind, and the couple's laughter is heard over the roar of the engine.

"It would be nice to have one of those," I say.

Daddy's quiet as he stares at the road ahead.

My eyes widen, and I point to the metal plate on the back, which reads *1913-258-GEORGIA*. "Does that mean they're from Georgia?" I ask with excitement.

He turns his head to the side. *Ptuh.* Brown sludge flies out his mouth and onto the passing road, leaving some behind on his lips. He wipes it off with his sleeve. "I reckon."

"Oh, it would be nice to visit there one day, wouldn't it?" I ask, doing my best not to grimace.

Daddy leans away from me, and his forehead wrinkles as he gawks at me. "How the *hell* am I supposed to know? I ain't never left the state of South Carolina, and I ain't plannin' on it neither." He shakes his head and turns back forward. "I got everythin' I need right here."

I look down at my hands, scraping under my fingernails. "Mama's expecting you to bring back only one pig and nothing else," I mumble without looking up.

"We'll see," he says and spits again. *Ptuh.*

I roll my eyes, but I look in the opposite direction before I do. If he catches me rolling my eyes at him, he'd whup me for sure. I can hear it now: *"You're not too old to pick a switch. I'll learn you a thing or two."* I've picked my share. Picking the wrong switch only gets you more licks. He likes the skinny ones, the ones that leave the sting a little longer than the others. I love Daddy, but he's a strict man; he doesn't tolerate disrespect.

We arrive at the auction near the edge of a deserted cotton field. The rows and rows of green plants are missing their little balls of clouds, not ready to be harvested yet. Empty wagons line the front of a rickety wooden fence that looks like it'll fall if the wind blows too hard. Trucks with metal cages filled with animals waiting to be sold are parked around the back of the old weathered barn set up for the auction.

We stop at a vacant spot, and Daddy pulls the brake on the side of the wagon. "Dagnabbit," he mutters as he jumps out, quickly ties the horse to a post, and hurries away, following the droves of men already heading toward the barn.

I sigh, climb down, and follow him inside.

When I get inside, my hand flies to my nose, pinching it. My eyes burn, and my mouth thickens with saliva. Without a breeze, the stench from animal droppings and body odor loiters in the air, making my stomach churn. I drop my hand to my side and take a few short breaths through my mouth, so I don't embarrass myself or Daddy. He wouldn't be happy.

Sunlight casts through the opened doors and the distorted wooden planks on the roof and walls, making it bright enough to see in here. With no chairs to sit on, other than a few bales of hay around the edges and hayloft, it's standing room only.

A group of men stand near the door collecting their numbers, but Daddy isn't among them. I step up on one of the hay bales and stand on tippy toes. I look over wide-brim hats and balding heads and find him near the front of the crowd, so I hop down.

"Excuse me," I say, squeezing through a cluster of hard shoulders and bony elbows. The heavy scent of sweaty armpits and stale cigars assaults my nose. *Blech.* I hold my breath and move faster.

"Watch it!" one man snarls.

"Where you off to, li'l lady?" another asks, banter in his voice.

"You can stand by me, darlin'," a third says lecherously.

I gasp and jump when a hand grabs my bottom. Too mortified to look back, I swat it away and keep moving.

When I get to Daddy, he's staring at the empty circle framed by men, waiting for the auctioneer. His hand twitches, whipping the lucky number fourteen card attached to a stick against the side of his leg, without looking in my direction.

I look through the smoke from cigarettes, cigars, and pipes, and notice I'm the only woman here. Old men, stroking their long gray beards with grimy hands and wearing filthy coveralls, pack the room. Some glower at me. Others stare at me with lustful eyes, grinning, showing more missing teeth than not. I scoot closer to Daddy and run my hands along the front of my white dress, feeling a bit overdressed. I should've worn the black one.

"One dollar, one dollar, one dollar, now two. Who'll give me two dollar, two dollar—"

The auctioneer grabs my attention when he begins his call. His rhythmic monotone chant is mesmerizing to watch, but my eyes keep wandering back to the number fourteen beside me going up with each bid. A bid that's not on a pig! Every time it goes up, my stomach shifts.

I drop my head with a frown and pinch the orange flowers on my dress, torturing them between two fingers. I really wanted a new dress.

"Four dollar, four dollar, four—"

Up it goes.

"Daddy," I whisper.

Up it goes…again.

My bottom lip disappears behind my teeth, fighting back the urge to repeat myself. I can't let him get mad at me for interrupting. He'll just have to deal with Mama when we get home. I stay silent for the rest of the auction and let him do what he wants to do. He'll do it anyway without my blessing—that's for sure.

XXX

I shake my head and cross my arms over my chest as I watch Daddy guide two pigs up the plank. "Mama won't like this."

Ptuh. "Don't care. My money, my *bizness.*" He slams the wooden slat in place, closing the pigs in, and picks up the chicken crate with four chickens and places it in the back of the wagon.

My shoulders slouch and when I turn, the world fades away and the only person left is a tall, lean, rugged man in Levi's stalking this way. His red-and-white flannel shirt is rolled up at the elbows, showing off his tanned muscular arms. His intense brown eyes are focused, and his strides are long and vigorous as he walks toward Daddy with his hands tapping the sides of his long legs with each step. He rakes a hand through his already ruffled nut-brown hair like it isn't the first time he's done so today.

My heart flutters while butterflies take flight in my stomach, and I realize my mouth is hanging open. I close my mouth and touch my stomach, but the darn butterflies won't land. My knees weaken, so I grab ahold of the wagon with my sweaty palms and step around to the other side. I need to get away from him. I've never felt like this before, and it terrifies me.

He stops behind Daddy and scratches his light stubble.

My eyes drift to his plump, desirable lips, and my finger strokes mine of its own accord. What would it be like to kiss him?

He wipes his hands down the sides of his Levi's before he fists his mouth, covering those tantalizing lips, and clears his throat. "Excuse me, sir."

Daddy turns and looks at the stranger up and down, giving him a once over. *Ptuh.* "Yes, what you want?"

The stranger extends his hand with a slight tremor. "Pierce Hayes."

After a solid few seconds of eyeing the hand, Daddy shakes it. "Henry Rutherford."

"I was noticin' the girl inside." Pierce tilts his head in my direction, but keeps his eyes on the man in front of him.

What—he noticed *me?* My cheeks burn, and my eyes dart all around, looking anywhere other than at him. Old grizzly men load squealing livestock in wagons, and others chat over the haze of smoky cigars. Their lips move, but I cannot hear their voices, because all the sound has dissolved around me. I pinch the collar of my dress out of habit, and I see both men turn in my direction out of the corner of my eye. When my eyes find theirs again, they both jerk their heads toward each other.

Daddy hooks a finger inside his mouth and chucks out the brown glob he had hidden behind his lip, almost hitting Pierce's dirty work boot. *Ptuh.* "My daughter? Wottabout her?" He crosses his arms over his chest.

Pierce lets out a long breath, and his shoulders relax. "I was a wonderin'…" He grabs a bandana from his back pocket, wipes his glistened forehead, and pockets it again. "Is she…is she spoken for?"

I gasp, hiding my mouth with my hand.

"Nope. Whatcha askin', son?" Daddy asks with a creased forehead.

Pierce looks at the ground while his fingers scratch his disheveled hair. "Her hand. How old is she?" he asks, before looking back at Daddy.

My stomach drops, and my heart bangs against the walls of my chest.

Daddy squints, eyeing the sky, and finally says, "Nearly eighteen, old 'nough, I reckon."

"I got a place, a farm, set up on ten acres in the next town over, Walterboro. I'm doin' fairly well. All the land ain't cleared yet, but I'm workin' on it." He inhales. "I'd sure like to marry your daughter. I'd like to do it right away, if that's all right with you." He glances at me and exhales.

I glare back at him with tight lips. This isn't happening. I shouldn't have come today!

"What's the hurry?" Daddy asks.

Pierce's shoulders lift. "I need the extra hand. It's plantin' season."

"But I'll be losin' one of my hands. Wottam I gittin' out of this?"

Pierce doesn't speak for a good minute while he stares at Daddy. His bottom lip disappears behind his teeth, and he shifts from one foot to the other. "Well, I gotta extra cow I can spare," he says. "I'll bring it by tomorrow if you set up the preacher to marry us. Would that be all right?"

What? I'm getting traded for a cow? A *cow*? I can't breathe. My heart beats faster, my mouth gapes, and my hand rubs the pain in my chest. I want to speak my mind, but I know better. Heat flashes through me as my temper rises, but there's nothing I can do about it.

Daddy looks at the ground, kicking a pebble back and forth with the side of his boot. There's silence around us, like we're the only three people here, even though people are mingling about.

After a moment without an answer, Pierce adds, "Sir, I'm an honest, decent, hard-workin' man. I'll take right good care of your daughter. You got my word."

Daddy glances at me and sighs before sticking out his hand. "I reckon we got us a deal. She'll be ready to leave after the 'I do's' tomorrow."

My shoulders drop when my heart sinks into my shoes, and all I can do is watch.

Pierce lets out a deep breath and shakes his hand. "Thank you, sir. I'll do right by her, I swear."

Daddy beckons me to join them in my marriage proposal with a flick of the wrist. "Pearl."

My feet shuffle, kicking up dirt as I mosey over to them, astounded.

"Hurry it up, girl. We ain't got all day." Once I'm in reaching distance, he grabs my shoulder and pulls me into a sideways hug. "Pearl, this here's Pierce Hayes, your soon-to-be husband."

"But Daddy, I want to graduate. Please, Daddy," I whine.

"When does school let out?" he asks.

"May. May 5th," I say.

He nods at me and then looks at Pierce. "Can you wait 'til after her schoolin' is done?"

I give him a hopeful smile before I see Pierce out the corner of my eye shaking his head. My smile drops.

"I need her now. I'm already workin' my fields and need the extra hand. I'm twenty-eight and ready to start a family of my own. She looks like she'll do." Pierce looks at me with apologetic eyes before turning them back at Daddy. "I'm sure you understand, sir."

Daddy glances at me, and his arm tightens. "I'm sorry, Pearl." He locks eyes with Pierce. "All right, be at the Grace Advent Christian Church on Cedar after service tomorrow, 'round noon. We'll do the weddin' there, then she'll be all yours."

With a wide grin, Pierce shakes Daddy's hand vigorously. "Yes, sir. I won't be late." Then he nods before he trots to his wagon and leaves without a glance back at his future wife. *Me.*

I watch the back of Pierce's head disappear down the dirt road with blurry vision. What just happened? I haven't moved from my spot, and I'm now standing alone.

"Come on, Pearl. Don't just stand there like a bump on a log. Let's git home." Daddy's in the wagon with reins in hand.

I wipe my eyes before I turn around and climb into the wagon. I don't speak. This is the worst day of my life—things couldn't get any worse. This is not what I expected when I woke this morning. I should've stayed home instead.

"You understand, doncha, Pearl?" he says, pulling onto the road.

My lips jut out, and I look down. This isn't fair.

"Don't worry, Pearl. You'll adjust, just like your mama did."

My eyes focus on a piece of wood shaving I'm picking at on the side of the wagon with my fingernail. "But I wanted to be a teacher," I moan.

"Ha, you can't be no teacher. Don't you got to go off to some special school for trainin' or somethin'?"

"Yes, sir," I mumble.

"And how you plan on payin' for this special school? I sure as hell can't pay for it. I can hardly keep you kids fed and clothed, let alone pay for some more schoolin'. The crops ain't payin' like they was, and we don't got the land like some folks 'round heres got. We hurtin', Pearl. Hurtin'. I'm not sure what we gonna do when the baby comes." He sighs and slumps. "We is barely survivin'."

I look at him with depressed eyes.

"Pearl, I tried to be a good daddy to you. Lord knows I didn't have one." He glances at me and hesitates like he's unsure whether to proceed. He finally looks at the reins in his hands and continues, "My mama was fourteen when the war come along. Those northern boys"—he scrunches his nose in disgust—"marched through town like they owned the place, takin' what they wanted," he says through clenched teeth. He doesn't look at me, avoiding my questioning eyes. "Pappy said he found her in the woods soaked in pee, blood, and—" He shakes his head and his jaw twitches. "They did things to her that... Well, the point I'm tryin' to make, Pearl, is you need a man to protect you. So you'll be safe from men like that." He leans over and spits.

"You never told me that story."

He glances at me and shrugs. "I don't like talkin' about it. I don't like knowin' where I come from."

I swallow with a gulp. "That's how you—"

He nods. "Mama died havin' me, and I didn't have a daddy. Pappy and Mamma was all I had. They was good, though."

"I'm sorry, Daddy," I say, understanding now.

"Listen, the only future you got is to git married. How many boys have courted you?"

I shake my head.

"I figured as much. This is your best opportunity to make somethin' of yourself. Shoot, you can be a good wife and a mother one day, just like your mama. Pierce seems like a gudnuf fella. I'm sure he'll treatcha right." He grins, but it's strained, I can tell. "Him comin' along is a blessin'."

I look straight ahead. He's right, as much as I don't like to admit it. Pierce may be my only chance to be a wife and mother, and maybe he'll be a good husband. I do want a family of my own, just as much as I want—wanted—to be a teacher.

I don't want to die alone.

He pulls out his chew bag from his pocket, letting me know the conversation has come to an end. The rest of the journey home is in silence other than the sound of the wheels rolling along on the dirt, kicking up loose rocks, and a *ptuh* every now and then. The birds have even gone quiet. They must realize now is not a good time to sing.

XXX

When we get home, Mama greets us with hands on her hips and shaking her head. "What happened to the one pig you was *supposed* to buy?" she asks, her small round belly protruding, barely showing she's three months pregnant.

"Don't go sassin' me, woman. They was a good deal I couldn't pass up." He plants a kiss on her cheek.

She pushes him away. "*Urgh*, you stink to high heaven. You smell like those filthy animals."

He shrugs, turns, and strolls back to the wagon. "We got a cow comin' after church tomorrow."

"You bought another cow? We can't afford that!" she says in a raised voice.

"Didn't. I traded." He takes the pigs to the pigpen, shutting the door behind them.

"What did you trade? We got nothin' to trade."

He comes back, getting the crate out the wagon. "Pearl," is all he says before taking the crate to the chicken coop.

She whirls around, facing me with an opened mouth and arched brow. "Pearl?"

With my head bent, I focus on my finger, which is tracing an orange flower on my dress. I can't meet her eyes.

He comes back, unhitching the horse. "Yep, she's gittin' married tomorrow after church. Make sure she knows what's expected of her. She's movin' to Walterboro." He walks to the barn, the horse trailing behind him.

Her hand covers her mouth. "Walterboro? Who you marryin', child?"

"Pierce Hayes," I mumble.

She looks up and rubs her chin. "Hayes, I don't know any Hayes. Is he a good man?"

I shrug.

"I don't know about this, Henry," she says when Daddy ambles back toward us.

"Don't go pitchin' a hissy fit. It's a done deal, and I ain't goin' back on my word. Supper ready?" he asks and disappears into the house without waiting for an answer.

She wraps her arm around my shoulder as we watch the door shut behind him. "This ain't what I expected when you left this mornin'."

"Me neither."

She sighs. "It'll be fine, Pearl. You just do the best you can to be a good wife."

"Yes, ma'am," I say, trying in vain to hide the tremor in my voice.

Chapter 3
March 22, 1914

Those darn butterflies have not left my stomach since I first laid eyes on Pierce yesterday. My body aches with tension and I'm nauseous as I stare at the whitewash on the old wooden building I've spent every Sunday in as a Rutherford. Today will be the last day I carry the name I've had for seventeen years. I'll be a Hayes when my feet touch the dirt again in a couple of hours, and I'm scared to death.

I glance around at the wagons and buggies lining the lot, under shady trees, and horses' tails swatting flies away and failing. Whose horse could I unhitch and ride away on? What would I do, where would I go if I ran? I have no money, and I wouldn't have a family or home anymore because Daddy wouldn't let me come back home. I'd be a disgrace. I guess my only choice is to marry a stranger, so I'll have somewhere to lay my head at night. Things could be worse, I suppose.

My eyes lift to the cross balanced on the steeple. "God, my life is in your hands. I trust you. Do as you see fit," I whisper, and then my feet find their purpose and take me inside.

My heart beats faster with each passing second I sit on the hard pew. I wipe my sweaty palms on my dress, over and over again. Mama pats my hand and my fidgeting stops…for a few minutes, but soon my hand forgets and fusses again with my dress.

Mama sighs and shakes her head but keeps her eyes on the preacher, like everyone else in this small room. Some stare forward, others bob their head in agreement, and a few raise their hands and say, "Praise the Lord." One elderly man in the middle with his eyes closed gets an elbow in the side by his wife. His head jerks and bobs like he wasn't just caught sleeping in the middle of service.

I, on the other hand, have not heard a word the preacher has said. I'm probably the only one in the room who hasn't, except for the man who'd been stealing a snooze. The preacher's lips move, but his voice doesn't reach my ears. Normally, during Sunday dinner, Daddy will ask about the sermon to find out who paid attention and who didn't. I guess I don't have to worry about not knowing this time since I won't be going home today—or any other day, for that matter.

I'm nervous about what is expected of me as a wife. I tossed and turned all night thinking about it. Mama told me being a married woman will come to me in time, whatever that means.

"Amen," the preacher says.

It's over. *Already?*

Everyone stands and files out, except us. We wait until the last person leaves before standing to greet the preacher, Mr. Anderson. Daddy asked him earlier if he would do the ceremony. With a smile and a pat of his oversized belly, he said he'd be happy to.

"I hear you're getting married today and moving to Walterboro, dear," Mrs. Martha says, her oversized belly matching her husband's.

"Yes, ma'am," I mumble.

"How lovely." She looks at the preacher with an affectionate smile. "I remember when Fred and I got married. Forty-two years come June." She turns back to me. "I hope you'll be as happy in your marriage as I am in mine." Her thick hand pats my arm.

"I hope so, too." I try to smile, but I can't.

"She will be," Daddy butts in as a throat clears behind us.

My spine straightens, and my heart pounds against my chest. I slowly turn around and my heart skips a beat when I see Pierce standing there in a wrinkled dark brown suit, looking just as ravishing as yesterday.

Pierce's eyes blaze into me like I'm the only one in the room while he twirls his black bowler in his hand. He smooths down his unkempt hair and plods toward our group without taking his eyes off me. "Are you ready, Pearl?" he asks in a soft and hesitant voice, speaking to me for the first time.

Daddy steps forward, ignoring Pierce's question. "You bring the cow?"

Pierce turns his chest toward the front of the church, finally takes his eyes off me, and nods at the door. "She's tied up behind my wagon. You want to see?"

"Yep, let's go have us a look," Daddy says, already walking in that direction.

Sixteen sets of eyes stare at me when I glance around. Elizabeth gives me a wide grin and bites her bottom lip. Mama takes my hand and gently squeezes it.

When they come back inside, Daddy has his hand on Pierce's shoulder, and they're both grinning like they're old friends. Daddy rubs his hands together and gestures to the preacher with a flick of the wrist. "Let's hurry up and do this. Time's a-wastin'."

Pierce takes his place next to me and smiles once more at me before turning to face the preacher.

I look down when my hand finds a button on my dress, toying with it. All I hear is the beat of my heart ringing in my ears. It's so loud I'm sure everyone can hear it. What kind of man is Pierce? Even though I'm becoming his wife, he's only said four words to me. He seems nice enough, but I can't be sure. I—

"Pearl?"

I look up. "Yes, sir?"

Daddy whispers in my ear, "Say 'I do,' Pearl," even though there's silence in the room and everyone can hear.

"Oh, I do," I say.

Pierce blows out his cheeks and his shoulders relax.

26

"Do you have a ring?" Mr. Anderson asks Pierce.

Pierce shakes his head at the preacher. "No, I'm sorry." He looks at me with remorse in his eyes. "I'm sorry."

"That's all right." I know he didn't have time to get me a ring. It hasn't even been twenty-four hours since he proposed…to Daddy.

I stare at the ground when I hear Mr. Anderson announce, "You are now husband and wife." I can't believe it.

I can't believe I'm married and got traded for a *cow*.

The men shake hands, and I follow them out the front door, with everyone else straggling behind. Pierce unties the big black beast from behind his wagon and hands Daddy the rope.

The exchange is done.

Pierce takes off his suit jacket, lays it on the back of the bench seat, and rolls up his shirt sleeves to the elbow. "Pearl, we need to get goin'."

I turn and see Mama's watery eyes and have to blink away my own tears. I hug my brothers and sisters, giving Elizabeth an extra-long hug while I pat her back. Her shoulders tremble and my own shoulder becomes damp. "Don't cry. I'll be fine," I whisper to her and smile to ease her mind. Or is it my own I'm trying to ease?

"I know," she says, wiping her eyes. "I'm going to miss you."

"I'll miss you, too."

Mama hugs me tight. "Come visit when you can, and write me letters. I want to know how you're gettin' along."

"Yes, ma'am." I turn to Daddy as he hands Pierce a large, battered black leather suitcase Mama gave me for a wedding present. It was hers when she got married, and now it belongs to me.

"Be a good girl, Pearl. He's your husband now. Obey him and make him happy," he says with a stern look.

I kiss him on the cheek. "Yes, sir."

Pierce places the suitcase in the back, and then he lifts me by the waist into the wagon with little effort, surprising me. I have to admit, he's a gentleman—and a strong one, at that. I'm not sure if he's doing this for my family or if this is indeed how he is. I'm hoping for the latter.

He hoists himself up on his side and gathers the reins. "You ready to go home, Pearl?"

I turn away and look at my family staring back at me. "Yes, I suppose I am," I mumble.

"We'll be on our way, then," he says, snapping the reins with a *tchk, tchk, swack,* and the horse ambles down the road.

I watch my family and Mr. and Mrs. Anderson as they get smaller and smaller in the distance before I turn around and face forward. I wipe a stray tear that got away. Realization has set in. I'm already dreading this, and I want to go to *my* home, especially when we pass under the brick archway, which reads *LET THE PINE BE SACRED*, letting me know I'm leaving Summerville, my hometown.

We don't speak for a good hour into the trip, and I'm constantly rubbing my naked finger; out of boredom or anxiety, I don't know.

"I'll get you a ring," Pierce says, breaking the silence. "I didn't plan on proposin' when I left for the auction yesterday mornin'. Took me by surprise, too."

"It's all right, I don't need one."

"Yes, you do. I'll get you one, I swear." He pauses, then adds, "You look beautiful today, Pearl. Your hair sure is pretty down like that, and your dress matches your eyes."

My hand flies to my hair, which is flying every which way in the gentle wind, and I pat it down. "Thank you." I look up at the endless sea of blue and faintly see the shape of a fish in the white fluffy waves. The warm sun plays peekaboo behind the passing trees, creating black flashes behind my eyelids, but it doesn't bother me much. The trees just got their leaves back from the dead winter and the pink-and-white azaleas are in full bloom. The purple wisteria cascading in the tree branches have a strong, sweet aroma. I take in a deep breath and smile before looking at my hands lying in my lap. "It's a nice day," I whisper, peering at him out the corner of my eye.

He glances around and nods. "It is. It is."

I look back up and now a horse bucks in the water like he's

splashing, causing a slight giggle.

"What are you doin'?"

My cheeks heat, and my head drops. "Oh, nothing."

"Pearl?" he asks softly.

"Just a childish game, that's all. I was making pictures in the clouds. Something to pass the time."

"Show me," he says.

Is he toying with me? When I look into his curious eyes, I realize he is not. "A-all right," I stammer and look back up. "Look over there." I point to the left. "A rabbit."

"Hmm, or a duck. See his long bill?"

I squint and smile. "Yes, I see it. It could be a rabbit or a duck."

"I suppose it could."

The rest of the leisurely ride is quiet, and I continue to look for pictures in the sky.

XXX

The sun is falling behind the trees and the sky is turning gray when we finally get to his house. When we pull into his short driveway, a small wooden house with a porch extending its entire length comes into view. My eyes follow along the porch until it reaches the end and stops at the enormous magnolia tree towering over the house with its glossy evergreen leaves sweeping along the rooftop. I close my eyes and take a deep breath, appreciating the lemony scent of the majestic white flowers already in bloom. When I open my eyes, I can no longer see the tree as we've already passed by the side of the house to the back.

The wagon comes to a stop. Pierce hops down and comes around to my side. His warm hands wrap around my small waist, lifting me and setting me on the ground. It's the second time he's touched me, and the warmth of his hands is the same warmth I have in the pit of my stomach. I feel adored.

His hands linger on my waist for a moment before releasing me.

He grabs my suitcase and his discarded suit jacket and hat, and walks into the back door of the house, leaving me standing here still thinking about his warm touch.

"Pearl, you comin'?"

"Oh, yes." I slug behind him into the house.

Smells of pine and cedar drift through the room as a lantern is lit, brightening the kitchen and displaying a large rectangular table.

"The table was the last thing I finished before the auction," Pierce says as he hangs his hat and jacket on a hook beside the door.

"You built this?" I run my hand over the smooth surface. "Did you build this house?"

He dips his chin. "Mostly, yes, with a little help from some kin. My father gave me this land when I turned eighteen. They live up the road"—he points at the wall on his right—"that way a bit. I've worked on buildin' and farmin' for the last ten years. I wanted to have it ready for when I got a wife. It's small…a kitchen, living room, and two bedrooms." He averts his eyes and swallows, his Adam's apple jumping as it slides up and then down again. "I can add on later when the young'uns come along. This will get us goin'." His eyes find mine again, but now I avert my own.

A single coffee cup with brown stains in the bottom sits in a deep white porcelain sink. At the end of a long counter, there's a black stove with a kettle for water on top and a few pieces of wood on the floor. It's a plain kitchen, but it looks no worse than our kitchen for eight back home.

He picks up the lantern and my suitcase and walks out the kitchen to another room, but he doesn't stop until we enter a small hall with two doors. He walks through the door on the left, the one facing the front of the house, leaving me in the dark. "The other one is empty. This is ours."

Sleeping in the same room slipped my mind. The gulp echoes in my ears when I swallow.

"Pearl?"

I wrap my arms around myself when I cross the threshold. The white lace curtain over the single opened window flutters in the mild breeze. I tremble, but I'm not sure if it's from the draft or something else.

"This is my side." He points to the side of the unmade bed closest to the door.

I nod and look to my left. My suitcase sits on the floor beside a tall mahogany dresser and a large matching wardrobe.

"Did you make those?" I ask, trying to keep my mind off other things.

He shakes his head. "No. I build what I can, but no. Like I told your father, the farm's doin' all right, so I can buy more furniture soon. I was…" He fists his mouth and clears his throat. "I was waitin' for you." He inserts his hands in his pockets and looks away.

"Oh," I mumble, wringing my hands.

"You can have the bottom two drawers. And there's plenty of room in the wardrobe. Outhouse is out back, to the left."

I nod as my eyes scan the room, avoiding his.

He lights a second lantern and picks it up, the orange flame glimmering on his cheek. "I have to go tend to the horse. I'll be back shortly." He walks out, leaving me alone in my new room.

I let out a long breath once he's gone. I'm tense around him, but I'm sure it will pass once we get to know each other better. I pick up the lantern and head to the outhouse.

A light is coming from the barn when I step out the back door. I walk the short distance to the outhouse, hanging the lantern on the hook above to free my hands. A tingle runs through my body when I relieve my full bladder. After the long, stressful day I've had, using the outhouse had slipped my mind.

The light is still on in the barn when I walk back to the house. It doesn't take this long to put away a horse, so I assume he's giving me time to make myself at home.

I rush inside as fast as my short legs will carry me and slip into my white cotton gown before he walks back into the bedroom, putting his lantern on his table. I blow out mine, slip into bed, and pull the covers to my neck as I watch him through innocent eyes. He has dark circles under his sunken eyes I hadn't noticed before, but I'm sure must have been there.

Mama told me what to expect tonight; she explained things the best she could. She said it's a wife's duty, and I have no choice. It'll be uncomfortable, but I'll get used to it in time. *It's best to just lie there and take it*, she said, *so it'll be over with quickly*. I don't know if I'm ready for *that* part yet.

He looks at me for a few seconds, strumming his fingers on the wall, and then turns and gets his gown out the dresser. After placing his gown on the bed, he unbuttons his dress shirt.

I turn on my side, facing the window, and squeeze my eyes shut. I'm strangling the blanket in my fists when I hear a *plop, swoosh, and rustle*. After a few minutes, he slips under the covers and snuffs out the flame of his lantern, sending us into darkness.

"I'm glad you're here, Pearl. I really am. I know it's a big change for you, but I'll give it all I got to make you happy."

"Thank you," I mutter.

"It's been a long day. Try to get some sleep. Night, Pearl."

"Good night, Pierce."

He moves, turning his back to me, and his breathing deepens almost immediately. I relax as I take in the sweet scent of the magnolia tree right outside the window, and soon join him in slumber.

Chapter 4

March 23, 1914

My eyelids flicker open when the sound of birds singing comes through the open window. I reach my hands above my head and arch my back. When I look at the other side of the bed to see if Elizabeth is still sleeping, I sit up straight. I'm not at home in my bedroom I share with my three sisters. I'm at Pierce's house, in Pierce's bed—*our bed*—alone.

My head turns toward the window when a strong lemon fragrance drifts through the room. I get out of bed and move the curtain to the side, getting a glimpse of the magnolia tree outside. Waking to the sight and aroma of the vast beauty every morning won't be so bad.

After I put on my black work dress, ready for a day of hard labor in the field, I head to the kitchen and freeze. Pierce sits at the table dressed in coveralls and a steaming cup of coffee at his lips.

Our eyes meet.

He sets the cup down without taking the sip. "Mornin', Pearl. How did you sleep?"

"Good." I wipe my hand along the front of my dress with a tremble.

"Water's ready." He points to the kettle on the stove. "You drink coffee?"

"Yes, thank you." I hesitate before walking to the stove, pouring hot water into a mug sitting on the counter, and stirring in a spoonful of coffee granules. I turn, facing him again while blowing on my own steaming cup.

He stands and places his cup in the sink. "I'll be in the field." He grabs his wide-brim felt hat from the hook and opens the door.

"What shall I do?"

He shrugs. "Woman stuff. Tend to the house and animals. I'll be back 'round nine for breakfast. Don't worry none 'bout dinner; breakfast and supper will do."

I set my cup on the counter and mince closer to him, wringing my hands. "What do you want to eat?"

"I'll eat what you fix. There's a smokehouse out back near the chicken coop and a garden. I'll take you to the store on Saturday."

"All right. Do you need help in the fields?"

"No, just the house and animals for now. I'll take care of the fields."

"But you told Daddy you need—"

He holds up his hand and narrows his eyes. "The house, Pearl. I don't want you in the fields; it gets awfully hot out there. That's man's work. A woman tends to the house and young'uns. And that's how it's gonna be."

"All…all right. Whatever you want."

He nods and walks out.

"Whatever you want," I whisper to myself.

XXX

The blazing sun is high above the perfectly still trees while I'm on all fours, pulling weeds from the small, neglected garden. A drop of sweat lands on my arm. I lean back, wipe my wet locks from my brow with the back of my hand, and notice Pierce in the field behind a plow being dragged by the horse. He stops the horse, takes his hat off, grabs a cloth from his back pocket, and wipes his forehead. He looks up at the punishing sun while pocketing the cloth and putting his hat back on.

When he moves again, he sways as he grabs ahold of the plow's handle. I shake my head as I stand and slap the dirt from my dress, and then I cross the field toward him.

When he sees me, he stops his plowing and meets me at the water bucket. He bends, grabbing a ladle of water, and straightens before saying, "It sure is a hot one today." He sounds winded. "Ain't it?" He takes a giant swig and lifts his chin toward the house. "How's it going down there?"

"It's going all right." I place my stretched hand over my eyes, shielding me from the sun, as I look up at him. "Are you sure you don't want anything to eat? I can make you something."

"I'm sure." He drops the empty ladle in the bucket and removes his hat.

"I figured you needed a break."

He nods, takes the rag out of his back pocket, and wipes his drenched forehead.

"What time would you like supper?" I ask while my hands twist my dress skirt.

"Oh, 'bout six is fine. Fix plenty, I work up an appetite." He replaces his hat and rag back to their rightful spots. "Let me get back to it, then."

"All right." I watch him saunter toward the plow before I turn and head back to the house.

A horse and buggy is parked next to the back door when I get back to the house. "Who could that be?" I mumble as I reach the door.

A stout, middle-aged woman with a sour expression on her face sits at the kitchen table. Her spine is straight and her hands are folded in her lap as she stares at the window over the sink. The faded yellow floral bonnet resting on top of her head doesn't match her navy-blue dress, which looks like it's a size too small. She doesn't move. Maybe the dress is cutting off her circulation, or maybe it's the white floppy bow tie around her neck. Perhaps that's what's causing her discomforted look.

She slowly turns her head to face me. Her small closed-lip smile doesn't reach her eyes, not by a long shot. "You must be Pearl," she says through clenched teeth. "Pierce's *wife*."

I stare at her without speaking.

She stands. "I'm Florence, Pierce's mother." Her eyes roam, taking me in from head to toe, and her lips pucker.

"Oh. It's nice to meet you," I fib uncertainly, not wanting to start off our relationship on a bad note. Her dark brown eyes are the same as Pierce's. By her gruff demeanor, I hope that's all he has in common with her.

After a few more moments of a silent standoff, she replies, "Yes, I'm sure it is. When Pierce came home Saturday from the auction, he stopped by the house to tell us he was getting married. We were surprised, to say the least," she says, shaking her head.

"Me too," I whisper under my breath, and give her my best fake smile.

She points to the basket filled with jars on the table behind her, but her eyes don't leave mine. "I brought over some extra vegetables I canned last summer. I figured you'd need them since I was sure you wouldn't bring anything with you," she says in a disapproving tone.

I walk around her to the table, ignoring her jab. "Thank you." I take the jars out the basket and place them on the table before handing the basket back to her.

"I normally bring Pierce over supper in the evenings, or he comes over to our house. We live up the road, next house on the left. I guess I don't have to do that anymore." Her brows disappear into her bonnet. "You do know how to cook, don't you?"

I nod. "Yes, ma'am. I've helped Mama in the kitchen since before I can remember."

"Hmm. Well, we always have dinner at our house on Sundays, right after church. I expect you there, so you can meet the rest of Pierce's family. I'm sure they're as anxious to meet you as I was."

"All right," I mutter, knowing I have no say where we have dinner on Sunday.

She looks at me from head to toe again and narrows her eyes. "You're awfully young. Are you even old enough to bear children, girl?"

Saliva gets caught in my throat when I try to swallow, and my breathing becomes increasingly difficult to control. My hands twist the front of my dress, and I can feel my upper lip glisten. *Please don't notice. Please don't notice.*

Her eyes dart to my restless hands, and one brow rises, followed by one side of her mouth, before she slowly raises her eyes back to mine.

"Yes, ma'am," I finally reply with a gulp. I don't know this woman. I don't even know my own husband. How did this happen so quickly?

"Very well. You will give my son the family he deserves. It's time. He's my oldest and should've already had kids." She pushes the door open. "I guess you'll just have to do," she says under her breath, but I heard it loud and clear. "I'll see you at church on Sunday." She steps out, leaving me standing in the kitchen pondering the idea of raising a family with a man I don't even know.

I watch her through the screen while she marches to her buggy and hurls the basket in. I hear her say, "*I can't believe he traded our meat for her,*" and, "*Katherine was a much better choice. What was he thinking?*" before she steps into the buggy and drives off.

Well, that didn't go well—and who is Katherine?

XXX

Pierce stuffs tobacco in his pipe and, with a quick flick of a match against the side of its box, lights it. Vanilla and cherry hits my nose almost immediately after he takes the first drag. I shut my eyes and take a deep breath of the sweet smell.

He shakes out the fire and drops the used stick onto the small table between us. "That was some good eatin', Pearl," he says as he pats his stomach.

"Thank you." I rock while staring at the road sitting in front of the house.

"I'm glad you're here." He pulls a deep drag off his pipe, his cheeks hollowing out, and blows a ring of smoke out of his mouth before adding, "Honestly." The cloud drifts over his head before being blown away by the warm, tender breeze.

"You may be the only one," I mumble under my breath.

His head whips in my direction. "What's that?"

"Oh, nothing." I shouldn't talk ill about his mother. My rocking increases when my fidgeting habit takes over my feet. Not wanting to meet his glare, I keep my eyes on the empty road.

"Talk to me, Pearl," he says, sounding irritated. "What's botherin' you?"

My rocking stops and I sigh. "I met your mother today."

He chuckles. "Oh, I see. And what did Mother say to you?"

I look at my tangled hands in my lap, keeping them from twitching. "Nothing, it's the way she acted toward me. I don't think she likes me much."

"Pay her no mind. She's just surprised I married so fast. She'll come 'round, give her time."

I nod. "All right, I'll try."

We sit in silence for a while enjoying the warm spring evening until a carriage goes past our house. I can't tell who's in it, but if it's a neighbor, I should be courteous, so I wave. That's how my parents raised me: *Always be nice to your neighbors, Pearl.*

"Don't." Pierce narrows his eyes at me.

I gawk at him. "Why? Who is it?"

"That there is Hazel Sullivan. She lives up the road." He lifts his pipe in the direction the carriage went. "Don't go messin' with her."

"Why?"

"Leave her be. She's a witch." He takes another drag off his pipe.

"A witch?" I laugh. "Oh, come on. You're telling me a story. There's no such thing."

He shakes his head. "I'm serious, Pearl. Stay away from her, that's an order. You'll have nothin' to do with her. Mind me now. You hear me? Mind me."

"All right." I slowly nod. "I'll leave her alone."

"Good. That's the end of it. I don't wanna yap about her no more. Nothin' good will come of it." He stands. "I'm gonna check the animals. I'll meet you in the bedroom," he says with a mixture of anger and eagerness in his voice before walking off the porch and disappearing around the side of the house.

I glance at the road again, but the carriage is already gone. Just because I'm young doesn't mean I'm stupid—there's no such thing as a witch. He's wrong, he has to be, but I'd never go against my husband. I don't need to be friends with Hazel, so I'll leave her alone.

XXX

I'm lying in our marital bed, staring at the empty doorway, when I hear thick, unhurried footsteps across the wood floor. Pierce emerges a second later, hesitates when his heavy-lidded, smoldering eyes land on mine, and treads into the bedroom. His eyes, dilated with want— no, need—watch me while undressing, not bothering with the gown tonight. His hands move with a slight tremor with each undone button. When he slides his shirt over his shoulders, I feel as if I'm inside my own skin, and I'm clawing to get out...but I can't. It's getting harder to get air to my lungs. My breathing increases with every stitch of clothing falling to the floor. I grip the blanket in a deathly choke, twisting it until it's damp from my sweaty palms, and squeeze my eyes shut.

"Pearl," he whispers in a caring drawl.

I clutch the blanket tighter, holding it to my chin. My upper lip becomes moist with sweat, but I'm too scared to release the blanket and wipe it away. It's so hot. It's stifling!

"Pearl, I'm your husband."

I nod. *Obey him and make him happy.*

"Pearl, open dem eyes."

I slowly open my eyes and they immediately widen, and I bite my lip when I see him…all of him. I knock my knees together when my body tingles in places I never thought could.

When he turns the lantern off, sending the room into complete darkness, all the air leaves with the light. Why is it so hot in here?

The bed dips beside me, and his knuckles caress my cheek. "Pearl, I know this is new and may be uncomfortable, but that's natural."

Lips replace the knuckles, and then his strong yet tender hands are on me…all over me. I'm clueless—I don't know what to do. So, I follow Mama's advice, and just lie here. I feel as if we are strangers—as we are—even though we are tied to each other…forever.

A heavy weight is on top of me, and I don't even notice my drawers are gone, but when he spreads my legs apart with his own, a cold breeze hits me where they used to be. My breathing surges even more. I'm petrified of doing something wrong, and all I can think about is making him happy.

I have to be a good wife. I have to be a good wife.

He lunges forward, and I draw in a deep ragged breath when a sharp pain erupts inside my womb. My mouth opens, but I don't make a sound.

I have to be a good wife. I have to be a good wife.

"Relax, Pearl. Need to…relax…a bit," he says with a grunt. "You okay?"

I have to be a good wife. I have to be a good wife.

I nod and take short, heated breaths, and the pain disappears. My shoulders relax first, followed by the rest of my body, and I close my eyes.

"That's it," he says as his moving becomes rhythmic and his breathing becomes erratic.

After several long minutes of thrusting, he grunts one last time and stills. Panting fills the room as he lies on top of me for a few moments, stroking my hair with shaky hands while his face is buried in my neck.

His gentle lips are on my neck before he finally lets out a long shuddering breath and rolls off me, onto his back.

I clench my legs together when warm liquid trickles out of me, but otherwise I don't move. I don't want to. I'm exhausted and relieved and...sad. I'm not sure if this is normal; I don't have anything to compare it to. While he was stroking my hair, I felt appreciated, but I feel abandoned now that he's not.

Neither one of us speaks. The room is quiet until a small sniff comes from my side of the bed.

He grabs my hand under the blanket, rubbing my thumb with his own. "*Shh*, Pearl. I didn't mean to hurt you," he says, his breathing steady. "I'm sorry. You'll get used to it, I swear. Next time will be better." He turns on his side, facing me.

My breath hitches, and I flinch. Is he going to do it again? Please, not yet.

He wraps his arms around me and tugs me close to him. I let out the breath and sink into him. My back is to his chest, and heat emanates from his body. I don't pull away—I'm...comforted. Am I supposed to feel this way? I hope so, because I like this feeling.

"Go to sleep." He kisses my cheek before settling his head on his pillow.

I don't say a word. I listen to his breathing as it goes deeper and deeper into a steady rhythm before sleep pulls my eyelids closed, and I drift off.

Chapter 5

March 24, 1914

Sunlight filters through the window, announcing morning. Pierce is already gone, and I'm glad. I don't want to see him this morning, although I know I will. I must face him sometime.

When I stand, I'm sore, like I rode a horse all day, and there is stickiness between my legs. "*Urgh.*". Is this how it'll be every morning when I rise?

A bucket of water sits on the floor by the dresser with a rag and bar of soap on top. I'm thankful Pierce brought me something to wash away his seed.

After I'm clean, I waddle into the kitchen expecting to see Pierce, but he isn't there. I see he's already working when I look out the window over the sink. Maybe he's trying to give me space, which I need. How am I supposed to feel this morning? I thought I would feel different—older, maybe—but I don't. I'm the same as always, other than a little sore and a little nervous about how Pierce will treat me when he comes in for breakfast.

My feet shuffle across the floor as I get busy making breakfast. They have little pep this morning, and they weigh a ton, but after a good night's sleep, I come to realize I *am* okay. I can do this. I can be the wife Pierce needs, and I'm looking forward to the next time. Maybe it will be more enjoyable for me.

Pierce doesn't speak during breakfast. He glances my way a few times, opening and closing his mouth like he wants to say something, but then continues eating in silence. Did I do something wrong? I can't tell from his quiet manner, but I hope I didn't upset him last night. The last thing I want to do is upset my new husband. I hope he isn't regretting marrying a young, inexperienced girl.

I didn't know what I was doing, but he can't blame me for that. I don't know what I'd do if he throws me out. Going home isn't an option; I'd be too ashamed.

When he's done with his breakfast, he grabs his hat from the hook beside the door and turns to me, staring with remorseful eyes, without saying a word.

I lumber to him. "Do you need something else, Pierce?"

He's quiet for a moment. "Are you all right, Pearl? Did I…" He pauses. "Did I hurt you?" he asks, his voice unsteady.

"I'm fine."

His shoulders relax. "Good. I never want to hurt you." He caresses my cheek with his fingers, leans down, and plants a soft, gentle, but electrifying kiss on my lips that only lasts a few seconds, and then his lips are gone. "Thank you, Pearl." He smiles and strolls out the door before I can reply.

My fingers rub my lips, and I can still feel the ghost of his lips on mine. No one has ever kissed me like that. An unexpected smile sneaks across my face. For the first time in three days, I'm excited about what the future holds.

I smile the whole time I'm washing the dishes and doing my chores, and I keep that smile for the rest of the day.

XXX

We sit on the porch, rocking in our chairs, as the sun disappears behind the curtain of trees. I'm enjoying the weather and the company and can't help but smile.

Pierce is stuffing tobacco in his pipe when he looks at me.

"What's with the beautiful smile you've had every time I've seen you today, Pearl?"

I shrug and look at my twiddling hands.

He grabs my hand, holding it in his. "Well, I like your smile. I'd like for you to do it more often."

Heat rises in my cheeks as I eye our linked hands, and I'm sure my face is a nice shade of pink.

He puts his finger under my chin and lifts it, forcing me to look him in the eye. "Do I make you happy, Pearl?"

"Yes, I believe you do," I answer honestly.

"Good, 'cause you make me happy." He leans over, giving me another soft kiss on my lips before releasing me and lighting his pipe.

I rub my bare finger, relieving my desire to fidget. I miss my family, but in time, I could grow accustomed to this life. I can fall in love with Pierce…my husband.

"I haven't forgotten about your ring, Pearl. I'll get you one when I get a little extra money. I have to repay my father and brother for somethin' first."

I look at him and shake my head. "Oh, you don't have to do that. I'm fine with not having one."

"Yes, I do. I want everyone to know you're married to me. When's your birthday, Pearl?" He blows a puff of smoke out of his mouth while squinting.

"June twenty-third."

He looks at the road and doesn't respond, like he's branding it into his brain, so as not to forget.

"When's yours?" I guess we should know each other's birthdays. We are in the "get to know you" phase of our relationship. Usually that happens before the wedding, but in our case, it didn't.

"September twenty-second."

We sit in silence for a few more minutes before he speaks again. "I want lots of young'uns with you, Pearl. I want strong, hard-workin' boys like me and beautiful girls just like you."

"I want that, too."

"And smart, they gonna be smart like you. I wasn't much into schoolin'. Didn't see a need in it. I was always meant to be a farmer." He points to his chest. "But our young'uns will be different."

"You *are* smart. You can build and do almost anything you set out to do. And to some, that's more important than any amount of book smart."

He looks at me with an appreciative expression and nods before turning back to face the road and taking a long drag from his pipe.

When we can no longer see anything but the moon and the stars above, we retire to our bed for the night. I expect the same thing as the night before. I'm right—except this time, it isn't so bad. Mama and Pierce were right.

I'm already getting used to it.

Chapter 6

March 28, 1914

The rest of the week is the same as the first couple of days. I get up, make breakfast, do my chores, cook supper, sit on the porch with Pierce, and go to bed. Other than the first night, our wedding night, Pierce hasn't been tired. In fact, he seems eager to go to bed at night. I don't mind because after he makes my toes curl, which I greatly enjoy, I feel loved when he cuddles me in his strong arms. If you can call it love already. It's absurd to have those feelings for someone you just met. But I'm sure in no time we will love each other like a husband and wife should.

Pierce takes me into town Saturday morning. On the way to town, we pass Hazel's small, wooden house. Its side planks are warped, and the saggy tin roof is losing its battle with gravity. It's tucked away behind large oak trees covered in Spanish moss. That's common for the Lowcountry, but the trees around her house are overgrown with the gray creeper, as if the lichen is trying to take over, claiming it as their own. Behind the two windows are torn curtains made from old burlap sacks, and the small porch houses one lonely rocking chair, so she must live alone. That's sad—no one should be alone. That's probably why Pierce thinks she's a witch, because she's an old woman who stays to herself in her creepy little house.

Pierce grabs my hand and shakes his head. "Eyes to the front,

Pearl. I don't want you lookin' over there."

"There's no carriage, so she must not be home," I say.

He squeezes my hand, so I do as I'm told and look at the road ahead.

We pass by a field of flowers dancing in the mild breeze. A sea of every color imaginable is covering the field as far as the eye can see.

"Wow," I say and gaze with my mouth hanging open.

"Beautiful, ain't it?" he asks.

"Yes," I say, still unable to look away. "I've never seen anything more breathtaking."

He looks at me with a grin. "I have." Then his eyes find the road again.

My eyes dart to my folded hands, which are resting in my lap, and my cheeks heat up. I'm not sure if I'll ever get used to his compliments, but I like them, and I don't want him to stop giving them.

"Mother would bring us here when we was little to pick flowers for the house. We loved comin' here. Maybe one day, you can bring our young'uns here. They'll love to run 'round in the field of flowers like I did."

"Yes, I'd like that. I may come back before then and get some flowers for the table."

He nods and points to the field right next to the flowers. "There's a bunch of blackberries over yonder. You can pick some of those, too. I got a hankerin' for some blackberry cobbler."

"I make a great cobbler. It's Mama's recipe." Mama always did say the way to a man's heart is through his stomach. If that's the case, Pierce is sure to love me.

The rest of the way to town is quiet, so I relax and enjoy the timbered scenery.

When we get to the small corner store, Pierce parks the wagon and helps me down. He pulls folded bills from his pocket and hands them to me.

I look at the money in my hand and lift my anxiety-filled eyes to his. "You're not coming in with me?"

He peeks over my head, toward the store, and scrunches his nose. "Nope, I'll be right over yonder talkin' to Charlie." He thumbs over his shoulder to a lanky man stacking lumber inside the back of a dusty flatbed truck. "He owns the saw mill."

"All right, I won't be long," I tell him reluctantly.

"Take your time and have fun." He grins and strolls away.

I turn around, facing the old wooden storefront and frown. The two windows on both sides of the door are coated in muck. One is missing its faded burgundy shutter while another is hanging on by one nail. The brown wooden sign with black letters over the porch's roof that's supposed to read *HOWARD'S GROCERY* is so worn and chipped, I can only make out some of the letters.

I step up the stairs while grabbing onto the wobbly railing, staggering, but I'm able to catch myself before I fall. "God, I miss home tremendously," I say when I reach the top and grab the tarnished door knob. I close my eyes and whisper, "Please don't let the inside be as bad as the outside," before I pull the door open and hear it creak as I walk into the store.

The strong smell of dust tickles the back of my throat, so I cover my mouth before letting out a soft cough, hoping no one noticed. I must've just missed the war between the jars and bags, considering how they're cluttering the shelves in a chaotic fashion. When I take a step, my footprints are stamped in the dirt covering the floor.

No one else is in the store other than the plump woman with white stringy hair behind the counter. She stares at me for a moment with half-closed eyelids as the smoke from a thick cigar lingers in front of her face. With cigar in hand, she takes a large swig of clear liquid from a glass jar, wincing and coughing as she slaps her chest. Once recovered, she flicks the long ash on the floor and turns back to the newspaper in front of her as though I'm not actually here.

I shrug and grab what I need.

When I walk to the counter with my things, I get a strong, rancid smell coming from the woman. It smells like she bathes in the cigar smoke, and I'm not sure if the strong moonshine smell is coming from her open mouth or the half-empty jar on the counter; it's probably the former. I do my best to hold my breath without causing attention to myself, so I don't hurt this woman's feelings.

She sets the cigar on the edge of the counter and looks at me with hooded eyes. They're so thin I can't tell the color of her eyes through the slits. "You new? Haven't seens you 'round heres bufore," the woman says in a raspy, strained voice, and with breath no better than the rest of her smells. She pulls a brown paper bag from under the counter, flicks it open and sets it beside the brown flaming stick. "Y'all just move heres?" She pushes a few buttons on the cast-metal register—*cha-ching*—and places the items in the bag.

"I just moved here," I correct her. "I'm married to Pierce Hayes."

She pauses, her eyebrows quirk. "Pierce Hayes, huh? Well, that sure iza fine catch if I do says so myself." She eyes me up and down as far as the counter will allow before she continues pushing, *cha-ching*, and bagging. "He sure weren't hit witha ugly stick, I tell ya that much. Fine fella, that one iz. You sure iza lucky lady." She looks at me once again before pushing the total key. "Didn't know he waz'a courtin' anyone."

I'm not sure how to reply, so I don't—I smile. I don't want anyone knowing our business, as I'm sure Pierce doesn't either, and I don't want to drag this conversation on any longer than necessary. I'm in need of some fresh air before I get sick from the awful stench. So, I hand her the money without responding.

"Didn't catch yer name?" She puts the money in the drawer and slams it shut with her hip.

"Pearl."

"Pearl, huh? Pearl Hayes. Well, it sure iza nice havin' ya heres, Pearl Hayes. Welcome to our town," she says, giving me a toothless yet genuine grin and passing me the bag. "Come back and see me real soon, woncha?"

"Thank you, I will," I say and hurry out the door. As soon as I hear the door shut behind me, I take a much needed deep breath of fresh air. It's rejuvenating. I'll never take fresh air for granted again.

Pierce is still talking to Charlie, so I place the bag in the back of the wagon, hop in, and glance around at the few people wandering the street.

A tall woman in her mid-to-late thirties, I imagine, and wearing a black dress, comes out of the chemist carrying a basket filled with different-colored bottles. She walks to a carriage parked out front with crows sitting on top. When the carriage dips as she steps inside, the crows fly off and chase after the carriage while it hurries down the road.

When I look back at Pierce, his eyes dart to mine. He shakes the man's hand before strolling back across the street with his hands in his pockets and a smirk on his face.

He climbs into the driver's spot and gathers the reins. "You meet Louise?"

"Who?"

"Louise Howard. Her husband owns the store, and she works behind the counter." He tilts his head toward the front of the dilapidated building. "She's a character—a little nosy, too. Don't mind her, she's harmless."

Tchk, tchk, swack.

"Oh, yes, she seems nice."

"How's your nose?" he whispers in my ear and lets out a small chuckle while he drives us down the road.

I shake my head and grin. "That's not nice."

"Well, it's true. She ain't much for bathin'. You get what you needed?"

"Yes, I did. Thank you for bringing me. You didn't have to rush on my account, I could've waited."

"Oh, I was just wastin' time. If you ever need to come to town, and I can't bring you, my sister Cora will be glad to. She's not much older than you, you'll like her. You'll meet her tomorrow at dinner with my folks."

"Okay. That sounds good." I'm not thrilled about seeing his

mother again, but I'm looking forward to meeting the rest of his family. I'm hoping to meet anyone in this town I can become friends with—preferably someone who doesn't smell like old cigars and moonshine.

Chapter 7

March 29, 1914

On the way to church on Sunday, I glance over at Pierce, who's wearing khaki trousers with black suspenders and a white, long-sleeve dress shirt rolled to his elbows. He probably doesn't realize how fetching he is. I grin sheepishly and bite my lower lip. Mrs. Louise was right; he sure wasn't hit with the ugly stick. I imagine all the single women at church fight over who will sit next to him each Sunday.

"What are you grinning about?" he asks with one brow raised.

I shake my head. "Oh, nothing. Just something Mrs. Louise said yesterday."

"And what was that?"

I look at my hands crumpling my dress skirt, and heat rises in my face with embarrassment. "That I'm a lucky girl," I mutter.

"*I'm* the lucky one," he says as we pull in the driveway of Jones Swamp Baptist Church. We come to a stop, and he hops out. "Come on, time to meet everyone." He comes around to my side and helps me down.

Pierce introduces me to the rest of his family. Pierce's father, Emmett, his sister Mabel, her husband and two sons, his brother Albert, his wife and son, and Cora all welcome me with curious but pleasant smiles. And then there's his mother, Florence.

"Mother, you remember Pearl," he says as we walk up to Florence, who is chatting with a woman in front of the brick building.

She glares at me. "Yes, well, you're cutting it mighty close this morning. I surely don't see how it took her *that* long to get dressed, but I hope it won't be like this every Sunday. Church is about to start." She tosses her nose in the air and walks away. "Let's go inside, Gladys. Why don't ya'll come for dinner after church?" she asks the woman as they stroll up the steps and disappear through the double doors.

I glance at Pierce as he gives me a sympathetic smile. "Just give her time, it'll get better," he says.

I nod to him. "It'll get better," I mumble as we walk inside.

Pierce leads me to an empty pew with his hand on the small of my back. People stare, mostly women with catty eyes, as we take our seats, and I see heads lean in toward each other out the corner of my eye.

"Who is she?"

"What is he doing with her?"

I try to hide my smile, a glint of triumph in my eyes. It may be childish, but the idea of others being jealous of me makes me gloat.

It's hard to concentrate, like it had been last Sunday. Only this time it's for a different reason. Last Sunday, I was nervous about my upcoming nuptials. This Sunday, however, it's because of the man, my husband, who sits next to me. The subtle rubbing of his fingers across the back of my neck, under my hair, is probably unnoticeable by others; but to me, it's like a million tingles running through my body. My heart flutters, and I glance at him. The edge of his lips turns upward, a hint of a smile, even though he's staring straight ahead listening to the preacher's sermon. I hope his father doesn't ask me about the sermon today, because I'm lost. I turn my attention back to the preacher and off the man who has taken over my entire life in one short week.

After church, we head to Pierce's parents' two-story lemon-yellow house with a wraparound porch, sitting on seventy-two acres of land. I'm impressed. It's bigger than what my parents own, a lot bigger.

"They gave ten acres to Albert on the other side of the property," Pierce whispers to me. "When my folks pass, me and him will split the rest."

His sisters Mabel and Cora wouldn't get anything, I know, just as I wouldn't get anything from my own parents. I cast a glance of appreciation at my new husband—without him, I might have been left penniless and alone.

"What about Cora?" I ask, knowing Mabel already has a husband and family.

"Don't worry about her," he says when he jumps out and comes around my side. He grabs my waist and lifts me out, setting me on my feet. "I'll take care of her. That's what big brothers are for." He smiles down at me and takes my hand, and we stroll inside the house.

The conversation around the full table doesn't seem to include me. I'd be more comfortable sitting at the kids' table in the living room. A woman with long, auburn hair in ringlets, Katherine, and her parents join us for dinner. Katherine looks to be about Pierce's age, and she's one of the women who kept eyeing me during the church service. She doesn't look at me now, though, as she sits across from me at the table with her blue eyelids, pink cheeks, and rosy lips.

I don't see us being best friends or friends at all, for that matter. But Florence, on the other hand, seems to love Katherine. She keeps praising everything about her, leaving me to glower. *"You look beautiful today, Katherine. Your dress is lovely, Katherine. My, my, Katherine, you sure are mature and not a child. I'll bet you'll make a fine wife and daughter-in-law."*

Katherine, however, keeps talking to Pierce. "How's the new field coming along, Pierce?"

"Fine," he says while shoveling food into his mouth, not looking at her.

"When do you think you'll have it all cleared?" she asks.

He shrugs and puts another forkful into his mouth.

Katherine keeps her eyes on the top of his head while he

continues to eat, but doesn't say anything else.

"Bless her heart. She didn't bring anything with her, so I had to stock the cabinet with the leftover canning I had from last year," Florence tells Katherine's mother, Gladys, like I'm not in the room. "I don't want my son to starve now that he has a wife. For Pete's sake, I sure hope she can cook."

Gladys glances at me, shakes her head, lifts her chin, and continues her conversation with Florence. "Well, if it was my Katherine"—she touches her fingers to her chest—"I would've made sure her new home was well stocked. It's proper etiquette, you know?"

"I know you would've. You good people." Florence cuts her narrowed eyes at me.

"And Katherine is an excellent cook. She would've put some meat on his bones," Gladys says with a hint of laughter.

Katherine smirks. She wraps a curl around her finger, twirling, and bats her long eyelashes at Pierce. He stands and walks over to the buffet, cuts a slice of pecan pie—my favorite—and strolls back to the table without glancing her way. She frowns and picks at her untouched plate of food with a polished fork.

With my face already flushed, I tune out the mother hens and take a bite of my fried pork chop. My eyes are closed when I slowly chew, savoring the delicious flavor. I have to hand it to Florence; she's a great cook, like Mama. I'm in a world all alone when the chatter around the table disappears. I put my fingers in my mouth, one by one, and I suck the grease off with a *pop*. When I open my eyes, Katherine's glaring at me with uneven brows like I'm a misfit.

"Where are you from, Pearl?" she asks in a haughty voice while dabbing a linen cloth to the side of her clean mouth.

"Summerville," I say, scoop a forkful of black-eyed peas and rice, and stuff it in my mouth like I haven't eaten for days. It's not ladylike, but I'm not the type for fanciness when the food is this good. I wasn't raised the way Katherine obviously was. She hasn't eaten anything at all—Florence should be offended.

Gladys speaks up. "What's your maiden name?"

I swallow the food in my mouth before opening it and replying, "Rutherford," like Mama taught me: *Don't talk with your mouth full, Pearl.*

"Never heard of them." Gladys taps her long fingernail on the table. "What does your father do?"

The tap, tap, tap is loud in the silent room, waiting for my answer.

I lay my fork beside my dinner plate. "He's a farmer," I say as my finger traces the fork's handle.

"How much land does he own?" Gladys asks.

I'm breathing faster and I'm getting uncomfortable with this line of questioning. My parents aren't rich farmers, not even close. They barely make ends meet. Pierce's parents seem like they're living high on the hog compared to my family.

Pierce leans into me and whispers in my ear, "You don't got to answer that. It ain't none of their business." The scent of pecan pie follows him when he straightens back up, leaving me longing.

"I'm not sure," I say as my eyes shift to the door, wishing I could leave.

"And where did you say you two met, Pearl?" Katherine looks at Pierce, but she's asking me.

"She didn't," Pierce answers for me while cutting a piece of pie with his fork and shoving it into his mouth, making me jealous my mouth must remain empty until the interrogation is done.

My tongue licks my lips. I would rather be eating sweet, sticky pecan pie.

"She was asking Pearl. Pierce, let your poor little wife speak for herself," Florence butts in, and all eyes are on me.

I glare at her before catching myself and lowering my eyes again. I wish I could say something back to her, but I'm to respect my elders, which she is. Anyway, I don't need to get any more on her bad side than I already am. I need to get along as best I can with his family, which includes his mother, unfortunately.

Pierce wipes his mouth with a cloth. "We met at an auction last weekend. Any more questions you want to ask while we're all here? Let's get this over with, so we don't got to bring it up again," he says in a firm voice.

"All right." Emmett slaps the table. "When we gettin' our money back for the meat?" He raises his eyebrow.

"I told you, you'll get it when I get it." Pierce buries a hand in his hair, sighing. "Just give me time. I'll have enough when the first crops of the season are sold."

"Don't worry about my share for now. You can pay me back when you get some extra," Albert tells him.

Pierce lifts his chin to his brother. "Thank you. I'll get it to you as soon as I can."

"Well, we want our money. I still can't believe you traded our meat." Florence glances at Katherine before turning back to Pierce with a smirk. "There were much better options you wouldn't have had to pay for. *Like some harlot*," she mumbles, her eyes shift to mine before they go back to Pierce. "You act like you ain't got a lick of sense. We raised you better than that."

"I swanee, woman," Emmett says under his breath, narrowing his eyes at Florence, silencing her. He turns his attention back to Pierce. "Know what, son? Don't worry about it. We'll make do with what we got. I just hope you're happy with your choice. That's all that matters."

"No, I'm gonna pay you back," Pierce says.

Florence grinds her teeth behind closed lips while glowering at me.

Heat rushes through me and, though I'm still uncomfortable, I sit up straight and force a neutral expression. I'll sit here and take it like a grown woman. My mouth's dry, so I grab my tea and take a small sip, like a prim and proper lady.

Katherine's eyes narrow when she glances at my naked finger. "Are you sure you're married? Where's your ring?"

Pierce slams his hand down on the table and the tableware rattles. "Of course we're married," he says through clenched teeth.

I shrink in my chair.

He looks at me and places a hand on my shoulder, gently squeezing. "She's gettin' one soon," he says in a calmer tone.

"You look young. Do you even know who the president is? How old are you?" Katherine asks, ignoring his outburst.

I raise my chin and say with pride, "Of course I do. It's Woodrow Wilson and I'm seventeen."

Katherine and her parents gasp.

Gladys' hand covers her heart. "Heavens to Betsy! Dear lord, that's awfully young. Don't you think, Pierce?"

"That's it. That's it. That. Is. It." Pierce stands and grabs my hand, pulling me out of my seat and throws his linen cloth on the table. "She'll be eighteen in a few months. She's old enough to be married with her father's blessin'. I chose her. We're *done* here with the questions," he says, his eyes dancing with fury.

We storm out the door hand in hand without saying goodbye. My arm is outstretched when he moves faster, and I have to jog to keep up with his long strides. "Pierce, wait!" I say and fall back behind him, not able to keep up with him anymore. I'm frightened. Will he take it out on me when we get home?

Pierce stops when we get to the wagon and turns, lifting me into the seat with ease. He smiles up at me and pats my leg with his loving hand. "I'm sorry."

I instantly relax and give him a smile back.

"Who's Katherine?" I ask when he hops in and gathers the reins, my voice cracking as I look at my hands twiddling with my dress.

He guides the horse onto the road. "No one. Or at least she's no one to me. Mother wanted me to marry her, but I don't like her that way, never have. She acts like she's better than everyone else, which she ain't."

My eyes find his. "Why *me?*" I ask with a gulp.

"I wanted a down-to-earth girl and the minute I laid eyes on you, I knew it was you I've been lookin' for."

Heat rises in my cheeks, and I look down, trying to hide my grin.

"What about the meat your father mentioned?"

"Me, my father, and Albert bought a cow. I picked it up the day before the auction, and we were supposed to slaughter it this week." He looks at me with his lips curled up. "Your father now owns that cow." He shrugs. "I need to pay 'em back for their part; I will, though. I'm doin' all right. Even though my father said I didn't have to, I will. I'm a man of my word, and it wouldn't be right if I didn't pay him back—"

The horse halts and bucks in the middle of the road.

"*Whoa*! Easy now, Buddy. Easy now," Pierce says.

Buddy snorts and stomps on the ground, kicking up dirt. Pierce stands, looks over the horse, shakes his head, and sits back down. He pulls the reins to the side, and Buddy begins turning us around.

"Did you forget something?" I ask, almost panicking. "I don't want to go back there."

"No, we need to go around."

"Why? The house is just a little further."

He nods to the center of the road.

I point to the big X etched in the middle of the dirt road. "What is *that*?"

"Hazel's X. Don't cross the X, ever," he says, almost snarling.

I glance at him—his shoulders are taut, his eyes steely. He always sounds so harsh whenever that woman's name comes up, and I can't see why.

Tchk, tchk, swack.

Buddy is now turned in the opposite direction, galloping, as he pulls the wagon behind him.

"Everyone in town knows to stay away from her and her X!" he shouts over the wagon's rumble.

I'm clutching the side with both hands. Once we get further down the road, away from the X, Buddy slows to a trot, and I relax my grip. "Why, what will happen?"

"Bad things. Stay away from Hazel and her X. Please, Pearl." He looks at me with concern in his eyes. "Promise me you'll stay away from her."

I shake my head and sigh. "All right, I promise." I'm not sure why Hazel has everyone so strung out. I don't believe in witches, but I won't go against my husband, so I'll do as he asks.

Better safe than sorry.

Chapter 8

June 22, 2001

"Did you ever cross the X, Nana?" Sara is sitting on the couch now with her legs tucked underneath her, flip-flops discarded on the floor, and clutching a can of soda to her chest.

Mary's returned along with a few residents. All their eyes are on me. Meredith's back from her important telephone call, sitting in a chair opposite of the sofa Sara's sitting on. I was too enthralled with my story to notice anyone join. I was there, living in that moment—it was so real.

I pick up my necklace and rub the ring attached to it. It won't fit over my swollen knuckles, and I can't even remember the last time it sat on my finger. I shake my head as I look at my wrinkled hands, now covered with liver spots. Time has not been good to my body.

"Well, I'll get to that, sure enough." I smile at the little girl who has my blood running through her. I wish I could stop her fate, but I don't think that's possible. The only thing I can do is tell my story and hope for the best.

"Go on, Nana, please continue with your fairy tale," Meredith says with an eye roll while sawing her fingernail with an emery board. She blows on her nail and adds, "We don't have all day. I have a date tonight."

I shiver, hating the sound of the nail file, and I can hear it perfectly fine.

She sniffs every so often and crosses her legs, one jerking up and down over the other. "Did your husband ever repay his dad and brother the money for the cow?" Meredith chucks the nail file into her bag and digs around without looking in my direction.

Is that all she cares about, the cow money? I snort. "Yes, Pierce paid them both in full."

She pulls a cigarette and lighter from her purse. "Well, that's good. I'd hate for our family to still owe someone for a stupid cow back in the early 1900s. I imagine the interest on that has skyrocketed." She stands, slinging the purse over her shoulder. "I'm going outside to have a smoke." She pushes the back door open and marches out.

I watch her through the tall glass window light a cigarette, take a long drag, throw her head back, and blow a cloud of smoke out of her mouth. Her shoulders instantly fall, relaxing. She opens her purse, drops the lighter inside, and once again digs through it, retrieving her telephone. She pushes the buttons while she sits on the black iron bench under a big magnolia tree in the center of the courtyard.

I love magnolia trees. I remember the one that sat in our front yard a long time ago. One of my favorite pastimes was sitting under it, smelling the fragrant aroma coming off its big white flowers. Is it still there? Is our house still there?

Meredith screams into her small telephone and slams it shut before dropping the cigarette, stomping it out with the sole of her high-heel, and lighting another one.

I shake my head and continue, "Well, the next five years were great." I look at the plain silver band that has tarnished over the years and smile. "We celebrated my birthday that first year, and he gave me this ring." I hold it out to everyone and beam. "It's about the same time I fell in love with Pierce." I shake my head and chuckle. "And no, it's not the ring that made me fall in love with him. I thought I was the luckiest girl in the world when he gave me this ring. It showed I was truly his, and he wanted everyone to know it. I wore it with pride. It was then he started showing me he cared. He may have showed me from the beginning, but I was too busy trying to be a good wife to him to notice. He opened up to me like no one ever has. People didn't know him the way I did. He wasn't quiet and shy like I first thought he was. It took time, but he broke out of his shell and so did I. I asked him one night while we rocked on the porch why he didn't let me graduate. He told me he couldn't let me go. He was afraid if he left without making me his wife, someone else would snatch me up."

I hear someone say, *"Aww,"* but I don't look to see who.

"He was nervous leaving me that Saturday; he was sure Daddy would change his mind. He was instantly drawn to me. I guess I felt the same way about him from the beginning. It just took me a while to appreciate how strong our connection was."

"Did you ever go back to school?" Sara asks.

"No. It was a different time back then. My course was set when I married Pierce. Being a wife and mother was top priority. Besides, there wasn't enough time in the day. Nine months after we married, we welcomed our first son, John Edward, on December 12, 1914. About a year later, William James was born on February 17, 1916. We were both so happy."

I can't believe my memory is so sharp now, as if everything had happened yesterday instead of over eighty years ago. I look at Mary.

She's smiling with her hands over her heart. "You're doing great, Pearl. Please go on," she says.

I nod at her. "The farm was doing well, and we were making our house a home, filling it with furniture and babies. John was only a year old when William came along, but he took to him like a big brother should. He had an instant bond with his little brother and, as they grew up, John was protective of William."

"Did you see Hazel again?" Sara asks.

"Yes, on occasion, but it was from afar. I never got too close to her, at least for the first five years. I tried my best to stay as far away from her as possible, even though I didn't believe she was a witch. Not at the time, anyway.

"I got pregnant again with our third child in January of 1919. We were so happy. Pierce always said he wanted a big family with lots of boys. They didn't have the technology back then as they do today, so we didn't know the sex of our third baby, but Pierce was sure it was another boy. He had great intuition. He turned out to be a great husband and a great father. I'm so happy he noticed me at the auction all those years ago."

"Was it a boy?" Sara asks eagerly.

Gravity finds the sides of my lips. "Yes, it was another boy. Jacob Matthew was his name."

"When was he born?" she asks.

I shake my head. "He wasn't. That was the first of many incidents that summer."

Sara looks at my stomach. "He wasn't born, Nana?"

I take a deep breath. "I've lived to see a lot of tragedies happen throughout the years like the Great Depression, World War II, and when JFK was shot, to name a few. Those were horrible events, but nothing—*nothing*—affected me deeper than my own tragedy. The one the summer of 1919 held in here." I tap my chest over my heart. "It was the worst summer of my life."

Chapter 9

May 1, 1919

I rub my small potbelly and look at the boys sitting on the kitchen floor, legs spread apart, giggling while drumming my pots and pans. Mama did the same thing, watched us kids play with her pots and pans while she cooked or cleaned. She was always in the kitchen doing something.

A sigh escapes through my frown. I miss my family. I've only been back to Summerville a few times in the last five years. I went home after the birth of my sister, Tammy, in September of 1914. Daddy died of a heart attack in 1917, and I, along with Pierce and the boys, went home for the funeral. My sister Elizabeth—I blink back the stinging in my eyes—married and got pregnant soon after. She and the baby died during childbirth. It breaks my heart to bury someone I love.

Elizabeth and her daughter dying scares Pierce, as it does me. But I assure him that I'll be fine. Mama made it through seven births, and she's fine. She was back piddling in the kitchen the next day after giving birth to us kids.

Thinking of her in the kitchen reminds me of her delicious cobblers. She made the best cobblers in town, still does. It brings me such joy thinking of filling my round belly with Mama's cobbler.

"Do y'all want to go pick blackberries?" I ask the boys.

"Yes, ma'am," John and William say at the same time.

"All right, let's get on some shoes."

I grab their hands, and we skip to their room. They drop to the floor and put on their scuffed, worn-out shoes.

"It looks like y'all need new shoes," I say as I squat in front of William. I make an X with William's shoelace, wrapping the bottom lace of the X over and through the top and pull it tight. Then I glance at John.

John's tongue darts out the side of his mouth while he makes his own X. He stops after it's pulled tight and studies the lace with a creased brow.

"Bunny ear, John," I remind him. I watch as his mouth forms an O, and then he makes his bunny ear.

"Can we get candy when we go to the store?" William asks.

"I don't know. It's up to your father," I say and finish his laces.

"Yay," William says. "Father always lets us get candy."

I roll my eyes and rise. "Come on. Let's go tell your father where we're going, so he won't worry."

We march to the kitchen and I grab two baskets from under the sink, giving one to each of the boys, and then we set off to the field. When Pierce sees us, he stops the horse and walks to the edge of the field where two buckets sit on the ground. He dips the ladle, filling it with water, and takes a long swig.

"I can tell the humidity this summer is gonna be higher than ever. It's gonna be a scorcher," he says once we reach him, his breathing heavy. He drops the ladle in the bucket, removes his hat, and sponges the sweat from his forehead with a rag. "And where are y'all off to?"

"To pick blackberries. I want to make a blackberry cobbler for Sunday."

He moves the rag to the back of his neck and glances up at the sweltering sun before turning back to me. "Why don't you wait? I'm fixin' to be done here, then I'll run y'all down in the wagon. It's awfully hot and you don't need to get too heated," he says with concern in his voice.

It warms my heart when he wants to protect me, but it isn't necessary. "No. It's not far, and it's good to walk."

"You sure?"

"Positive. We'll be fine."

He raises one brow and hesitates before replying, "All right, if you say so. Pick some extra, so you can fix one for us tonight. You know I love your cobblers." He lets out a winded chuckle and puts his rag away.

"I know. You remind me all the time," I say, rolling my eyes, and notice the half-empty water buckets. "Do you want me to get you more water before we go?"

"Naw, I'll get some in a bit." He glances over his shoulder at the field he's been working on. "I want to finish this row first. I'm almost done, then I'll take a break."

I take a step, leaning to the right, and note the long row still ahead behind him. I straighten, put my hands on my hips, and cock my head while narrowing my eyes at him. "All right, if you say so," I say, a bit nasally, with a big grin on my face.

He gives me a playful glare in response before leaning down. "Don't be gone too long." He kisses me and rubs my swollen belly.

"Eww!" the boys yell out the instant Pierce's lips touch mine.

Pierce, ignoring them, whispers against my lips, "Don't overdo it." Then he ruffles John's and William's hair and says, "Take care of your mama."

"We will," John replies, sticking his chest out.

Pierce shakes his head and replaces his hat, picks up the horse's bucket of water, and returns to the field.

With William's hand in one hand and John's in the other, we head to the dirt road, toward the blackberry field.

"And on his farm he had a cow," we sing and pause.

"C-O-W," I spell.

"C-O-W," William repeats, trying to hop on his shadow.

William points to the sky. "Birds."

I cover the top of my bonnet with my hand and look up,

squinting, to block the sun's rays from hurting my eyes. When my eyes adjust, I see a swarm of crows flying high above us. There are so many of them that the flapping of their ink-stained wings are clearly heard like a flag walloping on a windy day. They fly below the sun, blocking the light and making a welcomed shade for us. Their flapping sound is drowned out by their loud squawking, sounding like, *"murder, murder."*

The birds seem like they are trying to distract us, but that can't be, so I ignore them and return my focus to the boys.

"Yes, those are blackbirds. B-I-R-D," I say.

"X," John says.

Still walking, I lean down closer to him and ask, "What, sweetheart?"

He points to the ground behind us. "X," he repeats.

I turn to where we just walked and stop dead in my tracks as I stare at the big X etched into the dirt road. It's like the one Pierce and I saw five years ago after the first Sunday dinner at his parents' house. Except this time three sets of footprints cover the X—our footprints.

All the blood drains from my face. "We crossed the X," I whisper, my voice cracking.

I drop the boy's hands, and my hands fly to my opened mouth and racing heart. It's beating so fast I swear it will jump right out of my chest. I'm not sure why. Hazel being a witch is hogwash—I've seen nothing to prove it to be true.

But I have the heebie-jeebies anyway.

I scout around, but I see no one.

The bright blue sky has turned a brownish-green like a storm's coming, but there isn't a rain cloud in the sky. There's a silent calm and the crows have disappeared. Something's happening, but I don't know what. My heart crashes against my chest, and I need to calm down for my boys.

"What's wrong, Mama?" John asks as his brows knit.

"Nothing, nothing. I don't feel well." I touch my churning

stomach. Saliva builds in my mouth, so I swallow and take a few short breaths, hoping the nausea will go away. It does. It's nerves, it has to be.

"Mama, what about the blackberries?" William asks.

"Let's go home and pick berries another day," I tell them.

They take my hands without defiance and we walk to the edge of the road, near the shallow ditch, avoiding the X. I stare at it with wide eyes when we scoot past it like it will stand up and attack us. A chill runs through my body and the small hairs on my naked arms stand at attention. I can't believe I'm so afraid of an X. It's silly, but the terrifying feeling I have is real, very real.

I pick up the pace.

Something in the woods catches my eye. It looks like Hazel Sullivan, standing by a tree, watching us. I'm not sure if she's real; she doesn't look real. I can see the unfocused trees through the smoky mist of her black dress. She's perfectly still, and her unreadable face is blank.

When we get fully past the X, a small smile appears on her face before the sky turns blue again, causing me to look up. I glance back at the woods where I saw Hazel, but she's gone, so I focus straight ahead and hurry the boys down the road.

"Let's not tell your father about the X, okay? It's our little secret." I pray the boys don't tell Pierce about this. I don't know what he will do if he finds out about the X; I don't even want to know. It was an accident. A stupid, stupid accident. I'm so mad at myself right now I could chew nails. I should've been paying more attention. Stupid, stupid.

"We ain't supposed to keep secrets, Mama," John says.

"Just this once. Next time we go to the store, I'll buy you a piece of candy. Deal?" I shouldn't ask them to lie for me, but if Pierce never asks them, then it's not lying.

William nods vigorously at the mention of the candy.

"Okay, Mama," John says as he zips his pinched fingers across his closed lips and grins.

By the time we get back to the house, my stomach is unsettled, and I'm exhausted. "Boys, go to your room and take a nap," I say, nudging them toward their bedroom door.

"Yes, ma'am," they say and disappear into their room with their heads hanging.

As soon as their door is shut, I go into my room, climb in the bed, and fall into a deep sleep as soon as my head hits the pillow.

XXX

"Pearl?" Pierce shakes my shoulder.

I open my eyes and see his eyes dart back and forth between mine.

"Are you all right, Pearl?"

I nod and yawn, covering my mouth with my hand as I sit up. I swing my legs off the bed and slowly stand on wobbly legs. Pierce grips my arm until I regain my balance and focus.

"Yes, I am now. I wasn't feeling well earlier." His hand tightens, and I wince, regretting saying those words as soon as they leave my mouth. "I mean, I was tired, so I napped. It must've been the hot sun," I tell him, recovering from my blunder. "Where are the boys?"

"In their room colorin'. John came and got me. He said you was still sleepin', and he couldn't wake you." He lets go of my arm. "You never nap."

"It was the sun. It wore me slap out."

We mince into the living room, his arm around my waist, and I sit on the plain brown sofa we purchased four years ago. He pats his hand down my muddled hair. "I'll get you some water." He walks into the kitchen before I can object. When he returns, he hands me a glass and sits beside me, placing his hand on my knee. "You want me to get the doc?"

I place my hand over the top of his. "I'm fine. This baby wore me out today, that's all." After I take a sip of water, I give him a pathetic smile, but a smile nevertheless.

"I told you it was hot out today and not to overdo it. You shoulda waited for me like I told you to. You're hardheaded," he says, raising his voice slightly.

"I know. You were right—I'm sorry. But I assure you, I'm fine." And that's the truth. The nap was good for me, and I'm already feeling better.

"All right, as long as you're sure you and the baby are okay." He spreads his rough, calloused hand over my stomach and gently rubs it.

"Maybe this one's a girl. Girls can be a handful."

His brows quirk. "Didn't you say that about boys?"

"A handful is an understatement for boys." I stand, causing his hand to drop from my belly. "I cooked stew this morning. I just need to heat it."

"I can do it." He stands with me and pushes down on my shoulder with the same hand that was just caressing my swollen belly. "You sit and rest a spell."

I brush his hand off my shoulder. "No, I can do it. I'm good, honest." I touch his cheek and see him grin before I head to the kitchen.

He sneaks up behind me when I'm bent over, lighting the stove. "I don't suppose you had time to make a cobbler?"

I stiffen and straighten myself.

He wraps his arms around my waist and nuzzles my ear. "You know how I love your cobbler."

"We…we didn't get any blackberries," I say, looking at the wall in front of me and squeezing a rag on the counter. "I got tired on our way to the field, so we turned back before we had a chance to pick any. Maybe we'll go back tomorrow."

He turns me around in his arms, facing him. "That's okay. Maybe you should rest for a few days. I can take you and the boys in the wagon on Saturday. With the four of us, I bet we can get a whole mess of blackberries." He chuckles.

I nod and fake a smile.

He caresses my chin with his thumb before kissing me. "I'll get the boys for supper." He releases me and calls out, "Boys, supper's ready!" as he strolls out.

I let out a deep breath. I hope John and William don't discuss the X during supper. If Pierce doesn't ask, maybe they won't mention it. Maybe they've forgotten all about it.

XXX

As we sit on the porch watching the boys chase fireflies and the neighbors ride past the house, I look over at Pierce, smoking his pipe, and a sense of relief washes over me. The boys didn't mention the X during supper, and I couldn't be more grateful.

"I got one!" William yells, holding up his fist.

"Let it go before you suffocate it," I say and watch William's hand open. The little bugger flies away, and William takes off after it again.

I see Pierce out the corner of my eye concentrating on something. Before I can turn my head to find out what's caught his attention, he slaps my arm.

"Ouch!" I cover my arm with my hand and glare at him with hard eyes. "What did you do that for?

"Sorry," he says with a grin and points his pipe at my arm. "Did he getcha?"

I lift my hand and see a blood smear and a dead mosquito lying on my arm. I flick it off, wipe off the blood, and scratch the itch, the glare fading from my face. "Oh, I was wondering what you were doing. It's okay, I think I'll survive." I scratch once more before I make a cross with my fingernail on the raised skin, stopping the itch.

"I saved your life," he teases.

I roll my eyes. "Yes, my hero."

He chuckles before he turns to the boys. "I hear y'all didn't make it to the blackberry pasture today. We'll go on Saturday, so Mama can fix her famous blackberry cobbler," Pierce tells the boys while blowing out a swirl of smoke.

My heart skips a beat. "Wow, look at the moon, it's so big tonight! Isn't it, boys?" I rush out before the boys say anything about the X.

The boys look up and say, "Yes, ma'am." The glittering glow of the fireflies catches their attention once again. They both take off running, reaching for the little flickering lights.

I let out a small sigh of relief.

"It is. Looks like it's almost kissin' the trees," Pierce says. "I've never seen the moon so bright. It's a beautiful night, Pearl." He takes another drag off his pipe before pointing it at the boys. "Looks like the boys could use new shoes. After we pick blackberries, we should ride into town and order 'em some from Howards."

"Yes, that sounds good."

"Can we get candy?" John asks.

"If you're good, we'll see," Pierce says.

William looks at his hand and sticks out one finger and then another. "Yay, we get two pieces!" he shouts.

"One," Pierce corrects him.

"But Mama—"

I leap to my feet, sending the chair rocking and slamming into the house, and I clap my hands before William can say any more. "Come on, you two, it's time for bed!"

I open the door, allowing the boys to walk past, but they don't say a word.

Pierce blows out another ring of smoke. "Night, boys."

"Good night, Father," they both say with frowns on their faces and eyes stuck to the floor.

After they put their gowns on and crawl into bed, I pull the quilt over their little bodies.

"Remember, our *secret*," I say sternly, suppressing the panic in my voice as Hazel's expressionless face flashes through my mind. "I'll buy y'all a second piece of candy, but you can't tell your father."

They both nod. "Good night, Mama."

"Sweet dreams." I kiss them both on the forehead before extinguishing the lantern and shutting the door.

My eyelids are heavy and my feet drag on the floor all the way back to the porch. "I'm tired, and I'm going to bed," I tell Pierce when I reach him.

He grabs my waist and looks into my eyes, then at my stomach. "You all right, Pearl?"

I place my palm on his cheek and raise his eyes back to mine. "Yes, I'm fine, just tired. I'll be better after a good night's sleep." I kiss him on the lips and turn toward the door.

"I'll be in directly," he says before I shut the door behind me.

After a trip to the outhouse, I check on the boys one more time before I get my gown on and crawl into bed. When Pierce climbs into bed, I barely feel his light kiss on my pasty forehead.

"Pearl, you sweatin'." He places his hand on my forehead. "Are you hot?"

I shiver and pull the blanket to my neck. "No, I'm cold."

"I'll go get the doctor. Are you in pain?" He chucks the blanket off him, and puts a foot on the floor, but I grab his arm.

"No, it's too late to get him. He should already be in bed for the night. I'm not hurting, I promise. It's just a fever, probably from a sunburn. I'll be better in the morning." I shiver when a gentle breeze from the open window wafts through the room. Normally I would welcome it, but not tonight. "Can you shut the window?"

"It'll get awfully stuffy in here, you sure?"

I shiver again. "Yes, it'll help warm me up."

He gets out of bed, closes the window, and returns with a sigh. "If you ain't better in the mornin', I'm gettin' the doctor. Come here." He pulls me to him and cradles me against his chest.

"All right," I say before shivering myself to sleep.

Chapter 10

May 2, 1919

John, William, and I are singing while we're skipping along the road. I'm not sure where we're going; it doesn't matter. We're together, laughing and having a good time.

The sky is bright blue, the trees are a delightful shade of green, and the flowers along the side of the road are every color imaginable.

"Stop for a minute, boys. Let's have a smell."

We lean down and take a giant whiff.

William smiles up at me. "They smell so pretty, Mama."

"Yes, they do. Let's pick some and take them back home to put on the kitchen table."

The boys and I gather flowers of every color.

"Look, Mama. This one is red. R-E-D," William says with an enormous smile as he sticks out his chest.

"Yes, baby. R-E-D, very good. You are so smart." I ruffle his hair.

"This one is W-H-I-T-E," John says, holding up the little white daisy and sticking out his tongue at William.

I put my hands on my hips. "That isn't nice, John Edward. What do you say to your brother?"

"I'm sorry, William," he mumbles, looking at the ground.

"It's okay," William says.

I pat John's head, causing him to look up at me and smile. "Okay, let's keep moving, boys."

Pierce is up ahead, leaning against a tree and holding a small child, but then they slip into the woods, disappearing.

"Pierce, where did you go?" I call out. "Father wants to play hide and seek," I tell the boys. "Let's go find him."

They laugh and take off running into the woods.

"Wait for me!" I laugh too, but my laughter falls short when they also disappear behind the trees. I look up and see the bright blue sky has turned an eerie green, and black clouds are billowing like heaven is on fire and covered with smoke. "Boys, where did you go?"

Giggles weaken in the distance.

"Pierce! Boys!" I yell into the hushed air. I go into the darkened timber searching behind tree after tree, but no matter how much I look, I can't find a sign of them. "This isn't funny, boys. Let's go home before the storm comes. We don't want to get stuck in the rain."

I look up again at the black sky and then back into the dark woods. The flowers the boys had in their hands are on the woods' floor, forgotten. My heart beats faster, and I drop my flowers in a panic, joining theirs. I have to find my sons, so I go deeper into the thicket, faltering. The sunlight is no longer visible through the trees, so I pick up my pace.

I freeze when I see Hazel standing beside a big pine tree, staring at me and holding the same child Pierce had been holding earlier. The green leaves on the tree turn black and the surrounding woods disappear as they fade into the darkness. I see nothing except her glowing red eyes.

I turn around and shout, "Boys, time to go home!" My heart races and my panic escalates as I look behind every tree.

They're missing, Pierce is missing.

I take off running. But every which way I turn, she's in front of me, grinning.

I trip, falling to the ground. When I look back, I see the small child Hazel was holding, lying on the ground, not moving, not breathing. It's a baby. I reach for it, but Hazel's there, blocking me.

"Pearl," she says in a voice as black as night as she reaches out and grabs me, shaking me—

"Pearl, wake up. You're havin' a fit." Pierce shakes me.

I jerk and open my eyes, blinking to brightness. The sun is rising, and the room welcomes the light. Although the airless room is stuffy, I'm freezing, I'm shivering, and my stomach is cramping a little. "Bad dream. I'm all right," I say through chattering teeth, pulling the blanket to my chin.

"You are not all right. You need to get up and change, you're soakin' wet." He shakes me again.

I'm wet from the cold sweats, and I must've peed myself during my nightmare. I should be humiliated, but I'm not, not with Pierce. He's seen me at my worst and still loves me.

Pierce flings the blanket off me and gulps before returning the blanket back on top of me. "I'll get the doctor. Stay here." He flies out of bed. "I knew I shoulda gotten the doctor last night," he mumbles while slipping into his pants.

With his warmth absent, I'm colder than before. "Can you get me another blanket? I'm freezing."

He grabs another blanket out of the wardrobe, lays it on top of me, and straightens it out, making sure I'm well covered. He slips into his boots, not bothering with the laces. "I'll hurry. Don't move," he says and kisses my forehead before rushing out the door.

"I'm not going anywhere," I whisper to myself and pull the blankets back up to my chin as I continue trembling. My teeth rattle, and my fingers are numb. The cramping is getting worse, so I take a few labored breaths and shut my eyes…and wait. That's all I can do.

Pierce returns sometime later to find me in the exact same position. "Pearl, I'm back with the doctor," Pierce says, his voice tense.

I slowly nod without opening my eyes.

"Pearl, I hear you're not feeling well." Dr. Clayton touches my forehead with the back of his hand. "Yes, you definitely have a fever. Are you in any pain?"

"Cramps," I say through clenched teeth.

"Let's take a look." He uncovers me from my cocoon and exhales.

I look at my blood-soaked gown and shake my head in disbelief. "No!" I cry.

"Is she…will she be all right?" Pierce whispers to the doctor.

The doctor nods as he digs through his bag. "She's a strong, young woman, she'll be fine."

Pierce leans closer to his ear and whispers again, but this time the doctor shakes his head.

"I'll go tend to the boys." Pierce brushes my damp hair out of my eyes and kisses my clammy forehead. "I'm sorry, Pearl. I love you." He shudders. "I'm sorry," he repeats, wiping his glassy eyes and walks out, leaving me alone with the doctor.

The doctor pulls out a tarnished copper syringe and holds it in the air, flicks it a few times with his finger, and looks at me under his bifocals. "Pearl, I'm going to give you something to help you sleep." He sticks the needle into my arm and slowly pushes the plunger with his thumb.

I wince as I stare at his bushy gray handlebar mustache. "Is the baby gone?"

He removes the needle and sighs. "There's too much blood."

"Are you sure?" I whimper.

"There's nothing I can do. When you wake, you'll feel better." He looks at me with sympathetic eyes and pats my arm. "You rest now."

My eyelids feel as if they're filling with lead with every slow blink. He's blurry when he turns to his bag and pulls out some items I can't make out clearly, and my eyes shut once more—and they stay closed.

XXX

When I wake, Pierce is by my side, holding my hand with his eyes closed. The pain and shivering has stopped, but I feel empty and disoriented. What happened?

"The baby?" I mutter.

His eyes pop open, and I see his bloodshot eyes shine as depression fills his face. "Gone," he whispers. "You scared me." His

78

grip on my hand tightens. "I thought I was gonna lose you."

"I'm sorry. I should've let you get the doctor last night. Maybe if—" Tears form in my eyes and drip down my cheeks. I wipe at them with the palm of my free hand with anger.

He shakes his head. "No, it ain't your fault. Dr. Clayton said there was nothin' we coulda done." His voice cracks. "It was already gone."

I sniff. "What was it?"

He looks away and swallows. "A boy."

I don't smile; I can't. "You were right, then." The sun is setting through the open window, allowing an intense fire to shine through the curtain. I squint in confusion. "I've been out all day?"

"The doctor said you needed the rest. Cora helped with the boys. She cleaned you." He waves his hand at the new blanket on the bed.

"She's a good friend."

He nods.

I look back at his hand, which is massaging mine. "And your mother?"

"Don't worry about her. She'll get over it, same as us."

"She'll blame me," I whisper.

He squeezes my hand. "Don't worry about her," he repeats. "You just concentrate on getting better. Cora made some soup. You hungry?"

I shake my head, exhaling. "No."

"You need to eat so you can get your strength back. I'll send her in with a bowl of soup, and then you can go back to sleep. But you need to eat."

My nod is small, but my smile is smaller. "All right, if it'll make you happy, I'll try."

"Thank you." He stands and grabs the sides of my head with both hands, giving me a long, hard look. "You scared me."

"I didn't mean to."

"I know." He kisses me and walks out the door, closing it behind him.

I blow out a long breath and touch my empty stomach as I look at the closed door. Why did this happen?

XXX

I do eat, and I do gain my strength back within the next couple of days. Cora stays to help during the day while Pierce works in the field.

Florence comes by the day after my miscarriage with her normal repugnant attitude. *"This wouldn't have happened if you'd taken better care of yourself, girl. We won't be at the funeral. You shouldn't even have one."*

I blame myself, too.

Hazel's X is all I can think about. It's probably a coincidence, but I should've paid more attention where I had been walking. I should tell Pierce, but the damage is done, and there isn't anything I can do about it now. I hope it's the last time I have to worry about Hazel and her X.

We bury Jacob Matthew on May 4, 1919, in our church's cemetery. With only me, Pierce, John, and William in attendance, we say goodbye to the little boy we never knew inside the small pine coffin Pierce made, as it's covered with dirt.

Chapter 11

May 6, 1919

The boys are at the kitchen table eating dinner, and I'm cleaning collards from the garden for supper in the sink when I hear a creak from the front porch. I lean back, glancing through the living room at the screen door, and see nothing, so I ignore it and wash my hands when the smell of fresh-baked cookies hits my nose.

"Can we have a cookie, Mama?" William asks when I open the oven door and take the cookies out.

"No, these are for after supper." I slide the cookies onto a plate. "If you eat all your supper, you can have one."

The creak comes again; this time it's louder.

"Boys, stay here." I wipe my hands on my apron while walking to the front door and peeking out through the screen. I let out a stifled gasp and jump back.

Hazel is sitting in the rocking chair with her black hair pulled in a tight bun and wearing a dusty, long-sleeve black dress buttoned all the way to the neck. The only skin showing on this hot day is her face and hands.

I look toward the back of the house, making sure Pierce is nowhere to be seen. He's come in throughout the day, since we lost Jacob, to check on me. He'll surely be mad if he sees Hazel sitting in his rocking chair on our front porch. I need to find out what she wants and get rid of her, quick. With a sigh, I step out onto the porch, joining her. "Can I help you, Hazel?"

She's silent as she looks straight ahead, to the road, and rocks.

"Hazel?"

Silence.

I step forward, placing a hand on her shoulder. A sharp pain punches my gut, making me wince. I bend over and grab my hollow stomach and take in a few sharp breaths.

She collectedly turns her head and looks at me with a slight, closed-lip smile. "I heard about your baby."

"How?" I hiss through gritted teeth.

"Word gets around." She slowly taps a long red fingernail on the arm of the chair.

Tap…Tap…Tap.

The pain finally eases. I straighten and readjust myself, giving me a chance to scan her from head to toe with my inquisitive eyes. In the five years I've lived here, this is the first time I've seen her up close. With her long legs stretched, her feet push off the banister when she rocks, like Pierce, so she must be as tall as he is. Her black hair has only a handful of grays, and she has a few faint, thin lines around her eyes and forehead. I assumed she'd be older and unpleasant to look at, but she looks to be in her early forties, if that, and although she isn't beautiful, she isn't unattractive either…she's normal.

She doesn't look like a witch, but I don't know what witches are supposed to look like. Other than the red paint on the long middle fingernail on her right hand, she appears to be an ordinary woman. I've never seen anyone with paint on their nails—maybe she was painting before she came over today.

"What can I do for you, Hazel?"

"Do you have any *fresh* tomatoes from your *wonderful* garden out back? I could use some." She smiles, showing yellow crooked teeth.

I fight the urge to cringe, and swallow quickly. Maybe she *shouldn't* smile.

Her red fingernail continues tapping on the arm of the chair. The tap, tap, tap is drowned when she joggles her feet, making the chair creak with each rock. It gets louder and louder and the dull ache forming in my ears gets more intense with each pass. *C-r-e-a-k. C-r-e-a-k.* I raise my hands to cover my ears, but then it stops.

"Mama, who's out there?" John's walking toward the door.

I move quickly and stand in front of the door, blocking his view. "No one. Go get you and William a cookie. I'll be there in a minute to tuck you in for your nap." *I can't let him see her—he'd tell Pierce.*

"Okay," he says and skips back to the kitchen. "William, guess what? We get to eat cookies now!" he says with enthusiasm.

"Yay!" William says, echoing his brother's excitement.

"Only one!" I yell through the door.

"Aww," they both whine.

The rocking starts again, and I turn, facing the occupied chair.

"What *sweet* little boys you have there, Pearl. It's such a shame. *Tsk, tsk.*" She shakes her head slowly and looks toward the road where her horse and carriage are parked. Black crows gather on top of the carriage like a teenage gang waiting for their leader.

"What do you mean by that, Hazel?"

"You never answered me. What about those tomatoes, Pearl? I'm sure you grow *big, juicy* tomatoes in that *big* vegetable garden of yours. I bet you work in your lovely garden for hours and hours on end, getting those *prettay, young* fingers dirty."

Is that jealousy in her voice? Why would she be jealous? She doesn't know me. Is she envious of my garden?

"You can spare a few, can't you? What do you say?" She looks back at me with black-as-coal eyes, but they're like windows into her soul. The red-tinted slits down the middle expand, giving me a glimpse of the evil lurking inside. Her gaze slices through me, causing goosebumps, and a shiver scuttles down my spine before the slits close again, back to normal.

"I... I-I'm sorry," I stutter.

"Wha-what was that?" She fans her hand up to her ear, mocking me.

Pierce told me to have nothing to do with her, so giving her tomatoes will break his rules, and I don't want to disappoint him.

I clear my throat. "Pierce sprayed for bugs this morning. I can't let you have any. They're not good to eat," I rush out the lie.

"Ah, yes—your husband, your *handsome* husband who works all day long in that *big* field of his. His crops will surely be bountiful this year," she says, leering at me.

I cross my arms over my chest as anger swells inside me. "He is a hard worker, a very hard worker, and he won't take too kindly when I tell him you dropped by today. And I will!"

A red glow flickers in her eyes, and she slowly lifts her hand and places her red fingernail on her turned-up lips. "*Shh.*"

Did she *shush* me? My hands tighten into fists under my crossed arms, and my eye twitches. I need to get rid of her before I say something I'll regret. I exhale and relax my arms to my sides. "I'm sorry. I wish I could help, but I can't," I say calmly, and point to the door. "I need to put my boys down for their nap."

She stands and faces me. "Okay, Pearl," she says, appearing composed, before walking down the steps to her waiting carriage. The crows sitting on top of the carriage scatter, making loud *caw* sounds when she approaches.

When her carriage disappears down the road, I let out a long, unsteady breath. I walk back into the house and find the boys eating their cookie at the table. My fingers knead my temples against a slowly growing headache.

"Come on, boys"—I sigh—"let's take a nap."

XXX

We're sitting on the porch enjoying the calm night while the boys are already nestled in bed. The moon is hidden behind a gray blanket, making the night darker than normal. The only sounds heard are the crickets chirping and the frogs croaking. They seem louder tonight than usual. They must sense a storm is brewing.

Pierce lights his pipe. "Supper was good, Pearl. I love your fried chicken and collards. No one makes 'em better."

"Is there anything I cook you don't like? You'd be as big as a house if you didn't work so hard in the fields."

"Nope, I love it all," he says.

"I think you only love me because of my cooking," I tease.

He's silent for a minute, then nods before confirming, "I do love your cookin', that ain't no lie." He pauses. "But that ain't the only reason I love you. You mean the world to me, Pearl. You've given me two wonderful boys, and you're a great mother and wife. I couldn't ask for a better person to spend the rest of my life with. You was put on this earth just for me, I'm certain of that. I knew it the moment I put eyes on you. We're perfect together."

My hand goes over my heart. That is the most romantic thing he has ever said to me. I'm speechless.

"I know you feel the same way about me, Pearl, you ain't got to say it. Your eyes tell me every time you look at me."

"I do, I do," I say a little tearfully. "I love you, Pierce."

"I'm glad you went to the auction with your father that day. It was meant to be, us being at the same place at the same time. It was just meant to be, I tell ya."

I smile and whisper, "Yes, I agree."

We sit in a happy silence for a few minutes until I hear a creak. A pang of fear runs through me when I look over at Pierce's face, glowing red from his pipe's embers, and my eyes drop to his chair. He's rocking in the chair Hazel was sitting in only hours ago. That thought makes me quiver.

"You all right, Pearl?"

"Yes, of...of course," I stammer, still looking at the chair.

"You seem like you left me. Where'd ya go?"

I blink quickly and look back into his eyes. "Nowhere, I'm right here."

"I know you're still upset about Jacob. I am too. It's normal to be sad. It'll take time for both of us to get over it, but we will."

"No, it's…it's not that." I shake my head and look at my hands resting in my lap. "I need to tell you—" My tongue swells inside my mouth, unable to form the words. I feel as though I'm about to suffocate. Before the panic sets in, my tongue deflates, and I take in a deep breath.

What was that?

"Pearl?"

My eyes shift to his. "I'm fine," I say automatically and rub my throat. "Just tired, I guess." I stand with a slight tremble to my stance. "Maybe I should go to bed."

He seizes my hand. "You sure?"

"Yes," I say, feeling slightly better. "The boys wore me out today, that's all."

"All right, you ain't got all your strength back yet. You'll be better before too long. Once you're up to it, we should find a nice stone for Jacob's grave. The boys can help pick one out."

"Okay." I lean down, touching my lips to his. "Good night, Pierce."

"I'll be along directly, after I finish my pipe." He holds out his pipe and kisses my hand before releasing me.

I check on the boys once again before crawling into bed and falling asleep.

XXX

"Mama, where's Jacob?" William asks as he picks a ripe tomato from the garden and drops to the ground, sitting Indian style.

I drop a basket by his side. "Jacob is no longer with us, baby. He's in heaven with God."

Instead of putting the tomato inside, he takes a bite and sighs while tomato juice drips from his chin. "Why?"

"Because God needed his help," I tell him, picking a cucumber and placing it in the empty basket.

"He died 'cause we crossed Hazel's X." John picks a green pepper and puts

it in his own basket.

I narrow my eyes. *"That's not true, John. Don't tell him that."* I don't want William to think that. I don't want John to think that. I don't even want to think that. *"God wanted Jacob because he needed his help,"* I repeat.

"Why did he need Jacob's help?" William asks.

"I don't know. Maybe he wanted him to help keep an eye on the two of you. You can be a handful sometimes," I joke. *"Jacob may be your guardian angel."*

"What's a guardian angel, Mama?" William asks while John listens with open ears.

"It's someone to watch over you, to make sure you stay out of trouble."

"Oh." William frowns and looks at the ground. *"I miss him."*

"I do too, William," I mumble. *"I do too."*

"You didn't even know him. He wasn't even a boy yet," John adds and picks up a slithering stick and screams.

I run to him. *"Drop it, John. It's just a garter snake, it won't hurt you."* I slap his arm and it falls from his hand.

We watch the green-striped snake disappear into the pepper plants behind him. John's breathing is ragged as he stares at the plant.

"It's okay, John," I tell him. *"He's more scared of you than you are of him. Why don't you come pick some tomatoes with William?"* I grab his shoulders, turning him around, and freeze. The pepper plant the snake went under moves with intense fury. The small green-striped snake, now solid black, comes out of the plant, growing, until it's over ten feet tall and hovering above us. Its sides fan out like a king cobra with a yellow cross on its underbelly.

We watch with gaping mouths, paralyzed.

The scaly serpent sways back and forth like it's ready to pounce, deciding which one of us to strike first. It flicks its forked tongue and its diamond-shaped yellow eyes turn a deep maroon color, the color of blood. A hint of a smile is visible right before it opens its mouth wide, showing two large yellow fangs. Venom drops from the tips onto the plants below, burning them on contact with a loud hiss.

It rears back, ready to strike.

We all scream—

"Pearl? Pearl, are you all right? You're screamin'!"

I sit up and cover my trouncing heart with my hand, out of breath. I glance at Pierce before looking away quickly. "I'm all right, it was only a dream. I'm all right. I'm all right."

He exhales. "I was worried you was sick again. You want me to fetch some water?" Pierce tosses the blanket off him before I can answer.

I seize his arm. "No, I'll be fine. Just hold me."

"You sure?"

"Yes."

He lies back, taking me with him, and he wraps his arms around me. "What was the dream about?"

"It was nothing. Snakes. You know I hate snakes."

"All right, if you say so. Go back to sleep and don't dream about no more snakes." He lets out a small strained chuckle and tightens his arms.

I peck him on the lips. "I'll try. Good night, Pierce." I lay my head on his chest and close my eyes, but I'm not sure if I'm ready to go back to sleep. My heart still threatens to come out of my chest.

"Night, Pearl." He strokes my hair with his strong, comforting hands. Normally that would soothe me, but right now, it doesn't. I'm not sure anything can.

I don't fall asleep until well after Pierce's breathing gets heavier. When I do, my sleep is tortured and restless, as if I'm eternally trapped in this nightmare.

Chapter 12

May 7, 1919

Without opening my eyes, I feel the warm sunlight trickling into the room through the window, letting me know morning has arrived. I blink and when my eyes adjust to the light, I see a red glare on the curtain. I stretch away the restless night, get out of bed, and peek through the curtain. The sun's coming up over the horizon, making the streaks of clouds spread across the sky turn a reddish-orange. It won't last long, I know—the color will fade when the sun rises higher, but it's a sight I'm glad I'm blessed with seeing this morning.

I check in on the boys, who are still asleep, and stare at them for a few moments. They're so precious when they're out, like angels. I don't want to wake them yet because I get more done before they bound my day, so I tiptoe out of the room and close the door with care.

Pierce is sitting at the table, staring at his coffee cup with droopy eyes, when I walk into the kitchen.

I smile at him. "Good morning."

He looks up and points to the kettle sitting on the stove. "Water's ready."

"Thank you." I quickly make my coffee and sit, so I can have a few minutes alone with Pierce before the boys get up. "How long have you been up?" I close my eyes and breathe in the invigorating rich aroma before I take my first sip of the dark, bitter liquid.

He drinks his coffee, probably not his first of the morning. "A while. Did you get back to sleep last night all right?"

"Yes. I slept better the second time." I look at my finger tracing the edge of my cup, not wanting him to see my lie through my eyes. "You didn't?"

"I kept wakin' up. It scared me. The last time I woke you up from a nightmare…" He shakes his head, but doesn't finish; he doesn't need to.

I cover his hand with mine. "It's all right. I'm all right."

"I know, I know. I don't know what I'd do if somethin' happened to you. You're my world, Pearl." His eyes water before they fall to his empty cup as he fiddles with it in his hand.

"Don't worry, I'll be fine." I rise to my feet and take his cup to the sink, hoping my declaration will appease him.

He swipes his hands over his eyes, composes himself, and stands. "I'm gonna work for a couple hours. The new field is comin' along and should be ready to plant soon. Maybe after breakfast we can go into town. The boys still need new shoes."

"That sounds good. They're growing fast."

"Make a list of whatever else you need." He caresses my chin and kisses my lips before grabbing his hat from the hook. He looks at me one last time, as if he wants to say something else—but he doesn't, and then he walks out the door.

I open the cabinet and pull out a bag of grits when Pierce runs back through the door—it slams behind him. I jump and fumble with the bag, but I'm able to recover before dropping it on the floor.

"Pearl, come look!" he says with wide eyes.

I place the bag of grits on the counter and follow him out the door, stopping at my beautiful garden. The garden I've worked hard on for the last five years. The one that kept our family from starving.

The one that is now all black and dead.

Pungent odor ascends off the fly-infested rotten vegetables, making me pinch my nose with my fingers before it nauseates me. I fall to my knees, and with a shaky hand, I reach out for one of the black leaves of a tomato plant.

Pierce slaps my hand away. "Don't touch that, Pearl. We don't know what did this." He shakes his head. "It musta been a bug. I wonder if it got anyone else's garden."

My hand goes over my mouth while I choke back sobs.

Pierce pulls me up off the ground and into a hug. "Don't cry, Pearl. These things happen. We'll plant a new one." He leans back, holding me at arm's length. "We got plenty of canned food to last a while, don't we?"

"Yes," I mumble.

"I'll plow it today." He grabs my face with both hands, wipes my tears away with his thumbs, and kisses my forehead. "It'll be all right, you'll see."

I nod as my eyes search the ground, and my breathing gets labored. This had to be Hazel. I'm getting madder and madder at her and her stupid X. I believe she caused this—*know* she caused this. She must've snuck here in the middle of the night and sprayed something on my beautiful garden. That's exactly what happened. It was her!

I look at him with heated eyes. "Do you believe someone could've done this?"

"No. No one would do somethin' like this 'round here," he says slowly, before glancing off in the distance. "We'll fix this, I swear." He looks back at me and touches my cheek. "I'm hungry. Is breakfast ready?"

"No, I haven't even started it yet."

"Oh, yes." He smiles. "I guess you haven't had time to fix it yet. How about pancakes? The boys love your pancakes."

I narrow my eyes. "The boys, or you?"

He chuckles. "Both."

"I was about to put on a pot of grits when you came barreling back through the door. But I can make pancakes instead."

"I'll milk the cow and grab the eggs, then you can fix 'em."

"All right, I can do that."

He puts his arm around my shoulder and escorts me inside as I glance back at my once beautiful garden.

Once we get into the house, the boys come running from their bedroom.

"Slow down! What's the hurry?" I bend over and grab them both in a hug.

"We're hungry," John says, out of breath.

Pierce says, "Well, why don't you boys help me get the eggs and milk Bessie so Mama can make us breakfast? I hear she's fixin' pancakes this mornin'." He grabs a basket and the milk bucket from under the sink and hands one to John and the other to William.

William's beside the door, bouncing on his heels. "Yay, I love pancakes!"

I'm rewarded with a smile and a wink from Pierce while he shoves the boys outside. He turns back to me. "Don't worry, Pearl, we'll fix the garden," he says and disappears out the door.

XXX

Florence pulls up in her buggy as I'm putting seeds in the dirt of the new garden and covering it with my bare hands. Her head whips around to the side of the barn and sees the discarded plants Pierce threw over there, without getting out. "What did you do now, girl?" she says, her voice harsh and grating.

I purse my lips and continue to cover the seeds with the dirt. "Nothing."

"I've heard of a black thumb, but this is ridiculous." She huffs and drives off before letting me refute her.

"It's okay, Mama. We'll help get the garden back the way it was." John's warm, dirty hand grabs mine in a soft embrace. He looks at me and beams.

I smile back with a nod. "I know. It'll be better than before, with your help." I stand and brush off the dirt from my dress. "Let's wash off in the pond, then get a drink of water and take some to your father."

When we walk out of the garden, I see a familiar carriage pass around the corner of the house. I don't see the person inside, but I know it's Hazel. A shiver creeps down my spine like a million tiny ants carrying food back to their hill.

"Come on, let's go," I say to the boys.

We step to the water's edge and squat, dipping our hands into the cool water.

"Can we practice our swimmin', Mama?" John asks as he dunks his arms in the water.

"We'll see, maybe after supper." I touch his nose. "You're doing really well with your swimming. You'll need to make sure you help William until he gets to be as good a swimmer as you."

"I *am* a good swimmer," William says with a frown.

I straighten. "I know you are, but make sure you don't go in unless me or your father are with you."

"Okay, Mama," William mumbles.

"I'll help watch him," John says and grabs William's hand, both rising.

"Thank you. Let's get some water for Father."

"Okay," they both say, and we set out to do just that.

Once we get to the field and I hand Pierce a glass of water, he says, "You didn't need to bring me water. I still got plenty in the bucket."

"I know, but I wanted to see you. Besides, you need a break. It's sticky hot today." I fan myself with the collar of my dress, but the coolness doesn't come.

"Well, I'm glad you did." He takes a swig and picks up the horse's bucket, handing it to the boys. "Boys, take Buddy some water. He's been workin' hard."

"Yes, sir," John says. They each take a side of the handle and shamble toward the horse as water spills from its sides.

Pierce drinks the rest of the water in one large gulp. "How's it goin' down there?"

"Good. We're almost done, and we're taking a break to get something to drink." I pause. "Your mother came by," I say, a hint of distaste in my voice.

"Don't let her get to you."

I bite my tongue. "I try not to."

"What did she want?"

I shrug. "Who knows?" I look at the field, where the boys are petting Buddy while he slurps the water. "How are you doing?"

He glances over his shoulder at the field. "Good, good. Should be ready to plant beans in a few days."

I touch his sweaty arm. "I'll be glad when it's done. You need a break. You don't think what happened to my garden will affect the field, do you?"

"Naw, it's good, looking real good. This year's profits will be ten times better than last year's, you wait and see. This new field is gonna be good for us. We'll finally be able to sock away some money, some real money, Pearl. No more just gettin' by." He hands me the empty glass and picks me up, spinning me around and making me squeal. Then he sets me back down and kisses me. "Real money, Pearl."

"Come on, boys!" I call, fresh hope and happiness in my voice. "Let's go finish the garden, so I can start supper."

They run back to us. "Yes, ma'am," John says while William takes my hand.

"Real money." Pierce winks before heading back out into the field.

Chapter 13

June 5, 1919

John, William, and I gathered strawberries from the strawberry patch this morning. The boys are munching on a bowl of them while I'm making four pies. One for us, and the other three for Pierce's parents and Cora, Albert's family, and Mabel's family.

I take the first two pies out of the oven, replacing them with the other two, when I hear someone calling my name from the front porch. Who could that be? I close the oven and glance at my watch, noting the time.

"Who's that, Mama?" John asks without looking up. His tongue sticks out at the side of his mouth while he writes letters on a piece of paper at the kitchen table.

"Pearl," comes again.

"I don't know," I say as I take my apron off and place it on the counter. "Stay here and practice your alphabet. I'll be right back," I tell them both, and I jostle William's hair, who is scribbling on his own paper, before walking away.

When I peek out through the tiny holes dividing me from the outside, I see Hazel, standing with her back to me, facing the road. With hands clasped behind her back, the one long red fingernail sticks out, twitching. Her carriage is parked by the road again with the same black crows sitting on top. They seem to follow her like stray cats looking for milk.

"Your garden looks *lovely*, Pearl," she says without turning around.

"No thanks to you," I mumble.

She glances over her shoulder and lifts one eyebrow. "What was that?"

I shake my head. "Nothing. What can I do for you?"

I notice her black hair, in its usual tight bun, looks to have more gray than the last time she was here. The wrinkles lining her face are deeper, and she has more of them. Has it only been a month since the last time I've seen her?

She turns back around and doesn't speak.

I glance at my watch, toward the back of the house, and then back at her. "Hazel?"

She grumbles, "Eggs. Can you spare a few?"

You have to obey your husband.

My lips tighten as I look at the back of her head, and finally I say, "I'm sorry, but I've already gathered eggs today. We ate them at breakfast."

"Is that so?"

"The hens aren't laying many these days," I lie. "I'm sorry, but there's no more today."

"Are you sure, Pearl? I'm sure the chickens you have produced more than enough eggs for you, your *handsome* husband, and your two *sweet* little boys," she drawls, looking over her shoulder.

"I gave some to Pierce's folks this morning. His mother needed extra for baking," I say, the lies flowing easily out of my mouth, and I look at the floor, avoiding her eyes. "I'm sorry."

"Very well, Pearl. If you insist," she says before walking off the porch to her waiting carriage.

Once she's out of sight, I close my eyes and take a few deep breaths, in my nose and out my mouth, before returning to my boys.

The smell of burning pie floats through the kitchen when I enter. "Oh no!" I say to myself as I quickly slip on an oven mitt and take the pies out, plopping them on the stovetop. Not the smell I was expecting when I walked back into the kitchen. I let out a long, staggered breath and twist my lips while staring at the black crusts. I know I wasn't out there for that long.

I pick up the empty bowl on the table and look at the boys smiling at me with scarlet mouths. "You sure do love your strawberries, don't you?"

"Yes, ma'am," they both say with a snicker.

"It's okay," I tell them with a frustrated breath. "I guess two pies will have to do." I look back at the blackened pies. "The pigs will be in hog heaven tonight," I mumble to myself.

"Look, Mama. Look what I drawed. B-I-R-D," William says with a proud smile and holds out his paper to me.

"Look what I *drew*," I correct him and look at the paper. There's a black bird on it, like the ones we saw in the sky not too long ago. The letters are written on top in sloppy but legible handwriting. He's learning so well, so fast.

"Very good, William," I say. "You may be a famous artist one day." I tousle his hair and watch his smile grow.

His eyes light up. "You really think so, Mama?"

"Of course, you boys can do anything you want. The sky's the limit." I throw my head back and wave my hand into the air, being dramatic. But I do mean it.

"What does that mean?" William asks, looking up at the ceiling.

"It means you can do anything you put your heart"—I touch his chest—"and your mind to." I touch his temple.

He thumbs his chest. "Then I'm gonna be a famous artist."

"Artists aren't famous," John says.

I put my hands on both hips. "Yes they are, if they're good enough. Have you ever heard of Vincent van Gogh, Leonardo da Vinci, or Rembrandt?" I know he hasn't.

"No, ma'am. Who are they?"

"They're famous artists. I've seen their paintings in books when I went to school."

William's scratches his head. "Their paintins are in books?"

"Yes, well, pictures of their paintings. Their paintings can be seen on the walls of museums."

"What are museums?" William asks.

"Museums are buildings in big cities you can visit to see things from the past, like paintings from famous artists." I wink at William.

"Have you been to a museum, Mama?" John asks.

"No, but I've read about them. Maybe one day we can visit one. I'm sure Charleston has one, and it's not too far away."

"My paintins are gonna be in museums one day," William says with a smile.

"I'm sure they will." I touch William's nose before turning to my other boy. "How are you doing with your alphabet, John?"

"Just swell." John slides the paper across the table toward me. A large black X is in the center of the paper with hundreds of X's surrounding it. "I'm gonna be a school teacher."

My blood runs cold, and I know all the color has drained from my face as I stare at the paper for a moment before speaking with a gulp. "Very good, John." My voice shakes. "Why don't you take William outside and play?"

"Yes, ma'am." John reaches for his paper, but I place my hand over the top of it.

"Don't worry about that. I'll clean up." I shoo them out the door before they can protest, even though I know they won't. They love playing outside.

"Can we go swimmin'?" John asks before the screen door is shut.

"No. Stay away from the pond—and watch your brother. I'm going to start supper."

"Yes, ma'am." John takes William's hand and skips to the big pine tree that has the plank swing attached.

I stare at the X-filled paper and trace the large X with a trembling finger, feeling the burn of it. With shaky hands, I pick it up and rip it into small pieces before taking it to the outhouse and throwing it away, so Pierce won't see it.

He wouldn't be happy.

Chapter 14

June 6, 1919

"Boys, let's go for a walk. I want to pick some wildflowers in the field at the end of the road. Those flowers are the prettiest."

I grab the boys' hands and stroll to the end of the road. We stop and gaze at the array of color. The flowers sway like they're dancing to the wind's song.

William points to the performance. "Look, Mama, they're dancin'."

"Flowers don't dance, silly," John corrects him with a smirk.

"John!" I narrow my eyes at him. "William, they do look like they're dancing, don't they?"

He nods while picking blue forget-me-nots and looks up at me. "I like these. They're the color of your eyes."

I lean down and kiss his cheek. "I guess they are."

We gather as much as we can hold and head back toward the house.

On the way back, I look to my right and see Hazel's little old wooden house tucked away behind moss-covered trees.

She's on the side of the house, sitting on a stool and wringing a chicken's neck. Round and round the body goes. A pot of boiling water sits beside her, and feathers cover the ground around her feet. The gamy smell of scalding fowl drifts through the air. She looks at me while its neck snaps and grins, showing a hint of her corroded yellow teeth.

I stop and stare. I can't look away. Everything else around me disappears, because all my attention is focused on her.

She takes the chicken and dunks it a few times in the boiling water before she removes it and does a feather-pull test. She dunks it again, jiggling it a few more times, and yanks it out, repeating the test. When a feather pulls with ease, she plucks the rest off its body, discarding them to the ground.

I'm not sure why I'm so fascinated by this. I've done this a million times, but the way she does it, with such malice and structure, it's mesmerizing. Her eyes have not left mine since she noticed me staring. I try to look away, but I can't.

She stands and hangs the chicken by its feet on a string hung between two trees. The line houses several featherless chickens, eight in all. She takes a large rusty knife and slowly cuts the chickens down the middle, one by one. Blood and guts fall out each one and drip onto the ground, making puddles of deep ruby.

She stops with the knife midway through the air and looks at me like she didn't know I was still here, staring. She reaches into a chicken, pulls out the heart, and takes a bite as if she were eating an apple. Her eyes never leave mine and a smile forms on her face, showing her bloody teeth, and making me gag.

I jolt up and look around when I hear the loud pounding of my heart in my ears. It was only a dream, a vivid dream, another nightmare. I hate having nightmares, and they're becoming more and more frequent.

Pierce is gone, and the room is getting brighter by the second. There's no time to waste. I need to get up and start breakfast, because it won't make itself—so I sling the blanket off, rise, and quickly dress.

I crack the boy's bedroom door, peeking in at the sleeping angels, and quietly shut it again. Then I head to the barn where Bessie is waiting impatiently to be milked. "Good morning, Bessie. I'm sorry I'm late."

After I milk the cow, I walk inside the house and see the boys standing in the kitchen, dressed in their little coveralls. "Good morning, boys. Did you two just get up?" I place the full bucket of milk on the counter.

"Yes, ma'am," John says while William rubs his sleepy eyes and nods.

"All right then, let's go get the eggs." The boys help me if they're awake in the mornings. They love finding the eggs and seeing the chickens scatter, something that always brings a smile to my face as well.

When we get to the hen house, the door is ajar. I stop and throw my hand out to the boy's chests. They both halt and look up at me with drawn brows.

"What's wrong, Mama?" John asks.

I shake my head and look back at the opened door—a door that's always shut and latched. A strong, metallic, musty scent is coming from inside, and I jump in front of the boys, blocking their view. I slide my head through the crack, peering in, and I gasp. Feathers are scattered everywhere, as if a hundred pillows had exploded. Every chicken was slaughtered, leaving the flattened carcasses on the ground, drained of blood. Blood and innards drip from the ceiling, making pools of brownish-red gore, and it decorates the ground, the walls, and the bedding straw.

I turn back around and breathe through my mouth, fighting the nausea, and slam the door closed with shaky hands, so the boys don't see the horrific scene I'm sure will give me even more nightmares.

I heave a strangled sob. *Maybe I've already had this nightmare.*

William tugs at my dress skirt, his face scrunched with worry. "What's the matter, Mama?"

"N-nothing, baby," I lie through my teeth. "John, take William back inside and play in your room. I'll come get you when breakfast is ready." I turn them around and nudge them toward the house distractedly. *Please, Lord, don't let them protest.*

"What about our chores?" John asks staunchly, digging his feet into the dirt, but I keep pushing. "We're supposed to help get the eggs."

"I know, but not today. I forgot I need to go see your father first."

After making sure they get inside, I take off at full speed to the field. "Pierce! Pierce! Come quick!" I yell at him, and he turns around, bringing the horse to an abrupt stop.

He runs toward me with terror flooding his face, his eyes popping with tension. When I get close enough, he clutches my arms hard enough for me to feel his fear. "What is it, Pearl? Is it one of the boys?"

I shake my head. "No. It's the chickens. Something's gotten them," I pant.

We race back to the hen house, and Pierce slings the door open and freezes, looking inside. After a moment of silence, he says, "It musta been a wild animal. A rabid dog, maybe." He swings the undamaged door latch back and forth. "How could it have gotten in?" He looks at me. "Did you close the latch yesterday?"

"Yes, I'm pretty sure I did. I always do," I say and wring my hands.

His brow furrows. "How 'bout the boys? Could they have left it open?"

"They can't reach the latch. It couldn't have been them. Besides, if it had been a wild animal, wouldn't it have eaten the chickens?" I point to the house with an open hand. "All the chickens are still here, ripped apart."

He leans his head on his arms, which are resting on the door frame, and looks around inside. "I don't know. It don't make no sense."

*Hazel came over yesterday asking for egg*s, I remember with a creeping sense of horror. Just like the day she came over asking for tomatoes, and the next day the garden was dead. It was her—*she* did this. She killed my chickens. I need to tell him; I can't keep lying to him anymore. I take a deep breath, ignoring the swelling sensation of my tongue. "Pierce. I need to—"

A high-pitched scream comes from inside the house. We both jerk our heads toward the house, then pelt toward the scream.

When we barrel into the kitchen, John's standing on a stool, at the sink, with blood dribbling down his arm, crying. William's standing beside him, watching the blood drip with quivering lips and tears draining from his eyes. Pierce grabs John while I grab a towel and cover his hand, pressing hard to stop the bleeding.

"What happened?" Pierce raises his voice over the crying, and William steps back against the wall.

"I'm sssorry. I tttried to hhhelp with breakfffast. I wwwanted to cccut the tops off the ssstrawberries," John says through sobs.

"It's okay. Let me look." I uncover his hand and pump water over the wound before covering it back with the towel. I look at Pierce. "It's deep, but he'll survive. Get me the tin from the cabinet." I nod to the cabinet on the other side of the kitchen.

With a pale face, he shuffles to the cabinet.

"He'll be fine, Pierce."

I glance under the blood-soaked rag—the cut is still oozing red, but it's slowing, so I add more pressure to the wound. Pierce opens the tin on the counter, and I see what I need without taking my hands away from John's.

"I need some strips of gauze and the iodine."

Pierce tears the gauze, putting the pieces on the counter in front of me, and picks up the iodine bottle. After studying it, he looks at me with wide eyes. "This says it's poison."

"You're not supposed to swallow it. It'll be fine to put a little on his finger. It'll kill the bacteria and help it heal faster." I take it from his hand and gasp when I notice the cross and bones, in the shape of an X. I blow out the breath and shake my head, throwing away the unwelcome thought before dabbing the iodine on the cut, making his finger turn brownish-orange.

John screams. "It burns, it burns!" he cries as he jumps up and down on his heels.

William cries louder.

Iodine doesn't burn, but telling that to a hysterical little boy will do no good, so I blow on his finger to ease the nonexistent burning. "It's supposed to burn. That's how we know the medicine is working," I lie, and look at William. "He'll be all right, William."

William nods and juts out his bottom lip as his chin lands on his chest and his eyes find the floor. His hands are on the wall behind him, making his pudgy little belly stick out more than usual.

"Oh." John stops his screams and his jumping, but the tears still flow in a steady stream.

"Good boy." I wrap his finger in gauze, tie it off, and kiss his bandaged finger. "You'll live." I kiss his cheek.

Pierce puts everything back in the tin but lingers on the iodine bottle, shaking his head, before putting it away.

"Can we have pancakes?" Johns asks with a hiccup, holding his bandaged finger to his chest.

"Pancakes?" William asks, looking up with a smile on his face and dried tear streaks down his cheek.

"Of course we can, and you can even help," I tell them both.

"Don't you need eggs for pancakes?" Pierce whispers in my ear. "You want me to get some from Mother?"

I shake my head. "No, I can make them without."

"All right, you're the cook," he says, raising his palms.

XXX

After an eggless breakfast, I send the boys to their room to play, and Pierce helps me do the dishes. We're both gazing out the back window at the quiet hen house when I ask, "Do you really believe it was a wild animal?"

"Had to be. I'll go to town tomorrow and get some new chickens. It wouldn't hurt to get another latch, too. I'll make sure it doesn't come open by accident again."

"All right." I give him a warm smile. "Pierce, I need—" But my hand goes to my neck, and I swallow back a lump in my throat.

"We can get some eggs from my folks in the meantime."

I shake my head. I don't want Florence involved. This is another reason for his mother to dislike me. I can see her sour face as she blames me for the dead birds. I can hear her now, *"You should've put the latch on, girl. Maybe next time you'll be more careful."*

"I'll go. You don't have to see her," he says as he dries a plate with a hand towel.

"I don't know why she hasn't warmed up to me yet."

"Just give her time, she will."

I scrub the pan in the sink. "It's been five years. I don't think she'll ever come around."

He sets the dry plate on the counter, dropping the towel on top of it, and places a hand on my arm. "How 'bout we forget the eggs. You can fix grits or pancakes again. We'll go to town after breakfast tomorrow and let the boys pick out some new chickens. I'm sure there's a few things you might need at the store, too." He gives me a quick kiss and wraps his arms around my back.

"Thank you." I unwrap myself from his embrace and dry my hands on my apron. "Pierce, there's some—"

Pierce puts his lips on mine, silencing me. "No more talk about Mother. Don't worry, it'll be all right." He treads to the back door, opens it, and sighs. "I'll start cleanin' the chicken coop—it's gonna take awhile. Keep the boys inside, I don't want 'em to see." He grimaces before walking out and shutting the door behind him.

I nod at myself because he's already gone. I'm glad he's doing it because I couldn't stomach cleaning that mess.

I can't stomach the idea of telling him the truth, either.

Chapter 15

June 7, 1919

"Here, Pearl"—Pierce hands me a few bills—"get only what we need. We ain't got much money since I gotta buy more chickens. Not until I get all the wheat harvested and sold, then we'll have extra. Just not now."

We both look at the frowning boys sitting in the back of the wagon, staring at the empty chicken crate.

"Okay. I'll only get what we need." I turn and mount the steps to Howard's. I reach for the knob, but Pierce's hand catches mine before I can turn it, startling me.

He's standing beside me with troubled eyes. "You think we can do without somethin' so the boys can get a treat?" he whispers, glancing back at the boys still sitting in the wagon. "I hate the look on their faces. I want to see them smile again."

"I'll see what I can do."

"Thank you, Pearl. I'll be back shortly." He kisses me and retreats down the steps.

As I walk down the short aisle, my hand moves along the many items sitting on the shelf. It stops on a small black velvet bag. I open the bag and pour out colorful glass marbles into my palm. "Perfect," I mumble. They can both share this, and I only have to get one. I put the balls back into their bag and find the rest of the things I need, making sure I keep track of the total in my head so I don't go over.

I place the items on the counter and smile at Mr. Howard. He puts down the yellow pound cake he was eating, wipes his hands on his pants, and grins. "The widow Dorothy sent this over, think she's got a sweet spot for me. How you doin' today, Pearl?" he asks while ringing up my groceries and putting them in a bag.

Mrs. Louise passed away a few years back, and he has taken over running the store by himself. The store is in much better shape now. He dusted the shelves and floor, replaced the sign out front, fixed the shutters, and put a fresh coat of paint on the front. It's amazing what a man's touch will do to a store.

"Good. How are you, Mr. Howard?"

"Good, good, can't complain." He wipes his glistening forehead with the back of his hand. Beads of sweat run down his face, and his blue dress shirt, threatening to burst, is saturated. "It sure is a hot one out there today, ain't it?"

"Yes, it is. It's miserable hot," I say, fanning myself with the collar of my dress.

He picks up the bag of marbles. "And how are those two little boys of yours? They sure are growin' up fast, I tell ya. Every time I see them I think they've grown. I better start stockin' shoes just for them." He chuckles with a barking cough and drops the little black bag back on the counter as he covers his mouth with a handkerchief.

I let him recover from his fit before I say, "We had a wild animal attack our chickens the other night, and they're pretty upset about it. Pierce and the boys are getting some new ones. Have you heard of any wild animals around here? Rabid ones?"

His thick gray brows rise up. "Rabid?" He shakes his head. "No, no, can't say I have. I'll keep my eye out, though."

I hand him all the money out of my small green velvet drawstring purse. After counting, he looks at me with the lines of his forehead more pronounced than usual. "You're a little short. I need another dollar twenty-five," he says with a frown.

"Oh, I'm sorry." My face burns with embarrassment. "I must've added it wrong," I say while looking through the bag, but he places his hand over mine.

"Don't worry about it, Pearl. Y'all give me plenty of business." He picks up the marbles and drops them in the brown bag along with two pieces of butterscotch candy. He passes me the bag of groceries and smiles. "Give Pierce and those boys my best."

I pull the cord, closing my wristlet. "Thank you, Mr. Howard, I will," I gush, embarrassed and appreciative at the same time. "Thank you."

My face is still heated when I walk out on the porch to wait for Pierce. He doesn't leave me waiting for long. When he pulls up to the store, the chickens are clucking in the crate, and John and William are sticking their fingers through the small holes. The chickens peck at the boys' little fingers, making them giggle and jerk their fingers back out of the holes. Both Pierce and I laugh along with them.

Pierce takes the bag from me and places it in the back with the boys and chickens. "Did you get everythin' you needed?" he asks while taking my hand and helping me into the wagon.

"Yes, and then some."

"Good. Let's get these chickens to their new home."

Tchk, tchk, swack.

XXX

Emmett and Florence are sitting in their buggy behind the house when we pull up. My body stiffens, but I refrain from rolling my eyes. Pierce squeezes my hand, and I nod to him, assuring him that I'm all right.

Pierce helps me and the boys out of the wagon without looking at his parents.

Emmett comes up behind Pierce and grabs one side of the crate. "What happened, son?"

"Wild animal got the chickens. I spent all day yesterday cleanin' the chicken coop and buryin' the remains," Pierce says as they lift the crate out the wagon.

"You said a wild animal. Wouldn't an animal eat the chickens?" Emmett asks as he sets his side of the crate down inside of the hen house.

Pierce puts his side down—"Don't know," he says—and opens the lid on top. "Maybe it was rabid." He slants the crate on its side, and the chickens run out and scatter inside their new home.

John and William sprint after them. The chickens cluck and run away as they flap their wings. The boys laugh and point to the chickens as they call out names for each one: "Red, Spot, Speckle, Blackie…"

"So, you left the door open for a wild animal to kill all your chickens?" Florence asks with a smug grin on her face, still sitting in the buggy with her hands folded in her lap. "You need to be more careful, girl. Didn't you just have to plant a new garden?"

"It wasn't her fault, Mother," Pierce says. "It was an accident."

Now a deep scowl creases her face. "A careless—"

"Florence, let it rest," Emmett warns her before turning back to Pierce. "We're on our way to town. You need anythin'?"

Florence huffs in defeat but stays quiet otherwise.

Pierce grabs the bag from the back and holds it up. "Nope, just got back."

"All right. I'll see you tomorrow in church!" Emmett calls out as he steps into the buggy with Florence at his side.

Pierce nods when they drive past and puts an arm around me. I press myself closer to him, feeling comforted, but it does little to make me dread tomorrow any less.

Chapter 16

June 9, 1919

I'm at the kitchen table sewing a button on Pierce's white dress shirt, which had fallen off yesterday during Sunday dinner with his parents.

That was fun.

Florence couldn't stop talking about the chicken massacre. *"I can't believe you let a wild animal get to your chickens. You should've been more careful, girl. Chickens don't grow on trees here like they must do in Summerville."*

Pierce slammed his fist on the table, making my tea tumble over into his lap. He jumped up, hitting the edge of the table, and the button came right off. Needless to say, we didn't stay long after we ate. I hope the chickens are never brought up again.

I cut off the ending thread after securing it and hold up the shirt, admiring my work.

"Pearl." The voice coming from the front porch makes me jump.

My back stiffens and my lips tighten. What does she want now? I have nothing to say to her, so I toss the needle and thread in my sewing box, determined to ignore her. Maybe she'll go away.

"Pearl," she says, raising her voice a little louder.

"Well, dagnabbit." I throw Pierce's shirt on the table and stand. If I don't go out there, she'll probably keep yelling, and the boys will surely hear, so I might as well get this over with.

"I'll be right back, boys. Stay here," I tell them, peering out the screen of the back door.

"We will," they both say without looking up. They're lying on their bellies across from each other with a circle drawn in the dirt between them. Thirteen colored marbles are lined up in the shape of an X in the middle of the circle. John knuckles down and flicks a black shooter marble with his thumb, hitting a small yellow one out of the circle. "Oh, rats," William says, snapping his fingers while John grabs the yellow ball and sets it beside himself with a grin.

When I get to the front door, a tight-lipped Hazel glares at me through the screen, her hands behind her back. She looks the same— her hair is up in a bun, and she's wearing the same black dress— except she looks older, even more so than last time, but it's only been a few days since I saw her last. Her hair has more gray than black now, and she has more lines furrowing her face.

"It took you long enough. I don't have all day," she growls.

"I'm busy, Hazel. What do you want?" I bark.

Her flattened lips curl up slightly at the edges. "Well, ain't you a feisty one today, Pearl? I'd watch that if I were you."

She takes a step back when I open the door and join her on the porch. "Are you threatening me, Hazel?"

Her eyes narrow, showing no white, only the black. "I don't threaten."

"What do you want?" I repeat, getting testier.

"Milk."

"Milk?" I ask with a hint of laughter.

"Yes, milk. Can you spare a little?"

Obey your husband, make him happy.

I bite the inside of my cheek before answering, "I don't have any."

"You have a cow, don't you?"

"She's dry," I lie.

She tilts her head. "Are you sure?"

I cross my arms over my chest, ready for battle, and I want answers. "Yes, I'm sure. By the way, do you know what happened to

111

my garden and chickens?"

"I don't know what you're talking about," she says in a mocking tone, placing her hand over her heart, which I'm sure is black as a starless night's sky—if she even has one at all.

My lips tighten. I don't believe her, but I don't have any proof, so there's nothing I can do. It's her word against mine. "I have nothing to offer you, so can you please leave me alone? I'd appreciate it if you didn't come back."

"Oh? You invited me here," she says, grinning and showing her godawful crooked teeth that look browner than yellow now.

"I did not. That's a pure t lie!" I'd remember if I did. I've never spoken to her before the first time she came to my house, the day I found her rocking in Pierce's chair—the day before she ruined my beautiful garden. The back of my eyes burn, and I blink quickly, fighting back the tears.

"Yes, you did. You invited me the moment you crossed my X." A small, evil grin appears on her face. "Milk?" she asks again, raising one brow.

I shake my head. "I can't help you. Please leave," I say behind my teeth, feeling them grind back and forth to a dull ache.

Her red fingernail taps her chin while she glowers down at me. "Very well, Pearl. The cow has no milk." She turns and walks back to her carriage, waiting for her by the road. When she steps in, the crows resting on the top fly off, making their usual *caw* sound.

I march back inside. The door slams behind me, making me jerk my head toward it. "I'm so spitting mad!" I say to myself while I pace and bite my fingernails to the nub.

"What's the matter, Mama?"

"I can't believe she had the audacity to come here *again*," I say as I stare at the path I'm taking in the living room. "Why can't she leave me alone?"

"Mama, are you okay?"

"I know I didn't invite her, that's a lie. Just because I crossed her stupid X, I gave her a silent invitation? Ha! That is the most *ridiculous* thing I've ever heard, next to that awful woman being a witch, that is."

"Mama!"

I freeze and flick my eyes to John, who is standing in the doorway, frowning, his shoulders slumped.

He shuffles to me and takes my hand. "Are you okay?" he asks, his voice soft and concerning.

I relax when I look into the sweet chocolate eyes, eyes that look exactly like his father's, and touch his cheek. "Oh, John, my sweet boy. Yes, everything's fine. I thought you were playing outside."

"I was, but I heard the door slam."

"It was a neighbor wanting to borrow something. Don't worry about it." I look over him, toward the back door. "Where's your brother?"

"He's countin' his marbles. I let him win." He grins and walks away. "But I'll win them back."

XXX

The hint of petrichor in the humid air lets me know rain must be coming. The last of the sun's rays is disappearing, taking the blue with it until the morning. It's still light out enough to see, but I've already put the kids to bed. John was tired after supper, and William always wants to do what his big brother does, so they both went to bed early.

Pierce cracks open a boiled peanut with his teeth and sucks out the juice before popping the pods into his mouth. "I love your peanuts," he says with a slight chuckle.

"I know," I mutter. Other things fill my mind, like debating whether to tell Pierce about Hazel's visit today. I need to tell him; I'm *going* to tell him. I take a deep breath and open my mouth.

Before I can say anything, Pierce speaks again, this time his voice sounding sedated. "Pearl."

I close my eyes for a brief second and rub my scratchy throat, regretting not spilling everything that's been torturing me about that vile woman. "Yes?"

I've lost my nerve.

He lobs a shell into the waste bucket, wipes his hands on his pants, and gazes at the trees across the road.

After a moment of silence, other than the frogs and crickets having a sound war, I ask, "Pierce?"

"I…I think it's time we put our marriage back right," he says with hesitation. He wipes his clean hands again on his pants before taking the tobacco and pipe out of his shirt pocket.

"What?" I don't know what he's referring to—our marriage is fine, isn't it?—but by the tone of his voice, I'm not sure I will like whatever he's talking about.

He looks at the tobacco and pipe sitting in his hand before putting them back into his pocket. "The doctor said to give you a month. It's been over a month, and…and I want my wife back."

Oh. "Maybe we should wait a little longer. I'm not sure if I'm ready."

"You ready, Pearl. You's the strongest person I know." He smiles at me and rubs a knuckle across my cheek.

"Pierce, I don't know. Another miscarriage would—"

"It scared me to death when I saw all that blood. Lord, I was scared. I thought you was dying. If I had lost you, I don't know what I would've done. I'm not sure I can survive without you, Pearl."

"Pier—"

"But you made it through," he says. "We can't live our lives afraid of what ifs."

"Pierce, please."

"Another baby will be good for us. We need to put Jacob's death behind us and move on."

I shake my head.

He stands, steps in front of me, and leans down, placing both hands on the chair arms, caging me in. His warm lips capture mine. "I'll see you inside," he says and walks inside the house, leaving me on the porch with my jaw on the floor.

He didn't even give me the opportunity to make any more excuses.

Maybe this one will make it to full term. It has to. Pierce is right; we can't live our lives worrying about what ifs.

Pierce is sitting on the edge of the bed, removing his boots, when I step into the bedroom. He reaches for my hand and smiles at me. "Thank you, Pearl. It'll be all right this time."

I return his smile and nod. He's usually right.

XXX

The hot air whistling in my ear and the heavy arm slung around me that's burning me up isn't what's causing my insomnia. I lie here thinking about what has transpired in the last month, and my mind won't shut off. The garden and the chickens shouldn't have happened—it was my fault. What will happen to Bessie tonight if Hazel gets ahold of her? I can't let that happen. The chickens are one thing, but having to replace a cow...we don't have that kind of money right now.

I peel the hefty arm off me and gently climb out of bed. Pierce doesn't stir, so I take an unlit lantern and tiptoe out of the room. When I'm at the back door, I light the lantern and carefully open the door, slide out, and close the door without making a sound. Wet pellets beat down on my head while I track across the muddy dirt to the barn and swing the door open.

Bessie's lying on her straw on the other side of the room. When she sees me, she grunts, blowing snot out her nose.

"You're okay," I tell her as I set the lantern on the ground and turn back to the door.

I shut the double door, shove the wood beam into its place, and push down. I'm safe in here. Hazel will have a hard time getting in, if that's her plan. After pushing down again to make sure we're locked in tight, I rub my wet arms and toss my hair, slinging off the warm droplets before picking up the lantern.

"Hey, Buddy," I say while I walk past the draft horse and give him a small pat on his shiny black neck. He eyes me like I'm an intruder in his home. *I guess I am*. "Hey, Bessie. I'll sleep in here with you tonight. What do you say?" I set the lantern down beside her stall.

She turns her head away and chews on her cud.

"I thought that's what you'd say." I grab an old worn-out blanket from the corner and shake it out. Dust particles land in my throat, tickling it and making me cough. I look back at Bessie, but she isn't looking at me, and Buddy has disappeared behind his stall wall, ready for his nap.

I lay the blanket out beside Bessie's stall and sit, pulling my knees up to my chest and wrapping my arms around them. I wish I didn't have to be in here tonight. I'd rather be in Pierce's arms. He should be sleeping like a baby because of the steady shower hitting the roof, and our pre-sleep activities. I wish I would've told him the truth about Hazel. What's stopping me?

I don't know.

The smell isn't too bad in here, but sleeping won't be the same without the sweet smell of magnolia. But if this is what I have to do to keep Bessie safe tonight, I'll do it.

I blow out the lantern's flame, lie down on the hard floor, and close my eyes. The sound of an owl hooting outside sings me to sleep.

Chapter 17

June 10, 1919

I stretch my arms over my head, reaching for the ceiling, and arch my back. I can't remember the last time it felt like I hadn't slept in weeks and took a nap under a shady tree on a warm, lazy day.

The curtain is open, tied on the sides with a red tassel, giving me a perfect showing of the lustrous sky. The sunlight kisses the sky with shades of brilliant pink and baby blue this morning, inviting me to have a closer look.

When I throw the blanket off myself, I see a small red speck on the bedding between my legs. I put a finger in my mouth, dampening it, and then I wipe the spot, but it won't come off, it only smears. When I put my finger back in my mouth, I taste copper. It's blood. I saturate my finger with spittle and scrub the stubborn spot. The more I scrub, the more blood there is until it's soaking the bedding. My effort isn't doing any good, so I stop.

I'm wet between my legs, so I lift my gown. It's trickling out of me and drenching my underwear. I shift to get out of bed, but my legs won't move, they're numb, so I reach under my knees with my hands and lift, but they're dead weight.

"Pierce," I say to the closed door.

Blood gushes out of me and overflows onto the floor, spraying on the wall and coating it as it slides down. It's rising fast and my legs still won't budge. So I keep watching, until the blood is above the windowsill—that's all I can do.

I'm horribly dizzy. A thick coat of saliva fills my mouth, and I may throw up. I'm scared.

The bed disappears into a sea of what looks like warm, sticky Bordeaux.

"Pierce!" I scream, but he doesn't come. No one is coming, and I can't stay up any longer. The heavy logs that were once my legs drag me under. When I resurface, my arms fly about madly, searching for something to grab onto, but there's nothing, only an endless red sea. I gasp for air, gargling the salty iron before my legs pull me under again.

Once more, I fight my way back up and scream, "Pierce!"

Cock-a-doodle-doo.

My eyes snap open as if a bolt of lightning struck right beside me. I sit up, gasping for air with my hand over my painfully thrashing heart. It feels like it will jump right out of my chest, and I can't catch my breath. At first, I don't recognize where I am when I glance around, but when my breathing evens out and my heart calms, I remember last night's sleepover. I let out a deep quivering breath and wipe the sweaty hair from my forehead.

Cock-a-doodle-doo.

I rub the sleep out of my eyes with the heel of my palms, bend backward, and hear my back crack. Sleeping on the barn's floor isn't comfortable at all, and I hope I never have to do that again.

Bessie?

I jump to my feet and find Bessie at the other end of her stall with her tail tucked between her legs. Relief washes over me when I realize nothing happened to her. I peer over the stall's wall and rest my chin on my folded hands. "I'll come back soon, Bessie," I tell her before putting the blanket and lantern in the corner, waving to Buddy, who is eyeing me again, and leaving.

Pierce comes into the kitchen, buttoning his coveralls when I step inside. "Where was you? I was fixin' to come look for you."

I point my finger back the way I came, saying, "I was using the outhouse," as a tingle shoots between my legs, almost painful. Great. "Are the boys up yet?"

"No, still sleepin'."

"Good." I pump water into the kettle, making my situation unbearable, so I cross my ankles and bounce. "Can you light the stove for me? I need to go to the outhouse again."

The back of his hand touches my forehead. "You okay? You ain't gettin' sick, are you?"

"No, I'm fine." I brush his hand away and touch my stomach. "Just a little stomach ache, must've been the peanuts last night."

He looks at me for a moment before saying, "All right, if you say so. I'll get the water on."

As soon as his back is turned, I slip out the door and run to the outhouse.

After my bladder is empty and I'm dressed for the day, I check on the boys and see William's stirring, so I slink back out of the room. Maybe he'll go back to sleep so I can get my morning chores done without having them at my feet. I'm still tired, and I don't need the hassle this morning. Not after sleeping on the hard barn floor, and the terrible nightmare I had.

I walk into the kitchen and blindly reach for the milk bucket under the counter, but I grab nothing. The back door opens and closes, and I straighten myself.

Pierce stands there, fixed, with unfocused eyes, holding the milk bucket with a gray face, looking like a statue.

I point to the bucket. "I was looking for that. I want to milk Bessie before the boys wake."

Other than the veins in his neck pulsing, he doesn't move and he doesn't speak for several seconds.

"What's wrong?"

He blinks, coming back to me. "I figured I'd help you since you wasn't feelin' good." He hands over the nearly empty bucket.

"Is this all there is?" My eyes widen when I look in the bucket. I drop it on the floor and jump back as if it will bite me. Thick red liquid, so dark it's almost black, filters out of the bucket, spilling everywhere. My hand slaps my mouth. "What is that?" My mouth waters and I swallow back the sour acid fighting to erupt like a volcano.

"It looks like blood. Bessie's givin' blood today." He trawls his fingers through his hair, making it muddled. He looks at the floor and shakes his head. "I don't know what's goin' on. Why is she givin' us blood?" he asks, sounding distant. "I just don't know, Pearl."

I shake myself from my horrified trance, grab a towel, and drop to the floor on my hands and knees, not able to give him an answer. I watched her last night—or, at least, I was there with her. The door was still locked from the inside this morning. No one could've gotten in. We were safe, she was safe.

"I'll go to my folks. Maybe my father's heard of somethin' like this before. I'll get some milk from 'em for the boys."

I don't reply while I wipe the dark crimson off the floor, and he leaves me to clean Bessie's blood.

XXX

A thick layer of gray scatters along the sky, hiding the sun as it rises when Pierce returns with Emmett. I watch them through the kitchen window as they walk into the barn before joining them.

Emmett sits on the stool, poking Bessie's engorged udder, causing her to take a step back. Pierce places a pail underneath her and backs up, shoving his hands in his pockets. With his inspection finished, Emmett squeezes a teat, spraying red liquid into the pail.

Pierce glances at the balled-up blanket and the lantern in the corner, but he doesn't mention it.

"I don't know, son. I don't think it's mastitis, but I couldn't tell ya for sure." He pokes the udder again, making Bessie cry out. "Could be somethin' worse," Emmett says in a baffled tone, like he's talking to himself, while still eyeing the swollen gland. "You put her down." His voice rises as his narrowed eyes meet Pierce's.

"No!" I choke.

They both turn and look at me with dead eyes.

"Don't use the meat either, son, it might be diseased," Emmett says as they turn back toward each other. "You hear me?"

"I can't afford to get another cow right now. We just had to buy

120

more chickens and plant a new garden," Pierce says.

I walk to Bessie and rub her brown head, the coarse hairs feeling like a soft bristle brush under my fingertips. She looks at me under long eyelashes with her big shiny black eyes. She looks sad, like she knows what's going on. "Please, give her a couple of days. She may start producing milk again. Maybe she needs a calf. We can take her to Mr. Barker's for a stud." I don't know—I don't know anything about animals, but I don't want to see them put Bessie down. It's not her fault. This is Hazel's doing, I'm almost positive. She must've given her something to turn the milk into blood when I wasn't watching. It'll probably run through her system, and then she'll be back to normal.

"Don't fret, son. I'll loan you the money," Emmett says without looking in my direction. "It won't put us out none."

Pierce pauses, then shakes his head. "No, I ain't borrowin' no money."

"All right, then." Emmett nods. "We got enough milk for you until you can afford to buy another cow."

"Well, that I can do," he says to Emmett, and he turns to me, taking me by the arm. "You need to go inside and fix breakfast. Let the boys sleep a while longer. Keep 'em in the house."

We walk out the barn and stop at the wagon parked near the back door.

"Please don't kill her, it will devastate the boys. It's not her fault," I beg and look at him with pleading eyes.

"I'm sorry, Pearl, it's gotta be done. I can't let nothin' happen to our family. And we can't afford to keep her if she ain't producin'. The boys will get over it." He retrieves two full milk jugs from the back of the wagon and hands them to me. "Here, I'll be in directly."

"Please, Pierce."

"I won't hear of it, Pearl. Go." He pushes me toward the back door, and I plod into the house, defeated.

I'm in a daze as I place the milk jugs on the counter and mix the ingredients for biscuits while staring a hole into the wall.

I don't look at the barn on my way back from the hen house because Pierce, Emmett, and Bessie are no longer in there. The figures hiking in a distant field get smaller and more unfocused with each step. Bessie trails behind like an obedient child following her father.

Only her father is planning on using the shotgun he has in his hand on her.

I can't look, so I hurry inside and finish breakfast.

The gunshot echoing in the distance makes me jump, and a single tear slides down my cheek. I wipe it away with the back of my hand and clench my jaw in anger and frustration as I flip the frying eggs in the iron skillet. Poor Bessie—she didn't deserve that.

When Pierce walks in, he washes his hands in the sink. "I'm sorry, Pearl, it had to be done. If she started givin' us milk again, it may've been tainted—I don't know—and I ain't riskin' our family. Lord knows I'm tryin' the best I can, Pearl."

I nod, and put food on plates. "I'll go get the boys up. They need to get moving," I say softly and turn toward the door with my head hung.

Pierce grabs my waist, pulling me to him when I try to walk past him. "You didn't want her to suffer, did you?"

I shake my head.

"Don't be mad. I feel bad, too." His forehead touches mine. "I'm sorry. Please forgive me."

My smile is weak as I peck him on the lips. "I'll be fine." I push away from him, and he lets me go. He's doing what's best for our family, so I can't be angry with him. I just need a few minutes to adjust to what happened.

Why are the boys still sleeping? The sun is already up, and they never sleep this late. When I open their bedroom door, William is sitting up in the bed, but John is lying down with his eyes open.

They both turn and look at me.

"John ain't feelin' good, Mama." William scoots out of bed, walks over to me, and gives my legs a big hug.

"Good morning, baby. Did you sleep well?" I ask him as I rub his back and look over at a pale-faced John.

"Yes, ma'am." He hugs me tighter.

"Okay, go into the kitchen. Father is waiting for you. Breakfast is ready."

He looks at John once more. "I hope you feel better, John," he says, grabbing the little black bag off the dresser and walking out the door.

I brush John's wet bangs out of his eyes and put the back of my hand on his hot forehead. "What's the matter, John? What hurts?"

"All over, and I'm cold." He shivers and looks at me with dark, sunken eyes.

I retrieve another blanket and lay it on top of him. "I'll tell Father to get the doctor. He'll fix you right up." I kiss his forehead before walking out.

Pierce and William are at the table with forks to their mouths when I enter the kitchen.

"We couldn't wait. William was hungry, he's a growin' boy." Pierce ruffles William's hair and smiles at me, but his expression drops when he sees my somber face.

"John's sick."

"Bad sick?"

"Yes, he's running a fever and needs Dr. Clayton." I'm twirling my wedding band around and around as fast as my fingers will go.

Pierce wipes his mouth with a cloth, gets up without another word, and walks out the back door.

"William, eat your breakfast, then you can play in the living room. Stay away from John until the doctor can have a look at him."

His body droops and his bottom lip juts out. "Yes, Mama." He picks up his fork and stabs his eggs.

When I get back to John, he's sitting up with a green face. I run, grabbing a bucket just in time for him to lean over and lose everything in his stomach.

"I'm sorry, Mama. I didn't get my chores done this mornin'," he moans and spits in the bucket.

I rub his back. "It's okay, I'll get them done. You rest," I tell him and lay him back on the bed.

I leave him to get a wet washrag and a glass of water for him to clean his mouth with. I check on William, who's lying on his stomach on the living room floor. His feet spring up and down as they kick his bottom while he looks through the colorful marbles.

When Pierce comes back in with the doctor, I'm still sitting with John, wiping his face with the wet rag.

"I hear we have a sick boy." Dr. Clayton places his black doctor's bag on the end of the bed and opens it.

I stand and take a step back, giving Dr. Clayton room to do his examination.

"Yes, sir," John moans.

Dr. Clayton takes a seat next to John on the bed, making it creak. "Well, let's have a look. Shall we?" He pulls out his stethoscope, hooking it around his neck, and then his thermometer from his bag. "Open wide, John." He places the thermometer under John's tongue, removes the blankets, and lifts John's nightgown. "Good, no rash," he says with a nod, dropping John's gown back and putting the plugs in his ears. "Can you sit up for me?" He pulls John up by the arm. "Take a deep breath through your nose," he says while he listens, moving the metal ring around John's chest and back. "Another."

Silence.

"Good, John. Very good." Dr. Clayton covers John back with the warm blankets.

When the thermometer is done, he raises his chin, looking through his bifocals perched at the end of his nose. "101. I reckon you're not faking to get out of a few chores, boy," he chuckles, but his laughter turns into a wet, hacking cough. He yanks a handkerchief out of his suit pocket and covers his mouth.

He blots his shiny forehead with the handkerchief and puts it back in his pocket. "You have a virus, son." He pats John's leg and tosses his things in his bag. "You'll feel better in no time with a little rest." He pushes off the bed, struggling to get to his feet, and searches through his bag, pulling out a small bottle of pills. His arms stretch as he holds it out in front of him, and his lips move while he silently reads the label before passing it to me. "Here, give him one in the morning and one at night until his fever breaks. You can mix a little soda water and baking powder and rub it on his body—that'll help, too." He closes his bag, picks it up, and walks out the bedroom.

I follow him out, stunned, with Pierce close behind. "That's it? A virus? Are you sure?"

He turns back around with both hands clasping his bag in front of him. "From what Pierce told me, he was fine last night. This is a bug, nothing more. Kids get them from time to time. His lungs are clear, and his heart sounds good. Give him plenty of fluids and let him rest. The aspirin and soda bath should bring the fever down. That boy will be running around your feet in no time. He's a strong, healthy kid, he'll bounce back quickly." He walks to the back door, placing his hand on it, ready to push it open.

"What about influenza? Wasn't there a big outbreak last year that killed a lot of people? Isn't the pandemic still going on? There isn't a chance he could have that, is there? Should we take him to the hospital in Charleston?" I ask, my voice laced with panic.

He stops and turns, facing me again, and sets his bag on the floor. He takes the handkerchief out of his pocket, removes his glasses, and rubs the lenses with the cloth. He sighs. "I've been a doctor for nearly fifty years. I see kids and adults all the time with these same symptoms and they've all bounced back in no time at all. It's nothing to worry about, I assure you." He inspects his glasses before replacing them back over his eyes and stuffs the handkerchief back in his pocket. "He'll be fine in a day or two, maybe three. Give him time to recover." He picks up his bag and pushes the door open and turns back around. "Keep the other child away until he gets better. We don't want it to spread. You two better stay away, too, as much as you can, and cover your face with a rag when you check on him for the next day or two. Don't worry, everything will be fine," he says calmly and walks out the door.

"He'll be fine," I tell Pierce, who is looking at the closed door with his hands in his pockets.

He nods. "He will be. Dr. Clayton knows what he's doin'. He's a right good doctor."

"I'll pack some clothes for William, and you can take him to stay with Cora and your parents for a few days until John gets better. We don't need two sick kids on our hands." I fake laughter, to ease his mind…and mine.

He ignores my weak laughter, however, and simply nods again, still staring at the door. "A good doctor."

Chapter 18

June 12, 1919

"How are you feeling, sweetheart?" I ask as I sit on the edge of the bed and place the back of my hand to John's warm forehead. "Your fever is almost gone." I hand him a glass of water.

He sits up, leans his head back, and opens his mouth wide like a baby bird. I drop an aspirin into the back of his throat and rub his neck, coaxing it to slide down. "I'm feelin' a little better, Mama," John croaks and swallows a big gulp of water. "Don't worry 'bout me."

"I know you are. I bet tomorrow you'll be begging to do your chores," I joke.

John gives me a small smile before putting the half-empty glass of water on the bedside table and lying back. "Maybe William can come home tomorrow. I miss him. I need to let him win back his shooter." He opens his fist and lying in the palm of his hand is a red-white-and-blue marble.

I take it out of his hand and hold it in front of the lantern's light, getting a better look at the colorful glass ball. "That's a pretty one," I say before handing it back to him.

He frowns. "He was sad when he lost it, but I'll let him win it back."

"That's a real nice thing to do, son," Pierce says from behind me, putting both hands on my shoulders and peering over my head at John.

He shrugs. "He's my little brother. I love him."

"And he loves you, too." I stand. "You need to go to sleep now, so you can be all better when you wake."

"I am tired." He covers his mouth with his hand and yawns. "Good night."

"Night," Pierce and I say in unison before I douse out the lantern's flame, burying his room in darkness, and close the door behind us.

"He's getting better," I say while changing into my nightgown.

"If he ain't all better by tomorrow I'll go get Dr. Clayton again," Pierce says and we both crawl into bed before he snuffs out the light.

"That won't be necessary, because he'll be back to his old self tomorrow. He's already a lot better than he was," I say.

"Night, Pearl. I love you." He kisses my lips before he blankets me in his arms, my back to his chest, and settles in for the night.

"Good night. I love you too." I close my eyes and hope sleep will find me soon.

My mind wanders as we lie in silence. The steady rain pelting the roof doesn't drown my thoughts. Hazel pops into my mind, and I'm not sure why. Everything that has happened since I crossed her X flashes in front of my closed lids, coming to me in a torrential rush. My eyes snap open, expecting to see her shadowed face in front of me, but instead I find nothing but darkness.

"Pierce, are you still awake?" I whisper, rubbing my foot on top of his.

"What is it, Pearl?" He brushes my hair off my shoulder and kisses my neck. "You havin' trouble fallin' asleep?" He wiggles his hips, chafing me from behind. His bulge twitches against my backside, and he presses his hand on my stomach, pushing me closer to him. "Need my help?" he asks with a touch of friskiness in his voice.

I ignore his oh-so-subtle hint. "Pierce... Why do you think

Hazel's a witch?"

A flash of lightning cracks the dark sky the moment Hazel's name is mentioned, making me jump, and it reveals a large black hand reaching out to grab me—

No—it's a shadow on the wall, I realize, forcing myself to calm down. The magnolia tree's leaves are stretched out like fingers. I squeeze my eyes shut. *That's all it is.*

A rumble of thunder joins the rain, giving us a belated warning.

He sighs and unhooks his arms from around me and rolls onto his back. I roll over onto my back, look up into the darkness, and wait for him to answer.

"A lot of gossip 'round town. Things happen to folks who don't do what Hazel wants. I haven't seen it myself, it's all just talk. My folks got some of the lash, told me about somethin' that happened before I was born. They said she wanted two acres of their land."

"So she wanted to buy two acres? That's it? That doesn't seem like much compared to all the acreage they own."

"No, she didn't want to buy. She wasn't gonna pay for 'em, she's got no money. She wanted 'em to give her the land, the land that was just handed down from my father's folks to him. It wasn't as much as they got now. It was a starter, like what they gave me and my brother. My grandparents still owned most of it. My folks didn't get the rest until my grandparents died years later." He pauses. "My folks are stingy, as stingy as they come. That's why they *got* what they *got*. They ain't gonna give anybody anything unless they is kin. There's probably no one in town pinchin' a penny more than Emmett and Florence." I can feel him shake his head as the bed joggles. "They wouldn't give her the time of day, even if she had money. Bad as I hate to admit, their noses are stuck up in the air like everyone around 'em is stinkin' up the place. You know, like they been rollin' around in the hog pen, especially Mother. Always been like that and will always be like that. Ain't a cotton-pickin' thing you can do 'bout it neither."

"What happened?"

"The next two years, all their crops died before they could harvest 'em. It wasn't a good time. I'm glad I wasn't born yet. But they got along, they survived."

"Like what happened to our garden?"

"No," he says slowly. "I don't know—maybe. I didn't see it. But there ain't no reason she'd do anythin' to us."

I take in a deep breath—I wish that were true. "What happened after the two years?"

"Things were back to normal, I reckon. My folks never did find out what happened to their crops, but they believed Hazel was behind it. They and everyone else stay far away from her, turnin' and walkin' the other way when she's near. Everyone's afraid of her. And she draws her X all over town. No one knows what that's all about because no one is stupid enough to find out. That's why I told you to stay away from her and her X. We don't need no trouble."

"Wait. That was thirty-three years ago?"

"Yes, 'bout thirty-five, I reckon."

"How old was she when she tried to buy the land?"

"Not buy, take," he corrects.

"Whatever," I snap impatiently. "How old was she?"

"Don't know, never asked," he says, irritation in his voice. "Why?"

When I first saw her she looked like she was only about forty years old, if that. Does this woman never age? Of course she does, I remember; she ages every time I see her. Time is finally taking a toll on her appearance, I suppose.

"I was just wondering. She doesn't look that old." *Or at least she didn't.*

"I've never seen her up close, and I've never thought 'bout it." I feel his body stiffen. "Have you?"

I look at him as another bright shock lights up his face. The rain coming down on the window makes his face look like it's melting away, and then a thunderous boom shakes the bed.

My tongue swells inside my mouth and cuts off my air. I open my mouth and search for oxygen before my tongue deflates and brings me back to normal. "No," comes out of my mouth before I can stop it, ignoring the thunderstorm raging outside. "Well, I mean, once. I saw her in town walking out of the chemist when I was waiting for you. I didn't get too close." *Why can't I tell him the truth about her? I want to. I really do.* I can taste the truth in my mouth, but my tongue won't say the words.

"Pearl."

"Yes?"

"Stay away from her. Promise me."

"I promise," I say, trying to hide the guilt in my voice. "Good night."

His body relaxes. "Night," he says and rolls back onto his side and puts his arms around me once again.

I close my eyes, but sleep is far away. It will be difficult to sleep while thinking of Hazel. I'm still not convinced she's a witch. Maybe she's just an evil person who finds a way to make people's lives miserable. If crossing her X and not giving in to what she wants has caused all our misfortunes, I may have to do something I swore I would never do.

I may have to disobey Pierce.

Chapter 19

June 13, 1919

John dashes into the woods.

"I'm going to get you." I chase after him but stop when I hear black crows chanting, "Murder. Murder." I look up and see them flying in a disorderly manner, back and forth like they're not sure which way to go.

I look back at John, but he's gone. "Where did you go?" I ask, raising my voice in a playful tone.

A giggle comes from behind a tree.

I sneak until I'm right in front of the tree and reach around—"I gotcha!" I say—but he isn't there. "Huh?"

I go deeper into the woods, hunting for him. The deeper I go, the darker it gets.

"John!" I shout into the silent darkness. I can't remember the last time I heard his giggle. I don't know how long I've been out here searching for him, but it seems like hours. My feet want to drag, but I have to keep moving. I have to find my son. Fear is taking hold, so I pick up the pace.

"John, I give up. It's getting too dark, let's get out of here and go home. Please, John."

He doesn't answer. My heart punches my chest. I dash and look behind tree after tree, but he isn't behind any of them. Where can he be?

I stop and put my hands on my knees as I wheeze. I see John off in the distance and let out a long-winded breath. He's standing there with his back to me, motionless. I run to him.

When I get to him, I say, "John, you scared me. Never do that again."

He doesn't move or reply.

I grab his shoulder and turn him around, and I scream, the sound piercing through the quiet darkness. John faces me now—but he doesn't have a face. It's been wiped clean of all its features. He's all black, nothing more than a silhouette with hair, and then his clothes fall in a heap to the ground when he evaporates.

The wind is knocked out of me. I reach for him, but it's too late, he's gone. I only grab air.

"No! John!" I yell hoarsely.

I wake up screaming, out of breath. My jagged panting fills the room.

"Pearl, are you all right?" Pierce's eyes flare with concern.

I sit up, drawing in a shaky breath. "Y-Yes… Just another bad dream," I stammer.

He massages my back. "More snakes?"

"Yes. Snakes," I say, not wanting to talk about it. My eyes rise to the window when my breathing settles. The sun is already coming up, the room welcoming its light. The storm has already been forgotten by the day. I look back at Pierce, who is usually out of bed and gone by now. "I'll be back," I tell him, and before I know it I'm out of bed and hurrying to John's room.

My gut tells me that John's illness will be gone today.

I ease the door open to a dark room, walk over to his curtain and sling it open, letting in the sunlight. I turn around and prowl over to his bed with a smile on my face. My smile dies away quickly when I lean down and see his ashen face.

He's not moving.

My heart stops and the blood drains from my body. I can't breathe. The small room feels like it's getting smaller and smaller by the second, closing in on me.

"John?" I hesitantly reach out with a trembling hand and touch his cold, stiff body, and then I jerk my hand away, holding it against my chest, and straighten. My head shakes back and forth while I take a few…small…steps…back.

Then I let go.

I take a deep breath, and then the most gut-wrenching, blood-curdling scream I can muster comes out of my mouth. "John! John! No! John! *Pierce!*" I shriek and crumble to the floor. "John." I strike the floor with the palm of my hand. "No!" I strike it again, and again, and again. My chest tightens and my breath hitches, making it hard to breathe. I can't breathe. But the tears don't care, they come anyway.

Pierce runs into the room. He stops when he sees John.

"John?" He shakes John's lifeless body. "Open your eyes, son. Wake up!" he yells. "Son, please wake up," he says, sounding more desperate.

His back hits the wall and he slides down before he plants his head between his hands, resting on his raised knees, and weeps. "My boy. My boy."

This isn't happening. John isn't dead. This is just a bad dream, it has to be. This isn't real. This can't be real. "I want my baby back," I say in a soft cry I barely hear.

Pierce must've heard because now he's beside me, and I'm crushed against his chest.

My crying gets louder—my hands find my hair, and I yank hard, trying to pull myself out of this dream. I don't wake this time, though, because I'm already awake. I've already awakened from one bad dream to land inside an even worse nightmare. My heart has shattered into a thousand pieces, and I'm not sure how I'll ever put the pieces back together again. This is the worst thing that can happen. My sobbing is only interrupted when my need to breathe takes over, only to start again.

I'm not sure how long we've been slouched on the floor, but my throat is scratchy, and my head is pounding like a giant boulder is crashing into my brain over and over again.

Pierce squeezes once more before he lets me go. He rubs his eyes with the heels of his palms, wiping away his tears, before standing and leaving me on the floor. He looks at the ceiling with clenched fists at his sides and closes his eyes before letting out a long quivering breath. "I'll go get the doctor." He covers John's face with the blanket before touching my shoulder and walking out.

I crawl to John on my hands and knees. The wooden planks bite into my knees, but I don't care—I welcome the pain. I'll do anything to distract myself from the pain in my broken heart. When I get to him, I grab his cold, tiny hand under the blanket and hold in it mine. I bow my head and squeeze my eyes shut. *Please don't let this be real. Please don't let this be real. I'll do anything.*

I stay like this, oblivious of anything other than John's cold hand in mine, until another hand touches my shoulder. I jump, but I don't move from my baby boy's side.

"Pearl, you need to let go," Pierce says softly.

I shake my head. My eyes are still closed and tears are falling through the lids, but I don't wipe them away. "I don't want to let go," I whisper brokenly. "He's my son."

Pierce grabs me by the waist and stands me up, making me let go of John's hand. I reach for his hand again, but Pierce picks me up and carries me into our bedroom, not letting me get to my son. He places me in the bed and covers me with the blanket, cocooning me in.

"I'm sorry, Pearl, I'm so sorry." He kisses my forehead. "Stay here." Then he walks out the door and shuts it behind him, leaving me alone to mourn our son.

I'm in bed, gazing at the wall in an almost comatose state when Pierce comes back in sometime later. He looks at me with bloodshot, glassy eyes. He's been crying again, or maybe he never stopped.

I sit up. "Pierce?"

He sits on the bed beside me and weeps into his hands. His shoulders tremble with every sob.

I touch his shoulder. "Pierce?"

"I had to tote him out and lay his little body in Doc's wagon. That's the hardest thing I've ever had to do." He shakes his head and wipes his tears with fury.

"He…He took him?"

He runs his fingers through his hair and rubs the top of his head. "Yes, he said he had to. They need to find out what happened. He's gonna have him sent to the hospital in Charleston. Someone will bring him back after they take a look, so we can bur…" He blows out a long ragged breath.

I lie back and Pierce joins me, seizing me in his arms like he's afraid to let me go. "How long?" I want my baby back. I want him back alive and well.

"The doctor said a couple days. I'll start on his…" He pauses, catching his breath. "…I'll start on his coffin later today. I'll make him somethin' nice."

Tears spring from my eyes. "I know you will, just like you did with Jacob."

"I'll get Mother to make the arrangements. I know you won't be up to it."

"Thank you." I sink into his chest and his arms tighten around me.

We stiffen when we hear William's and Cora's laughter as they come in the back door.

He lets out an exasperated moan, and his arms unwrap from around me. "I'll go tell 'em. It's gonna break William's heart." He pushes up off the bed and stops at the door. "The doctor said we should scrub everythin'. I'll get Cora to take William for a couple more days until we get the house cleaned," he says and leaves, shutting the door behind him.

I throw the covers over my head and cry myself to sleep.

Chapter 20

June 16, 1919

The day of John's death, I stayed in bed all day. I couldn't get up no matter how hard I tried. I remember repeating over and over again, *"Please let this be a dream. Please don't let this be real."*

Pierce went to town and called the preacher at Mama's church, Mr. Anderson. He had someone rush to get Mama, so Pierce could tell her the sad news. She was shocked to hear about John and promised they would come for the viewing and funeral—which should give me comfort, but it doesn't.

Nothing can.

When Pierce got back home, he spent most of the time in the barn making John's coffin. I haven't seen it yet. I'm afraid to. Seeing it will make it all too real, and I want to live in denial for a little while longer. John was my firstborn, a part of my life for four-and-a-half years. I'm not sure how I'll go on after this, but I have to…somehow.

John's body arrived at the house yesterday, and we laid him on Florence's best linen tablecloth. It was spread out on the kitchen table, which we had moved into the living room. When Pierce told me the autopsy concluded John died of influenza, I wanted to scream and rip my hair out, and then wring that so-called *doctor's* neck.

I still might.

With two sons gone, I'm keeping William close, not letting him out of my sight for more than five minutes at a time. Every time I don't know where he is, my throat tightens, and I feel as if I can't breathe until I see his beautiful chocolate eyes again. I can't let anything happen to William. I can't…I just can't.

I crack open the door to William's room, the one he once shared with his brother. He's lying on his bed with his head propped up by one hand while he shuffles through his marbles with the other. His eyes are dry, but his frown is large.

I close the door and put my forehead and palms against it. *How am I going to get through this?* Without an answer, I push off and head to my room.

Pierce is wearing a pair of khakis and buttoning his white dress shirt when I enter the room. I grab a navy-blue dress from the wardrobe and slip into it.

He sits on the unmade bed and puts on his shoes. "You okay, Pearl?"

"No." I press my lips together and yank the brush through my hair. "But I will be, in time, I suppose." I snap in a clip to hold my hair back and drop the brush on the dresser with a clunk.

He walks up behind me. "I'm sorry you're hurtin', but so am I. We need to do this together, for us and for William." He tugs me, turning me around, and holds me against his chest.

I don't resist.

"I love you, Pearl. We'll get through this." He stands back, still gripping my arms.

I hang my head, avoiding the sadness in his eyes. It doesn't matter if they're contagious or not, mine's affected too, and I'm not sure there's a cure. "I love you too," I mumble.

"Your family should be here soon," he says.

My family. My eyes swing up, meeting his. "Did you set them up to stay at the neighbors?" I ask with a little more eagerness.

"Yes, I took care of it. Don't worry."

The sound of neighbors and church members coming to see our little boy echoes through the house, causing reality to set back in and complete sadness to seep back through my heart.

"Take your time. I'll start receivin'." He squeezes my arms before he lets go and walks out.

My eyes narrow at the perfectly made bed.

Why did this happen? Why my baby? A horrible burst of agitation erupts inside my head, making me dizzy. My jaw tightens, barely suppressing my snarl of anguish, as my chest heaves quickly and desperately against an all-encompassing feeling of suffocation.

I grab the freshly made blanket tightly with both hands and yank it off the bed, the force of my grip stretching it to its breaking point before I whip it violently against the now empty bed. My mind is consumed with rage.

Then the anger is gone, and a terrible feeling of emptiness creeps its way over my eyes, making my vision go black. I hold the blanket to my face and sob and sob into it until I can't anymore, but the emptiness remains.

The blanket falls from my hands back on the unkempt bed, and I cover my mouth and blow hot air into my palms. I close my eyes and take a few harsh and uneven breaths through my nose. One last deep breath and a shaky wipe of my wet face, and I'm back to normal, as normal as I can be.

I drop to the mattress and slide into my black Edwardian pumps like I'm getting ready for church, not my son's wake.

Not able to stall any longer, I emerge with a brave mask which I know Pierce will see right through, just like I see through his.

"Florence," I say as she walks past me with her nose in the air to greet her friends.

Emmett touches my arm, lightly squeezes it, and gives me a small, kindhearted smile before he retreats to the other side of the room where a group of men are gathered.

"You doing okay?" Cora asks as she wraps her arms around me in a gentle hug.

I nod and look at the floor when she releases me. "I'm all—"

"Cora, don't be rude! Come say 'hi' to your Aunt Verona,"

Florence calls out from the middle of a group of elderly woman dressed in their Sunday best, all staring in our direction.

"I better get over there. I'll talk to you later," Cora says and hurries away before I can say anything.

My eyes find William, sitting cross-legged on the living room floor, staring up at his big brother. I walk over to him and hold out my hand. "Come on, let's go swing on the porch."

He takes my hand and stands. "Okay, Mama. Is Tammy comin'?"

"She sure is," I say and hold the door open for him. "They're all coming—Mamma Alice, your uncles, Thomas and Samuel, and your aunts, Helen, Ethel, and Tammy."

"I'm not callin' Tammy *aunt*," he says as he climbs up on the double swing Pierce made for the boys.

I sit and push my foot off the floorboards, making us swing. "Well, you don't have to."

He crosses his arms over his chest. "*Humph*. Good, cause I ain't gonna."

I can't help the small smile on my face when I look behind us and see my family's wagon coming down the road. "They're here," I say and quickly stand, making the swing sail high. When it comes back down, I throw out my hand and stop it with a jerk. William jumps off and stands beside me as my family pulls into the driveway and stops. I grab William's hand and we sprint off the porch to their wagon.

Mama hops out and holds out her arms. "Come give your mama some suga." She gives me a warm hug. "How you holdin' up, Pearl?"

"I'm doing the best I can." I hug her back, and then I hug my brothers and sisters. "Y'all are all growing up so fast, especially you, Tammy."

"I'm almost five," she says.

"You sure?" I ask and cock my head to the side. "I thought you were almost fifteen."

Her eyes light up and she inhales. "Really?"

"Yes," I tell her with a small chuckle and look at Mama. "Let's go inside, so I can introduce you to Pierce's family."

"All right," Mama says and slings her arm around my shoulder and walks me up the steps.

I open the door and we step through. "I can't believe Pierce and I have been married for five years, and this is the first time you'll have met his family."

"I know, we should've come out sooner," she says as we approach Florence.

"Florence," I say and she slowly turns around, cutting off her conversation with her friends. "This is Alice, my mama." I turn to Mama. "Mama, this is—"

Florence's eyes narrow as she looks right into mine. "I guess you didn't notice I was talking with my friends. I guess you were never taught any manners," she says and turns back around.

My jaw drops and heat floods my face.

Mama puts her arm through mine and takes me to the other side of the room. "It's okay," she says in an understanding voice.

"It's not you, Mama, it's me. She doesn't like me very much," I say.

"Oh, now that's not true, Pearl. It's a sad, stressful time for everyone. She'll come around, just give her time."

I sigh internally. "Yes, ma'am."

"Alice, I'm glad you came." Pierce kisses Mama's cheek.

"I wish it was under better circumstances," she says.

"Me too." Emmett comes up behind her and she turns around. He extends his hand and adds, "You must be Mrs. Rutherford. Emmett Hayes."

Mama shakes his hand. "Yes. Please call me Alice."

He smiles warmly at her. "All right, Alice. It's good to finally meet you."

"Same here."

"Emmett, Owen's looking for you!" Florence calls out from across the room and narrows her eyes toward our group.

"Please excuse me," Emmett says before walking away.

"Yes, of course," Mama says to his back.

"There's plenty of food in the kitchen. Make yourselves at home,"

Pierce tells Mama, and touches my arm before catching up with his father.

Mama turns her head toward John. She takes the three steps it takes for her to be at his side and touches his hands that are crossed over his chest. "He sure is a handsome fella, just like his father"—she tilts her head—"but the nose and lips are yours." She shakes her head. "Too young, too young," she whispers and looks at me. "How about let's make us a plate and sit a spell on the porch. It's a quite nice evenin'."

"Okay," I say, and I walk her into the kitchen, where casseroles are spread on the countertop.

"Now that's a spread!" she says as she picks up a plate.

After we make our plates with a variety of food, we take them to the front porch.

"Guess what?" Helen asks me as we settle on the porch steps.

"What?" I ask.

"I'm getting married." Her grin spreads from ear to ear.

"Oh, Helen, that's wonderful." I smile, but I can't feel the happiness I should. "When?"

"October 18. I wanted to wait until it cools down and the leaves start to change."

"I'll make sure we come. This is joyous news." I hold back my tears as a surge of emptiness washes over me again. My eyes drop to my filled plate, and I pick up the fork. "News we need right now," I whisper.

"Yes, it is," Mama says and sips her tea.

My fork is at my opened mouth, full of potato salad I don't have an appetite for, when a familiar carriage passes in front of the house. I drop the fork, and it clanks on the plate.

Hazel slows and glances my way but doesn't stop, which I'm grateful for.

"Who's that?" Mama asks.

I shake my head and look at my plate. I pick up my fork and stab an innocent potato over and over again. "No one, she's just a neighbor who stays to herself." I wouldn't know how to explain everything that has happened that may or may not be the result of Hazel and her X. If I told Mama about Hazel being a witch, she'd think I was foolish.

"Well, it's rude for her not to come by and give her condolences. You're her neighbor, that's what good neighbors do." She watches the carriage disappear behind the trees surrounding Hazel's house.

"I didn't say she was a *good* neighbor, Mama."

"Now don't be ugly, child."

"Just leave it," I snap. "It doesn't matter anyway, John's gone, and he isn't coming back." Tears threaten, so I blink them back in a hurry, ignoring Mama's look of pity. I look at William, who is observing me closely.

"Can I go play with Tammy?" he asks.

I kiss his forehead, savoring the moment. "Yes, but don't go too far. Stay where I can see you, in case I need you."

"Okay, Mama." He rushes off the porch, chasing Tammy while she shrieks in laughter, making me smile.

"He's the spittin' image of Pierce. He's gonna grow up to be a fine young man," Mama says softly.

I watch my son run carefree. "Yes, he will."

XXX

"Can John sleep with me tonight?" William asks while I tuck him into bed.

I sit on the bed next to him and stroke his tapered hair. "No, baby. He needs to stay out there tonight. Tomorrow he'll go to his new home, the one that's next to your little brother Jacob. Do you remember?"

He frowns. "You think John's still sick?"

"No, John's not sick. In fact, he will never be sick again. God will take good care of him, I promise," I say with a tearful smile.

He doesn't understand, I know, but he knows something is wrong.

He gives me a big hug.

"I love you, William," I say, fighting back another surge of tears as I kiss him on the cheek and stand. "You're such a sweet boy."

"I love you, Mama."

I blow out his lantern, shut his door, and wander out into the quiet living room where Pierce is studying John. I stop in the doorway and watch him for a minute. Maybe he's stamping John into his mind so he'll never forget his precious face. I know I've done it many times over the last couple of days. I never want to forget what John looks like, ever.

Pierce sighs and says, "He looks like he's sleepin'," without taking his eyes off him.

I walk to him and look down at my "sleeping" son. "Yes, he does. He looks so peaceful and out of pain now. He'll never hurt again." I'm not sure if I'm saying it for Pierce's sake or mine. Maybe both.

I rub Pierce's back while we stare at our son for a long time. Neither one of us are ready to say goodbye yet. The silence stretches off into the distance, but I can barely detect the passage of time.

Then, "I'm gonna miss him, Pearl," he says with a sigh.

"I am too," I whisper.

Pierce takes my hand. "Let's go to bed. It's been a long day, too long."

I look up at the dark, puffy circles he has under his eyes. "Yes, it has."

Chapter 21

June 17, 1919

The sun's light hits my eyelids, and I wake from another restless night. I'm not sure how much sleep I've gotten in the last week, since the night I slept with Bessie, but it can't be much. My heart is breaking off, chipping away little by little, piece by piece. I hope nothing else bad happens, because I don't know how much more I can take.

Pierce is wide awake with his arms tucked under his head, staring at the ceiling like he's thinking or avoiding starting the day—possibly both.

"Did you get any sleep?" I ask.

He shakes his head and sits up. "Not much. You?"

I toss the covers aside and put my feet on the floor. "No," I say on an exhale as I stand and cross the room to the wardrobe. I pause a moment with my hand on the knob. *I can do this*, I tell myself, before I pull open the door and take out the black dress I bought for Elizabeth's funeral.

"You gonna be all right today, Pearl?" He walks over to the opened wardrobe and takes out his only suit.

I shimmy into the dress. "I'll do my best. How about you?"

He slips his arm through the sleeve of his white dress shirt and then the other before replying, "I'll be fine, I have to be."

"I'll check on William," I say and walk out.

I open William's bedroom door—and he's gone. My heart plunges. I run into the living room and freeze. William is lying on the sofa with his hands tucked under his cheek and his eyes closed. I clutch my chest and let out a sigh of relief.

I guess he really wanted to sleep with John last night. I won't punish him. It's the last time he'll sleep with his brother, so I'll let him have this. He'll miss him as much as Pierce and I will, maybe more, if that's possible.

John still looks peaceful like he did last night, but his hands are no longer crossed over his chest. One hand is off to the side with his palm facing up. Inside his palm is a big red-white-and-blue marble.

I rush out into the front yard and fall hard to the ground, covering my weeping eyes with my hands. The grass, wet from the morning dew, is making wet spots on my funeral dress, but I don't care. That's the least of my worries. This is the last morning I'll have both my sons with me. The last time I'll see John's face, other than what's embedded into my memory.

I jump when a hand touches my shoulder.

Pierce kneels beside me. His breaths are short and quick. He pulls me into a hug and strokes my hair while letting me cry into his shirt. "It's okay, Pearl. Let it all out."

After a few moments, the pain lessens slightly, so I wipe my tears and slowly rise to my feet. "I'm okay, I'm okay. I'll be fine."

He follows me up and grabs my face with both hands, making me look at him. "Pearl, it's okay to be sad. It's okay to cry. I'll stay out here with you for as long as it takes. We can sit and rest a spell."

"No, I'm fine—or I will be," I say and remove his hands from my face. I don't want to be a burden on him or anyone else. I know he's hurting as much as I am.

"You sure?"

I nod.

"Okay, then. Let's go inside." He takes my hand and we stroll onto the porch like he's dropping me off after a first date. "Your mama got here early and made breakfast. Can you eat?" he asks when we walk through the door.

"I'll try." My eyes are focused on the floor as we walk past John toward the kitchen. "I thought I smelled something cooking," I say softly as he puts his arm over my shoulder and squeezes.

Mama's in front of a big pan of eggs cooking on the stove when we enter the kitchen. "Morning, Mama." I hug her from behind while she stirs eggs in the cast iron. "You didn't have to make breakfast."

"Oh, don't you fret none." She waves her free hand in the air. "That's what mamas are for."

"Somethin' smells good." Pierce kisses Mama's cheek.

"I wanted to help. We'll leave right after the funeral, so this may be the only chance I get to spend time with my daughter. We don't get to see each other often," she says, still looking at the eggs, avoiding my eyes and making me feel guilty.

"We'll see each other at Helen's wedding." I glance at my wedding ring as I turn it around my finger.

She turns off the stove and shovels eggs into a big bowl. "We sure will. That will be a good visit."

There's already bacon, ham, and biscuits on the counter along with a pot of grits cooking on the stove. Plates and silverware, which includes John's baby spoon, sit on the starter end. I caress the handle of his spoon, fixating on it for a few seconds. I shake my head and blink away the moisture forming. When I turn around, Pierce's eyeing me with folded arms. I mouth, *I'm okay.*

He nods and takes a seat at one of the few chairs left in the room.

"What time did you get here?" I ask Mama while I pour hot water from the kettle into Pierce's cup and stir in the coffee.

"Oh, 'bout an hour ago. I saw little William sleepin' in the livin' room with John." She sighs and wipes her hands on a dish rag. "That's the saddest thing I've ever seen. He's surely gonna miss his big brother."

"Yes, he is." I hand Pierce the cup with unsteady hands, but they still when his finger runs along mine. "Did you see the marble

William left for John?" I ask Pierce.

"Thank you. I did." He sips the dark brew but keeps his regarding eyes on me. "You gonna be okay?"

"Stop asking," I say, annoyed. "Please, just stop asking." I turn away and try to calm my breathing. "I'll go wake William and get him dressed." I march out, needing to get away from inquisitive eyes.

When I get to the living room, I shake William gently until he stirs. "William, wake up." I shake him again. "It's time to get dressed, baby."

His eyes flicker open, and he looks at me with droopy eyes. He sits up and yawns as his fingers rub the sleep from his brown eyes, which look just like his brother's. He scratches his head and looks around. "I'm not a baby, Mama. I'm a big boy. John told me I have to be a big boy now." He stands and stretches, looking taller than he did the night before.

"What? When did he tell you that?"

"Last night," he says and walks out the room.

I look back at John, who is still lying on the table. William must've been dreaming. I follow him into his bedroom and pick out a dress shirt from the dresser, holding it up for him to put his arm through.

He crosses his arms over his chest and shakes his head. "Nuh-uh, Mama. I'm a big boy now. Remember?" He uncrosses his arms and thumbs his chest. "I can do it all by myself."

"All right. All right." I hand his shirt to him and hold my palms up in surrender. I take a step back and watch as he removes his gown and slides on his shirt.

Maybe he *is* growing up. I shouldn't baby him anymore—but he's all I have. I blink back the tears, but a few escape.

After he's dressed, sans shoes, he smiles with outstretched arms as he looks down at his buttoned shirt. "See, Mama. I told you. I can do it all by myself." He looks up at me and his smile disappears. "Don't cry, Mama. John doesn't want you to cry and I don't neither." He wipes my tear-stained cheek when I bend to look him at his level. "You can tie my shoes."

"Thank you, I'd like that. And I'll try to do better." It's a promise I'm not sure I can keep.

XXX

Albert and Mabel's husband, Wayne, carry the small wooden coffin from the barn to the living room and place it on the floor. With one at John's head and the other at his feet, they lift his body and the marble falls out of his hand before they place him in the box.

William slides on his knees across the floor and grabs the marble before it disappears under the sofa. He stands and blows on it, making sure it's dust free. "Here, John," he says and places it back in John's hand before stepping away. With his chin up, his face turns red and his eyes mist over.

Everyone's watching William. Some have gaping mouths while others dab their wet eyes with a handkerchief.

William stands straight, hands crossed over his stomach, and his eyes drop to his brother as the lid closes. "Bye, John."

I burst into tears and Pierce grabs me, crushing my face into his chest. I promised William I wouldn't cry, but I can't help it. I'll never see John again.

A ping brings my head up, and I see Emmett hammering nails on the lid. My head finds refuge in Pierce's chest once again.

When the pinging stops, Albert and Wayne pick up the coffin, carry it outside and down the front steps, and place it in the back of our wagon. After everyone is loaded into their own wagons and buggies, we begin the procession to the church. This will be the last time Pierce, William, John, and I ride in this wagon together as a family. I glance behind and see Pierce's family, my family, and the neighbors, who have gathered at the house, following us down the road.

We pass Hazel's house, which is tucked away in the woods. She's sitting on her front porch rocking in a chair. I can't see her expression since her house sits back away from the road, but I know she's staring at me—the tingling in my spine tells me.

"Don't look over there," Pierce says.

"I'm sorry," I whisper, turning my eyes back forward and pulling William closer to me.

XXX

After the graveside funeral, and the last of the dirt is covering John's coffin, I hug Mama longer than I should. I don't want to let go. "I'm not ready to say goodbye."

"I know, sweetheart." She pats my back. "But we really need to get goin'. We'll see you soon, I promise."

I nod into her shoulder, press closer, and tighten my grip.

"Pearl, let go." Pierce tugs my arm. "They got a long ride ahead of 'em."

I nod again and release my death grip as I wipe my wet eyes. "Bye, Mama. I love you."

"I love you, Pearl." She hops up on the wagon as Thomas flicks the reins, sending them promenading down the road. "Take care of Pierce and that sweet boy of yours!" she shouts with a final wave, the rest of my family waving with her.

"Yes, ma'am," I say to myself, and I wave back while I watch them ride away.

XXX

My head bows and my shoulders drop when I enter the kitchen. Leftover food caked in dishes is scattered on the counter and in the sink. With a heavy sigh, I shuffle to the sink and gather any spoiled food, slinging it into the slop bucket. Then I fill the sink with sudsy water and grab a dirty pot.

"You don't need to do this now. It can wait." Pierce grasps my wrist, stopping me from scrubbing a pot. Water and soap suds cover my hands while they linger over the sink.

150

I don't look at him before speaking through gritted teeth. "I need to stay busy, Pierce. He's not coming back, and I need to keep myself busy, so I don't think about it." I try to pull my hand away with a yank.

He lets go of my wrist and rolls up his sleeves. "Okay, Pearl. What can I do to help?"

I point to the slop bucket. "Feed the pigs."

"All right." He grabs the bucket. "I'll get William to help me, and then I'll let him ride on Buddy. He likes that."

"Pierce," I say before he walks out.

He pauses, and I can hear him turn around. "Yes, Pearl?"

I inhale sharply, keeping my eyes firmly on the dishes. "Don't let anything happen to my baby."

"I won't." He walks out, leaving me to my thoughts and dirty dishes.

XXX

Pierce and I are lying in bed, staring at the ceiling in silence. The glow of the moon is coming in through the open window, giving us a hint of light.

I can't take the quiet any longer. I work up the nerve to ask the question I've been thinking about all day. "Do you think there's any more to John's death?"

A good minute passes before he says, "No, Pearl. He was a sick boy."

"But—"

"Bad things happen to good people. People get sick and sometimes they die. We didn't know he was so sick." He pauses before quietly saying, "It was my fault. I shoulda took him to the hospital."

My arms slam against the mattress. "No! We trusted the doctor. We both did." I'm angry at everyone. Hazel, myself, Pierce, the doctor—we're all at fault. "This shouldn't have happened. John should be here, sleeping in his room with his brother, where he belongs." My hands ball into tight fists and slam onto the bed again, making it vibrate.

Pierce gently covers my fist with his hand. "Pearl, we can't blame him, he didn't know. I talked to him today. He thought it was just a bug, and he feels right awful about it. He said he's gonna retire as soon as he finds someone to take over."

"*Humph.* Good. He *needs* to retire," I say viciously. My hand breaks free from his tender hold, and I cross my arms over my chest. "But it won't bring back John." My bottom lip sticks out in a childish pout.

He turns to his side, facing me, and puts an arm around me. "There's nothin' we can do to change what happened. We just gonna have to move on the best we can."

I take two quick, deep breaths, trying to control myself. "I know," I say quietly.

"Try to get some sleep. We both need it." He constricts me in his arms like he's terrified I'll disappear. "I love you, Pearl. I love you so much."

"Me too," I whisper.

Hazel still seizes my mind, the way she stared at me when we passed by her house this morning, and then she floats away. I close my eyes for some much-deserved sleep.

Chapter 22

July 19, 1919

All is quiet, and we are slowly getting back to normal, as normal as we can. Pierce and I have moved forward again as husband and wife, as we should, and William has adjusted to being an only child. Pierce is hoping we can add to our family soon, and I'm ready too. I need to hear the laughter of children at my feet.

We finally have enough money for a cow, so Pierce took William with him this morning to Mr. Barker's farm to inquire about one. I'm looking forward to getting a new cow instead of getting milk from his parents every day, and hearing about it from Florence.

I'm shelling peas at the kitchen table when I hear, "Pearl," in a low, raspy voice coming from the front porch.

My spine straightens and I sit, motionless, holding my breath. Will she go away if I don't move?

"Pearl," she says, louder this time. "I know you're in there."

I let out the breath since there's no getting around this, so I wipe my hands on my apron and untie it from the back. Whatever it is she wants, I hope it's minor.

As slow as I can, I slip the apron over my head and stand.

"*Now*, Pearl!" she yells, making me jump.

My hand knocks the pea bowl, but I'm able to catch it before it falls onto the floor. I throw my apron on the table and mosey through the living room in defiance. When I get to the front door, I take a deep breath before peeking out through the screen's security.

Hazel is sitting in Pierce's rocking chair, and she must sense me without looking. "Can you go fetch me a glass of water? It's *hot* out today." She fans herself with a black lace hand fan. "*Stickaaay* hot."

Without saying a word, I turn around and stalk to the kitchen. I remember what happened with the vegetable garden, the chickens, and the cow when I denied her, and I don't want anything to happen to our water. If I give her a glass, maybe she'll drink it and leave before Pierce comes back.

I grip the handle of the pump until my knuckles turn white as the water fills the glass. "I should spit in it," I mutter. I glance over my shoulder at the front door and shake my head. No, Mama didn't raise me like that; and besides, she'd probably know I had.

When I get back to her, I hand her the glass and notice the brown liver spots on her wrinkled hands, like my great-grandmother had when I was a child. Her hair is solid white now—there's no black at all. The lines around her mouth, eyes, and forehead are deeper and more noticeable than before. She looks like she's aged significantly since the last time I saw her, and that was only a month ago. Has it been that long since John's death?

I don't know how old this woman is who's sitting in my husband's rocking chair. Before, I assumed she could be in her forties, but now, taking a good, long look at her, she looks around seventy, maybe eighty. Time is not her friend.

"You finally figured it out, Pearl. But you're too late." She sets the glass on the table beside her without taking a sip. "Of course, it's been too late from the beginning." She fans herself again and rocks, making the chair creak with each pass. The sound is different than when Pierce rocks in it. It's relentless. She points her red-tipped nail at the empty rocker beside her, my rocker. "Why don't you have a seat, so we can chat a bit before your *handsome* husband and your *last remaining* son comes back?"

I don't move.

"Sit, Pearl!" she hisses, venom in her voice.

I sit at the edge of the seat, ready to dash out of the chair in an instant. All the muscles in my body are tense. My hands are in my lap, and I'm twirling my wedding ring around my finger and tapping my foot. I need answers. "Did you have anything to do with my vegetable garden?"

She doesn't speak. She rocks and fans herself, looking straight away to the road where her crow-covered carriage is parked.

"The chickens or the cow?"

Still nothing.

"What about my sons? Did you have anything to do with Jacob's death—or John's?" I raise my voice.

"Oh my, dear. For a smart girl, you sure is dumb. I thought you was one of those *educated* girls."

My temperature rises. I suck in a lungful of air and grab the arms of the chair. How dare she speak to me like that in my own home! I leap to my feet. "You can't—"

"Sit *down*, Pearl," she says, baring her teeth. She locks her narrow eyes with mine, and I see the rampant warning pulsating in them.

The heat in my body takes a dramatic nosedive. I slowly sit, feeling defeated, and place my hands back in my lap and wait for her to continue.

"You should've never crossed my X. That was a foolish thing to do. Weren't you warned?"

"Yes, but…but it was an accident. I wasn't paying attention."

"You should've paid more attention, Pearl. You were doomed the minute you stepped over my X." She smiles, making her wrinkles become more defined, and showing her once yellow, now brown, decayed teeth.

"Please, I gave you water. Can't you leave us alone?"

"This will be the last time you see me. I'm afraid our little conversations must come to an end. Oh, how I enjoyed them, though." Her tone is light, making me wonder if she has.

I relax my shoulders and exhale, trying to let go of the hatred I have for this woman. This is the end of our relationship, and I'm glad. I never want to see Hazel again for as long as I live. "Okay, thank you. Thank you, Hazel."

She turns her head back toward the road and continues to calmly fan herself. "My time on Earth is almost over. My last breath will be taken when the sky turns a fiery orange, and a black cloud disappears into the night's sky." Her red-tipped nail points to the sky above where her house sits behind trees.

My mouth drops open. Did she predict her own death? "What are you saying?"

She looks at me. Her eyes flash red before turning back to their normal shade of black. "But it doesn't have to be that way."

I think, but come up with nothing. "What? I don't understand."

"Forgiveness can drive out the darkness of hatred." She wobbles as she stands and shuffles her feeble body to the edge of the porch, still fanning herself while looking at the road. She drops her head and mumbles, "I never could forgive." Her head snaps up. "And I never forgot," she says with bitterness.

"One more thing, Pearl, before I go." She turns and glares at me, cutting me deep with her eyes. "If you don't stop it, you will live a long, miserable, and lonely life until your blood runs through no other. *Your* fate lies in *your* own hands now." Her eyes flicker red as she holds up a wrinkled hand and points her red fingernail at my mouth. "*Speak*," she says in a hushed tone, like she's speaking to herself rather than to me. Then she turns and tramps off the porch quicker than her frail legs should.

My hand covers my gaping mouth. I rise to my feet and walk to the edge of the porch. "What does that mean?" I yell, because she's already at her carriage, the crows scattering.

She doesn't reply, and she doesn't turn around. She gets inside and drives down the road with her flock following.

"What does that mean?" I whisper. Why didn't she just tell me what she wanted me to know?

I walk back into the kitchen and throw her water in the sink. I grab a clean glass and fill it with my own water. What did she mean? I raise the glass, hold it up to the window and study the clear liquid in the sun's light, before taking a big swallow.

It's fine. Maybe since I gave her a glass of water, which she didn't even drink, she'll leave it and us alone. I can only pray.

XXX

I'm pulling the last fried pork chop out of the frying pan when I hear the wagon return. "Just in time," I say to myself as I wipe my hands on my flour-coated apron and walk out the back door.

Pierce and William are both sporting big grins when the wagon comes to a stop.

William sees me and jumps off the wagon. "Look, Mama! We got a new Bessie." William bounces while pointing to the black-and-white cow tied behind the wagon.

"I see that. Maybe we should come up with a new name for her." I rub the top of William's head.

William closes one eye and puts a finger under his chin as his lips twist. After only a second, he snaps his fingers. "Naw, I like Bessie. She looks like a Bessie."

"Okay," I say, smiling at his childish resolve, "Bessie it is."

Pierce steps down from the wagon and grabs me by the waist. "I've missed you," he says right before planting a soft kiss on my lips.

I wrap my hands around his neck and pull him in for a deeper, longer kiss. "I've missed you, too."

He takes a step back and smiles down at me. "That was nice." He releases me and unties the cow. "How was your day?"

"Oh, nothing out of the ordinary," I lie, knowing I need to tell him, but I don't want to ruin the moment. I can't hide it from him any longer, so I'll wait until tonight when William isn't around, because the conversation will surely get heated.

We all three take the new Bessie into the barn, getting her settled.

"Look, Mama, she likes it here," William says while we all watch

Bessie tread to the other side of her stall, already feeling right at home.

"It seems she does," I say.

Pierce picks William up and carries him into the house with me trailing close behind. "Is supper ready? I'm starved."

"Yes, I just finished," I say and Hazel enters my mind once again.

XXX

I need to tell Pierce about Hazel's visit today. I'm not sure how he'll react, and I'm scared of what he may say or do. He has never raised a hand to me, and I don't think he ever would, but I'm still terrified of disappointing him.

William is in bed and we're sitting on the porch when I finally work up the nerve. "Pierce. I—"

"William sure does like the new cow." He chuckles, takes a drag off his pipe, and blows it out, granting me the sweet scent I love.

"Yes, he does." I look at my folded hands lying in my lap. "Pierce, I need—"

"He talked to her the whole way home from old man Barker's today. He told her all about her new home like she could understand him. It was somethin' else. Havin' a new cow will be good. It's just what we need."

"I guess it is."

"I can't believe he wanted to name her Bessie."

"Bessie's a good name for a cow, I suppose."

He nods a few times, looking out at the road, and rocks. "It is. It is."

His chair creaks, and I twirl my ring around my finger as my heart races.

I take a deep breath. "Hazel came by today," I say without hesitation before he has time to interrupt me again, and before I chicken out. I let the breath out, relieved I told him.

Pierce's rocking stops, and his pipe halts midway in the air to his mouth. He turns his head, glaring at me with narrow eyes. "What did you say, Pearl?"

I'm sweating and the temperature seems to have risen ten degrees. My throat feels like it's closing, so I gulp, opening it up again so I can speak. "Hazel…she stopped by for a glass of water."

He raises an eyebrow. "And did you give her water?"

I slowly nod.

"How come you went and done that?" His jaw twitches and he hasn't taken his tapered eyes off me since I first told him. I'm not even sure he has blinked.

"She was passing by, and it was hot. I was scared something would happen to the water. With everything going on lately, I…I thought she may be behind it all."

Pierce shoots out of his chair. He paces back and forth in front of me, his chest rising with each breath. He stops, bends at the waist, and points the pipe in my face.

I shrink back in my chair and turn my head away.

"I told you to stay away from her, and I mean it," he spits. "Do you understand me, Pearl? Stay away from her. Nothin' good can come of it."

I look at him with honest eyes. "I won't see her again. I told her to leave us alone, and she said she would never come back."

"Good. Good." He rights himself and takes a few small steps back, still damaging me with those resentful eyes. He stabs his pipe in my direction a few times like he wants to say something else, and then his eyes shift to the porch's ceiling. "I'm gonna check on the animals," he says through gritted teeth, marches off the porch, and disappears around the side of the house.

My shoulders drop, and I let out a choppy breath, relieved I told him—but now he's mad at me. It's not my fault she kept showing up on our porch, but I'm glad she said she will never come back.

It's over.

Chapter 23

June 22, 2001

"Wait a minute. Just wait a minute." Meredith holds up a hand and tilts her head. "Are you telling us some old woman put a curse on you?" She rolls her eyes and twirls a finger next to her temple. "You're crazy to believe that."

"It's the truth." I grind my teeth when heat rushes through me. I don't normally have a temper, but no one will stand here and tell me that I'm crazy to believe what I know. "Everything I'm saying is the truth." My thumb punches my chest. "I should know. I lived it."

"Oh, please. This isn't a story you should tell a child. A dying kid, a witch, and a curse, it's insane." She grabs her purse and slings it over her shoulder, but it falls to the floor, spilling the contents everywhere. Her eyes widen and she falls to the ground, her knees thudding on the floor. She nabs a small vial, a silver flask, and a pack of cigarettes from the floor and chucks them in her purse.

Everyone stares at her except Mary, who is kneeling beside the couch. She picks up a prescription bottle, and Meredith snatches it away. "That's mine. I don't need your help," she says and stuffs it into her bag.

Mary stands and backs away. "Fine."

"All because of this woman and her stupid X, you and your whole bloodline is cursed? Ha!" She zips the bag and stands, hooking it over her shoulder. "It's ludicrous."

Mary throws her hands up and pushes the air. "Let's calm down. I need you to calm down, Meredith."

"Did you hear what she said to my daughter?" Meredith stabs a finger in my direction. "She's crazy!"

I narrow my eyes. "I am *not* crazy! It's true, and you should be warned." I point to Sara, whose eyes are nearly popping out. "Sara should be warned. She needs to know the rest of the story. You two are the last of my bloodline."

"Come on, Sara. We're leaving." She pulls Sara out of her seat. "We're not listening to any more of this nonsense. Get your shoes on."

Sara slides her feet into her flip flops. "But I don't want to leave. I want to hear the rest," she says, planting her feet on the ground.

Meredith shakes her head and jerks Sara's arm, dragging her away. "We're done here. Come *on*, Sara."

Sara pulls her arm free, turns around, and runs to me. She gives me a tight hug, one which I know will probably be our last, and kisses my cheek. "It was great meeting you, Nana."

"It was great meeting you too, dear." I pat her back and give it a soft rub. "Don't cross the X, Sara. Stay away from X's," I whisper in her ear.

"Come on, Sara, let's go. Now!" Meredith yells.

"I will," Sara whispers back. "Bye, Nana." She waves with a frown as she moseys down the hall with her head hanging.

Meredith waits with her hands on her hips. "Any day now, Sara, any day." When Sara gets to her, Meredith narrows her eyes at me. "Goodbye, Nana," she says harshly. "Have a great life." She pivots and stalks down the hall with Sara following.

I turn back around and see every head is twisted toward the hall. Once Meredith and Sara are gone, they all turn back to me like dominoes.

"That's a depressing story, Pearl. I can't believe you lived through all that," a big-chinned woman with no teeth comments.

"And all that happened in one summer?" another woman asks, shaking her head. "Such a shame." She grabs a prune from the plate beside her with shaky hands and stuffs it in her mouth. Her jaw twitches with each chew while prune juice runs from the side of her mouth. She wipes the juice away with her hand and wipes her hand on her housecoat before reaching for another prune.

I take my gaze away from Pruny and her prune bath. "There's more to the story. It's not over with yet. I wish it were, but there's still more to tell."

"Please continue. I want to hear the rest," Mary says, taking her seat again.

I glance once more at the empty hall before continuing, "Where did I leave off?" I ask, tapping my finger to my lip.

"You told Pierce about Hazel stopping by for a glass of water, and he was mad," Big Chin says.

"Oh, yes. Well, after that it was quiet for a couple of weeks without incident. Everything was back to normal, as normal as it could be with the loss of John. I thought Hazel would leave me alone, but she wasn't finished with me yet."

Chapter 24

August 5, 1919

"When will Father be home?" William says as he climbs into bed.

I pull the covers over him. "Soon. Remember the terrible storm we had the other night?"

He nods.

"Well, it caused a big hole in Uncle Albert's barn, so your father is helping fix it," I say with a big yawn that brings tears in my eyes. I've been extremely exhausted lately, but today it seems worse. I may be pregnant—and I hope I am, because we need it—but I won't say anything until I'm sure. I'll go see Dr. Clayton in the morning when I have more energy. I hope I *will* have more energy.

"You tired, Mama?"

"A little. I may take a nap, too. If you get up before I do, you be sure to wake me, okay?"

"I will, Mama. Sleep tight."

"Don't let the bedbugs bite," I finish for him and kiss the tip of his nose. "I love you, sweetheart."

"Love you, Mama," he says as he rolls over to his side and closes his eyes.

I back out of the room and shuffle to my own. Not having the strength to take off my shoes, I collapse on the bed still wearing them. As soon as my head hits the pillow, I fall into a hard, deep sleep.

I hear sweet giggles.

"William, where are you?"

I look behind a tree, but he isn't there. The giggles come louder, like they're right behind me, so I twirl around and reach out to grab him, but all I grab is air. "William, come out, come out, wherever you are!"

I search behind tree after tree, but I can't find him. He's always been a good hider. I keep walking until the woods open into a meadow with colorful flowers everywhere. It's peaceful here, like all the world's troubles have vanished.

John and William are hand in hand, skipping in circles in the middle of the field with another boy, a smaller boy. I can't see their feet through the tall flowers. They stop and all three pick up a dandelion and blow with fat cheeks and puckered lips. They giggle when the small petals float away, and they chase after them with hands in the air, trying to grab them. I laugh, too, and pick my own dandelion. I make a wish to always have my family be happy and healthy, and then I blow, allowing the white seeds to fly off the stem and into the air like snowflakes.

The wind picks up, making the flowers dance. The boys laugh even louder.

I walk closer to them, lean down, and ask, "What's your name?" to the little boy who's staring at me with familiar chocolate-brown eyes.

"Mama, this is Jacob," John says.

I cock my head to the side, getting a better look at the little boy. They all look at each other and take off running.

"Wait, don't go!" I yell with my arms outstretched, trying to reach them even though they've already sprinted away. I gather my long skirt with both hands and run after them, stumbling over the thick flowers. My feet drag because there's so many that it's hard to walk, but the boys run freely.

The boys stop and turn around right when I fall into a body of water I hadn't noticed. I go under and take in a mouth full of muddy liquid. When I surface, I gasp, struggling for air. My fingernails claw the edge, but I can't get out because it's too slimy and my hands slide right off, over and over again, sending me back under.

The boy's faces ripple above the murky water as they stare down at me from the water's edge. When I come back up, I reach for them. "Help me, please. John, help me," I say, wheezing.

They all have the same smile on their faces. My heart beats faster and faster and the panic intensifies. I will drown if I don't get out now. I reach out one last time before something grabs my legs and pulls me under—

"Pearl, wake up." Pierce shakes me.

I jerk and look at him in a daze. When my eyes focus, I let out a deep, ragged breath. I sit up and rub my tired eyes. "What time is it?"

"Almost six. How long you been sleepin'?"

"Since one, I think." I've never slept that long, even with my last pregnancies.

He puts the back of his hand on my forehead. "You sick?"

I push his hand away and stand, swaying. Pierce grabs my arms, steadying me. "No, I'm fine, just exhausted."

"You sure? I can get the doc—"

"No, I'm not sick at all. I promise." I give him a trivial smile. "I'll check on William."

I walk past him to William's room before he can ask me anything else. When I open the bedroom door, my heart hammers in my chest—he's gone.

I turn to Pierce, who's right behind me with a creased forehead. "Where's William?"

He looks past me into William's room, and his face blanches.

"I'll check the front, you take the back," I rush out.

We both take off running in different directions of the house, calling out William's name.

I run out the front door. "William!"

He doesn't answer.

The back door slams. "William!" Pierce shouts.

I race around the side of the house toward the back and stop at the outhouse. I fling the door open.

Empty.

Pierce comes out of the barn, shaking his head at me.

I place my hand on my forehead, shielding the sun from my eyes. "He's not in the fields. Where can he be?"

"I don't know." He goes inside the hen house, coming back empty-handed.

I don't have a good feeling. "William, please come out! It's not funny anymore." I wring my hands and bite my lip as my breathing becomes labored.

Pierce's eyes widen before he charges toward the pond, and I take off after him, but I'm unable to keep up with his long legs.

"William, no!" He runs into the pond, splashing water as he stumbles. He picks up William, who was face down. "No!" he shouts and holds William to his chest. "No."

I plunge to my knees and explode in wails. "No! No! *No!*" I scream raggedly. "Not my baby, God, please, not my baby!" I beg, but I know it will do no good because Pierce has now come from the pond with our lifeless boy clutched in his arms.

Pierce cries into William's neck and drops to his knees in front of me. William's shriveled, pale hands hang by his sides, not moving except for the small jerks caused by Pierce's sobs. Droplets of pond water drip from his hair and clothes to the ground, making small craters. My eyes drop to the dents, and I gasp. Underneath Pierce and William is a big X drawn into the dirt.

My hands fly to the sides of my head, and I snatch a handful of hair. I can't stop the hot lava from burning my throat, so I turn away and vomit on the ground beside me. I heave until there's nothing left in me.

"Pierce," I say while spitting the last of the chunks out of my mouth. I turn to Pierce, who still has his face buried in William's neck. I point to the ground under him and cover my mouth with my free hand. "Pierce."

He looks at me and then to where I'm pointing, and freezes. His face turns white and his jaw drops as he shakes his head and slowly rises. He takes a few steps back, still clutching William in his arms and glaring at the X, and he finally looks at me again. "What have you done, Pearl? What have you done?" he roars.

I push myself off the ground, trembling and shaking my head. "I didn't do anything," I screech while stepping to him with outstretched arms. "I didn't do anything, Pierce, I swear."

He backs away, glowering at me with hard eyes and tight lips, without speaking.

"I didn't do anything," I drop to my knees and slump, defeated. "Please, Pierce. I can't do this alone. I need you," I plead with my head bowed, sobbing into my hands.

After a few agonizing moments, he kneels in front of me. He pulls me into him with one arm while still clutching William with the other. We sit on the ground, crying in each other's arms for what seems like hours.

When we have no tears left to shed, Pierce stands. Still holding onto William, he grabs my hand and pulls me to my feet. With distorted lips, he looks at the ground again and kicks the dirt until the X is gone. Dust flies up, sticking to our wet faces and making us both cough.

"Come on, let's take our son inside." He tugs me with him while I'm still staring at the invisible X.

Pierce places William in his bed and stands back, taking a stuttering breath. He stares at him for the longest time before saying, "I'll go get the doctor." He looks at me with glossy eyes and touches my arm before walking out.

I crawl into bed beside William and wrap him in my arms. I rock back and forth and sing to him like I did when he was a small baby, my voice soft and cracking, barely audible. "Rock-a-bye baby, on the tree top. When the wind blows, the cradle will rock."

Nightfall arrives, darkening the room. I'm gazing into the darkness, humming, when the lantern lights, making me jump. Pierce and Dr. Clayton are staring at me as I hold William in a tight embrace, still rocking back and forth.

Pierce grabs my hand. "Pearl, the doctor needs to look at William."

I look at him with distant eyes and nod. I gently lay William on the bed like he is the most fragile thing in the world and kiss his forehead before getting up. Pierce takes my hand in his and wraps the other around my back and escorts me out the room. He sits me on the living-room sofa and touches my wet, dirty cheek.

"Stay here." Then he's gone.

I do as I'm told and sit where he places me without moving, staring into space for I don't know how long. Since everything around me is hazy, I don't see the doctor leave, but when Pierce sits beside me and places his hand over mine, I know he's gone.

"He said William died three or four hours ago, so it musta been right before I got home. I don't understand it. He knows…" He pauses, looking away from me. "*Knew* not to go into the pond alone. He knew."

My lips quiver and hot tears drain from my eyes and trickle down my face. I don't bother wiping, because I don't deserve to wipe away the tears caused by William's death.

"Pearl, I didn't know you was sick. If I'd known, I'd come back sooner. I'm sorry."

I don't blame him, I blame myself.

He squeezes my hand. "Pearl, please talk to me."

I should've never slept for so long. I should've never taken a nap to begin with.

"Pearl?"

I hate myself for causing this.

He hugs me, but I don't return the hug. My arms hang from my sides because I don't deserve his sympathy. His arms tighten.

I'm the worst mother ever. I don't deserve to live.

He pulls away and gently grabs my head with both hands, forcing my eyes to meet his. He thumbs my wet dirty cheeks, wiping away the tears I refused to discard. "I know you're in shock, Pearl, but so am I. We'll get through this, I know we will. We got to. We just got to."

I nod, once.

He hugs me again before he stands. "I won't be able to sleep tonight. I'll be in the barn makin' William's…" He pauses. "William's coffin." He bows his head and sniffles while he walks out, leaving me alone.

When he's out of sight, I slowly rise and amble to William's bedroom, where I pause in the doorway for a moment and look at the puffed bedding, and then I shuffle to it and pull down the blanket covering my son. I gaze at his pale face and sigh before I crawl into bed next to him and wrap him once again in my warm embrace. "You're so cold, William."

I cover us with his blanket and rock us both to sleep.

Chapter 25

August 7, 1919

I'm alone in the living room holding William's small, stiff hand, not wanting to let go yet. I never want to let go. He's lying on the kitchen table with Florence's best tablecloth underneath him like John was almost two months ago. I can't believe it's been almost two months since John died. It seems like yesterday I was dressing John in his church clothes, the same as I did with William yesterday evening for the viewing. I didn't want to see anyone, so I hid in John and William's room where I feel closer to them while Pierce's family, neighbors, and church members gathered once again in our small house to view another one of our dead sons.

I still haven't spoken a word to anyone, other than William, since I begged Pierce not to leave me after he pulled William out the pond. I've kept to myself, lying in the bed with William, singing and talking to him continuously until Pierce made me give him up from my hold yesterday afternoon. It was hard to let him go. I wanted to fight it, but I've lost all my fight. I have nothing left in me. Remembering to breathe is becoming more and more difficult every time I think of my precious sons no longer being with me. I want to join them, because going on without them seems impossible. Pierce is the only thing saving me from going crazy by constantly checking on me, but it may be too late. I can't imagine what my life will be like with my two little boys gone. I'm still hoping I'll wake from this awful dream—no, this horrendous nightmare.

An arm wraps around my shoulder, making my body twitch, and I look up into Pierce's bloodshot eyes as he frowns down at me. "We'll get through this, Pearl, I swear." He squeezes my arm and sniffs.

I nod and glance around at our little house, now bursting at the seams with grievers and spectators who I hadn't realized were there. I shouldn't feel alone, but I do.

Albert and a neighbor, Timothy, bring in the wooden coffin and place it on the floor beside the table. It's so small—smaller than John's, but bigger than Jacob's.

I lean down, brush William's dark, combed hair from his forehead, and with quivering lips, I kiss him there one last time. "Mama loves you, baby," I whisper to him and step back.

Pierce picks up William, kneels beside the coffin, and gently places him inside. Then he crosses William's arms over his chest, and kisses his forehead before standing and wiping his wet eyes. He straightens his suit jacket and nods to Albert as he sniffs.

Albert and Timothy lift the lid off the floor.

I hold up my hand. "Wait."

They freeze, looking at each other, and then at me.

I sprint to William's room, and with a trembling hand, I grab the small black bag of marbles from the dresser and clutch it to my chest. I close my eyes and take a deep, shuddering breath, wishing I could crawl into bed and forget about the world, but I can't...not today. So, I turn back around and walk out to face it head on.

The room is quiet, and everyone's eyes are on me when I step back into the living room, making me uncomfortable. I am the center of attention, which I'm not used to, and don't much like. I slowly stagger to William and tuck the bag under his crossed hands lying on his chest. I kiss my finger and place it on his lips before stepping back and nodding.

The lid is put into place, closing my son away from me forever, and Emmett nails it shut.

Albert and Timothy place the coffin in the back of our wagon, and we start down the road to our church with everyone behind us, just like John's funeral. I turn around and notice there is one difference—my family isn't here. I turn back around, facing the front. We didn't tell my family. They don't know.

It's probably for the best. I'm not sure if I could bear to see them, especially little Tammy. It would be too painful to see her vibrant youthfulness. I'll call them when I visit the doctor next week.

My eyes swing to Hazel's run-down house, without her on the porch this time, when we pass. The torn curtain in the window twitches. She's behind it, I know she is. And I can almost hear her laughing at me like I'm a hilarious joke. *"You fool girl, you so dumb. I thought you was one of those educated girls."* My hands ball into tight fists in my lap of their own accord until my knuckles are white. My eyes narrow and my nostrils flare as my breathing increases. I'm glad I can't see her horrid face, because if I could, no one could stop me from jumping off this moving wagon and beating her to a bloody pulp. The rage I have boiling through my veins for this woman right now consumes me. It's disgraceful, this isn't me, I hate this person—and I hate feeling like this. I take a few deep breaths and stretch out my hand in my lap, trying to get my anger under control.

Pierce grabs my hand and squeezes, making me jump, but he doesn't say a word. I hear his silent request loud and clear, so I turn back and face the road ahead, trying to forget about the foul woman behind the curtain.

The rest of the day passes in a blur. I'm still in shock, and it's all I can do to stand without my legs giving out, but I don't fall, thanks to Pierce.

William is buried beside John and Jacob. William was such a sweet boy, the same as John.

Everyone will miss him, especially me.

Chapter 26

August 10, 1919

"Pearl, how you feelin'?" Pierce asks as he comes into the bedroom and sits beside me on the bed. "Can I get you somethin' to eat?"

I look at my folded hands in my lap. "I'm not hungry."

"Pearl, you've been lying in bed for three days now. You ain't ate nothin'. You gotta eat." He shakes his head. "I'm worried."

My fingers move to my ring, slowly turning it around and around.

"Pearl, maybe you should see the doctor. I know you is upset, but I can't lose you, too."

"I'll go see him in the morning," I say, my voice barely above a whisper.

"I can get him. He should be done with supper by now." He stands, but I catch his arm, and he sits back down on the bed beside me. "What is it, Pearl? You can tell me."

I'm twirling my ring and biting my lip.

He seizes my hand, stopping its movement. "Just tell me."

"I need to tell you what happened. I thought everything was in my head, but I think it's true."

His eyebrows lift. "What's true, Pearl?"

My heart beats faster as the nerves take over, making my chest ache. The bravery that was just there is gone, but I can't back down now. I have to tell him. I swallow hard, before admitting, "Everything that happened is because of Hazel. She caused it all."

The blood drains from his face and the hand holding mine tightens. I wince and it loosens. "What do you mean, Pearl? What happened?"

"The day, back in May, when John, William, and I went to pick blackberries for a cobbler—"

He nods. "Yes, I remember."

It all comes out of me in a mad flood, before I can stop myself. "Well, we didn't make it, because of the X," I rush out. "I was looking up at a swarm of crows William saw, and I didn't notice the big X in the middle of the road. We crossed over it. John saw it and pointed it out after we passed it. I got scared, and we came back. I may have seen Hazel in the woods, but I'm not sure."

Pierce releases my hand and turns away from me. He rests his elbows on his knees and drops his head, covering it with his hands. "Go on, Pearl. Tell me everythin'."

I take a deep breath. "I miscarried that same night. Hazel came by a few days later and asked for tomatoes out the garden. Pierce, I swear I did obey you. I didn't give her any." I see his head nod, but he stays silent. "The next day, the garden was dead. The same thing happened with the chickens and Bessie. Hazel stopped by for eggs and milk and, each time, the next day..." His head dips lower and he lets out a frustrated breath. "She may have had something to do with John's death, but I can't be sure. That X on the iodine bottle..." My eyes swell with hot misery, and I cover my mouth with my hand. "Water."

His head whips in my direction. "What?"

"She came by and asked for water. I was so scared something would happen to the water, so I gave her a glass to keep our water safe. That's what happened to William, he drowned in the pond. It had to be her, Pierce. It had to be," I say through clenched teeth.

He bites his tight fists and looks away. "Is that it?"

"She told me I'd live a long, miserable, and lonely life until my blood runs through no other." I touch my stomach, but he isn't looking at me to notice.

He jumps to his feet and paces back and forth a few times while clenching his fists at his sides, his knuckles turning white with each flex. His chest heaves, the veins in his neck bulge, and with each pass, his face gets redder and redder until it's almost the shade of a ripe tomato. He stops, screams, and slams his fist through the wood lath on the wall, busting right through.

I recoil. I've never seen him so angry. All the air seems to escape from the room—maybe it's scared, too.

His eyelids droop when he looks at me. "I'm sorry, I didn't mean to—" His jaw twitches. "I'm not mad at you, Pearl. I'm mad"—he waves his bloody hand in the air—"at all this."

"All right," I say with a tremor and hold out my hand for him to show me the damage.

He looks at his hand and wipes the blood on his coveralls. "I'm fine," he says tightly as he clasps his hands behind his neck and looks at the ceiling. "Is that it, Pearl? Is that all of it?"

I put my hand back in my lap, feeling the sting of rejection. "I think so. What does it all mean?"

"I don't know," he says, sounding defeated.

"I'm sorry. I should've told you when it first happened. I should've never kept anything from you."

He glowers at me. "You're right. You shoulda told me from the beginnin'. I'm your husband, Pearl. You shouldn't keep anythin' from me."

"I know," I whisper. "I'm sorry. I'll never keep anything from you again, I promise."

He sighs. "Okay, Pearl."

I shift my head, absently swiping away a strand of hair from my eyes. "What would you have done?"

"I don't know." He shakes his head. "I'm not sure. But I will not sit by and watch that witch"—he points at the window and his voice rises with each word—"destroy any more of my *family!*" he yells and slaps his chest with his hand so hard I imagine it'll leave a bruise.

I jump. My nerves are shot.

He stands there for a moment longer before looking down at me. "I'm sorry." He treads over to me and strokes my cheek with his undamaged knuckles. "I love you, Pearl. I really do." He kisses me on the lips and walks out the door.

"Where are you going?" I throw the covers off myself and run after him. I follow him out the door and into the barn and step to the side, feeling blindly along the wall and stalls as I watch my husband.

He picks up a jug of kerosene and shakes it, hearing it slosh around, before he picks up another and does the same. He grabs three glass jars from a shelf and pours kerosene in each, filling them before screwing the lids on tight.

Something wet nuzzles the back of my hair, and a gust of wind blows my hair apart. I whip around and see Buddy looking back at me. I step out of the horse's reach and continue to watch Pierce's mission.

The old blanket I slept on the night of my sleepover with Bessie is in his hands, along with a pair of shears. He cuts it into strips without saying a single word to me and stuffs the strips and a box of matches into his pockets before he grabs the jars and marches past me.

I follow him. "Pierce, what are you going to do?"

He ignores me while he puts the jars in the back of the wagon and walks back into the barn, only to emerge a few seconds later carrying the two kerosene jugs and putting them both in the wagon with the jars.

"Pierce, please!" I yell after him when he disappears back in the barn.

He brings Buddy out, backs him up to the wagon, and picks up the harness.

"Pierce, *answer me!*" I stomp with my arms to my sides like a two-year-old having a tantrum.

He stops, the muscles in his neck and arms stretched taut—then, he rolls his head before finishing hitching the horse to the wagon. "I'll be back later. I'm gonna go to Father's to see if he's got more kerosene. When I tell'um what happened, he'll help." He steps up into the wagon and takes the reins.

I reach up and grab his arm. "Pierce, what are you going to do?" His eyes are red with fury as he stares down at me, and it scares me. "You can't kill her."

"She killed my boys. She destroyed my family," he says through clenched teeth. "I sure as hell won't let her get you, too. Step back, Pearl."

I do as he says, letting out a whimper.

"Stay here." *Swack*—"Ya!" he yells and speeds off.

I walk back through the house and keep going until I'm standing on the front porch. I slowly sit in my rocking chair and stare off into the distance, thinking about everything that has happened. What does the future hold? I don't know, but it has to be better than the last few months.

Twilight turns into a blanket of darkness, and I wait.

And wait.

Two hours pass, and I'm still waiting. The orange moon has risen high above and there has to be a million stars twinkling in the black sky. It's hot and muggy and all I can hear are the sounds of the crickets and frogs. They're louder tonight than I've ever heard them before. It's a beautiful night, and I wish Pierce was sitting here next to me in his rocking chair to enjoy it. Even though I've been queasy lately, I wouldn't mind smelling the sweet vanilla-and-cherry scent of his pipe right now. I'd give anything to have him here with me and not off killing another human being—if that's what she is. If that's really what he's doing.

A gentle breeze grants me the smell of smoke, making my head jerk toward Hazel's house. A small orange flicker dances through the trees. I stand and walk to the edge of the porch, hugging the column at the top of the steps, not able to look away. The strong aroma of kerosene and wood burning floats through the air, tickling my throat.

I hold my breath as the flame gets bigger and bigger until a full blown red-and-orange blaze is licking the sky. The roaring fire heats my skin like it's right in front of me, even though it's not.

A high-pitched scream echoes in the distance, so loud it sounds like it's on the porch beside me, torturing my ears. I know it's Hazel because the hairs on the back of my neck stand at attention, and the blood drains from my body, making me shiver with a chill. The scream weakens, and then it's gone. The crackling of the fire is the only sound I hear; even the frogs and crickets have gone silent.

A black cloud of smoke resembling Hazel lingers above the flame. It reminds me of the black dress she always wore. As I stare at the smoke, it turns into the shape of an X, and then it vanishes quicker than it arrived. My mouth hangs open in horror. It was just like her prediction.

Blindly, I step back until my legs bump the chair, and I sit as a deep sense of foreboding hangs over me. The fire engulfs what was Hazel's house and all I can do is watch until Pierce pulls into the driveway and goes around back. I get up and hurry through the house to get to him.

Pierce is already unhitching the horse when the back door slams behind me. I follow him into the barn and as soon as I cross the threshold, the stench of smoke churns my stomach, so I cover my mouth and nose with my hand.

"I'll make you a bath." I grab a bucket and head to the well. I fill the tub we have in the barn with the water and help him remove his smoke-covered clothes while holding my breath.

He steps in the cold bathwater and sits without flinching. "It's over, Pearl. She's gone. She won't hurt us no more." He doesn't look at me. He stares over my shoulder and his eyes grow like he's watching a mad scene play out before him.

I glance over my shoulder, but nothing's there. When I turn back around, he's still staring at the invisible specter. "Pierce?"

He focuses his eyes back on mine. "It's okay. She won't hurt us no more," he repeats.

I nod and scrub the ashy smell of Hazel's burned-down shack off him with soap and water. "Did your father help?"

He shakes his head but doesn't say anything else. He's quiet, and I don't ask him anything more about what had happened. I don't need to.

After he's washed and dressed in clean clothes, I take his hand. "Let's go to bed." I'll tell him about the baby. The doctor hasn't confirmed it yet, but I'm a woman, I know. I want to start fresh, and now that Hazel is gone, it's the right time. I don't want to keep this from him any longer. He needs this. We need this.

"You go ahead." He releases his hand from my grip. "I'm not tired, and I got a few things to work on out here. I'll be in shortly."

"I want to talk to you about something," I say quietly.

He shakes his head. "I can't. Not now. Later."

"Are you okay, Pierce?" I ask, concerned and afraid of his answer.

"Yes. Yes, I just got a lot on my mind right now. I won't be able to sleep just yet." He looks around the tidy barn. "I want to straighten up out here a bit. I'll be in soon."

I look into his eyes, still averted from my own. He killed someone, I know, and perhaps he's still shaken and doesn't want me to see. I'll give him that. If I fall asleep before he comes to bed, I'll tell him about the baby over breakfast tomorrow.

"Okay. I love you." I kiss him softly.

His eyes soften as he traces my cheeks with both hands. "I love you too, Pearl. Things will be better now." He kisses me again before turning me to the door. "You go on now."

When I get inside, I change and crawl into bed, feeling a great sense of relief before falling asleep.

Chapter 27

August 11, 1919

"I'll be out in the field." Pierce grabs the hat hanging from the hook like he always does. His eyes glimmer when he smiles at me, and then he plants a long tender kiss on my lips. *"I love you, Pearl. This baby is just what we need."* He rubs my stomach. *"Maybe it'll be a girl this time."* He grins before walking out the door.

I smile and bite my lip, imagining a baby girl. I'll make her pretty, little frilly dresses and show her off to everyone I know. I'm in a good mood, the best I've been in a long while, so I hum while making breakfast.

A creak comes from the front porch. I shriek and drop the bowl of pancake batter, spilling it all over the floor.

It can't be her—she's gone, out of our lives, forever.

I step over the spilled batter and creep to the front door. When I peek out through the mesh, my jaw drops. A woman in a dirty, long black dress is hunched over, sitting in the rocking chair. Her white hair is sitting on top of her head in a messy bun, like a bird's nest. The one long red fingernail is the only thing resembling the Hazel I first met.

"H-Hazel?" I stammer.

"I'm not done with you yet, Pearl," she says in a low, scratchy voice.

I open the door and walk out, joining her on the porch. *"Please... I'm sorry."* I touch her shoulder, and it burns my hand, causing me to jump back and shake the sting away.

She slowly turns her head toward me. Her face, deeply engrained with crusty wrinkles, bursts into an orange-and-red flame. She's on fire! "Pearl," she wheezes, blowing out smoke, and then she turns to ash all over the chair.

I scream and run back through the house to the backyard.

"Pierce!" I yell, and the door slams behind me, making me jump.

I don't see him in the field.

"Pierce!" I yell again, but he doesn't reply.

I run to the barn, but he isn't there. My heart races. I run toward the pond and stop, sighing, with my hand over my heart. He's standing with his back to me at the edge, staring into the water.

I jog to him and say, "Pierce, thank God I found you. Hazel was here, on the porch."

He doesn't move.

"Pierce?"

Silence.

I move in front of him and look up at his handsome face. His focus is on the pond, but then he slowly drops his eyes to mine. His skin dissolves, melting away, forming a puddle of flesh, muscle, and blood on the ground around his feet.

"No." I shake my head and stagger back until my feet hit the water, soaking my shoes. "No. No! No!"

He's nothing but a skeleton. Maggots and worms crawl out of his hollow eye sockets, and his bony fingers reach for me as he searches for air he can't find.

I scream—

I jolt upright, panting. I place my hand over the heart flaying my chest and wince at the pain. But the pain eases when I realize it was just another dream.

Another dream!

My eyes widen when I look at Pierce's side of the bed, his empty side. *Oh, God.* "Pierce!" I rush out of bed and crash to the floor, tangling my feet in the blanket. I'm in a panic as I kick my feet with fury until they're free, and I jump up and dash out of the bedroom.

"Pierce!" I yell when I enter the kitchen frantically, nearly slipping when I turn the corner, and I grab the door frame to stay upright. My heart sinks when I find the room empty, so I scramble to the window, banging my hip on the sink, and look out. I drop my head into my hands, shaking my head back and forth, and giggle. I keep giggling until it turns into a full-blown laugh.

Pierce is in the field. He's okay. He's okay.

I stop laughing and wipe my eyes with my gown skirt. The tears I shed now are happy ones, ones that haven't occupied my eyes in a long, long time.

XXX

"Good morning, Bessie," I say as I sit on the milking stool and pull teats until I get a whole bucket of milk. I smile and scoot the bucket out of the way before rising.

"Thank you, Bessie." I pat her bristly head and lead her out of the barn, passing Buddy, to graze in the pasture, and then I take the milk inside.

After I've finished making our typical breakfast of eggs, ham, and biscuits, I put the food on plates and take them to the table along with two coffees. He'll surely have worked up an appetite when he comes in from—

I turn my head to the side and look at the floor. Was Buddy in the barn this morning when I milked Bessie? I think he was. That's odd; he should be in the field with Pierce. I rush back to the sink, look out the window, and see Pierce like I did earlier, but he's too far away for me to tell what he's doing.

I step outside and cover my forehead with my hand, shielding my eyes from the rising sun as I walk toward him. The closer I get, the better I see Pierce's actions. He's in the field wandering around in circles and drumming his fingers on his forehead. His head bobs as he stares at the ground, and his lips are moving frantically.

I stop and cup my mouth with my hands. "Pierce!"

He stops and turns, facing me. He smiles and his lips move, but I'm too far away to hear what he's saying. His smile drops, and his eyes widen like something has spooked him. He takes a step but quickly stops, clasps his chest with his hands, and falls to the ground.

It all happens so fast.

An abrupt sense of dread shoots through me like a winter chill. My throat tightens and my heart stops for one, two, three full seconds, and then it twists like the wringing of a wet rag before it thrashes forward at full speed and beyond. I hear the hammering in my ears and my fear heightens to an extreme level. "Oh, God, no!" I gather my skirt in my hands and bolt to him so fast my muscles burn and I stumble twice. "Pierce!"

When I reach him, his vacant eyes and mouth are open wide like something frightened him right before he fell. He isn't moving. He isn't breathing. His body is absent of the vibrant life he once had. I crumple to the ground and shake him. "Pierce!" I cry out. "Please, don't leave me! I need you!"

He doesn't move.

I clasp my hands together, bringing them over my head and dropping them with all my strength on his chest, beating him over and over again. *Thud.* "Pierce, please don't leave me." *Thud.* "I need you." *Thud.* "We're having a baby. Please, I need you." *Thud.* I stop and fist his shirt in both hands. "You said everything would be all right now, you *promised*," I cry. "We were supposed to grow old together! You're my soul mate, my life." My voice fades as my head falls to his chest, and I sob into his shirt, soaking his shirt with my tears. "Please don't leave me. I don't want to do this alone, I can't. Please, Pierce," I whisper. "I love you."

I sit up, close my eyes, and let out a loud, thunderous scream. I scream at the top of my lungs until it burns, and I choke on the salty tears that fall down my throat. I gag, but I'm able to compose myself before I retch. Taking a deep breath, I wipe the tears, but they keep flowing. They won't stop, but I don't care.

I stare at his body, smashing the bean plants underneath him. With shaky fingers, I close his eyes and mouth. "Why?" I yell and look up to heaven. My eyes pop when I see a flock of crows flying above us. My head snaps back to Pierce. *They'll eat him.*

I slowly rise, shaking, and take a few steps back, watching Pierce, watching the birds, until I'm closer to the barn than my husband. Then I turn and race to the barn and saddle the horse as quick as I can.

On the ride to Pierce's parents' home, I hear a constant heavy flapping, like sheets drying on the line during a tornado. I look up at the murder of crows following me, hundreds of them. There are more now than before, like they're multiplying.

I lean in and ride faster.

"Mr. Hayes!" I yell when I reach the front porch.

Emmett comes out first, wiping his hands on a rag. "What's all the ruckus out here? What is it?"

Florence emerges a second later with pressed lips. "What in tarnation is going on, girl?"

"Pierce is in the field. He isn't moving. I need you to come quick," I rush out and watch them run to their buggy without another word and take off without a second glance.

Once we get to the edge of the field, I point to Pierce. "He's over there," I say and hop down from Buddy.

Emmett runs past me, followed by Florence. I keep up with their pace as best as my short legs can.

Emmett drops to one knee and jostles Pierce's lifeless body. "Pierce. Son. Son?"

Nothing.

With his hand on Pierce's chest, Emmett bows his head and closes his eyes for a brief pause. He is either praying or feeling for any movement from Pierce; which, I don't know. Then he rises and looks at Florence with remorse in his eyes. "He's gone."

Florence throws the back of her hand over her eyes and faints dramatically, hitting the ground with a hefty thump. Emmett rushes to her side, kneels, and slaps her face until she stirs.

"What happened?" she asks, slurring her words and sitting up.

Emmett glances at me over his shoulder. "I'm gonna get her inside. I'll round up a few men to help tote him into the house." He pulls her up and she wobbles, so he wraps an arm around her waist and looks up at the crows. "Stay here and make sure nothin' happens to him."

Then they leave.

The caws above me sound as if they're laughing at me. I ignore them and drop to the ground next to my husband. "Pierce"—I pick up his hand and hold it against my cheek—"why did you leave me? We have a baby coming. What am I supposed to do now?" My lips quiver and my head falls to his chest. "Why, Pierce? Why?"

I don't notice for a while that I'm no longer alone until Emmett grabs my arms and says, "Get up, Pearl. We gotta get him inside," and pulls me up. I watch four men—their faces are a blur—pick Pierce up and walk toward the house. I follow along obediently like a lamb to slaughter.

When I enter the back door, I notice two plates full of eggs, ham, and biscuits along with overturned cups with brown liquid dribbling out are in the bottom of the white sink. The table I left them on is gone.

I shuffle into the crowded living room filled with people, and the room goes silent. Everything fades around me as I stare at my soul mate lying on the kitchen table.

Why did this happen?

When the doctor arrives, he moves around my hazy vision, placing his stethoscope on Pierce's chest and two fingers on his wrist.

Hazel's gone. She's gone. This shouldn't have happened.

Fingers snap in front of my eyes. "Pearl. Pearl, can you tell me what happened?" Dr. Clayton asks sympathetically.

"He...He...He didn't come in for breakfast," I stutter, unblinking. My eyes can't look at the doctor because they won't leave Pierce. When my eyes water, I finally blink, making the tears slip down my face. I wipe them away and sniff before continuing, "I walked outside, and he was walking in circles, talking to himself. When I got closer, I called for him. When he saw me"—I swallow— "he put his hand on his chest and collapsed in the field. I rushed to him, but when I got there, he wasn't breathing. He was staring at me with empty eyes and an opened mouth." I bury my face with my hands, not able to stop my sobbing.

"They were closed when we saw him," Florence snaps.

"I-I closed them," I say between quickened breaths and wipe my face with my palms.

Dr. Clayton unbuttons Pierce's shirt. Several red marks adorn his chest. The doctor swipes his hand along one and looks at me with a raised brow.

"I…I hit him."

"You *hit* him?" Florence practically yells at me.

"I tried to…I tried to revive him."

"I'd say it was a heart attack," the doctor says. "Do you want me to send him to the hospital for an autopsy? They'll tell you the same thing." He looks at me, then at Emmett.

"I'm sure that's what happened. Write it up," Emmett tells the doctor. "Can we get him buried then?"

"I don't see why not. I'll let you get to your grieving." Dr. Clayton turns to me. "I'm sorry, Pearl. You've been through so much." He squeezes my arm before leaving.

Yes, I've been through so much. Too much.

"Timothy!" Emmett yells, startling me.

Timothy steps forward. "Yes? What can I do?"

Emmett flicks his wrist at the front door. "Go to town and see about a casket. Tell James I'll settle up later. Get whatever's cheapest."

"Yes, sir," Timothy says with a small head dip.

"Louis, go to the church. Let the preacher know I'm buryin' my oldest tomorrow. Have his men dig a grave next to his sons'."

Louis nods as Albert walks in and gapes at his brother lying on the table and asks, "What happened?"

Emmett turns to two old women wearing large straw hats, who are perched on the couch in the corner, and ignores Albert. "Janie, Esther, let everyone know of Pierce's death. A viewin' tonight and burial tomorrow." He looks around at everyone still standing in their same spots and claps his hands together, making a loud smack echo in the room. "What are y'all waitin' for? Go! Now!"

Everyone scatters at his command, and I watch in disbelief.

"Wait!" I yell and everyone freezes. "That's not enough time. I need time to say goodbye. Why are you in such a hurry to bury your son?"

Emmett swings in my direction. His lips tighten and his eyes narrow before he charges across the room like a raging bull and I'm holding a matador's red cape.

Everyone stares.

He snatches my arm and drags me into the bedroom, slamming the door behind him. He releases me and points his callused finger in my face, which causes me to take a step back. "This is all *your fault,*" he spits. "You caused the death of your entire family, includin' my son"—he slaps his chest—"my first born. He told us what happened when he came by last night and because of you"—he sticks his finger back in my face—"he is dead. I told him not to do it, but he wouldn't listen. We'll bury him before anythin' else happens to this family. After the funeral tomorrow, take the wagon and leave town, for good! I don't want to see you here ever again. You hear me, girl? You've caused enough damage." He grips my arm once again, squeezing so hard his fingernails bite into my skin. I try to jerk away but he holds me steady before throwing my arm away like trash. I stumble back, catching my balance on the dresser.

He walks to the door, calmly turns like he didn't just rip into me, and curls his upper lip in disgust. "I suggest you leave without any argument. You don't want to cause any more trouble for yourself. You understand that, girl?"

I nod with a tremble and rub my sore arm.

He walks out the door, leaving me stunned and speechless. I can't believe he talked to me like that. He has always been kind. I expected it from Florence, but not Emmett.

I look at my arm and see half-moon-shaped marks as I ease into bed and cry. This can't be real. I'll wake any moment and have Pierce and my boys back. This can't be real.

But it is real, because I'm all alone. I hear people coming and going, but I don't bother leaving my safe haven. I bury my face in Pierce's pillow, smelling his musky scent, and wait until I hear nothing at all.

XXX

When it's quiet, I sneak out to find an empty house and a kitchen full of dirty dishes. It looks like a drunken tornado whipped through, tossing dishes in its path. When did people have time to make all this food? Well, it's not my problem, because this isn't my house anymore, or at least it won't be after Pierce is in the ground tomorrow.

I pick up a dirty glass and wash it out before filling it with water and quenching my thirst. My eyes roam the chaos in the sink. Among the many dirty dishes lies a small silver spoon: *John's spoon*. The glass drops from my hand, shattering in the sink. I pick up the spoon and clean it off with a rag before slipping it into my pocket and walking out.

Pierce's body is lying on the same kitchen table and the same white-lace tablecloth that our two sons had lain on not too long ago. I grab Pierce's cold, stiff hand and talk to him, even though he isn't truly here.

"Pierce, I love you, and I will love you until the day I take my last breath. I'm so sorry all this happened, but I know you're up there with our sons." My eyes dart to the ceiling. "Take care of each other. I'll see you again one day." I lean down and kiss his blue lips, wishing he would kiss me back one more time. I climb onto the table next to him and put my arms around him like I've done many nights. My eyes close, and I fall asleep next to my husband for the last time.

Chapter 28

August 12, 1919

After I fold my last dress and put it in the old black leather suitcase Mama gave me on my wedding day, which seems like a lifetime ago, I turn around and see Pierce's red-and-white flannel shirt hanging inside the wardrobe. I take the precious material out and caress the soft woven fabric between my fingers.

I remember the first day I laid eyes on him. He was wearing this shirt with a determined expression on his face as he stalked toward Daddy at the animal auction. I thought he was the most handsome man in the world—still do. I loved this shirt on him and he wore it many days. I hold it to my nose, and inhale. "*Aaah*." The vanilla-and-cherry scent I love so much is still there. My lips quiver, and there is a piercing sensation behind my lids, so I open my eyes and quickly blink. I'll miss sitting on the porch in the evenings, smelling his pipe.

My head whips to the closed door when I hear the sound of people talking in the other room. I shake my head and tuck the shirt along with John's spoon and William's baby blanket under my dresses and close the lid with a heavy sigh. I'm burying my best friend today, and I'm dreading it immensely.

No one speaks to me or looks at me when I enter the living room, so I stand in the corner, like a two-year-old being punished, and watch.

Florence sobs into Albert's chest. The people around her pat her on the back, consoling her. Emmett stands beside the casket with his crossed hands low and in front of his waist, holding a hammer and nails. His eyes are bloodshot as he looks at the ceiling and snuffles.

Four men pick up Pierce and place him gently in his bought casket. I drop my head in my hands and bawl when the lid is closed and the pings of the hammer hitting the nails echo throughout the room. No one comforts me, but I don't expect them to, nor do I want them to. I'm all alone.

At ten o'clock, when Pierce is laid in the back of his parent's wagon, the procession begins. I'm parked at the side of the house, waiting for my turn to follow. After Pierce's parents pull out, I inch forward, but Albert passes without letting me in. Mabel's husband, Wayne, does the same. Timothy stops and dips his head, giving me entrance. I mouth, *Thank you,* and snap the reins, moving forward.

We pass Hazel's house, or what used to be her house. Nothing escaped the fire; it's all gone. The moss-covered trees are charred with black soot, scarring them. Tiny needles prick my back when I see a swarm of black crows, the same black birds that flew over Pierce's dead body—Hazel's birds—hovering over the smoldering ashes, making me shiver. They all turn their heads and look at me like they know I was the one responsible for this. I guess I am.

If Pierce had let Hazel be, would he still be alive today? I should've never told him the truth. I stare off blankly into the distance. Pierce's family may be right; I caused his death, and I'll live with it for the rest of my life.

When we get to the cemetery, my eyes quickly find John's and Jacob's headstones. We couldn't afford tombstones, so we found two flat white stones at Bull Swamp Creek perfect to mark their graves. After we took them home, Pierce worked hard chiseling their names and dates of their birth and death on them. Pierce's love is reflected on those stones.

A small wooden cross with William's name carved on it sits at the base of a dirt mound. Beside it is a six-foot-deep hole. I shake my head and wipe my tears before climbing down from the wagon.

No one moves such that I can stand in the front near the open grave, where family and spouses are supposed to be. So I stand back while the preacher begins his sermon.

"Today we celebrate the life of a great man. Pierce Hayes was…"

How do I go on without him? It's only been a day, and I already feel like I can't. Yesterday was one of the worst days of my life, but I wish it would have gone on forever regardless, because yesterday was the last day I spent on this earth with my Pierce. The last day we spent breathing the same air and sharing the same heat of the sun. I'll never again look into those beautiful brown eyes I've grown to love so much. I'll never again be wrapped in his warm embrace, nor will I fall asleep listening to the beat of his loving heart.

I'll never have another day on this earth with my beloved Pierce, and it breaks my heart knowing that. I loved him more than life itself, and I'll live the rest of my life missing him. The sadness will last until my dying breath.

"Amen," the preachers says.

Everyone scatters and I lumber to the open grave. I gaze at the hole while men shovel hard clumps of compact soil and clay on my husband's casket. The loud thud drowns out everything else around me. I can't look away.

"Make sure you *never* come back," Florence says from behind me.

My shoulders slump and I close my eyes before turning around and opening them to the brown eyes resembling those of the man I loved, except these are possessed with hatred. My own eyes, now worn out and distraught, go unfocused behind my droopy lids as I wait for her wrath.

"You killed my son. You're nothing but trouble. I knew it from the moment I laid eyes on you. Stay far away from me and my family, girl. You hear me? Stay away." She spins and stalks toward the wagon. She steps into the wagon next to Emmett and Cora, and all three narrow their eyes, giving me a harsh stare down before taking off down the church's driveway.

I slowly turn back around and look at my three sons' graves. "Boys, you will always be in my heart. I'll never forget you as long as I live. I'll see you again one day." I give one last look at where my husband's body will rest for eternity. We will never be buried side by side, I know. "Goodbye, Pierce. I will always love you." Then I mope away, dreading the long journey home to Summerville.

Chapter 29

August 12, 1919

SUMMERVILLE: THE FLOWER TOWN IN THE PINES. I pass under the familiar brick archway, which welcomes me back home. The thick moisture in the air and the dark clouds scudding in tells me rain is on its way. I hurry through town without stopping so I can get home before the sky opens and drenches me.

When I pull into our long driveway and the trees break away, I see my family home—or where my family home was. It has burned to the ground, like Hazel's house, which I saw this morning.

"*Whoa.*" I pull on the reins, stopping the horse, and my mouth drops open. I stare, dumbfounded, for a few moments before hopping down from the wagon and sinking to my knees in front of the charred boards and ashes. "This can't be happening," I mumble. My eyes look at the ground—I pick up a handful of dirt, and throw it at the scorched remains as I scream at the top of my lungs. I scream again until I taste ash from the seared wood, hunch over on all fours, and hack until saliva floods my mouth. I take a few quickened breaths and claw at the dirt in front of me. Once the queasy feeling subsides, I sit back on my heels and look at the clouded sky. "Why?" I hold up my outstretched arms. "Why is this happening? It's not fair!"

I can't do this any longer. I want to give up.

No, they got out in time. Yes, they're all well and staying somewhere else.

They're all fine.

The sound of wheels behind me grabs my attention, and I look over my shoulder. It's the preacher from my old church, Mr. Anderson, and the man who owns the general store, Mr. Holton.

I wipe my face with the skirt of my dress and rise, brushing the dirt away the best I can before they approach me. I imagine I'm a sight to look at.

"Pearl, you came home. I see you got the letter." Mr. Anderson grabs both my arms and leans back. "You haven't changed a bit since I saw you last year." His face turns down when he looks over my shoulder.

"What letter? What happened? Where's my family?"

He shuffles his feet, looking deeply uncomfortable. "I'm sorry, Pearl. When we got here, the whole house was in flames." He shakes his head. His hands harden around my arms before softening again. "There was nothing we could do. All six perished in the fire."

The world spins. "No," I whisper, and slump into his grip. This can't be happening.

His grip tightens. "Do you need to sit down, Pearl?"

I shake my head and steady myself before stepping out of his reach. "I'm okay," I say and rub my hands up and down my naked arms. My lips quiver from the cold chill rushing through my body even though the weather is hot. The August heat is sweltering, even at night. The still air without an ounce of breeze can be intolerable.

Mr. Holton steps forward holding his hat with both hands. "We were outside the store when you passed. We assumed you got the letter."

"No, sir."

"We weren't sure what you wanted to do about the funeral. You're the last living relative we know of. I had volunteers from church make the coffins, since I know your family didn't have a penny to their name," Mr. Anderson says.

"Thank you," I mutter as my eyes fall to the ground.

"A group of men dug the graves next to your father and sister.

They've worked all day. Everything should be in order for a funeral tomorrow. You got here just in time." Mr. Anderson looks up at the sky when a raindrop lands on his shoulder. "We should get you inside. Looks like it's coming up a cloud. You can stay with me and Martha until you need to go back home to your husband and son." He puts his arm around my shoulder and leads me to his carriage while Mr. Holton jumps into my wagon.

I step into the passenger side. "When was the fire?"

He taps a finger to his pursed lips. "It was Sunday night after the evening bible study. Again, I'm so sorry. I wish your husband would've come with you. He should be by your side at a time like this." He snaps the reins, and as we pull away, I tremble. *He should be here with me.*

"Sunday night was the same night…" I whisper to myself as I look over one last time at the remains of my family home, and in the middle of the ashes are blackened, charred boards crossed in the shape of an X leaning against where the door should be. A tremor overtakes my body. I lean over the side of the carriage and heave.

"Whoa." He stops the horse and pats my back. "I know it's upsetting to find your family like this, but they're with the Lord now. That should bring you some solace."

I spit and lean back against the seat. With leaden eyes, I look at him and slowly nod while I wipe my mouth with the back of my hand. My whole family is with the Lord now, every last one of them.

XXX

Mrs. Martha comes out of the house with an umbrella protecting her white beehive from the light drizzle. "I'm so sorry, dear. How are you holding up?"

"I'll be all right, I guess." I've cried so much in the last few days I don't think I can cry any more.

Mr. Holton hands me my suitcase from the wagon and pats my shoulder. "You come by the store if you need anything while you're in town."

"Thank you," I mumble with a nod, and my lips turn down as I look at the wet ground. I'm not sure how long I'll be in town. I don't know what I'm supposed to do now. I have nowhere to go, no place to stay, and no one left.

"Come in before you catch a cold, dear. The boys will take care of your horse. Right, Fred?" Mrs. Martha cloaks her hefty arm around my shoulder and escorts me inside.

"Sure thing!" Mr. Anderson calls out while unhitching his horse.

"Yes, ma'am," Mr. Holton says before the door closes behind us.

Once inside, she takes me to the guest room and lights a lantern, illuminating the room. A full-size black-iron bed with a white quilt, two mahogany side tables, and a matching dresser are crammed in the modest room. A single window dressed in a thin lace curtain tied back with two pink cords shows the rain hissing across the sky.

She walks to the window and glances out. "Ah, it's starting to come down out there. Looks like you got here just in time, dear." She turns to me, clasping her hands together in front of her.

I rock on the sides of my foot and lift a shoulder. "I suppose so."

Her eyes scan me and she frowns. "How would you like a nice warm bath? I'll draw you one and you can soak while I warm you up some supper. How does that sound?"

"Good," I say appreciatively. "Thank you."

"Let me show you to the bathroom." She walks past me out of the room, and I follow behind her with my suitcase still in hand.

My eyes widen when she opens a door in the small hallway. "You have a bathroom inside? I've never seen a bathroom inside a house before." This is exciting and foreign to me. It helps me forget everything that has happened in the last several days for a few seconds…almost.

She giggles and lights lanterns hanging on the walls on each side of the door, and a bright, white-tiled bathroom comes to life. Everything is white except for the two pink towels hanging on a rack. *Mr. Anderson must love that.*

"Yes, we had it built on last year." She steps in front of the sink and lights another lantern mounted on the wall. "We saved enough money and had it done ourselves. The congregation had to vote on it, of course, but we paid for it," she says while plugging a hole at the bottom of a claw-foot tub. She turns a knob, and water rushes out the neck of the faucet like a waterfall.

I set my suitcase down and hesitate by the door for a moment before I plod to the pedestal sink. My hand runs along the smooth surface until it reaches the shiny silver faucet, but I don't turn it on. I pull back my dirty hand, inspecting it, and then my eyes find the mirror over the sink. I frown. A pale, thin-faced woman with dark circles under her sunken eyes and black smut across her cheek is staring at me. Her long brown hair and black dress are both wet and disheveled. She's a mess, a complete and utter mess. She isn't the same person I knew, far from it. I can't look at her anymore, so I turn my back on her.

A white porcelain commode sits in the corner. I step in front of it and slowly lift the lid. It's different from the outhouse I'm used to— it's shiny, clean, and the water looks good enough to drink. I grimace at that thought.

"The handle on the side is the flush." Mrs. Martha points to the silver handle on the tank.

I push the lever and the water in the bowl swirls and disappears through the hole at the bottom with a loud gush. I jump and take a step back.

Mrs. Martha chuckles and turns off the water to the tub. "Why don't you bathe and change into dry clothes?" She points to my forgotten suitcase by the door. "You'll feel better once you're clean and dried. You can use this towel." She taps one of the pink towels on the rack with her finger. "I'll put water on for coffee and warm your supper."

"Okay. Thank you," I say.

She walks out and shuts the door behind her.

The water looks inviting, so I quickly use the toilet and peel off my wet clothes. I step in and once I get used to the warmth of the water, I sit, lean back, and close my eyes. My shoulders instantly relax. I forget where I am and who I am for a moment, because this feels wonderful. I could soak in here for days. I've never had a warm bath before. The baths I always took were outside in a barn with cold water, the ones you rush through before you freeze to death.

Coming back to my senses, I pick up the soap and rag from the edge of the tub and scrub away the dirt and grime. If only I could wash away everything that has happened this summer.

When I'm clean, I dress and follow the delicious aroma drifting from the kitchen. Mrs. Martha has her back to me as she faces the counter. My stomach growls on cue as soon as I enter the room, rewarding me with a small giggle from the older woman.

"Have a seat." She turns and slips a plate of food on the table in front of an empty chair.

I take the seat and my dry mouth salivates when I see the fried chicken legs, mashed potatoes, brown gravy, and fried squash in front of me. My tongue darts out, sliding along my lips.

She sets a cup of coffee beside the plate. "You look like you haven't eaten in days."

"I haven't," I whisper and look at her. "Thank you," I say, and I mean it.

"You're more than welcome, dear. I'm so glad you could come on such short notice. Fred didn't know what to do with your family since you're the last of it. We didn't know if you would come back for the funeral."

I pick up my fork and shovel a scoop of mashed potatoes into my mouth. *Oops.* I drop my fork, lower my head, and close my eyes, saying a silent blessing. Grace is something I shouldn't forget, but once I smelled the food, I forgot everything I've ever known except for how starved I am. When I open my eyes, she's smiling.

The chair squeaks, begging for relief, when she sits. The wedding ring on her finger looks like it's cutting her finger in two as she fiddles with her coffee cup. "I'm glad you're here, but I wish it were under better circumstances. The news must've been a shock." She takes a sip.

I swallow the piece of chicken I put in my mouth and shake my head. I open my mouth to explain when the door opens and Mr. Anderson waddles in. He removes his hat and hangs it on a hook by the door and takes off his drenched suit coat and does the same. "I'm glad you're eating," he says. "The supper was delicious, but Martha always makes too much for just the two of us." He pats his oversized stomach.

She stands and makes him a cup of coffee while he sits at the table next to the seat she vacated. "It is nice to have another mouth to feed."

He nods at her when she hands him the cup. "Thank you, darling."

She smiles at her husband before she goes back to the counter and cuts an apple pie, putting slices on plates and setting them in front of the three of us. "So tell us, when do you need to go back home?" She sits and takes in a mouthful of pie.

My eyes sting and I blink quickly.

She stops chewing. The pie slips down her throat with a big gulp. "What's the matter, dear? Did I say something wrong?"

My eyes focus on the fork I'm twiddling in my hand. I feel like I'm fading away, day by day, until there will be nothing left. "I...I don't have a home," I mumble, my voice laced with grief as my heart is filled by profound sadness. "My husband and sons have all passed this summer. I don't have anything or anyone anymore." Tears spill out of my eyes and down my cheek.

Mrs. Martha places her hand over her heart. "Oh, dear Lord. What happened? We knew about your oldest passing. We didn't know about your little one or your husband."

"Here," Mr. Anderson says as he hands me a clean handkerchief.

"William drowned and...and Pierce...he...he had a heart attack." I open the handkerchief and wipe my wet eyes and tear-stricken face.

"You poor child," she says, shaking her head.

"What about your house?" he asks. "It belongs to you, being Pierce's wife."

"Yes, Fred's right, dear. It's your house, so you do have a home."

"His family blames me for everything," I say behind tight lips. "They told me to leave and never come back, so I did." I strangle the innocent handkerchief, twisting it with my hands until it looks like a corkscrew.

"That's just not right," Mr. Anderson says after a pause, sounding genuinely affronted. "We can help you fight it. A new young lawyer just moved into town, I'm sure he'll be glad to help."

"Yes, David Hall. He and his wife have a young boy, Joshua. He's a cute little fella, but he's got the terrible twos or threes," Mrs. Martha says. "He sure does give his parents a fit and…" She looks at me with a disheartened look. "Oh, I'm sorry. I shouldn't have said anything about the boy."

I shake my head. "That's all right," I say and place a hand over my stomach. "And no thank you, we'll be fine. I'll figure something out. They were mean to me after everything happened. I don't want to go back."

"We?" he asks.

She leans forward and places her hand on my arm. "Are you with child, dear?"

I suck in a deep breath. "I'm not positive, but I think so. I never had time to go to the doctor or tell Pierce with everything that happened with William, and then Pierce's…" My voice breaks. I can't finish. I unravel the cloth corkscrew and rub it hard against my eyes.

She stands and before I know it, her arms are around me. "You can stay here with us as long as you want." She straightens herself and pats my shoulder. "Isn't that right, Fred?"

"Of course, stay as long as you need. We could use the extra help around here. We aren't as young as we used to be. You can help us, and we'll help you and your baby. How does that sound, Pearl?"

"It sounds…good," I say with a weak smile. Maybe there's hope for me and my baby after all.

Mr. Anderson claps, rubbing his palms together as he stands. "Good, it's settled. I need to work on the sermon for your family's funeral." He looks at me with sadness in his eyes before turning to his wife. "I'll be down at the church. I won't be long." He kisses her on the cheek. "Pie was good, as usual." Then he grabs his hat from the hook and an umbrella from the stand, not bothering with his suit coat, and walks out the door.

Chapter 30

August 13, 1919

I open my eyes to the sound of a light drizzle showering the roof and the smell of bacon and eggs drifting through the gap under the door. My tongue darts out and runs across my parched lips, making sure I'm aware there is food to be eaten. So, I sling the covers off me and rise, ready to get this day over with. I quickly make up the bed and hurry to the food that waits.

I'm in the doorway with my hands folded in front of me, watching Mrs. Martha glide around the kitchen.

"Good morning," she says and sets a full breakfast plate in front of an empty chair and nods for me to sit.

"Good morning." I sit and, before I lift the fork, I bow my head and close my eyes. "Dear Heavenly Father, thank you for this meal, and let it nourish my body. Amen." I open my eyes and see Mrs. Martha standing in front of me with a smile on her face and a glass of milk in her hand.

"The baby needs milk, so you need to drink it all," she says as she sets the milk on the table.

My throat aches with thirst on cue. "Yes, ma'am," I say before I take a big gulp of the liquid—the *cold* liquid. Milk sprays out of my mouth and nose as I choke. I slap my chest, trying to get straight.

"Are you all right, dear?" She pats my back and holds my arm in the air.

I nod and she lets my arm go. I wipe the remnants of milk from my burning face with a cotton napkin and exhale. "I…I guess I'm not used to cold milk," I stammer.

I dab the table with the napkin, but she puts her hand over mine, stopping me. "Let me do that. You eat," she says and gets a rag from the counter.

"Yes, ma'am."

She wipes the milk off the table and grins. "It'll take a little time to get used to. I'm sure you're used to drinking straight from the cow."

I nod while I push a forkful of eggs into my mouth while she tosses the soiled rag into the sink.

"We don't have a cow, if you haven't noticed. Even if we did, I surely don't think neither Fred nor I could milk it anyway." She spoons coffee granules into a cup sitting on the counter. "We're getting too old for that mess. We get our milk delivered from the milkman in his automobile." She quickly turns around, her eyes dancing with excitement. "Can you believe it? An automobile! And it's cold because of the icebox." She points at a small wooden rectangle cabinet standing in the corner, then fills her cup with steaming water from the kettle. "It keeps everything cold. I can't believe all the advances that have come about in the last decade. Who would've known?" She lumbers across the kitchen and sits beside me.

"So many new things…so many," she says softly to her cup, like she's hypnotized by the thought. She perks up and speaks to me again. "Everyone wants everything nowadays. Earnest is taking so many orders from the Sears Roebuck catalog, he can't keep up."

I smear strawberry preserves on my biscuit. "Earnest?"

"Earnest Holton, over at the store. He's taking care of everyone's orders for supplies. People are putting in bathrooms all across town." She sips her coffee.

"Oh," I say absently. "I guess I never knew his first name."

"And there's businesses popping up everywhere. The future is now." She stabs her finger on the table and leans back. "I never thought I'd live to see it. Our little town is growing fast."

"I noticed the new buildings on Main Street when I passed by yesterday evening. It does look like the town is growing, and there are more automobiles on the road, too."

"Oh, those things scare the dickens out of me. I'll never ride in one, that's for sure."

"I think it would be fun."

"Well, you're young, I'm old." She smiles. "I'd surely have a heart attack. Oh, and that reminds me! We have a new doctor in town, Dr. Murrell. You'll like him." She glances at the table hiding my stomach. "We've never had a baby around here before. The good Lord never blessed us with kids of our own. And with your family passing, it's just what you need to get you through this tough time." She pats my arm before standing and walking to the sink.

"Yes, I suppose you're right. Breakfast was good, thank you." I get up and hand her my empty plate. "Can I help?"

"No, dear, you relax. Today will be a trying day for you. We'll leave soon to go down to the church. Fred's already there getting things in order." She looks out the window. "I wish it wasn't raining today. It's so nasty outside. It's a bad day to be outside for a funeral in this weather." She turns to me. "Did you know we have a funeral parlor in town now?"

I shake my head. "No, ma'am." I stand on my tippy toes and look outside at the rain hammering down in a steady downpour. I forgot about standing outside in the rain.

"They'll do everything for you. You don't have to lift a finger. Of course you have to pay a pretty penny to not lift that finger." She waggles her finger. "The caskets there are outrageous. Fred went over after the fire to see about purchasing some. He was going to take up a church offering to help bury your family, but once he saw the price, he quickly changed his mind. There was no way the people in the church could afford to buy six caskets, and your family had no money. Your parents never trusted the bank, so any money they had burned with the house. Some men from the church pitched in and built coffins for your family. I'm certain you'll be pleased."

"I'm sure it'll be nice," I say, staring out the mullioned window as the squall of wind picks up, whipping the droplets and taunting the sky until it rushes down in wet sheets to the ground, splashing into mud puddles. The house across the street isn't visible through the torrential rain. Yes, today is a bad day to be outside for a funeral.

"Don't worry, we have umbrellas. It'll be all right." She pats my arm and turns toward the door when it opens.

Mr. Anderson steps inside as a brilliant shock of white cuts through the rain right outside the window and a loud crack rumbles through the house. He shakes his umbrella, and then he puts it in the stand before shutting the door and hanging up his hat. "It's really coming down now." He takes the cup of coffee Mrs. Martha offers. "Thank you, dear." He kisses her cheek and sits at the table. "How are you doing this morning, Pearl? Did you sleep well?" he asks while fanning out his suit jacket and making rainwater spray on the floor.

"Yes, sir." I take a seat in the chair next to him.

"Fred!" Mrs. Martha drops to her knees in front of him and wipes up the small puddle with a dish towel.

"Sorry, dear," he says, smiling at her.

She struggles as she gets to her feet, narrows her eyes at him playfully, and tosses another soiled rag into the sink.

He glances out the window. "I saw the sky this morning. I knew the rain was coming, so I had the men go ahead and bury your family. They've been working for the last couple of hours."

I look out the window with wide eyes. "I hope they aren't still out in this weather."

"Oh, they're fine. They should be done by now," he says nonchalantly and takes a sip of his coffee. "I figured we'd get them covered before it started pouring. We couldn't have a viewing anyway."

"Oh...Okay," I say, my voice faltering as I twist my wedding ring around my finger. Not having a viewing and not seeing my family one last time slipped my mind. The news devastates me, but he's right. My family was burned, unrecognizably so, I imagine, so having them seen would not be possible. I'll never see my family again…none of them. *What am I going to do?*

"We're expected to start at eleven," he says, bringing me back from my miserable thoughts. "If it slacks up a bit, we can do it in the cemetery. If it's pouring, we can have it in the church. We'll play it by ear. Okay?"

I slowly nod and blink back the stinging sensation in my eyes. "Thank you for everything you're doing."

He flicks his hand. "It's not a problem. I liked your family. They were good people. After your father died, the congregation took care of your family. We didn't want anything bad to happen to them. I wish we could've caught the fire in time. We still don't know what caused it." He shakes his head. "We'll probably never know. Accidents happen all the time." He leans back and drums his fingers on the table.

I know.

"I'm making potato salad and ham for after the service." Mrs. Martha grabs a large pot from the stove and takes it to the sink. She leans over while pouring boiled potatoes in a strainer as smoke engulfs the air. Her face stays put during the steam bath.

"We'll eat in the church's basement like we did all those potluck Sundays. Do you remember them, dear?" she asks while putting the pot of boiled eggs into the other sink and turning on the cold water.

I stroll over to the pot of brown, speckled eggs cooling in the running water. "Yes, ma'am. I enjoyed them very much."

"Well, good. We still do it every first Sunday of the month. There will be a lot of food to eat today, so bring your appetite." She smiles. "The baby needs to eat."

I just finished eating breakfast, and I can't think of eating any more food right now. I'll be as big as a cow if I carry this baby to term staying here. My hand flies to my stomach. I hope I carry this baby, Pierce's baby, to term. If I lose this one, I'm not sure what I'll do. I'll have no reason to want to stay on this earth any longer.

She turns off the water. "Do you have a dress to wear?"

"Yes, ma'am," I say absently as I pick up an egg from the pot and stare at it lying in the palm of my hand. "I have the black dress I got for Elizabeth's funeral." The same black dress I wore to Jacob's, John's, William's, and Pierce's funerals. My shoulders sag. The weight of it all hits me again. *I'm all alone.*

She takes the unpeeled egg out of my hand. "Why don't you go get ready?"

I look into her compassionate eyes, which give me comfort. "Oh," I say and blink a few times, bringing myself back to the here and now. "It won't take long to get dressed. I can help you with the salad." I reach for another egg, but she places a gentle hand on top of mine.

"No, it won't take me but a minute to whip this up. You go." She turns me around and nudges me out the kitchen.

I do as I'm told without a fuss.

When I enter the bedroom, I see the black dress I wore yesterday lying on the dresser. *Was that yesterday?* I hold up the dirt-covered dress and bite my lip. "Shoot, I can't wear this." So, I fold it and put it back on top of the dresser to clean later. I pick up my suitcase and drop it on the bed before opening it and taking out a brown dress. "This will have to do," I whisper and slip it on.

I take out William's blanket and Pierce's flannel shirt and hold them both to my nose, inhaling. Their scent lingers on the fabric; I can still smell them both. And when I close my eyes, I can imagine them being right here with me.

They're right here with me! I smile but it fades quickly when I open my eyes and realize they're not here. They're gone. My eyes burn as the sadness surfaces and I blink, coming out of my thoughts. I put the possessions under one of the pillows on the made bed, trapping their scent. Then I pull out John's spoon, kissing it on the bowl before placing it on the bedside table. I put the rest of my clothes in the dresser and slide the suitcase under the bed.

After I pay the bathroom a visit, I walk back into the empty kitchen. The potato salad and ham are on the counter. My tongue darts out on cue, licking my lips, and my stomach growls. I glance at my watch. It's ten-thirty—

"Are you ready?" Mr. Anderson asks from behind me.

I jump and turn around and see him and Mrs. Martha standing in the doorway in changed clothes.

"It looks like the rain is easing up. A graveside should be fine. What do you say?" he asks while adjusting his navy-blue bow tie with red and yellow stripes.

I look out the window and notice only a slight drizzle is falling now. "Okay."

"That's a brown dress, not black. Are you colorblind, dear?" she asks, concern and curiosity in her voice.

I run my hands along the dress. "No, ma'am. The black one was dirty."

She grins. "You will love my new wringer washer."

This confuses me. "Wringer washer?"

"Yes, advances, remember? Fred, grab the ham while I get the salad." She picks up the salad and saunters out the door with Mr. Anderson closely behind carrying the ham.

"Advances," I mumble, shutting the door behind us.

XXX

At eleven sharp, I'm huddled under an umbrella staring at the mud mounds over six graves. I'm burying Mama, Samuel, Thomas, Helen, Ethel, and Tammy. Their final resting place sits beside Daddy, Elizabeth, and her daughter Addie Marie.

The knuckles clutching the metal rod of my umbrella turn white with red streaks as I choke the handle. My fingers skid over the four hard stones under my skin, and the tear gates open when I realize I have no family left. It's just me…me and my unborn child. I wipe the tears away with the embroidered handkerchief Mr. Anderson gave

me and look down at the FA on the cloth with blurry vision.
   I'm all alone in this world—for now.

Chapter 31

June 22, 2001

"Here, Pearl," Mary says, standing in front of me and holding a small plastic cup.

I look at the pill inside the cup, confused for a moment, and rub the pain in my engorged knuckles, but it doesn't go away.

"A pain pill," she says.

"I forgot where I was for a moment. It seems so real, talking about my past." I look at her and cock my head to the side. "How did you know I needed one?" I take the pill from the cup and swallow it down with a sip of water.

"You've rubbed your knuckles for the last twenty minutes until they're almost purple. I thought you needed one."

"Thank you, Mary. What would I do without you?" I ask with a crooked smile and rub my knuckles again. "Rain must be coming."

"They're calling for it," she says as she takes her seat.

"You lost your entire family in one summer?" Big Chin blows her nose, and the tissue billows with air and snot. "That's so sad."

"Yes, all in one summer," I say with a heavy sigh.

"Were you pregnant? What happened to the baby?" a petite woman hunched over the side of her wheelchair asks. Her clouded eyes are fixated on the floor, so her vision must be worse than mine. The large lump on her back reminds me of a hunchback.

I nod. "Yes, I went to the doctor the day after my family's funeral. I was pregnant with Pierce's child, and he never even knew. It wouldn't have made a difference anyway. He was doomed when he crossed the X getting William out the pond. Or maybe he was doomed when I crossed the X a few months before."

"Did you ever remarry?" Hunchback asks, still eyeing the floor.

I trace the ring on my necklace and frown. "No, I never remarried, never wanted to. My heart was broken—no, it was torn to shreds, and I built a wall around what was left. I didn't want any more heartache, and I couldn't have found anyone else to hold a candle to my Pierce."

"So you've lived alone for all these years?" Pruny's rippled forehead is more pronounced than before when her eyebrows draw up.

"Yes. Other than my daughter, then my granddaughter, I lived alone with no one else touching my heart."

"What happened to Pierce's family?" a man with a long gray beard asks as he leans back in his chair and stretches his long legs, taking up too much room and blocking the path for anyone who would want to walk in front of him. His large hand rests on the curved head of the cane standing beside him. It looks like a shepherd's staff. He reminds me of Moses.

"Oh, I don't know. I left Walterboro the day of Pierce's funeral and never returned. I didn't care what became of them. They wanted me gone, so I left and never looked back. Of course, a part of me always hoped they would find Hazel's wrath." A touch of that old bitterness stays with me even still, I note, and I know it will be there until the end.

"This is some story, Pearl. You should've written a book," a young woman in a chef's jacket, whose hair is covered with a black-and-white bandana covered in crossbones, says with a slight snicker. She looks like she's been nipping too much on the old folk's food for far too long. Her white smock is unbuttoned, and the *GIRLS DO IT BETTER* T-shirt does a poor job of hiding the rolls she has underneath.

"Sandra." Mary gives the cafeteria worker a hard glance before returning her attention back to me. "Go on, Pearl. Please go on."

"I'm sorry, Mrs. Pearl. I didn't mean nothing by it," Sandra says and removes her bandana, showing the black spiked hair that was hidden underneath. "I just mean it's an interesting story. Please continue."

I nod to her in acceptance of her apology and take another sip of water with a nervous hand.

"Let's see." I lift my eyes and think for a moment. "I lived with the Andersons and helped them around the house. They were getting old, so they welcomed the extra help. After the sale of my parents' land, since I was the only heir, I received $345. While the land wasn't much, that was a lot of money for a single woman back then. I offered to pay the Andersons for letting me stay, but they wouldn't have it. They were such sweet, kind people. So, I went to the bank and opened my first bank account. It felt good to have a cushion in case anything happened. I knew the Andersons were getting old and couldn't live forever.

"A neighbor let me clean her house for extra money. After working for her for several weeks, she referred me to a few more people. It was hard work being pregnant and cleaning houses like I did, but I didn't mind because I was used to hard work. I knew it would all pay off one day, and I saved every last dime I could.

"Angela Marie Hayes was born May 2, 1920. The same day, the year before, I miscarried with Jacob. I named her Angela because she was my little angel. She was always a sweet, well-behaved girl, but she was quiet, shy. At least we believed she was. We soon found out she wasn't like the rest of the kids." I tap my temple. "Her brain would never mature past the level of a seven-year-old's. She would always be a child in a woman's body. The doctor told me she would never be a functioning adult, and I should commit her to a nursing home to ease my burden." I shake my head. "I couldn't do that—she's all I had.

"Martha died at the end of 1927, and Fred died less than a month later. It devastated him when she passed away. I guess his love for her was so strong it broke his heart when she died, and he couldn't live without her. Since they had no children of their own, they treated me and Angela like family. They left me a little bit of money to help us along after they passed away. I think Fred knew his time was almost up and wanted to ensure Angela and I were taken care of.

"I had to move out of the house after his funeral, since it belonged to the church and the new preacher was set to move in soon after. Angela and I moved into a small one-bedroom apartment in town until I could find a house we could afford close by. I bought a house in town right before the Great Depression hit." I pucker my lips and shake my head. "There surely wasn't anything *great* about it. Right after I signed the papers, the stock market crashed"—I wave my hand in the air—"and all hell broke loose. People lost their jobs and couldn't afford to feed their families. Most of my employers dropped me because they couldn't afford to pay me anymore, and no one was hiring. I struggled to keep myself and Angela fed and clothed, but it wasn't anything new. We managed."

Chapter 32

September 13, 1939

"Angela, time for supper!" I call out, glancing at the back door, as I put food on the plates and carry them to our small round wooden table in our tiny kitchen in our cute little house. I look around and beam.

We've come a long way.

I walk back to the sink, turn the water on, and look out the window at the busy street, which has been flooded with cars. "What would it be like to drive one of those?" I ask myself while I absentmindedly scrub a pot and daydream about being behind the wheel of a convertible—a burgundy one, maybe—so my hair could fly in the wind. I smile at that thought, then my smile fades, and I sigh. If only I could afford to buy one.

A stray calico cat darts across the road, making a shiny blue car suddenly stop. The olive-green car behind it slams on its breaks, stopping mere inches from the car in front of it, and blows its horn.

I jump and shake my head. No, I would be terrified to learn. I'd end up killing myself in one of those things.

I turn off the water and reach for a towel. A drop of water falls from my wet hands and lands on the mail scattered across the countertop. I pick up a flyer lying on top that came in the mail today.

I've never been to a play, and I bet Angela would love to go.

Huh? The flyer falls from my hand onto the counter, and I turn toward the door. "Angela!" I yell when I get to the door and peek out through the screen.

The backyard is serene, familiar. The metal yard chair, with peeling paint, that I've spent countless hours reading and sipping sweet iced tea in, is empty. The big oak tree casts in its shadow, a shadow that Angela loves sitting under to play with her doll, Dolly—but it's vacant. She's always there; she never leaves the yard. No fence marks our yard from any other because it has always been safe, no need to keep anyone in…or out, for that matter.

Where could she be?

I step out and hold my praying hands to my jutted lips as my eyes dart around frantically. "Angela, time to eat, sweetheart!" I say, my voice cracking, as I walk around the side of the house.

Empty.

My heart picks up its pace, and my feet join in when I hurry to the other side of the house. "Angela!"

The boxwood shakes and whimpers. My heart jumps. Two feet stick out of the bush, one with a Mary Jane, the other one without.

I sprint and kneel beside her, getting a whiff of fresh cut grass and…*Oh, God, no!* My hand slaps my opened mouth, and my eyes water. Her face is smeared with dirt, her long brown hair is tangled with pieces of leaves in it, and her ripped underwear is lying off to the side.

I pull her into my arms, probably more forcefully than I should, and rock her gently. "No, baby, no," I choke out between sniffles.

She stops whimpering and looks at me under droopy lids and frowns. "I'm okay, Mama. Don't cry," she says, her voice wavering. She touches my cheek with her dirty hand like John and William did.

I glance around, but see no one. "Who did this to you?" I hiss through clenched teeth as I pull dry leaves from her hair with shaky hands.

She slumps and hangs her head, avoiding my eyes.

I take a deep breath through my nose and release it before I raise her chin with my finger. "Angela, baby, I'm sorry. I'm not mad at you. You did nothing wrong." I look around again at the empty yard. "Whoever did this is the one who should get into trouble, not you. Don't be afraid."

She nods but remains silent.

"Come on, let's go inside." I stand and pull her up by the hand. I slap at the grass stains on the back of her frilly pink dress, but they remain.

When we get inside, I deposit her on the sofa. "You stay here, I'll be right back." I retreat to the kitchen and pick up the phone book, opening it and flipping through the opaque, stiff pages until I land on the page I wish I didn't need. I grind my teeth as I lift the telephone's handset and hold it to my ear. With a quivery finger, I turn the dial and wait until it goes back into the correct spot before turning it again. It seems to take longer than normal to dial a simple number.

"Summerville police department," a woman says in my ear.

"I need a police officer to come to my house." I pause and bite my lip. "Some…someone assaulted my daughter," I tell the operator, while I twist the spiral cord around my finger, turning it purple.

"What's the address?" she asks, sounding annoyed.

"105 South Cedar Street."

"Someone will be right out," she says and hangs up before I can thank her.

I gently place the receiver back in its cradle and look at Angela. Her arms are wrapped around her as she stares a hole in the floor. My shoulders drop. I wish I could take her sadness away, but I don't know how. I'm lost, useless. I scowl harshly at myself. A mother's job is to protect her child, and I failed.

"Where's Dolly?" she asks without looking up.

My hand squeezes the fingers on the other hand as I falter toward her. "I…I think I saw her outside." I point to the screen door. "I'll get her, sweetheart," I say when I pass her and head out of her sight.

I find her best friend near the bush I found Angela in and drop to my knees. With a nervous hand, I slowly pick her up and brush the dirt and leaves out of her brown-yarned hair the best I can. My lips quiver, and I slam the doll into my chest, squeezing the ever-loving life out of it. *Why did this happen to my baby girl?* I scream internally, and I scream it again and again in my mind. I hold the doll out and glower at it, and then I slap her plaid dress like I did Angela's, but harder, much, much harder, until I deem it's clean enough. I take a deep breath through my nose and hug the doll before standing and going back inside.

XXX

"Can you tell me what happened?" the young police officer, Jacob Bennett, asks Angela while steadying his pencil on his notepad.

She looks at the floor, still clutching her doll. She doesn't speak, and she doesn't move. She's like one of those mannequins in the store's window downtown.

"Can you tell me who did this to you?" he tries again.

She shakes her head and hugs her doll against her chest tighter. Her sad eyes haven't left the floor since the policeman got here.

He closes his notepad and sighs. The door opens and another officer walks in. "Excuse me," Bennett says, then stands and greets the man at the door. They speak in hushed tones for a few minutes, shaking their heads and nodding, before Bennett walks back toward us, leaving the other one by the door.

I squeeze Angela's hand. "What's going on? Did he find anything?" I ask Bennett.

"I'm sorry," he says remorsefully. "None of the neighbors have seen anything and there is no visible evidence at the scene." He looks at the other man and then back at me with uneasiness in his eyes. "Listen, ma'am. We'll file a report, but there's little else we can do if she doesn't talk. We don't know who we're looking for."

I turn to Angela and plead with my eyes. "Angela, please talk to them. What did he look like? Can you tell them?"

She shakes her head.

"I'm sorry. There's not much else we can do. If she remembers anything—anything at all—give us a call. We'll canvass the area and keep a lookout for anyone suspicious, but I can't promise we'll find anything." He looks at Angela. "I'm sorry this happened to you," he says, his voice showing benevolence and regret.

She remains silent while studying the floor.

I nod and push down on my knees before I rise. "I understand," I mumble. "Thank you for coming," I say as we approach the door.

"She should go to the doctor," the other police officer says as he opens the door.

"I'll take her in the morning."

"Just let us know if she remembers anything," Bennett says.

"I will."

I watch the men get into their black-and-white and drive away before I shut the door and lean my forehead against it. I feel numb. Why did this happen to my baby?

I pad over to her and sit, putting my arm around her shoulder. "Why don't you go take a bath while I warm up supper? You'll feel better after you're clean and fed."

She stands and walks down the hall with her head hung low and her doll clutched in her arms without saying a word.

When I hear the water turn on, I step out onto the front porch and glance around. No one is outside, so I walk to my neighbor's house, where Jack, Audrey, and their two little boys live, and knock on the door.

As soon as the door opens, two arms wrap around me and pull me into a tight hug, squeezing the air out of me. "Pearl, I'm so sorry. Is Angela okay?" Audrey asks with concern and shock in her voice.

"Yes…Yes," I say when she lets me go and I can breathe again. "She's shaken, but she'll be all right." *I hope.* "Thanks for your concern."

She opens the door wider, but I don't move. "Do you want to come in?"

I shake my head.

"Is there anything I can do?" she asks.

I glance down at my ring and twist it around my finger. "You didn't see anything?" I ask, looking back up at her with uncertainty.

"No, I'm sorry. I've been inside with Stephen all day. Earache." She shakes her head. "I can't believe this happened. It's always been safe here. I was shocked when the policeman knocked on the door." She gulps and looks down at her folded hands. "I thought something happened to Jack. He should be home by now. Don't get me wrong, I love Angela and don't want anything to happen to her, but I was so terrified—"

I lay my hand on her arm. "I know. It's okay."

She looks up, her eyes misted over, and she blinks rapidly. "I tried to call him at his office, after the policeman left, but he wasn't there. I was worried." She wipes her eyes and lets out a small, strangled laugh. "He just called to let me know he's working late tonight because he had to step out of the office today, and I was so relieved. God, I feel so bad."

"Mommy." Stephen comes up behind Audrey with glossy red eyes and a giant frown on his face, and tugs on her shirt.

"I won't keep you. You take care of your boy," I say and take a step off the porch.

"Okay. I'm sorry, Pearl." She picks the sick boy up and cradles him to her chest, and then she gives me a pitiful smile and shuts the door.

When I get back to the house, I see my other neighbor, Josh, putting a suitcase in the trunk of his car.

"Josh, I'm sorry about your grandfather," I say when I approach him.

"Hiya, Mrs. Hayes. Thanks." He slams the trunk shut, turns and faces me with dark, solemn eyes.

"I'm glad you got to come home for the funeral. How's your mom?"

He sighs. "Still sick. She didn't even go to the funeral this morning."

"Do the doctors know what it is?" I ask out of curiosity and concern.

He shakes his head. "She has more tests this week. Hopefully they'll find something out."

"I hope so, too. It's got to be hard on her and your father, not knowing."

"Yeah."

"How's law school?"

"It's good." He lifts his chin toward my house and furrows his brow. "What's going on? I saw the police at your house earlier. They talked to my dad." He puts his hands in his pants pockets and fiddles with his keys, making them jingle.

I glance over my shoulder at the quiet house then turn back to him. "It's Angela. Someone attacked her earlier."

His eyes widen. "Really? Angela? What happened?" he says, his voice rising.

I shake my head, not wanting to elaborate. "Did you see anyone suspicious around here today?"

He frowns. "No, sorry, I haven't. After the funeral, I was busy packing and doing some last-minute studying, so I haven't seen anything other than my room for the last several hours." He glances at his watch. "Speaking of which," he says softly, as if he were speaking to himself, before looking back at me, "I've got to get on the road. I've got an exam tomorrow. I wish I could stay and help, I really do."

"No...no, it's okay. I won't hold you up any longer. You drive safe."

"Yes, ma'am." He opens the car door and slides into the seat. "I hope you find out who hurt Angela," he says as he turns the key and the engine roars to life.

I nod and give him a small, pathetic wave as he shuts the door and backs out of the driveway. I turn around and see my small house, located on what had been a safe street, and sigh.

My baby's innocence has been lost to a monster.

Chapter 33

September 14, 1939

I glance up from my magazine and look at Angela, who is sitting beside me stroking Dolly's hair. She never told me who attacked her yesterday, but I didn't expect she would. I'll probably go to my grave never knowing who did this to her, and that kills me. My teeth grind behind my tight lips. I want to hang the SOB in the town square, and then I'd castrate him while he hangs from the—

"Angela Hayes," a short, plump nurse no taller than me appears from behind the glass-block wall and calls out into the nearly empty room occupied only by us.

I put the magazine on the side table, stand, and grab Angela's hand, but she doesn't move, making me jerk back when I try to move forward. At nineteen, she's bigger than I am, and it's hard to move her by force. She isn't a little girl anymore, even though she acts like it.

"Angela, you promised you would do this, remember? I said I would buy you a piece of candy if you're a good girl."

She shakes her head, and the hand gripping her doll to her chest turns red.

"Please, for me? When we get finished, we'll go by the grocery store, and I'll buy you two lollipops," I whisper, feeling the nurse's eyeballs at the back of my head.

She shakes her head.

I tilt my head back, looking up at the ceiling, and sigh. "And tonight for supper, I'll make grilled cheese"—I look back at her—"and you can help me."

She slowly stands, clinging to my hand, and walks with me down the wood-paneled hallway to the examining room. I knew that would change her mind. I smile sadly.

When we step into the small room, my hand trembles, but it isn't because of me. I look at our joined hands. "Angela, it'll be all right," I whisper, but she continues to shake as she looks at the floor.

"Have her step out of her underwear and wait on the table for the doctor." The nurse gives me a small smile before leaving and closing the door behind her.

Angela's shaking her head when I turn back to face her.

I pry my hand out of her death grip and say, with authority in my voice, "Angela, I will not bribe you anymore. If you want me to take Dolly until you do as you're told, then I will."

She squeezes her eyes shut and continues to shake her head while strangling the doll tighter against her chest.

I dig my palms into my eyelids. I shouldn't punish her, but I'm so tired, and she needs to do this. I'm at my wit's end. Having a nervous breakdown isn't an option. It's hard to raise a child on your own, especially a child like Angela. I wish every day Pierce were here to help me, and I need him more than ever right now.

A note of desperation creeps into my voice. "Angela, please."

She whimpers and hesitates before she cautiously lifts her pale yellow dress and slides out of her underwear without dropping her doll.

"Good girl, Angela," I tell her, relieved, yet also guilty I'm making her go through with this. "I'm proud of you. If you let the doctor do what he needs to do, it'll be quick, and I'll let you put double cheese on your sandwich tonight."

She nods, still whimpering, and hands me her balled-up underwear.

I turn to the door when there's a knock, and Angela steps behind me. A man in a white laboratory coat with receding, sleek black hair parted down the middle comes in, the nurse following shortly behind.

"Hello, I'm Dr. Harris. I hear there was an incident yesterday"—he looks at his clipboard—"Angela." He smiles, bending at the waist to look around me.

Her head digs into my back, and I take a small step forward, but she moves with me.

The nurse whispers in his ear, and he looks at me, comprehending. "Ah. I see. Well then, Angela, can you lie back on the table for me, so I can examine you?"

Angela shakes her head into my back, but he doesn't see because he's facing the counter. He snaps on a pair of latex gloves and slides on a leather strap with a headlight attached over his head.

I turn and hold my hand out, palm up. "Angela—Dolleee."

She jumps on the table, lies back, and closes her eyes tight.

When I turn back to the doctor, he's eyeing me with a thick, raised brow. "She loves her doll. Sometimes I have to threaten to take it away."

He shrugs. "Whatever works." He drags the metal stool, scraping it along the black-and-white-checkered floor until it's at her Mary Janes, and sits. "Okay, let's take a look," he says as he places her feet on the stirrups and tries to push her knees apart, but they won't budge. His eyes dart to mine.

"Angela," I say in a firm tone.

After a moment, she slowly opens her legs.

He picks up a duckbill gadget resting on a metal tray beside him and leans forward. "Just relax, Angela. This is a little cold," he says right before the instrument touches her opening.

She jumps and whimpers.

"You're doing good, Angela. Just another moment," he says over the clicking sound echoing in the room and disappears under her dress skirt like he's mining for gold.

I grab ahold of her hand and give it a light squeeze. "*Shh*, it's okay, Angela. It'll be over in a minute."

When he comes up and takes the speculum out, he places it back on the metal tray and turns off the light attached to his forehead. It seems like it takes forever for him to give me an answer, but when he looks at me with compassionate eyes and nods, I know.

I turn my head and blink away the threatening tears. I can't believe this happened to my baby—my poor, innocent, sweet baby.

He stands, removes his gloves and tosses them in the metal trash can in the corner, and takes off the headlight and puts it back on the counter. "It's too soon to tell if she's pregnant. You'll need to come back in two weeks."

"Okay." I look at Angela, who still has her eyes closed and is still whimpering. I tap her on the shoulder. "He's done, Angela. You can relax."

She opens her eyes and looks at me with shiny blue orbs while letting out a deep breath and relaxing her shoulders. I can see the tension leaving her already.

"You can get dressed now, Angela. You did good." Dr. Harris pats her arm and helps her sit up.

"Just come out front when you're done, and they can help you set up another appointment," he tells me, and then he looks at Angela. "We won't have to do this next time." He smiles at her before he and the nurse walk out, leaving us alone.

I slide Angela's underwear up her legs when she hops off the table. "Angela, I'm sorry this happened to you. I wish I could take it back, but I can't. You did good today by letting the doctor do what he needed to do. I'm proud of you."

"Yes, ma'am," she squeaks.

I hope she isn't pregnant, but if she is, we'll deal with it the best we can.

After making an appointment for two weeks, I grab her hand, and we walk out the front door. "Let's go to the store and get your candy."

"And cheese." She smiles for the first time since yesterday afternoon.

I put my arm around her shoulder and pull her in close. "And cheese. Lots and lots of cheese."

Chapter 34

June 22, 2001

"Oh, dear. You mean to tell me someone raped that poor innocent child?" Big Chin covers her mouth with her hand.

I nod with a sigh. "Yes."

"Did they ever find out who did it?" Hunchback asks.

I shake my head. "No, and nine months later, after a very difficult labor, she gave birth to Lillian Grace Hayes on June 15, 1940. Lillian was normal and healthy as far as anyone could tell. Angela had…a time with her pregnancy. She didn't understand why she was sick or getting fat and she hated going to the doctor. I had to bribe her every time with lollipops and grilled cheese. It always worked, though." I chuckle.

The laughter fades from my face, and I remember the pity I felt for my daughter. "She was miserable. I tried to comfort her the best I could. I knew I'd be the one raising Lillian from the beginning, but I didn't mind. It was only me and Angela for twenty years, so having Lillian come along made for a refreshing change."

I close my eyes and see Lillian as a baby. "She was beautiful. She reminded me of Angela when she was a baby with her curly brown hair, and eyes that were the color of the brightest blue ocean. An ocean I've never seen, but can only imagine. Lillian was a fussy baby; but it didn't matter. I loved her as much as a mother could love a child—or, in my case, a grandchild. Angela hated it when Lillian cried. She would cover her ears and run out of the house into the backyard, behind her big oak tree. That was her safe haven. She had little to do with Lillian. She preferred her doll, the one that didn't cry or have dirty diapers. Angela gagged every time Lillian had a dirty diaper, but she never changed one. I always did it. I'm the one who did everything.

"When I had to work, my next-door neighbor, Audrey, watched Lillian for me. She was a stay-at-home mother with two little boys of her own. I remember Daniel and Stephen running around their backyard laughing and chasing each other. They reminded me of John and William. I always wondered what they would've become if we hadn't crossed the X that dreadful day."

"Did you see an X when Angela was raped?" Sandra asks as she sets a tray of dried-out meatloaf, lumpy mashed potatoes, and runny creamed spinach on the table beside me, making my nose scrunch in disgust, and takes a seat.

I press my fingers into my forehead, trying to remember. "No, I don't think so. I don't know if Hazel had anything to do with Angela's rape. I didn't see an X for over twenty years, so I didn't look for one because it never crossed my mind. My whole focus was on Angela and making sure she was okay."

"So Hazel's curse was done—no more X's?" Sandra's inquisitive eyes show her fascination with my story.

"I wish, but that wasn't the case. Hazel would bide her time, letting me think she was done with me, and then she'd show up unexpectedly."

"What happened next?" Mary asks.

"Well, about two months after Lillian was born, Angela started coughing. I gave her some cough syrup I got from the pharmacy, but it never eased up. I thought it was a cold, but when she coughed up blood, I took her to the doctor and he sent her to the hospital right away. They diagnosed her with tuberculosis and sent her to a special hospital in Columbia—The Crestview Hills Sanatorium, two hours away. I hated her being so far away from me, but I didn't have a choice.

"I could only see her on Saturdays. Audrey watched Lillian while her husband, Jack, drove me to see Angela every Saturday during visiting hours. They never asked for any money for gas or babysitting. They were such a nice couple. I couldn't have asked for better neighbors.

"Angela hated being there. She was depressed because I wasn't there with her, but I couldn't be. I had to work and take care of her daughter. She didn't understand. It saddens me, the idea that Angela thought I didn't love her anymore, but I did. I loved her so much, and I missed her every day she was in that place.

"Angela was to remain in the sanatorium getting treatment. They informed me from the beginning it would take months and months until she got better, but her prognosis was good. So, she went into The Crestview Hills Sanatorium on August 9, 1940." My eyes drop to my hands resting in my lap. "But she never came home."

Chapter 35

January 18, 1941

I pull the door open and step inside the sanatorium for the twenty-second time. The overwhelming smell of disinfectant lingers in the air, and I can't help the automatic crinkle of my nose, so I rub out the burning sensation. It happens every time without fail. I should be used to it by now, but I'm not. I hate the smell of hospitals, and I hate coming here.

I've come every Saturday since Angela's been here except twice. Lillian became ill in November. When she had a fever and was coughing, it scared me half to death. I thought she may have had what Angela has, so I took her to the doctor right away. He took one look at the rash she had on her face and diagnosed it as rubella. He assured me she was fine and to keep her away from everyone for a week or two until all her symptoms were gone. So, I kept her away from everyone for two weeks to be sure—better safe than sorry.

Those were the longest two weeks of my life. I was on pins and needles the whole time. I thought Lillian may have been misdiagnosed and would die like John had many years ago. Luckily, that didn't happen. She has a good doctor.

I follow the hard gray terrazzo paving the way to the nurse's station.

I smile when I see Claudia, one of my favorite nurses, behind the counter shuffling through paperwork. She stops, turns her head toward me, and frowns.

My smile fades. "What's wrong?"

She comes around the counter and stands in front of me. "Oh, Pearl, we tried to call you this morning, but you must've already left."

The blood drains from my face and my heart skips a beat...or two. "What is it, Claudia, is she okay?" A lump gets caught in my throat, and I hear a big gulp when I swallow hard.

"The doctor looked in on her this morning. Her left lung collapsed." She sighs. "She's lost her appetite. The poor thing has barely eaten this week, like I told you on the phone the other night, and her fever is back. We have her on medicine, so it should take care of it, but it'll take time."

I twirl my wedding ring around my finger. I bite my lip until I taste copper, masking some of the pain in my shattered heart. "Can I see her?"

She shakes her head. "I'm sorry. The doctor said no visitors until we get her fever down. She was doing so good last week. I don't understand it."

I plead with my eyes without responding. Like any mother in my position would want—would *need*—I need to see my daughter.

After a moment of looking into my desperate eyes, she glances over her shoulder and takes a step to her right and looks behind me. Her eyes shift to the other nurse sitting behind the desk, who nods at her. She peeks at her watch, hurries to the cabinet, grabs a thin, white paper mask, and hands it to me. "Okay, just for a few minutes. The doctor won't be back until this afternoon."

"Thank you. I appreciate it," I say quietly, fear and gratitude clouding my voice in equal parts. "I really do."

She leads me down the hall to Angela's room while putting on her own mask. "Just a few minutes," she repeats when she opens the door and steps aside, giving me room to pass.

"A few minutes," I agree and look at my mask in my hand. It reminds me of the time Pierce and I had to cover our faces when

John was sick. This is a different illness, but the outcome can be the same, I know, and I dread that every day. I put the mask on over my mouth and nose and tie the back before stepping inside the sanitized room, with Claudia right behind me.

Angela's sleeping with Dolly and another doll tucked under her right arm, and there's a plastic tube going inside her flimsy pink hospital gown under her left arm. It's helping her breathe, I assume.

I'm at her side in four steps. I look down—lying in the middle of her chest is a wooden X. Old fears return to my mind. I guardedly pick it up and study it methodically, as if fascinated by it.

Claudia takes the cross from my hand and places it back on the wall above Angela's head the correct way. "I'm sorry. It must've fallen off."

I shake my head at the thought of Hazel's X once again haunting me. It couldn't be. That was a long time ago, and nothing has happened in over twenty-one years. It must be a coincidence, but something deep within me twists in fear as I look at my sweet daughter, who now has the dark look of death itself. My heart seizes.

Her face is pale, she has dark circles under her eyes, and she's lost weight since I saw her last week. She doesn't look like my vibrant Angela. But then again, she hasn't looked like herself in months, not since she got sick.

I pick up her hand and hold it in mine. "Baby, Mama's here." My eyes gloss over, and I blink quickly, halting my tears. "Mama loves you, Angela." My voice breaks despite myself.

She doesn't stir.

Claudia touches my shoulder. "We gave her fentanyl to keep her comfortable. She hated the tube we put in her to help her breathe. She won't wake up for some time."

"I can imagine she probably put up quite a fuss. If it happens again, threaten to take away her doll." I look at the other doll and run my fingers down its curled yellow hair and hard plastic face. "That always works for me," I say, my voice almost a whisper when I look back at Angela's closed eyelids.

"Okay, but she calmed down when we gave her the medicine. I hope you don't mind, but I gave her the other doll. She named her Grace."

"It's fine. Thank you. Please let her know I was here when she wakes," I say, still staring at my fragile child.

"I will. She's a sweet girl."

"She looks…" My eyes water again, so I hurry and wipe at them. I'd think she were dead if I didn't see her chest moving up and down while she breathes. Please, God, let her come out of this. *I can't bury another child.* "How long will it take for the lung to heal?"

"A week, maybe two," Claudia says, sounding uncertain. That scares me deeply, even more than seeing Angela in this state.

"Is she going to…" I stop and take a deep breath. "Is she going to die?" I whisper to Claudia, but I'm still looking at my sweet, innocent baby. She doesn't deserve this.

"The lung can heal, but it's the fever we're concerned about. We've given her medicine and have been making sure she has plenty of fluids." She points at the bag of fluid attached to the IV running into her arm. "She'll be fine once the medicine starts working. We'll keep her monitored."

I nod and rub Angela's hand. *Open your eyes, Angela. Please.*

They stay closed.

"I love you, baby. Please get better. I need you, your daughter needs you," I plead to her one last time before I walk out, fearing I will never see her again.

Claudia walks with me to the double doors of the main entrance.

I take my mask off and hand it to her. "Will she be all right?"

"Don't give up," she says compassionately. "Just keep praying. I'll call you if anything changes." She touches my arm before turning and walking back to the nurse's station, never giving me a direct answer.

I open the door and step out into the frigid, cloudy day as Hazel pops into my head. I take a deep breath and look up at the sky. "I'm begging you. Please don't let *her* take another one," I say before descending the steps.

When I slide into the passenger side of Jack's car, he dog-ears his book and places it on the seat between us. "That was quick. Is everything okay?" he asks and brushes the brown locks away from his wrinkled forehead.

I shake my head and my fingers twist the ring around my finger. "No. She's running a fever, and she has a collapsed lung."

He pats my hand and gives me a weak smile before turning the key and starting the engine. "She's in a hospital. They'll take good care of her. Don't you worry, Pearl, everything will be fine," he assures me. He pulls down the lever to drive and slowly pulls away from the sanatorium.

I look at the brick building as we pass by it. "Yes, I'm sure it will be," I mumble, but I don't believe it. If the X lying on top of her chest is a sign, nothing will be.

Chapter 36

January 19, 1941

I'm sitting on a chair in the backyard with my bare feet propped up on a stool. I take a sip of sweet tea and pick up a LIFE magazine with Katharine Hepburn on the cover. I run my hand over her flawless face. What would it be like to be a beautiful, famous movie star, to have handsome men flock all over me, and to buy whatever my heart's desire? Her life must be grand.

I close my eyes, tilt my head toward the sun shining on my face, and take a deep breath of the sweet scent of my blooming rose bushes. Laughter brings my attention back to the backyard. Angela and Lillian are sitting under the big oak tree having a tea party with their dolls. They're both seven years old. They've been this old for as long as I can remember, never getting older, but it seems normal.

Lillian whispers something in Angela's ear, and they both giggle, their shoulders shaking with laughter. I love to hear them giggle, so I do the same. Nope, I love my life and my girls, I wouldn't change a thing. Everything is perfect.

Both girls get up and run around the tree, round and round they go. One is chasing the other, but I can't tell who is chasing who. Something tickles my arm, so I look down and see a small white flake. I reach for it, but a light breeze blows it off my arm and onto the ground. Is that snow? It can't be; it's a spring day in the south. No, I realize, it's not snow. A storm of dandelion petals pour from the sky and covers the ground.

A peaceful feeling washes over me, and I look at the girls still running around the tree with dandelion-white hair that match their white dresses. It's beautiful.

The girls freeze and look up. I follow their gaze and see the blue sky turn dark gray, with black clouds wheeling in fast. A strong wind yowls, influencing the branches on the trees to totter.

Then everything stills. The tree trunk turns black like it's charred, and the color runs all the way to the top. The branches turn into long arms, and the beautiful green leaves turn into razor-sharp claws.

I fly out of my chair. "Girls!" I yell, but they don't move, as if they're hypnotized by the tree.

"Girls, get away from the tree, now!" I try again, but they're stunned motionless.

I try to run to them, but my bare feet won't move. They're stuck to the ground. I look down and lift my foot, but black sludge is attached to my sole and it makes it impossible to walk. My outstretched arms reach for the girls, but I'm too far away. My fear is increasing by the second.

"Please, somebody help me!" I yell at no one, because no one is here. I'm helpless.

The hole that once housed an owl turns into a mouth with protruding, pointed ochre-yellow teeth. It opens wide, takes Lillian into its mouth, and chews. My hands fly to the sides of my head and I scream, still unable to move from my spot. I hear bones crunching and blood oozes from the sides of its closed mouth as it swallows with a loud gulp. A large lump slides down the throat of the beast, and then it smiles at me with blood-stained teeth.

I scream again and my whole body shakes. "Angela!" I shout, trying to get her attention, but she's still staring at the tree, paralyzed, like she didn't just witness the maddening scene before her.

The tree wraps its claws around Angela's arms, picks her up, and rips her apart like a rag doll.

"No! Angela!"

"Angela," I pant, sitting up drenched in sweat, looking for air. It was just a dream. I can't remember the last time I'd had a nightmare. It was—

My hand flies to my mouth and I shake my head. "Please, no," I whisper.

Lillian stirs in the next room, drawing my attention away from the atrocious thought. I throw the covers off myself and get out of bed. "I'm coming, Lillian," I say loud enough for her to hear me.

Thoughts of Hazel's wrath are put on hold when I enter Lillian's room. She's sitting up in her crib, holding her outstretched arms to me and waving her palms. I stand in front of her and smile at the muddled hair on top of her head. "That's not going to be any fun for either of us to comb out," I tell her.

Her hands move faster and her legs mimic them.

"All right, all right," I say and pick her up before the fussing begins. Her fist goes into her mouth, and I can see the sides of her mouth turn up. "Let's get you dressed for church, young lady."

I lay her on Angela's bed, take off her gown, and change her cloth diaper. I'm pinning the second side when the telephone rings from the kitchen, startling me. Her blue eyes, eyes matching her mom's, look up at me, and the sense of trepidation rushes back in, flooding my thoughts. I pick her up, position her on my hip, and put a fake smile on my face. "Who could that be this early in the morning?" I ask her in a playful voice and wide eyes while I tickle her exposed belly, trying my best to hide my troubled feelings. She giggles while gnawing on her fist. "Well, let's go find out," I tell her on the walk to the kitchen. My pace slows with each step as I dread who the caller is.

The ringing stops and I blow out a breath while looking at the silent phone.

The ringing starts again, and I pause with my hand hovering over the receiver. If I don't answer, another piece of my heart won't break off. It rings again, and I snatch it out of its cradle before it has a chance to ring any longer, and I slowly bring it to my ear. "Hello," I answer softly while holding a half-dressed baby on my hip.

"Pearl, this is Claudia…"

I close my eyes and my heart flutters.

When she doesn't continue, my eyes open and I hold out the receiver, glance at it, before putting it back to my ear. "Claudia, are you still there?"

"Yes, I'm still here. I'm sorry, but"—she sniffles—"Angela passed away last night."

I stare at the wall in front of me. Tears swell in my eyes, and my lips quiver. "What…What happened?"

"Her other lung collapsed, and she couldn't get enough air," she says as she sniffs again. "She must've accidentally pulled out her breathing tube during the night. She…she suffocated, Pearl."

Lillian cries. "*Shh*, it's okay." I bounce her up and down on my hip while tears wash down my face. With my hands full, I can't wipe them away.

"You'll need to go to a funeral home to make arrangements. They'll contact us. Let them take care of everything, Pearl, that's what they're for. You don't need the added stress."

I stand here, dumbfounded and in shock before I realize I should respond. "Right," I reply absently before shaking myself. *This can't be happening.* "I'll go in the morning, if that's all right?" I'm not sure if they're even open on a Sunday, but I can't deal with it today anyway. I want to crawl under a rock, but since I have Lillian, I can't do that.

"That's fine. If you need anything, please let me know."

"Okay," I mumble.

"Will you be all right, Pearl?"

I let out a strangled laugh as I look up at the flat ceiling. "Yes, of course." I have to be, for Lillian.

"She was a sweet girl. I'll miss her. We all will miss her immensely."

Me too. "Goodbye," I say in a daze.

"Goodbye, Pearl. Take care of yourself."

I nod at the phone but don't answer before hanging up and dawdling to the sofa with Lillian. Once I'm seated, I pull Lillian into a hug and cry into her neck while I rock us back and forth. She wails too, but I'm sure it's not for the same reason. She didn't know her mama, and she never will.

Chapter 37

January 20, 1941

The temperature seems to drop with every step, making my fingers and toes numb by the time the home comes into view. When I get to the BURNS AND SONS FUNERAL HOME sign in front of a large white two-story house, I stare at it while I huddle in my coat and blow cold breaths out of my mouth, stalling.

I can't believe I'm about to walk in there and arrange Angela's funeral. This can't be real. I'm not sure if I can do this.

I need Pierce.

After a few more minutes of deliberating whether this is real or not, I mosey up the nine brick steps divided by an iron railing until I reach the top of the porch. I inhale deeply through my nose before I turn the brass knob and enter reality.

The open room is peaceful and the air is clean, refreshing—almost too refreshing, but not quite. The wood paneling on the lower walls and fake flowers on pillars create a homey, inviting atmosphere.

A crackling sound sends my focus to the large mahogany fireplace on the far wall, which is decorated with pewter candlesticks on each side of the mantle. The small orange and yellow flames dance over a few pieces of crisscrossed wood, sending warmth throughout the room.

A large picture of an angel, looking down from the clouds at two small children crossing a wooden bridge overlooking a field of flowers hangs in the center above the fireplace.

Twin mauve high-back chairs across from a matching sofa sit in front of the fireplace. A shiny gold metal box with a tissue coming out is in the center of the oval mahogany coffee table between the seats. I can imagine people sitting in those seats in front of a cozy fire, crying, and grabbing tissue after tissue like a magician pulling an endless piece of cloth out of his pocket.

I've never been in a funeral home before, but it's soothing. Now I know why people want a place like this taking care of their deceased loved ones.

"Arthur Burns," a man says, bringing me out of my thoughts, as he extends his hand.

His salt-and-pepper hair, mainly salt, parts to the side and his large crooked nose sits under black horned-rimmed spectacles. The crisp black suit and fat red-and-white-striped tie he's wearing looks to be on the expensive side. Nothing like the old worn suit Pierce had, and I'm sure this man owns more than one.

I wish Pierce were here.

I take my gloves off and stuff them in my coat pocket before shaking his soft, cold hand. "Pearl Hayes," I say and unbutton my coat.

"Shall I take your coat?" His eyes shift to the brass coat rack beside the door as he adjusts his eyeglasses.

"No, thank you. I'll leave it on," I say and tug my coat closed. "I need to be at work soon."

"As you wish." He holds his arm out, his hand pointing down the hall, while his other touches the button on his suit jacket. "Let's go into my office."

"All right."

He leads me down a short hallway with pictures decorating the wall, and I stop at the one of Jesus. A sharp pain punctures my heart as I stare at the cross holding up the man who is supposed to be our savior. I know I shouldn't have any doubts, but—

"Mrs. Hayes?"

I look at Mr. Burns, who is standing in front of an opened door, and he steps aside, motioning me to go first.

"Yes…Yes, of course." I glance at the picture again before I enter the office and sit in one of the two black leather chairs across from the large, uncluttered oak desk. A picture frame cocked up by its flimsy foot, a pencil holder with six ballpoints, a crystal dish half filled with white-and-red-swirled candies, a yellow-flowered box of tissues, and a gold horse statue are the only things on the desk.

Behind the desk is a massive painting of horses racing in an open field with their manes waving in the wind as they pass by the gray mountains in the backdrop. On the side wall are floor-to-ceiling twin cherry bookshelves, filled with books of every color and size, with several small horse statues placed in front.

He takes a seat behind the desk, his spine straight. He places both hands, folded, on the desktop. "How can I help you today, Mrs. Hayes?"

I miss Pierce.

I slouch and twirl my wedding ring on my finger. "Please, call me Pearl."

He glances at my ring. "Oh, I'm sorry," he says consolingly. "You're here for your husband."

I stop my twirling and straighten. "Oh, no, he's been gone for a long time now. It's my daughter Angela." I glance down at my lap, trying to hide my frown, but I'm not sure why. He's probably used to the sadness shadowing people in here.

"Oh. I'm so sorry for your loss. I know it must be difficult to lose a child. May I ask how she passed?" he asks with a calm but compassionate look on his face. He pulls open a drawer attached to the desk with ease and retrieves a piece of paper and a pen from the pencil holder sitting on top.

I cover my mouth with the side of my fist and clear my throat. "Tuberculosis. Saturday night. She's at The Crestview Hills Sanatorium in Columbia."

He jots something on the paper.

"They told me to come here, and you would help me. I've never done this before," I admit, feeling a little embarrassed and sad at the same time. I wish Pierce were here with me.

"We're here to help you, Pearl." He looks at me with kindhearted eyes. "We here at Burns and Sons can take care of all your needs. We'll make everything lovely, I assure you. We know how difficult it is to lose a loved one," he says sympathetically.

I nod. "Good, I'd like that."

"We'll arrange for her to be transported here. You'll need to send over a dress for her to be buried in, and we'll need to know where her final resting place will be. Don't worry, we'll take care of the rest." He hands me another sheet of paper and a pen from the desk. "We'll need some information so we can put her obituary in the paper. If you would fill out this form."

I look at the paper, and I write Angela's details on the form behind blurry eyes.

Mr. Burns stands and leans over the desk, pulling a tissue from the flowered box, and hands it to me.

I quickly wipe my eyes and nose. "Thank you."

"You're welcome." He sits again, back straight, and folds his hands on top of the desk…and waits.

Once I'm done, I hand him the paper, and he scans over it. "This is good. I see you're a member of Grace Advent Christian Church on Central Avenue. That's a nice church. We've done several funerals there." He stands and walks to the door with an outstretched arm. "Let's go pick out a nice casket for Angela."

"All right." I stand and smooth down the front of my coat before following him down another hall. Then he disappears through thick, burgundy floor-length drapes, parted and tied back by gold tassels on each side.

I stop and gawk when I pass over the threshold into the parlor filled with caskets like the ones Mr. and Mrs. Anderson were buried in, but better. Mahogany, oak, black, white, gray, and even a baby blue one congregate in the room.

He turns from the center of the room and must notice my resistance, because he strolls back to me and places his hand on my upper arm. "If you don't find anything here you like, we can order one from the catalog. It can be sent here within two days." He glances around. "But I'm sure we'll find something you'll like." He points me to a dark, almost black, casket gleaming in the overhead light, displayed proudly in the center of the room like it won first place in a beauty pageant. With the substantive gold handles and silk-cushioned lining inside, it looks inviting…and expensive. "This is the Manchester Mahogany. It's our top-of-the-line model," he says in a delighted tone and a sparkle in his eye.

My eyes drop to the floor. "I don't think I can afford this one," I mutter.

"That's perfectly fine."

I look back at him as he runs his clean, callous-free hand along the silk lining while he stares at it.

"Few people have the money to afford this one," he says softly, still staring at it as if he were talking to it instead of me. "It's out here just in case." His eyes shift to mine. "We have more that may be more suited for your budget. We also have a financial plan you may be interested in."

"Yes, I'll need to do that." Any money I've saved will be gone after Angela is buried, and I know it won't be enough.

"I'm here for you, to make this as painless as possible. I have one over here that may be perfect, and it's one of our cheapest." He leads me to a polished white one, just as pretty as the expensive mahogany one. "This is the Coral Mist."

We buried our other kids in pine boxes with no cushion. But this one, this one isn't just a box, it's a chest…a treasure chest.

I run my hand down the smooth, shiny chest and touch the velvety light pink pillow. "It's soft. Angela loved pink. She has a pink dress." I frown, pulling my hand away quickly from the plush headrest as if it stung. "She loved dressing up in her pink dress," I whisper. I will only see her wear it once more, right before they shut the lid. I dab my wet eyes with the wadded tissue he gave me earlier.

"That's perfect." He smiles. "She will be beautiful. Let's go back into the office and take care of the details. Shall we?" He holds out his arm toward his office.

I nod.

"I'll send someone out today to get Angela, so we can prepare her," he says as we enter his office and he takes a seat behind the desk. "Please, have a seat." He points to the black chair I vacated earlier.

I sit.

He opens the bottom drawer of his desk and his arm moves as if he were rifling through it. "Ah, here we are"—he pulls a paper out and holds it up as he pushes his eyeglasses back up his nose—"the Coral X."

I draw in a breath as Hazel pops into my mind. "Wha-what did you say?" I stammer.

His forehead creases as he frowns and slides the paper toward me. "The Coral Mist. Isn't that the one you wanted?"

My eyes water and I blink quickly. "Yes. I thought you said…" I shake my head. "Never mind."

"Just look over this and sign your name." He taps the bottom line on the paper with his finger. "And if you can bring her dress by as soon as you can, we can have her ready for a viewing tomorrow night."

"I have to go to work, but I can bring it by later this afternoon, if that's all right?" I ask while scribbling my name at the bottom of the financial papers with trembling hands. It feels as if I'm signing my life away. I guess I am, sort of.

God, I miss Pierce.

"That's fine. I'll contact the church to see what time on Wednesday is suitable for the funeral." He looks at his watch. "I'll call *The Post and Courier* and have her obituary run in the morning and again on Wednesday. I'll give you all the information when you come back with the dress."

"Okay." I stand and shake his hand, my hand still trembling. "I appreciate all your help."

"You're welcome. That's what I'm here for. If you need anything, please don't hesitate to call. I'll walk you out." He escorts me to the front door and opens it while I slip on my gloves and button my coat. "Again, I'm sorry for your loss."

"Thank you," I mumble as I walk out the door and turn toward the house I have to clean today, still drowning in thoughts of Hazel.

Chapter 38

January 22, 1941

My elbows rest on the kitchen table as I hold my coffee cup to my lips. I take a sip in a daze and watch Lillian, sitting in her highchair and chewing on a teething ring with heavy drool dripping down her chin. She's content…at the moment.

Knock. Knock. Knock.

I jump, nearly spilling my coffee, but recover with a slight grin and set it on the table. I stand and say, "I'll be right back, Lillian. Be a good girl."

She smiles, showing one small tooth.

When I open the door, Jack is standing there in a black three-piece suit with a gloomy look on his face.

"What's the matter?" I ask and grip the door knob.

"You just lost your daughter and you're concerned about me?" He shakes his head, and his blue eyes flicker past me to Lillian. I follow his gaze, and when I turn back around, his eyes are on me again. "How are you holding up, Pearl?"

My eyes glance at my bare feet, and I frown. "Oh, I'm doing all right." *I have to be.* I grip the knob tighter. "Do you want to come in?" I open the door and step aside, but he doesn't move.

"No, I just wanted to bring you this." He hands me a rolled-up newspaper. "I picked up an extra one for you. I assumed you'd like a copy of Angela's obituary."

"Thank you. I didn't think about that." My face heats with embarrassment and disappointment as I hold the paper to my chest. Our sons didn't have their obituaries printed in the paper, and I don't know if Pierce did either—but I wish I had the clippings now.

"We'll leave around ten fifteen, so you can get there a little early before everyone else shows up to say your..." He exhales. "Your goodbyes."

"I was going to walk. It's not far. I don't—"

He holds up his hand. "No. You're riding with us. You're not walking to your daughter's funeral," he tells me firmly, before his face softens and he gives me a small smile. "Besides, Audrey will kill me if you don't agree to ride with us. She sent me over here to let you know what time we'll be leaving. You know how she can be. She won't take no for an answer."

I nod, grateful in spite of the trouble. "All right, I'll come over at ten fifteen then. Thank you. Thank you for everything you did."

"It was no problem. I'll see you soon." He glances to Lillian again before he turns and walks back to his house.

Lillian cries, so I shut the door and hurry to her. Her face is flushed and her lips quiver as she reaches out in front of her. Her teething ring is on the floor in front of the chair, so I pick it up and rinse it off before handing it back to her. "Here, sweetheart. Try not to drop it again."

When it reaches her tiny hand, she shoves it back in her mouth and chews, silencing her sobs. Slobber gushes out of her mouth and drips, coating the tray. I dab a cloth to her chin, but it does no good. Her mouth is a running faucet, and I know it aches. I hope she doesn't get fussy at the funeral today.

I sit and open the paper. *Franklin D. Roosevelt's Third Inaugural Address* doesn't hold my interest. I flip straight to the obituaries.

OBITUARY

ANGELA HAYES

Angela Marie Hayes, age 20, passed away peacefully on Saturday, January 18, 1941, at The Crestview Hills Sanatorium in Columbia SC. She was born on May 2, 1920, to Pearl Grace (Rutherford) Hayes of Summerville, SC and the late Pierce John Hayes of Walterboro, SC. She is survived by her mother and daughter, Lillian Grace Hayes. She is preceded in death by her father and her three brothers, John, William, and Jacob Hayes of Walterboro, SC. Friends may call at the Burns and Sons Funeral Home in Summerville from 9 a.m. to 8 p.m., Tuesday. The family will receive friends from 5 to 8 p.m. Tuesday, at the funeral home. Funeral services will be held on Wednesday, January 22, 1941, at 11:00 a.m. at Grace Advent Christian Church, 349 Central Avenue. Pastor William Faulk will officiate. Arrangements under the direction of Burns and Sons Funeral Home in Summerville, South Carolina.

I cut the obituary out of the newspaper, walk to the living room, and grab Angela's children's bible off the bookshelf. She didn't read it, but she liked to look at the colorful pictures. When I open it, Jesus is hanging from the cross. I tilt the bible, making the cross turn on its side and look like an X. I shake my head, ignoring this absurdity. "Your obituary doesn't belong on this page, baby girl," I whisper to myself and flip through the pages until I find her favorite story, *Noah's Ark*. I place the clipping alongside the animals making their way to the large vessel before closing it and placing it back on the shelf.

I walk back to the kitchen and pick Lillian up from the highchair, her legs kicking in the air while she bites the soft ring. "Come on, Lillian. Let's get ready to say goodbye to your mama."

XXX

248

I'm standing in front of my daughter's grave, listening to the young preacher talk about my sweet baby girl. Lillian pulls at her white bonnet, trying her best to take it off. After I've had enough of her squirming, I one-handedly take it off and stuff it in the diaper bag draped over my shoulder, cradle her in my arms, and give her a bottle. The moment she gets the nipple in her mouth, her eyes shut and she goes limp.

"Do you want me to take her?" Audrey whispers.

I shake my head and look at Lillian drain the bottle with her eyes closed. "No, she's fine now." Milk dribbles out the side of her mouth and drips down to her neck. I wipe the milk away and stroke her curly brown hair. It looks like how Angela's did when she was a baby. It'll straighten when she gets older, I can tell, like Angela's. She looks like her mama.

"As we mourn this life that is no longer with us, we lift up our sadness and grief to you. Lord, we ask that you would comfort us in our pain and bring us an abundance of your gentle healing mercies. Jesus' name we pray, Amen," the preacher says, and everyone scatters.

"Thank you for coming. You didn't have to come all this way," I tell Claudia when she approaches me, holding Dolly and Grace in her hand.

"Don't be silly. We all loved Angela." She looks at the two dolls, stroking their hair, before carefully handing them to me. "I wish she had left under better circumstances."

"I know," I say as a small hand reaches for the dolls. I look down at Lillian's droopy eyes, still sucking on the bottle, and hand over Grace. Her eyes close again when the doll touches her hand and she brings it to her chest. I keep Dolly clutched in my hand and adjust, struggling to hold Lillian.

"I need to head back now," Claudia whispers.

"Okay, drive careful."

She nods. "Take care of yourself and this little one." She smiles and gently places a hand on Lillian's chubby leg, making it twitch, before she turns and walks away.

"The congregation took up an offering to help out with the funeral costs," Pastor Faulk says as he hands me an envelope.

I take the envelope and put it in the diaper bag along with Dolly. "Thank you. The service was beautiful."

"You're welcome. Angela was a sweet girl. She will be missed." He touches my upper arm. "If you need anything, please don't hesitate to ask. We're your church family, we're here for you."

I nod. "Okay," I say tentatively.

"We'll see you two on Sunday." He smiles at Lillian and touches her leg, making it twitch again before he leaves.

"Pearl, I'm so sorry for your loss," a voice calls out from behind me.

Lillian jumps in my arms, and her eyes fly open before they slowly flutter closed again.

I turn around. "David? David Hall. I haven't seen you since…" I look at Lillian. "Since Lillian was born, I guess. Where did y'all move?" I ask, looking back at him.

He shrugs. "Just across town. Mandy needed a change."

"How is she?" I ask with concern.

His eyes drop to the ground and he shakes his head. "Cancer got her." He looks back at me with sadness in his eyes. "Three months ago."

"Oh, David, I'm so sorry. I didn't know," I say, feeling awful.

"She'd been sick for a while. It was only a matter of time." He peeks at Lillian and frowns.

"Josh isn't here?" I glance around. "How is he?"

"No, he couldn't make it. He's good, and in his last year of law school." He puts his hands in his pockets. "I won't keep you. I wanted to tell you how sorry I am to hear about Angela. Take care of yourself, Pearl," he rushes out.

"I will," I say, my voice unsure. "Thank you."

He looks at Lillian again with an expression I can't make out, but he doesn't touch her like most people do, and then he hurries away.

I tilt my head as I watch him walk away. Then I look back at

Lillian still sleeping with the bottle in her mouth and Grace in her hand.

"Here, let me have her," Audrey says as she takes Lillian from me, making her wake with a small cry as she lets go of the empty bottle. "How are you holding up?" She catches the bottle as she takes the diaper bag from me and shoves it inside.

"Thank you." I give her a strangled smile and rub out my tired, free arm. "I'm okay," I lie, trying to convince myself.

"Do you want us to wait?" She points to the car where Jack and her sons are nestled inside.

"No, I want to walk. Clear my head. But thank you."

"I thought you'd say that. I'll take her home with us, so you can have some time to yourself. You can pick her up later." She bounces Lillian on her hip, making her giggle.

"I won't be long." Lillian reaches for me, and I kiss her cheek. "No, you go with Mrs. Audrey. I'll be there soon to get you."

Lillian cries out and puts her fist in her mouth and her head on Audrey's shoulder.

"She's teething," I tell Audrey.

"Take your time. Don't worry about Lillian, I've got her," she says before walking to the car and getting in with Lillian on her lap.

After they're gone, I turn and look around. Everyone is gone except for the men throwing dirt over Angela's casket. There's a chill in the air, but I don't bother buttoning my coat. The cold air is refreshing.

While the men finish the last of the dirt mound, I walk around, noting the tombstones decorating the graveyard. Some are cracked and look like they've been here for a long time. Some have green algae growing on them, like no one has ever taken the time to clean them. Are Pierce's and our son's headstones ever cleaned, or are they neglected like some of these have been?

Hardly any of the graves have flowers on them; the ones that do have wilted and died. Angela has fresh flowers on hers from all the people who came today. Angela loved flowers. She loved helping me with my rose bushes, even though she got pricked by the thorns every time.

I'm all alone when I walk back over to the now finished grave. The headstones surrounding her grave have the name Rutherford carved in large letters on them. There's a lot of my family buried here—all except four.

Tears pool in my eyes. I've done well today, not crying during the funeral. I didn't want Lillian to see me cry and upset her. But now that I'm alone, I can't stop the overwhelming feeling to let the tears all out. I drop to the ground, lie on top of the dirt, and weep. *I still can't believe my baby is gone.* My head shakes back and forth with a hysterical tremor. Angela was my last remaining connection with Pierce, and now she's gone. *Gone!* A hard box and six feet of dirt separate us.

The *caw* of a crow catches my attention. I look up and see it sitting on a moss-covered oak tree towering above me, staring at me. Hazel pops into my mind. The sleek black feathers remind me of Hazel's birds, and the tree reminds me of those that hid her house many years ago. The crow's eyes flash with a red twinkle before flying away and disappearing into the sun's rays.

Once it's gone, I turn back to the dirt mound lying underneath me, and drop my head to my praying hands resting on her grave. "I'm so, so sorry, my sweet Angela. I caused this. It was all my fault." I don't want to go on, but I have to—for Lillian.

I stay at her grave, sobbing for hours, it seems, because I'm not ready to let go. When my head is about to explode from a massive headache, I pull out a handkerchief from my pocket. I trace the *FA* embroidered on the white cloth with a dirty finger. I miss the Andersons. I wish they were here to help me now like they did when I came back to Summerville all those years ago. I wish I had someone, anyone.

"God, I miss Pierce," I mumble as I wipe the tears and snot with the handkerchief and rise to my feet. When I look down at my coat, I sigh. "I'm a dirty mess," I say and slap at my coat with anger and frustration before I look up to heaven. "Take care of our babies, our angels, Pierce. I love you all," I say, before I walk away to get the only living relative I have left: my granddaughter.

Chapter 39

June 22, 2001

"How can you tell that story without shedding a tear, Pearl?" Mary sniffles and wipes her nose with a tissue. Her face is so red and blotchy; it reminds me of Lillian's face when she had rubella.

"I've cried my share, believe me. I've cried enough for a hundred women to last a lifetime." I take a sip of water "What time is it?"

Mary glances at her watch. "It's almost six. Do you want your supper?" She points to the tray on the table that looks like it's been sitting there for a while. "It's cold, but Sandra can reheat it."

Sandra stands. "Sure thing, Mrs. Pearl."

My nose crinkles. "No, I'm not hungry." I push the tray away, not wanting to smell any more of the grotesque food.

Sandra quickly sits back down, backward in her chair with her arms resting on the back. "Please tell us more, Mrs. Pearl."

"Did Lillian survive?" Moses asks.

"Of course she survived. Where do you think her great-granddaughter came from who was here earlier?" Hunchback answers.

"Could everyone stop talking so Mrs. Pearl can finish," Sandra says, sounding annoyed. "I want to find out if anything else happens with Hazel's curse."

"All right then, where was I?" I pull the little black hair that's always under my chin. Mary plucks it from time to time, but it always grows right back. "After the funeral I raised Lillian alone, but I guess that was always the case since Angela hadn't been able to be a mother to her. It was sad Lillian never got to know her mama. When she spoke her first word, she called me 'Mom.' I didn't correct her. I let her do what she wanted. When she got older, I explained to her that her mama had died, and I was her grandmother. She still called me 'Mom.' I didn't mind; I enjoyed being someone's mom again.

"After Angela's funeral, I got a job working at the counter at the post office. One day after visiting Angela's grave, I saw an ad in the post office window. I was feeling the aches on my body from cleaning houses for so many years, so I inquired within, just like the sign said. They hired me right on the spot." I smile. "The pay was good compared to what I was making cleaning houses, and the work was easier, that's for sure. Jack got a new job in New York, I think." I rub the ridges on my forehead. "He moved his family, and I never heard from them again. I lost my babysitter, so the extra money came in handy when I had to find another one, and I started saving money for Lillian's future. I wanted her to go to college and be successful. I loved Lillian and would give her anything I could to keep her happy. She was a good girl." I shake my head and touch my wedding ring. Lord, I miss Pierce. I've never stopped missing him.

"What happened to her?" I hear, but I don't know who asked the question because I'm seeing Lillian in my head and remembering what she did.

"*Shush*, let…her…finish," Sandra says, punctuating each word slowly.

I shake myself from my reverie. "Lillian graduated from high school and went to college to become a nurse. When she graduated from college, it was one of the happiest days of my life. I haven't had many since before the summer of 1919. The days after losing my Pierce and our sons were sad and lonely times. But when Angela, and then Lillian came along, things were looking up for me. When Angela died, I knew I needed to make Lillian's life the best and happiest I could, and I did. I was so proud of her, and I couldn't have asked for a better granddaughter.

"I missed her when she was away at college, but after she graduated, she came back home to live with me and get a job at the hospital in town. She loved working there. She met a doctor, and they got married in…" My finger taps my puckered lips trying to recall the date. "Oh yes, it was 1964."

Chapter 40

May 16, 1964

Lillian's sitting at the vanity while the hairdresser's taking out the curlers from her long, straight brown hair. I remember when she had curly hair before it straightened, like I knew it would. She hated it. One time, I caught her with her head on the ironing board, and her hair was all fanned out on top. She had my iron in one hand and a mirror in the other. I nearly had a heart attack. I stopped her, of course. She could've caught her hair on fire, I recall with a smile and a small chuckle. She must've only been eight or nine at the time.

"What are you giggling about?" she asks as she squints at me through the foggy mirror while the hairdresser coats her hair with hairspray.

"Oh, nothing. I was remembering how curly your hair used to be, and how much you hated it."

She stands and turns around. "The ironing-board incident again?" she asks, cocking her head to the side and putting her hands on her hips. "Will I ever live that down?" She shakes her head with a smile and steps toward me.

"Not in my lifetime," I say distractedly. My eyes scan her floor-length, white-satin, off-the-shoulder dress with pearl beads running down the back. "You look so beautiful, Lillian, like a princess." I lean in to her and whisper, "I can't imagine what your dress cost, let alone the entire wedding."

She lifts a brow. "Well, thank goodness I'm marrying a doctor, and his family owns the biggest chain of furniture stores throughout the state. So you don't have to worry about it."

"I could have pitched in if they needed some money."

"Don't be silly." She playfully slaps my arm. "I'm just glad you're here to enjoy this day with me."

"Me too, sweetheart." I glance at the bridesmaids sitting on the couch sipping champagne out of crystal flutes while they speak to one another in hushed tones. Their matching short—very short— peach dresses with bows wrapped around the front ride up, nearly showing their… "They look more like party dresses," I whisper and tilt my head toward the girls. "I've never been to a big wedding. Actually, the only one I've been to is my own, and it was nothing"—I wave my hand in the air—"like this."

"I promise you'll have a good time tonight." Her mouth forms an O and she claps her hands together, holding them to her lips. "Oh, I have to give out presents." She hurries to the corner of the room, grabs a big teal shopping bag and opens it, pulling out flat black square boxes. She hands each of the bridesmaids one and gives me one with a big grin on her face.

"You didn't have to give me anything," I say and run my hand over the soft velvet box.

"Thank you, Lilly!" all the girls shriek.

"You're welcome," she tells the girls, but her eyes stay on me as she bites her colorful red lip. "Just open it."

I open the box revealing a strand of pearls. My jaw drops, and I'm speechless while I gaze at the delicate beads in the opened box. "Here, let me help you." She picks up the pearls, puts the strand around my neck, and clasps it in the back. "They look fabulous on you," she says and stands back, admiring the necklace.

I step to the vanity and look into the mirror. "Thank you, Lillian. These are so beautiful," I say, touching the smooth milky white gems. My eyes mist over, and tears land on the hand stroking the beads.

"I've never owned real jewelry before"—I hold out my hand and look at the ring on my finger—"except for my wedding ring."

She leans over my shoulder and brings her hand up under mine. "I wish I would've met him," she says softly and stares at my ring. "I bet he was a great man."

"He was." I nod. "My Pierce was one of a kind. I'll—"

Our heads whip to the door when it flies open and Ruth, Robert's mother, sashays in wearing a beaded cream dress that sparkles like diamonds—she's holding a small white box with a jeweled bow on the front. "Okay, ladies"—she snaps her fingers—"it's almost show time." She puts her hand over her heart and smiles. "Oh, Lillian, darling, you look ravishing." Her eyes land on me, taking me in, and her smile becomes restrained. "I do declare, Pearl, you look simply *gawgeous*."

"Thank you, Ruth, and so do you," I say and return her smile.

Ruth's a little fancy for my taste, but I still like her. She drives a big expensive car around town but never forgets to wave at me when I walk down the sidewalk carrying an armful of groceries. She's tall and beautiful and always holds her head up high. She's always dressed in clothes I could never afford, wears a lot of makeup, and she's always coated in jewelry. Richard, her husband, is the complete opposite. He seems to lack the confidence his wife has, and where he's deficient in height, he makes up for it around the waist.

"Okay, Pearl, Johnathon is waiting outside to escort you to your seat." She opens the door and holds her arm out toward me.

"All right." I walk to the door and glance back at Lillian. "Lillian, I'll see you out there."

"Okay. I'll see you out there," she repeats with a glowing smile and a twinkle in her eyes.

Before I close the door, Ruth opens the box and shows Lillian what's inside.

Lillian draws in a quick breath and covers her heart with her hand. "Oh, Ruth, it's beautiful."

"It's your 'something old.' It's been passed down from generation to generation," Ruth tells her. "Sit and I'll put it in your hair. It should sit right above your veil." They walk over to the vanity and Lillian takes a seat.

Whatever it is, I'm sure it's beautiful and expensive. The Garnetts come from a long line of money. I close the door and head to the foyer.

Johnathon, Robert's younger and only brother, stands by the door leading into the sanctuary with his elbow out. "Ready, Mrs. Pearl?" he asks with the corners of his lips turned up.

I slide my arm through his and take a deep breath. "As I'll ever be," I say as I take a step into the enormous sanctuary and freeze.

Johnathon bends to my height. "You okay, Mrs. Pearl?"

All the mahogany pews are filled with people that I don't know. People are even standing along the side and back. "Yes, it's…just a bit overwhelming."

"Yes, it can be. You'll sit in the front," he says and we walk down the long aisle to the front of the church.

When we reach the first set of pews, I take my seat beside a woman I've never met.

"I hope you don't mind, we're a bit crowded," he whispers, leaning down at my side. "We had to fill in the seats."

"Of course. No, I don't mind at all," I say, confused. I'm just glad I don't have to stand.

He awards me a smile before he straightens and leaves, returning to the back.

I glance down at my hand twiddling my ring, and my head jerks up when a glint of light catches my eye. Sunlight shines through the stained-glass windows, making tiny little rainbows dance on the walls.

Beautiful, colorful flowers covering the stage remind me of the field John, William, and I picked flowers in. I miss that field. *Is it still there?* It'd be a shame if they destroyed it by building houses on top of it.

Robert and the preacher walk in from a side door and step up on the stage. Robert is a handsome man. He reminds me of my Pierce, in a way. They're both tall with short brown hair and strong facial features—just about flawless.

I miss Pierce. Every day that passes is another day closer to when I'll get to see him again, and the thought fills me with hope. I'm looking forward to that day. But for now, I need to stay here for Lillian.

The music plays and all the bridesmaids and groomsmen walk elbow-in-hand down the aisle, the same way Johnathon brought me in. He's now walking with one of the bridesmaids.

When the last couple steps up on the stage, the music changes to a different song and everyone jumps out of their seats, catching me by surprise. I slowly and awkwardly rise to my feet, since I guess it's customary to stand when the bride comes down the aisle. I didn't know.

When I see Lillian, and she sees me, we smile at each other. The tears in her eyes are happy ones, I assume. I'm so glad she's happy, and I'm thankful I'm here to share this moment with her.

When she passes me, I see the gift Ruth gave her. It's a big diamond hair comb—in the shape of a cursive X. My breath hitches, and I cover my mouth with my hand. The lady beside me looks at me with a creased forehead.

"She's so beautiful," I whisper, covering my discomfort.

"Yes, she is," she whispers back.

It couldn't have anything to do with Hazel. Could it? It's been twenty-three years since I saw the last death marked with an X. It's just a coincidence, I convince myself. This is a *joyful* event.

I sit when everyone else does and try to listen to the ceremony, but my attention keeps wandering back to the X staring at me from the back of Lillian's head. I shake my head and throw away the appalling thought.

It's just a coincidence.

XXX

"Sir, how much further?" I ask the young driver.

"My name is Jimmy, ma'am," he says, and I can see his warm grin from the rear view mirror. "It's not much further."

"It was nice of Lillian to rent this car for me. Is this your car?"

"No, ma'am. It's the company's, I just drive it."

"Oh. Well, the seats are so comfortable." I rub my hand over the plush leather. "I sure hope I don't fall asleep back here."

He chuckles. "You wouldn't be the first, ma'am. Relax and enjoy the ride. And if you need anything, let me know."

"Okay, Jimmy." I sit back and look out the window at the buildings and homes passing us by.

The sun falls behind the trees and my eyes get heavier, but when we pass through an iron gate with a brick fence attached on each side and a globe brightly lit on top of each column, I sit up and roll down the window. We make our way up the circled driveway, and I hear the gurgling of water from the giant stone fountain in the center. My jaw drops, and I stretch my head out the window when the car stops in front of a colossal, three-story pale golden brick Georgian mansion. A large double door and eight black rocking chairs are sheltered on the wide porch, which is supported by four enormous columns. Two identical glass rooms are brilliantly lit and stretched out on each side of the porch.

The door opens, and I step out into the warm night air. "This is…wow," I say, still unable to close my mouth.

"Yes, ma'am," Jimmy says with a smile before he shuts the door behind me. "Would you like me to walk you up?" He points to the double doors at the top of the stairs.

I shake my head. "No, I got it."

"I'll be right out here when you're ready to go. Have a lovely evening, Mrs. Pearl," he says with a tip of his chauffeur hat.

"Thank you." I cautiously hold the iron railing as I step up the stairs, still gazing around in awe. As soon as I walk inside, past the foyer and into a grand ballroom, I stop. Soft music plays in the background, and the whole room is decorated with round tables with white and peach tablecloths. A large vase of a dozen or more white roses sits in the middle of every table, and big peach bows are tied to the back of each white cloth-covered chair. A big long table decorated in the same fashion is on a raised platform in the front of the room.

Large columns on the sides of the room are decorated with wraparound white lights like Christmas trees. I lift my chin and see hundreds of frozen rain drops hanging from the ceiling. I feel like I need an umbrella to stand underneath the gigantic chandelier.

The biggest cake I've ever seen is on its own round table in the corner. By the looks of the throng of people here, it will all be eaten. It has seven round tiers with peach flowers draped all around from the top to the bottom like a vine. I guess the glass bride and groom sitting on the top is supposed to resemble Lillian and Robert, but it doesn't. Nevertheless, the cake is magnificent, and I'm sure it tastes just as good.

Two men in white dress shirts and black bow ties behind a counter are busy making cocktails. People surrounding the bar are laughing and chatting away as they sip their drinks. I've never had an alcoholic drink in my life, and I won't start now, even if this is a celebration. I'm too old for that. I shake my head. The last thing Lillian needs is for her drunken old grandmother to humiliate—

"Can I help you find your seat?" a young man in a black-and-white uniform asks from beside me, making me jump. "I'm sorry. I didn't mean to startle you."

"It's all right," I say with a slight chuckle. "And yes, you sure can. I'll never find it by myself."

"What's your name, ma'am?"

"Oh, I'm Pearl Hayes, grandmother of the bride."

He points an outstretched hand to the front, near the stage. "You'll sit with the rest of the family near the wedding party." He escorts me to one of the round tables and scans the place cards. "Here you are." He pulls back a chair.

"Thank you," I say and take my seat, scooting the chair back to the table with my feet.

"Can I get you something to drink while you wait for the bride and groom? A cocktail, maybe?" he asks with a raised brow and clasped hands.

"Do you have sweet tea?"

"Why of course. We are the birthplace of sweet tea, after all," he says with a smile. "It would be a downright sin not to have it. I'll be right back." He motions to another waiter holding a tray with a wave and walks away.

The other boy walks over and bends at the waist, showing me the top of the large silver tray covered in an assortment of appetizers. "Hors d'oeuvres?"

"They all look tempting," I mumble while I take a mushroom and smile up at him.

He doesn't move.

I quickly take a meatball. "Thank you," I say as the other waiter brings my tea. "Thank you," I repeat to them both before they nod and walk away.

I'm sipping my tea when everyone jumps to their feet and claps, startling me. "Oh, gosh," I say, nearly dropping my tea, but I'm able to set it on the table without spilling a drop. I sigh and shake my head.

Lillian and Robert walk hand in hand through the door. Robert has a big smile on his face, showing his perfect white teeth while he looks around and waves. Lillian is smiling, too, but her smile is strained and her eyes are tense.

They go straight to the long table on the stage followed by the rest of the wedding party. Waiters flood the room, setting plates in front of the guests. I'm not sure where they were all hiding before, but there are a lot of them.

After I've taken the last bite of my lamb chops, roasted potatoes, and asparagus, someone takes my plate away and refills my glass of tea.

When The Duprees' "You Belong to Me" starts playing, the small chatter around the room silences and everyone turns their attention to the center of the room. Lillian and Robert stroll hand in hand to the dance floor. I turn my chair, facing the dance floor, and place my hands in my lap as I gaze at the duo dancing in sync.

Once the song ends, everyone in the room claps. Robert's father, Richard, walks up behind Robert and taps him on the shoulder. Robert turns, places his new bride's hand in his father's, and scans the room until his eyes land on mine.

He saunters over to me with a bright smile, bends at the waist with one hand behind his back, and reaches for my hand with the other. "May I?"

I look at his outstretched hand, and I feel my brow crease. With my hands still in my lap, I slowly lift my eyes to meet his. "May you what?"

His smile drops, and he looks momentarily confused before plastering on the same smile again. "May I have this dance?"

My hand flies to my chest, and I shake my head with a slight tremor. "I don't think so," I say with a soft laugh. "Can't you find someone else to dance with? How about your mother, can't you dance with her?" I rush out.

"I will soon, but it's customary for the groom to dance with his mother-in-law for the second dance." He looks at Lillian and his father standing there…waiting, staring at us. "Just like it's customary for your daughter to dance with my dad," he says, without withdrawing his hand or relinquishing his smile.

My heart flutters, and my eyes sweep the room. Eyes, too many for me to count, stare at me. *Why didn't Lillian warn me about this?*

I purse my lips when I see Robert's blank expression. His smile is now absent. "I can't dance. In fact, I've never danced a day in my life. Besides, I'm not her mother. I'm her grandmother."

"I know, but you raised her like she was your daughter." He glances around quickly, and then he looks back at me. "Please don't leave me standing here. Everyone is waiting," he says, his bottom lip pokes out ever so slightly.

I roll my eyes, place my hand in his, and stand. "Oh, all right."

His smile is back, this time more wicked, as he leads me to the dance floor. I see Lillian with one too. If I can put a smile on her face, then my humiliation is worth it.

"I've never done this before," I tell him again and put my free hand on his shoulder while he puts his around my back.

The music starts playing Kathy Young and The Innocents' "A Thousand Stars," and he takes a step and sways. "It's okay, just follow my lead."

I move with him, doing my best to keep up with him without stepping on his toes, but I feel like a waddling penguin. "You'll take good care of my baby, right?"

He slowly turns me fully around before we sway again. "Of course." He peeks at his wife, then back at me. "I love Lillian with all my heart. I'll never hurt her. I'd lay down my life before I let anything happen to her. I'll do everything I can to make sure each and every day we have together on this earth is the happiest. I promise."

I nod. "I believe you."

"She has your eyes."

"She has her mother's eyes." My eyes fall to his black dress shoes moving with the music as I try hiding my sadness from him. "She's beautiful, just like her mother was."

"I wish I could've met her."

I look back into his knowing eyes. "Me too," I say softly, wishing Angela were here to see her daughter get married.

We dance to the rest of the song in silence. When the song finishes, he takes me back to my seat.

"Thank you for the dance." He kisses my hand.

"You're welcome."

"I think you lied—you're a great dancer to have never done it before."

"I didn't lie. You're a good teacher."

He chuckles. "Enjoy the rest of your night, Pearl." He bows before turning and strolling over to his mother and taking her to the dance floor.

I let out a deep breath and notice Lillian walking toward me, but every time she takes a step, another person stops her. So, I sip my tea and wait.

When she finally reaches me, she takes the empty seat next to me and exhales. "Are you having a good time?"

I yawn. "I am, but I'm getting tired. It's time for me to go home."

She frowns. "Are you feeling all right?"

"Yes, of course. I'm old, dear, remember?" I joke, but I'm also being honest.

"You're not old. Stop saying that." She grabs my hand and squeezes.

I look at her sullen eyes, hard. "Is everything all right?"

She looks at Robert, who has finished dancing with his mother and is handing her off to Richard. "Yes," she says in an unconvincing tone. She doesn't look at me as she quickly blinks, trying to hide her tears, but I notice.

"Lillian?" I press, not convinced.

She turns to me when Robert comes up behind her and puts his hand on her shoulder. He smiles down at his wife when she touches his hand with hers, but she doesn't look at him. "I'm drained." She sighs. "It's been a long, busy day."

"Yes, it *has* been a long day." I glance at my watch. "It's getting late, and I'm going to go." I stand and kiss her on the cheek.

"You're not leaving yet, are you, Pearl? Don't you want to stay and have some cake?" Robert asks.

"No, I'm tired. That dance wore me out," I tease and kiss his cheek.

Lillian stands beside Robert. "I love you, Mom."

"I love you too, Lillian." I look at Robert. "Take care of my girl."

He wraps her in his arms and smiles. "I will, I promise," he says when I stroll away.

Jimmy is out front talking to the other drivers when I get outside. When he sees me, he hurries to the car and opens the back door.

"Leaving so soon, Mrs. Pearl?" he asks with a hint of confusion.

I get inside and sink into the plush leather, feeling instant relief on my aching body. "Yes, I'm tired. Take me home, please."

"Yes, ma'am." He tips his hat at me and closes the door.

Chapter 41

March 9, 1966

I smile at the sleeping baby in my arms and stroke her thick brown hair. "She's beautiful, Lillian. She looks like you did when you were a baby."

"That hurt. I will never do that again, so enjoy her," Lillian jokes but doesn't laugh.

Well, I think she's joking. She doesn't know the meaning of the word pain. The little pain right before they gave her some miracle drug, making her numb, doesn't count. She couldn't even push Meredith out on her own. I gently caress the side of Meredith's flat head. The doctor said it will pop out, and I'm sure it will. I hope it will.

"You don't mean that. I've been there, and I can assure you, you will want other children. Meredith is going to need brothers and sisters to play with, to bond with. There's no bond like a sibling's bond. I remember how close my boys were."

She huffs and crosses her arms over her chest. "No, I'm serious. That hurt like nothing I've ever had to endure in my life. She is it for me. I don't want any more children if they have to come out like that."

The door opens and Robert walks in as she says those words. He leans down and kisses her on the lips before taking a seat next to the bed and crossing one leg over the other. "Now, come on, Lil, it wasn't so bad. You didn't feel a thing once they gave you the Demerol," he says while he rolls up the sleeves on his dress shirt and leans back in the chair. "You'll forget all about the pain, and next year we'll have our boy." His face lights up like fireworks on the Fourth of July.

"I don't think so." She jabs her finger at him. "If you want another, then you go through nine months of sickness and getting so fat your ankles swell and you have to wobble. Then YOU"—jab— "go through fifteen hours of labor before pushing a watermelon out of your—"

"Lillian! Do not finish that sentence," I say a little too loud, and Meredith wakes with a screech. "Oh no, I'm sorry, little one." I rock her, but she screams louder. "*Shh*, it's okay. Nana didn't mean to wake you."

Robert stands. "She's probably hungry. I'll go get a bottle," he says and hurries out the door.

I rise, bouncing Meredith and patting her bottom. "*Shh*. I didn't mean to scare you, Meredith." She's still crying, so I hand her to Lillian. "I'm sorry, Lillian. I shouldn't have raised my voice. I know better."

"It's okay. Babies cry." She gives me a pathetic smile, and I can see the tired bags under her eyes. "She's probably hungry. It was time for her to wake up anyway, so she can eat," she says and looks at Meredith rooting for her nipple.

I put my hand on her shoulder. "You don't wake a sleeping baby to feed. She'll let you know when she's hungry."

"Robert said we need to keep her on a schedule." She rolls her eyes. "You know how strict he can be for schedules."

"Well, Robert isn't a mother. Mothers know what's best for their child. Is he the one who'll be looking out for Meredith?"

A frown develops on her tired face and she sighs. "No, he'll be back at work next week working eighty hours."

"Are you all right?"

She nods and looks at Meredith, who is sucking on her finger, trying to get milk. She gave up on getting milk from its rightful source. Lillian isn't planning on breastfeeding like I had. I breastfed all my natural children until they could take regular milk. But Lillian was formula fed since Angela would never let Lillian anywhere near her. She hated being around Lillian, so having her latch onto her breast was out of the question.

I look at her. "Is everything all right with you and Robert?"

She nods again without taking her eyes off her baby. But I see her glistening eyes, and they tell the truth. Eyes always tell the truth, even if you beg them not to.

"Lillian, you can talk to me. You know that, right? Is it his long hours working?"

She blows out a deep breath. "Everything is fine. Robert is a great husband, he truly is. I'm just…tired, I guess."

The door swings open and Robert walks through, making Meredith wail. "I got the bottle." He holds the warm bottle to me. "You want to feed her, Pearl?"

"No, no, I can't. I need to leave."

"Okay." He grabs Meredith from Lillian and takes her over to the chair and sits, cradling her in his arm. When he gives her the bottle, she immediately clamps onto the nipple and sucks furiously. "See, she was hungry." He beams at his daughter.

"Why do you need to leave so soon? It seems like you just got here." Lillian asks when I grab my purse and shove it under my armpit.

"I need to make an appointment." I kiss Lillian's forehead, and then I kiss Robert and a content Meredith both on the cheek. "She's beautiful, Robert. You take care of our girls."

"I will." He smiles at me with the biggest smile I've ever seen on his face.

"What kind of appointment?" Lillian asks behind me.

"Oh, it's nothing, just routine. I'll see you later." I hurry out the door before she can ask any more questions. When she needs to know, I'll tell her about my cancer, but not before. No need for her to lose any more sleep than she already will with her newborn daughter.

Chapter 42

March 31, 1966

I'm having a double mastectomy today, like my doctor recommended. I don't need my breasts anyway; they just get in the way. Gravity took hold of them a long time ago and never gave them back.

I dreaded telling Lillian; I chickened out many times because I knew she would worry. Everyone believes cancer is a death sentence, which may be the case, but I'm not scared. I'm in God's hands. If he feels it's my time to go, then it's my time to go. No need to argue, because there's nothing I can do to change it.

When I did tell Lillian about my cancer, she cried for what seemed like hours. I'm glad I waited until the last minute to tell her about my operation. It gave her a little more time to get used to being a new mom. She was mad at me, but she got over it fairly quickly. Her anger turned into concern and then worry. I'm not sure if it's better to have her angry at me or worried about me. Both break my heart.

"How are you doing?" Lillian asks, breaking me out of my thoughts.

I look up at her. "I'm good."

"Are you nervous?"

"No, what happens will happen," I say truthfully. "If I don't wake up, I've lived a full life, so don't you go worrying about me. You just take care of that precious baby of yours." I have lived a full life—I meant that—and if it weren't for Lillian and Meredith, I wouldn't want to wake from this surgery. If it weren't for them, I wouldn't be here right now. I'd beg the cancer to take me.

"Don't talk like that. Everything will be fine. You'll be bouncing Meredith on your knee in no time," she says and smiles at me.

I lift my head from the pillow, and my eyes dart around the sterile room, looking for any signs of Hazel lingering around. No—no X's as far as I can tell. The last X I saw was in Lillian's hair. That was two years ago and nothing has happened yet. Maybe I will wake after all.

"I'll be here when you come out of surgery." Lillian squeezes my hand. "I love you."

"I love you too, sweetheart. You have always been such a good girl. I'm proud of you, and you will be an excellent mother."

Her eyes turn glassy. "You talk like you'll never see me again."

My eyes dart around the room once more before landing on Lillian again. "I'll wake up, I promise." I give her a big smile, which I get back in return.

"Okay, are you ready, Pearl?" the anesthesiologist asks.

"Ready as I'll ever be," I tell him, but I keep my eyes on my beautiful Lillian as she squeezes my hand again.

"Count backward from 100 for me," he says and puts a shot into my IV.

"100, 99, 98…97…96…" My eyes flutter. "95…" I look at Lillian as tears run down her cheeks before closing my eyes.

XXX

My nose twitches at the smell of disinfectant. *Am I in Angela's room at the sanatorium?* When I hear the hum of the fluorescent lighting, I open my eyes and squint at the bright light. I sigh internally. No—Angela's gone.

I sit up and wince at the pain from my stitches.

"It's okay, don't sit up. Just lie there and relax," Lillian says, placing a hand on my shoulder.

I lie back and glance at the darkness through the single window in the room. "What are you still doing here?"

"I wanted to make sure you were okay before I left. But I can stay with you tonight if you want me to."

"No, no. You should go home to your family."

"They're fine. Robert came in a few hours ago, after he got off work, and checked on you. Then he went and picked up Meredith from his parent's. She's probably sleeping right now anyway."

"A baby needs her mother. You go home to her and your husband. They both need you. I'll be fine. You can come back in the morning." Another shot of pain runs under my breasts, or where my breasts should be, and I grimace.

"I'll go get the nurse to give you some pain medicine. It'll help you sleep."

"Then will you go?" I say through clenched teeth.

"Yes, then I'll go," she says as she turns and walks out the door.

I close my eyes and breathe through the pain. It's not the worst pain I've ever had, but I couldn't sleep with it, that's for sure.

Lillian comes back through the door, followed by a petite blonde in a white uniform.

"This will help with the pain," the nurse says as she sticks a shot in my IV. "You should feel some relief soon."

She's right—I'm better almost immediately. The pain dwindles, my head gets foggy, and a smile soars across my face.

"That's good. Thank you, Rebecca," Lillian says to the nurse who takes her cue and leaves.

I lift my head and watch the door close behind her.

"How are you feeling now?" Lillian gently takes my hand and holds it.

I look at her as she becomes blurry, and I drop my head back on the pillow.

"Good, gweatt, nefer befferr," I slur. My eyes feel as if someone is filling a bag of bricks, one by one, on my eyelids. I try to blink, but it's getting harder and harder to open my eyes. "Go," I tell her, trying to lift my hand to motion her out, but failing.

"Okay, I will." She giggles. "I'll come back in the morning."

I feel a delicate kiss on my cheek before I fall into the best sleep I've had in years.

Chapter 43

April 4, 1969

A pile of mint-colored squares and a stack of small, thin paper books are scattered across the kitchen table. I have enough to fill at least three pages and half of the blocks on another. I slide the Greenbax catalog closer to me and rifle through the pages until I land on page twenty-four and press down the center to flatten it out. But I'm still nowhere close to getting the new electric mixer I want. I gaze at the opened catalog and run my finger over the ad. "Your personal kitchen helper. Nine speeds. Fast, perfect, uniform mixing," I read to myself with a giddy smile.

I slide the rubber band off the books, pulling it over my wrist for safe keeping, and open a half-filled saver book, spreading it out on the table. I pick up one of the stamps and stick my tongue out when I hear the front door open.

"Mom, you here?" Lillian calls out.

"Of course I am, where else would I be?" Since I no longer work, I have nowhere I need to be. Lillian doesn't like for me to walk much anymore. Not since I broke my hip last year trying to change a light bulb. After that, she's begged me to stop walking all over town. I don't want her to worry, so I stay around the house I bought forty years ago, tending to my rose bushes and small garden I have in the backyard. Lillian keeps asking me to move in with them, but I always refuse. I'm content here.

"I'm putting in my Greenbax stamps." I drop the dry stamp back on top of the mound and stand. "Did you bring me any?" I glimpse at my watch. "Is it Saturday? Are we going to Piggly Wiggly?" I ask, passing her and walking into the living room.

She follows me. "No, ma'am," she says with annoyance in her voice.

"Well, why aren't you at work? It's not shopping day." I plop down in my dark green recliner Lillian bought me for my birthday last year, brace my hands on the arms, and lean back, making the footrest fly up—and then I notice her empty hands. "You didn't bring me any stamps? I need more. I really need that new mixer." I flex my sore, swollen hands with difficulty. "You know I can't use the hand one anymore because of my arthritis. It has two bowls and nine speeds. I can even choose the color, and I want the baby blue one."

She shakes her head and sits on the sofa. "No, sorry, I didn't. I took the day off," she says while she twiddles her purse strap.

"What's the matter? Where's Meredith?" I sit up and touch my wedding ring, which is now attached to a chain around my neck. I can't wear it anymore. My hands hurt from arthritis, and my knuckles are swollen. Two years ago, the ring cut off my circulation and my finger went numb and turned purple. I'm not sure how long it was like that; I didn't want to take it off. I never wanted to take it off, because Pierce gave it to me—it's mine. Lillian rushed me to the emergency room and had it cut off. I was fighting mad and furious at her, but she fixed it. She took it to the jeweler, got it soldered, and bought me a gold necklace to put it on. I haven't taken it off since, and I never will. I'll die with it on.

"She's fine, Mom, don't worry about her. Ruth has her tonight because I wanted some alone time with Robert." She's studying her own wedding rings. The big ones covered in diamonds on her little finger.

"Oh, thank God. I thought something was wrong. I'm glad everything's okay." I let out a deep breath, lean back, and grab the multi-colored crochet blanket I'm working on from the side table. "I'm hoping to have this finished by Christmas for Meredith. I can't work on it much with my hands, but if I can do a little every day, it'll get done." I pick up the long needle and start a loop. "It's good you two will spend some alone time together. It's good for the marriage for a husband and wife to—" I look up from the blanket and notice her disheartened expression, so I place my work back on the side table. "What's wrong, Lillian?"

She looks at me with tears in her eyes. "Everything is *not* okay. It hasn't been okay for a long time. I'm leaving Robert, and I'm telling him tonight when he gets home. I don't want Meredith to be there when I tell him I want a divorce."

I sit up again, pushing the footrest back in place. "Oh, Lillian, no. Maybe you can work things out! What about Meredith?"

She shakes her head. "We've been drifting apart for a long time, since the wedding, to tell you the truth. I was so happy that day. I really was." She grabs a tissue from the flowered cardboard box on the coffee table and wipes her tears. "I thought it was what I wanted, but right after I said 'I do'"—she pauses and looks away, like she's remembering—"no, it was when his mother gave me that diamond comb. It didn't feel right anymore, but it was too late by then. I tried to make it work, I honestly did. I believed having a baby would fix things, but it didn't. I've been hanging on by a tiny thread." She takes her rings off and drops them into her purse. "The spark is gone. It's been gone since our wedding day. I don't blame Robert. He's a great husband and a great father to Meredith." She sighs. "It's me. I take full blame in this."

"I remember the comb," I mumble. Did Hazel have anything to do with her failed marriage? I grind my teeth. I won't let her win this one without a fight. "What about Robert and Meredith? She loves her father, and he adores her. He's a good father."

"He *is* a good father, I'm not disputing that. I'll ask for joint custody. I wouldn't dream about keeping them apart from one another." Her lips turn up in a tense smile. "Everything will work out for the best, you'll see."

"Lillian, don't do anything rash. Have you talked to Robert? Maybe you both can cut back on your hours at work to get to know each other again. All marriages have problems. You can work through this. There has to be—"

"I've been having an affair." She closes her eyes and drops her head.

My hand covers my mouth when I suck in a lungful of air, trapping it to survive this conversation. "Oh no, Lillian, you didn't!" I exhale, shaking my head. "You didn't."

She looks up with glazed-over, guilty eyes and nods. "He's a doctor on my shift at the hospital. It's been over a year. We didn't mean for it to happen, it just did."

I'm still shaking my head in disbelief. "I don't like this, Lillian. Not one bit."

She covers her face with her hands, shamefully sobbing into them. "I'm sorry."

I narrow my eyes and stare at her trembling head. This is such a disgrace.

After a few minutes, she gets herself under control, wipes her eyes, and looks at me with sad baby blues that melt my heart every time. I can never stay angry at her for long. "I'm hoping Meredith and I can stay here for a few weeks until I can find an apartment."

I slide to the edge of the chair and push myself up. I'm at her side in an instant, putting my arm over her shoulder and pulling her into a hug. She falls into my embrace like she did when she was a little girl, and I pat her back. "Of course, dear. You both are welcome to stay here as long as you need. I could use the company."

"Thank you." She rises, leaving my embrace, and grabs her purse, hooking the strap over her shoulder. "I need to go."

"All right. If you need to." I get up and follow her to the door, my eyes focusing on the floor. Her dark-brown penny loafers glide across the hardwood, stop when they reach the door, and turn around, displaying two round Abraham Lincolns. I look up into her eyes, noticing the newfound energy.

"I have a couple errands to run, then I'll go home and pack some things for me and Meredith before Robert gets home. He won't be happy, and I want to have everything in the car ready to go when I tell him." She pulls a necklace out from under her shirt, rubbing it between two fingers while it dangles around her throat.

I've never noticed it before, so I reach for it.

She lifts her chin and looks at the ceiling. "Xavier gave it to me this morning. Do you like it?"

When I touch the X-shaped diamond pendant, it burns, and the blood rushes from my head. I quickly let go, dropping it back on her chest. I swallow with a gulp. "I need to tell you something," I say softly as I stare blankly at the X.

"It's his initial," she says, ignoring me, and lowers her face to mine. "He gave it to me when he begged me to leave Robert. He's leaving his wife today, too. I'm so tired of sneaking around," she says in an exasperated tone.

My mouth drops open. "He's married, too?" I ask, my voice rising with each syllable. *Where did my sweet Lillian go?*

She nods and clasps her hands in front of her mouth. "I know he's going to ask me to marry him as soon as our divorces are final," she says as she lifts her shoulders and smiles.

I glance back at the X on her chest and grab her forearm. "Lillian, come sit down. I need to tell you something."

She unhooks herself from my grip. "Not now. I've got to get home and pack. If you want to tell me what a big mistake I'm making"—she rolls her eyes—"it will have to wait until later."

"No, it's not that. Well, it is, but I need to talk to you about something else…about my past."

She turns around and raises her hand, palm toward my face, while the other one opens the door. "I gotta run, Mom. We'll talk later. See you tonight," she says and hustles to her car.

I slowly raise my palm and give it a trivial shake. "I love you, Lillian."

She must not hear me because she gets in without looking at me and drives off.

I close my eyes and rub my aching temples. *This just isn't right.*

Chapter 44

April 5, 1969

Meredith is sitting at the kitchen table, hunched over, and her little arm is in constant motion. I tiptoe behind her and look over her shoulder. A black train comes to life when she fills inside the lines with a crayon.

She lays the black crayon on the table and exchanges it for a red, but doesn't look up when I sit beside her.

"What are you coloring?" I ask.

She jumps.

I grin. "I didn't mean to scare you, sweetheart."

She slings her long, curly brown hair over her shoulder. "You didn't scare me," she says adamantly. "It's a train."

I lean in closer to the picture and squint. A wooden bridge overlooks a field of colorful flowers that look almost real is drawn in behind the train, along with a railroad crossing sign in the shape of an X that doesn't look like it was there before. A chill runs through me, but I don't know why. "Those are beautiful. Did you draw those?" I ask as I point to the additions. I can't believe a three-year-old can draw so skillfully.

"Yes, ma'am." She focuses on the paper again and frantically colors the red caboose like her life depends on it. "I'm going to be an artist one day, just like William," she says without lifting the crayon off the paper or taking her eyes away from it.

"Who's William?" I ask. "Is he a boy from daycare or church?"

Her hand freezes, drops the crayon, and she looks at me with a creased forehead while reaching into her pocket. "You don't know who William is?" She brings her fist out of her pocket and puts it on her leg, like she's hiding something.

"No," I say and point to her fist. "What do you have there?"

She leans toward me and whispers, "It's a secret."

"Meredith, you know we don't keep secrets. What do you have in your hand?" I turn her hand over.

She looks at me with sad eyes. "William gave it to me. He told me to keep it safe until I see him again." She slowly opens her hand and in the center of her palm is a red-white-and-blue marble.

I tilt my head to the side. Where have I seen that marble before?

Knock. Knock. Knock.

I turn my head to the front door and stand. "I'll be right back. You stay here and finish your coloring," I tell her and walk away.

When I open the door, two young boys are standing on the porch with their hands in the pockets of their coveralls.

"Can Lillian come out to play?" The taller brown-haired, brown-eyed boy asks.

"You mean Meredith? She's at the table coloring." I point behind me. "I'll go get her."

I turn around and walk back into the kitchen, but she isn't there. The marble is lying on the picture of the train, abandoned. "Meredith, where did you go?"

Laughter comes from the backyard, so I walk to the door and peek through the screen. The two young boys, along with a smaller boy, are out there with Meredith, sitting Indian style on the ground in a circle beside the big oak tree.

I step outside and walk closer to the children.

Marbles are scattered in the circle drawn in the dirt between them. An empty black bag is sitting off to the side next to the boy who shoots a yellow marble into the circle.

"You forgot the pretty marble inside." I point at the back door. "Would you like me to get it for you, Meredith?"

I turn around and take a step.

"She's not Meredith, she's Lillian, silly," one of the boys says.

I stop and turn back around. "What?"

They all giggle without looking up from their game.

Meredith shoots a blue ball into the center, knocking the yellow one out. "I'm Lillian, and this is John, William, and Jacob," she says as she grabs the yellow marble.

The boys look at me with big brown eyes and a smile looking all too familiar.

I shake my head. "No, you're Meredith. Boys, I don't know who you are, but I think it's best if you leave now. It's getting late."

I glance up at the darkening sky that was as blue as the ocean a few minutes ago. Now it's almost black as a starless night. I look back at the kids, but they've disappeared.

"Meredith?"

"She's LILLIAN!" a deep, threatening voice yells from behind me.

I whip around and see someone dressed in all black standing behind my sweet girl and holding a gun to the side of her head. But she's no longer the little girl who was here a few minutes ago—she's a grown woman.

"Lillian?"

"I love you, Mom," she says calmly before a loud bang slices through the quiet night.

Knock. Knock. Knock.

My eyes shoot open and my breathing is erratic. "Lillian," I say with a pant as I cover my chest with my hand. "No." I shake my head, and my eyes land on a little animated space man talking to his space dog inside the television.

Knock. Knock. Knock.

My head turns toward the door then at my watch. *It's eight in the morning.* I get out my chair as fast as my old body can and turn the knob on the console, killing the little space family.

When I open the door, a man wearing a loose, dark blue uniform and a shiny gold badge on his chest is standing on my front porch, not surprising me.

"Um, Mrs. Pearl Hayes?" he asks, his voice soft and unsure.

I stare at him for a moment before I realize he has asked me a question. My eyes land on his name tag, which reads *JACKSON*. "Yes, that's me, Officer Jackson."

He takes off his peaked cap and fiddles with it in his hand. "May I come inside?"

I slowly open the door wider and step aside, knowing he's about to tear my world apart. "Come in. Have a seat." I wave to the kitchen table after he enters, and I shut the door behind him. "Would you like some coffee?" I ask as I shuffle into the kitchen and turn on the kettle.

He takes a seat. "No, ma'am."

I shovel a scoop of instant coffee grounds into my cup with a trembling hand. "I need my coffee, if you don't mind. I just woke up." My eyes shut on a long blink. "And I believe I'll need it," I whisper to myself before looking in his direction.

He glances at his watch. "No, I understand. It's pretty early. Please, take your time." He places his hat on the table and takes out a notepad from his shirt pocket. He flips through it and stops on a page, studying it.

When I get my coffee ready, I join him at the table, relieved he gave me some time before breaking what's left of my heart. They never come with good news, always the bad, and the thought fills my tired brain with a high-pitched whine of terror that pierces through the haze. I take a sip of my coffee absently, dreading what the man will tell me, but feeling oddly numb at this point. Once I saw Lillian's necklace, at some level, I knew. "Tell me," I whisper, my voice hoarse and scratchy with emotion.

He takes a deep breath. "I hate to come here and give you bad news. I'm here about your granddaughter Lillian Garnett."

I look at the quiet hallway with heavy eyes. "What happened?"

He taps his finger on the table, hesitating. "You were her only living relative besides her daughter"—he looks at his notepad—"Meredith," he says, before putting his notepad back in his shirt pocket and buttoning down the flap.

I close my eyes. "Were?" I swallow hard and my mouth salivates.

"Last night around seven, the neighbors heard gunshots," he says slowly, sounding tired himself. "Lillian's husband, Robert... He shot her before turning the gun on himself. They both died instantly. I'm sorry." He places his hand over mine for a second before retracting it. "His parents told us you were her only relative, besides her daughter."

I nod with my eyes still closed, trapping the tears. "What about Meredith?" My lips quiver. "What...what will happen to her?" I open my eyes and quickly grab a tissue from the table, dabbing it to my wet eyes. Keeping them closed wasn't doing any good, because the tears escaped anyway.

"She's with his parents. They said they will be the ones to raise her. I don't get involved in custody battles." He glances around at my petty house. "If you want to fight for custody, you'll need to go to the courts."

I shake my head. "I'm too old to raise any more children." I look at my wrinkled hands and rub my tender, engorged knuckles. "They're the most logical choice. Richard and Ruth have enough money to give her everything she could need or want, for that matter," I say a little above a whisper.

He stands and grabs his hat off the table. "Again, I'm sorry for your loss."

I struggle getting out the chair and my whole body aches. I feel like I've aged ten years in the last ten minutes. "Thank you," I mumble as I walk him to the door and open it.

He turns to me before he steps out onto the porch. "Take care, Mrs. Hayes." He settles his hat on his head and walks out.

As soon as I shut the door, the floodgates open, and I fall to my knees.

"Lillian," I cry, and I weep into my hands for the first time in years.

Chapter 45

April 8, 1969

I take a sip of my coffee and open the newspaper to the obituaries.

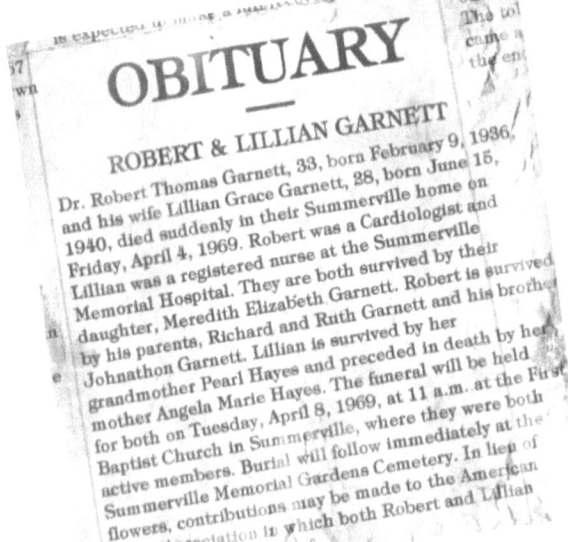

OBITUARY

ROBERT & LILLIAN GARNETT

Dr. Robert Thomas Garnett, 33, born February 9, 1936, and his wife Lillian Grace Garnett, 28, born June 15, 1940, died suddenly in their Summerville home on Friday, April 4, 1969. Robert was a Cardiologist and Lillian was a registered nurse at the Summerville Memorial Hospital. They are both survived by their daughter, Meredith Elizabeth Garnett. Robert is survived by his parents, Richard and Ruth Garnett and his brother Johnathon Garnett. Lillian is survived by her grandmother Pearl Hayes and preceded in death by her mother Angela Marie Hayes. The funeral will be held for both on Tuesday, April 8, 1969, at 11 a.m. at the First Baptist Church in Summerville, where they were both active members. Burial will follow immediately at the Summerville Memorial Gardens Cemetery. In lieu of flowers, contributions may be made to the American Heart Association in which both Robert and Lillian were great supporters of.

I'm sure the Garnetts don't want anyone knowing about what truly happened. The obituary reads as if they were saints, but of course I know better.

I cut out the obituary and place it with Angela's in her bible, and then I walk into my bedroom and pull out the same black dress I wore to Angela's funeral. I haven't worn it since that day, but I'm sure it still fits. My body hasn't changed much except for my lack of breasts.

I slip it on, and it fits—*thank goodness.*

Knock. Knock. Knock.

I hurry down the hallway and open the door to find young Jimmy standing there in a dark suit holding a black chauffeur hat.

"Ready, Mrs. Pearl?" he says with a small sympathetic smile.

I grab my purse from the kitchen counter and hook it over my arm. "As I'll ever be," I mumble and shut the door behind me.

XXX

The stage is covered with large vases and urns filled with flowers of every color. Robert and Lillian's wedding picture sits on an easel between two closed mahogany caskets with a large spray of white roses and greenery on top. It reminds me of when I had to pick out Angela's casket and was shown the most expensive one, which I could not afford. I glimpse at the other side of the church where Meredith sits between Robert's parents in the first pew. Of course, Richard and Ruth don't have that problem.

Behind the podium, the preacher says, "Robert and Lillian had an ideal marriage that we all…"

He must not know the truth. Do Richard and Ruth know about the failed marriage and Lillian's affair? Is Xavier here? I narrow my eyes and look around the church filled with people who were here five years ago to celebrate Robert and Lillian's massive wedding, trying to see anyone who appears at all guilty, but I don't see anyone in particular. Was he at their wedding?

"Amen," the preacher says. A group of men, sixteen in all, gather to the front and grab the casket's brass handles, eight on each. They carry them out while everyone looks on. Sniffles and cries are heard throughout the church. I'm surprised at myself, because I haven't shed a tear yet. At least I haven't today.

Johnathon extends his elbow to escort me out like he did at the wedding. Only this time the corner of his lips are turned down instead of up. "I'll walk you out, Mrs. Pearl."

"Thank you, Johnathon. I'd appreciate it," I say, hooking my arm through his.

We all gather outside and watch the pallbearers slide the caskets into two black hearses and shut the doors closed.

Johnathon takes me to my car and deposits me in the back. He leans his head inside and looks at me with pain in his eyes. "We'll meet you at the cemetery, Mrs. Pearl."

"Oh…okay," I stammer.

He straightens, nods to Jimmy over the roof of the car, and shuts the door.

"You all right, Mrs. Pearl?" Jimmy asks when he shuts the door and looks at me through the rear-view mirror.

I turn to look out the window and reach for the ring attached to my necklace, gingerly tracing it with my finger. "I guess I have to be," I whisper, and I feel the vibration under me as he starts the engine and pulls away.

The ride to the cemetery is long and quiet, but the thoughts about Hazel in my head are so loud, they're tormenting my brain. I shut my eyes and rub my temples, trying to relax, but the ache doesn't ease.

"We're here, Mrs. Pearl," Jimmy says at the opened door, making me jump. He holds out his hand for me.

"Oh, I didn't realize we had stopped." I take his hand as he helps me out of the car. "Thank you, Jimmy."

"My pleasure. I'll wait right here. Take your time."

I give him a weak smile before I toddle alone to the gravesite, where people are already gathered around the two caskets already on their platforms, ready to be lowered. More luxurious bouquets of flowers surround the open graves, but the strong, sweet smell isn't coming from these flowers. I tilt my head back and see the wisteria cascading down in the trees like purple waterfalls. I close my eyes and take a deep breath in, remembering the first ride of many I had with Pierce, my new husband, all those years ago. That day is etched in my brain as if it were yesterday. The smell is the same, but the atmosphere is so different.

The preacher says, "Oh God," bringing my attention back to the now as the caskets descend into the ground, "by whose mercy the faithful departed find rest, bless these graves, and send your holy angel to watch over them…"

Everyone sobs, including me. *My Lillian is gone!* I angrily wipe away the tears with the same hands that have wiped away so many tears throughout the years, more than any one person should.

"Amen," the preacher says and everyone slowly departs as four men shovel dirt into the holes.

I stay where I'm at, watching. I'm silently crying now. Will my tears ever come to a stop? I've cried enough in this lifetime to create a small pond. I'm so tired of crying. I'm so tired of being miserable, of hurting, and being lonely. The emotional pain is getting unbearable. When will this all *end?*

"Nana!" I hear come from behind me.

I quickly swipe my tears away before I turn around and see Meredith running toward me. I lean over and wrap her in a hug. "I wish I could pick you up, honey, but I'm too old." When I straighten, Ruth is behind her with an arrangement of flowers from the church.

"Grandma says I have to live with her now. Mommy and Daddy are in heaven." Her lips jut out in a pout and her eyes gloss over before she looks at the ground. "They're not coming back."

I touch her soft cheek with my palm, wishing I could take away her pain. "I know, sweetheart. I know. But they're in a better place, and they'll always be watching over you. You be a good girl for your grandparents, okay?"

She looks up at me behind long, thick lashes. "Okay, Nana," she mumbles with a big frown casing her face.

Ruth hands me the flowers she was holding. "For you," she says bitterly, and she smiles behind tight lips.

"Thank you, Ruth. Everything was beautiful today. Lillian would've been pleased."

Her eyes fly to the ground, and her jaw twitches. Her eyes slowly find mine again, but this time they have more malice in them. She grabs Meredith's hand and glances back at the awaiting car. "We need to get going. Take care, Pearl. I'll try to bring her by to see you sometime," she rushes out.

I tilt my head slightly and look into Ruth's cold eyes. Does she know about the affair? "I...I'd like that," I stutter. "Please, take good care of Meredith for me," I say, doing my best to be cordial.

"Of course," she says with a hint of cynicism and a lift of a brow.

I have a feeling this will be the last time I see Meredith. My shoulders drop. It tears me up, but a part of me is too tired to fight, too tired to go on. I blink quickly and lean down again, wrapping Meredith in a one-armed hug while I clutch the flowers with my other. I kiss her cheek before releasing her. "Bye, sweetheart."

"Bye, Nana," Meredith says softly before she walks away with her head down.

I watch my only living relative stroll away and get into a black stretch limousine. I stare until I don't see it anymore.

When I turn back around, I'm startled by a tall man wearing a sleek gray suit and a skinny black tie staring at Lillian's grave. His bronzed skin makes him look as though he has been kissed by the sun. His jet-black hair is a little chaotic, obviously from running his hands through it too much, and he looks like he hasn't shaved in days. If this is who I think it is, then I'm not surprised Lillian was attracted to him, but it still doesn't justify their actions.

He turns his intense, bloodshot emerald eyes to me. "You're Pearl, aren't you?"

"Yes," I say, and my lips tighten.

"Lilly told me a lot about you. She loved you very much."

I stare at him, frozen.

He extends his hand. "I'm sorry, I'm Xavier. I worked with Lilly at the hospital."

I glance at his outstretched hand before my eyes slowly find his again.

He retracts his hand, putting it in his pants pocket. "I guess you've heard of me."

"I've heard of you. You were having an affair with my baby girl, and it got her *killed!*" I say, my voice climbing with every word.

The gravediggers, still throwing dirt on the open graves, stop, drop their shovels on the ground, and amble to a nearby shaded tree. All four grab cigarette packs and lighters from their pockets and light up.

"I'm sorry. I didn't want it to happen," he says just above a whisper. "We were both unhappy in our marriages, and we were attracted to each other. We tried not to succumb, but it was inevitable. I was in love with her, and she was with me." He sighs and looks back at Lillian's grave. "I told my wife the same night. We're getting a divorce."

I narrow my eyes and clutch the vase in my hands. "Well, I'm so sorry for your loss," I say bitingly. "You lost your *wife* due to your infidelity, but my Lillian lost her *life* due to hers. Her daughter lost her mother and father." My face burns with raging blood.

He turns to me once again with wet eyes. "I know you're angry. If I could change places with her I would, in a heartbeat. I loved her, and I wanted to marry her. I don't know how I can go on without her." He wipes his face with the sleeve of his jacket and exhales. "I want to think I made her as happy as she made me the short time we were together. We just went about things the wrong way. When she told me she was—"

"I agree with you there," I say through clenched teeth. I'm gripping the vase so tight I'm afraid I'll break the glass, and my blood pressure is rising with every passing second. I can't do this anymore, or I may have a stroke. I close my eyes and take a deep breath through my nose and release it out of my mouth before opening them again. "Xavier, I need to leave before I say something I will regret."

I turn and march away before he can reply—I'm not interested in anything else he has to say.

Jimmy opens the back door when I approach with concern in his eyes. "Are you okay, Mrs. Pearl?"

I drop in the seat and pull my legs inside. "Yes. Just take me home," I grumble. I lean my head back and close my eyes.

"Yes, ma'am," he says and shuts the door.

Chapter 46

June 22, 2001

"I found out later that he committed suicide." I shake my head and lower my eyes. "So many lives ruined by that affair," I say in disgust as I wrinkle my nose and perch my lips.

"I can't believe you lived through such tragedies, Pearl." Mary sniffs and wipes her eyes with a balled-up tissue. When she opens and stretches it, it breaks into a cluster of small holes like Swiss cheese. I'm afraid of what might shoot through those little holes if she blows her nose.

"Did you ever see Meredith again?" Pruny asks.

"Not until last month, apparently. Her grandmother wouldn't be bothered with visits. I called, but they were always too busy." My two fingers rub the soft material of the throw wrapped around my legs, and I frown. "I made this blanket for her and sent it at Christmas time, but the package came back unopened from the post office. *Rejected, Return to Sender,'* it said." I shake my head and sigh. "I didn't bother after that. She was better off without me anyway," I say in a miserable tone, still looking at the blanket. "I was too tired, and a part of me was hoping Hazel would leave her alone if she was away from me."

"What did you do after the funeral?" Big Chin asks.

"Well, nothing. I sat in my recliner and watched TV for fifteen years, depressed. I was lonely and miserable like Hazel said I would be. My next-door neighbor tried to get me out of the house, but eventually gave up when she figured it was no use. Church members delivered groceries, so I didn't starve."

I shrug and look up. "After doing nothing for fifteen long years, I realized Hazel had been winning. But I couldn't let her win. She'd been winning since I crossed her X. So, I decided to *live* until the day I met my beloved Pierce and children again. I got out of my chair and cleaned my house until it shined. Then I craved fried chicken, so I marched down to the Piggly Wiggly and bought a four pack of chicken legs. When I got home, I seasoned and floured the drumsticks and placed them carefully in the pan when I heard, 'Thank You for Being a Friend,' the theme song for *The Golden Girls*. I loved that show," I say with a small smile. "I went into the living room and sat in my recliner and watched nearly all of it when a loud ringing blasted in my ears and smoke filled the room. I jumped up and hurried to the kitchen, filled a glass with water, and threw it on the fire. It not only didn't put it out, it made it worse, much worse. Flames engulfed the kitchen. I had the sense to step out of the kitchen but not enough to leave the house. A neighbor found me watching the intense blaze from the living room. He got me out and waited with me until the fire department and ambulance showed. They took me to the hospital to make sure I wasn't hurt.

"My doctor suggested I move into a retirement community. With my house being unlivable and I having no family to stay with, I had little choice. The fire ruined the kitchen and part of the living room, but I salvaged my most treasured possessions and moved in here, where I've been ever since. I don't even know if my house is still there."

"What's the address?" Moses asks, straightening.

"It was on Cedar Street." I pause, raising my chin and squinting at the white-panel ceiling. "105 South Cedar Street."

"Oh, that's gone, torn down. Strip mall now," he says and leans back in his chair. "Whole street ain't nothin' but shops."

"Oh. I loved that little house." I frown and look at the floor with heavy eyes. "It's a shame," I say absently as haziness floods my mind. Shame? What's a shame? My head is cloudy and I can't think straight, so I rub my temples and shake my head, hoping it will ease, but it doesn't.

"That is some story, Mrs. Pearl," the cafeteria worker—I can't remember her name—says with a hint of sadness in her eyes. She wipes her nose with a black-and-white bandana.

I tilt my head and look at her, confused. "What's wrong, child?" I ask the girl and look around, seeing Mary and many unrecognizable faces with the same sadness in their eyes, staring at me.

Why are they all staring at me? Who are these people?

"The story," she says.

"Story?" I mumble as I scratch my head and look out the back windows. The sinking, fiery tangerine sun peeks through the cracks of the big tree in the center of the courtyard, painting the sky a rustic red. I cover a yawn with my hand. "What time is it?"

Mary stands. "It's almost eight. I'll take you to your room and get you ready for bed before I head home."

"Yes, please. I'm awfully tired."

"Thanks for sharing your story with us." Some old lady who has a big hump on her back says. But I don't know who she's talking to because she's staring at the floor, so I ignore her.

Mary pushes my wheelchair toward the hallway.

"Good night, Pearl," I hear people say in harmony, like they're a church choir.

I hold my hand up and wave but don't look back. I don't know any of those people.

"Mary, what are you doing here so late? You shouldn't work this late," I say when we go under the red *EXIT* sign with the X flickering, on the way out of the cafeteria.

"I couldn't miss your amazing story. I'm so proud of you for remembering all that stuff today. What you lived through was so heartbreaking." She quivers under her breath. "I couldn't do it, that's for sure. You're the strongest person I know."

I'm confused, and it's so frustrating. "What story?"

She stops the wheelchair and squats beside the chair, looking at me in the eye. "The story you just spent all day telling everyone. Don't you remember?"

I shake my head and twist my lips.

She touches my hand before standing and pushing me forward again. "It's okay. It's hard to remember things sometimes. I forget things all the time."

When we enter my room, she flicks on the light, pushes me to the bed, and kicks the brakes. She removes the afghan from my legs and tosses it on the bed before helping me stand on rickety legs.

My hand touches something on the arm of the chair: a string. I tug it and follow it up with my eyes to a blue balloon. "What's this?" I ask as I turn and plop down on the bed and kick off my slippers.

"That's the balloon Sara brought for your birthday."

"Who's Sara?"

"Oh, Mrs. Pearl." She shakes her head and lets out a small strangled breath as she grabs a nightgown out of the dresser and quickly changes my clothes.

She must be tired.

After she helps me with the bedpan and tucks me in for the night, she disappears into the bathroom with the bedpan.

I grab the flannel shirt I like to sleep with and hold it to my nose, sniffing. I search for the sweet scent, but it's not there anymore.

My mind opens once again and Pierce and my children are there. They've always been there, but have been hidden in the darkest corner, unable to surface. My breath hitches, and my mouth turns into a delightful smile. "Pierce!" I snatch up the multi-colored throw, feeling the softness, and press it against my chest along with Pierce's shirt.

Mary appears in the bathroom's doorway, wiping her hands on a towel. "You okay, Mrs. Pearl?" she asks with concern and tosses the towel on the counter.

"Yes…Yes!" I say with excitement in my voice and point to the closet. "Can you grab my suitcase off the top shelf of the closet?"

She ambles to the closet. "Of course," she grunts as she pulls the old black leather suitcase down and places it beside me. When she sees me having trouble with my hands, she sits on the other side of the bed. "Here, let me help," she says and flips open the tarnished brass snaps that had been holding it closed.

"Thank you, Mary."

The lid creaks open, displaying the contents, and my eyes widen like I've uncovered a chest full of treasures. *I have.*

My praying hands flies to my mouth and my eyes mist over. I quickly blink them away and clear my vision. "Oh lord, I haven't looked at these in years."

"You remember them?" she asks.

I nod and with a shaky hand, I remove John's spoon, William's baby blanket, Angela's Dolly, and Lillian's white bonnet that has now turned yellow, and place them on the bed beside me. I pick up a flat square black box and hold it out to Mary. "Can you—"

"Sure," she says and opens the lid, revealing a strand of pearls. "They're beautiful."

I run a finger over the smooth beads. "They still feel the same. I only wore them one time, the time Lillian put them around my neck at her wedding. I never had a reason or occasion to wear them again."

I close the lid and put the box on the bedside table, and then I take out Angela's children's bible and flip through the pages until I locate Angela's and Lillian's obituaries. I carefully pick up the unreadable, faded yellow clippings and stare at them for a moment.

"Oh, Mrs. Pearl, they haven't held up over the years. You can't even read them."

"It's all right. I couldn't read them anyway with my eyes." I gently put them back inside the bible and place it on the black box lying on the table. Then I take off my glasses and put them on top of the bible. I grab the rest of my mementos of my husband and children and hold them close to my heart, releasing a long breath with a smile.

"Mary."

"Yes, Mrs. Pearl?"

"Promise me that, when I go, these all go with me." I squeeze my family's possessions. "I can't stand the thought of my things being thrown out or burned like trash."

She touches my hand. "Mrs. Pearl, don't talk like that."

"Promise me."

She frowns and nods. "Okay, I promise." She looks at the red *8:32* on my clock and slaps both knees. "It's time for me to go. I'll let you get some sleep. You had a long day." She stands, closes the empty suitcase, and puts it back on top of the closet before pulling my curtains closed. "Good night, Mrs. Pearl. I'll see you in the morning." She walks to the door and looks at me one more time and smiles.

I take my teeth out and put them in the bowl next to my bed. "Good night, Mary. Drive safe," I say with a yawn.

I close my eyes before the lights are turned out and the door is shut.

Chapter 47

June 23, 2001

Mary

I rush into The Pinewood Nursing Home and place a bouquet of assorted flowers on the counter. "Good morning, Debra"—I give her a strained smile—"I'm sorry I'm late." I hurry behind the counter, tossing my purse in the cabinet.

"Don't worry about it, it happens," she tells me as she eyes the bouquet and raises her chin to them. "Nice flowers. Who gave them to you?" She smirks.

"I picked them up last night on the way home. They're for Pearl...for her birthday." I turn the vase, smiling, and look at the beautiful flowers proudly. "I figured it would brighten up her room. Her room is so plain. It's sad." I heave a sigh and shake my head. "I should've helped her decorate it a long time ago."

"That's so sweet." Her mouth forms an O and she lifts a finger in the air. "Oh, *Live5News* and *The Post and Courier* both called again this morning."

"I asked her yesterday, but I'm not sure she's up for an interview. How is she this morning?"

"When I checked on her last night, she was sleeping. I haven't heard a peep out of her," she says absentmindedly while she jots down notes in her nightly report. "She's a sweet woman; never complains about anything. I wish they were all like her."

"That was some story yesterday, huh?" Sandra comes up behind me and swipes her badge in the time clock.

"What story?" Debra asks.

"Nice flowers." Sandra leans over the bouquet, closes her eyes, and takes a deep breath in with a smile. She opens her eyes and looks at Debra. "Mrs. Pearl told a story about a witch. It was cool to hear, but if all that stuff really happened, I feel sorry for her. She's been through the ringer, I tell ya."

"I hate I missed it," Debra says.

Sandra pulls out a red-and-white bandana from her back pants pocket and ties it around her head. "Yeah, I stayed late to hear the ending."

I stretch the cord attached to my badge, sliding my badge down the small slit of the time clock and letting it go—it snaps back in place on my shirt pocket. "Any problems last night?"

"No, everything was quiet." Debra grabs her purse out the cabinet and adds, "As usual." Then she clocks out.

The TV sitting on top of the tall cabinet behind the desk is turned to the news station. I glance at it, and she follows my gaze.

"This must be a recap from last night. It aired on the late night news. It's so sad." Debra shakes her head. "People need to watch those warning signals. They should know better than to take the risk and try to cross the tracks while the lights are flashing."

"I had to take a detour last night when I left, so it must've been bad. I didn't see what happened." I nod to the TV. "Turn it up."

Debra grabs the remote from the desk and turns up the volume. We all three gape at a white car, crushed, and turned upside down beside the track where a train is stopped.

"That looks like an expensive car, such a shame," Sandra says, clicking her tongue and standing with legs apart and arms crossed over her chest.

I turn my head toward her and narrow my eyes. *What is wrong with her?*

She looks at me and shrugs. "What?"

I shake my head and turn back to the TV.

"Breaking news," the anchorman says. "We just found out the identity of the ones involved in last night's horrific accident. The granddaughter of the late Richard Garnett of Garnett Furniture, Meredith Garnett Curtis, thirty-five, and her daughter Sara Curtis, eleven, were killed in the accident. No other injuries were reported. Police found drugs at the scene. We will have to wait for the toxicology reports to see if the drugs found were a factor in this tragic accident. Johnathon Garnett, the only living heir to the furniture king, asks for privacy at this time."

A picture of a younger and healthier Meredith and Sara posing on a wooden bridge appear on the TV screen before showing a picture of the accident once again. A railroad crossing sign in the shape of an X is clearly visible in the background.

I gasp and my hand flies to my open mouth.

Sandra's eyes widen and she points to the TV. "Did you see that? Did you see the X?" Her face pales as she turns to me. "It's true."

"What's this about an X? What's going on?" Debra looks back and forth from me to Sandra with a creased brow.

"I need to go tell Pearl," I say in a rush, ignoring Debra. "She'll be devastated."

"I'll fill Debra in—you go." Sandra pushes me into the hall.

"Okay." I leave them and hightail it down the hall to Pearl's room and stop.

Before I enter, I take a deep breath and relax my shoulders. I pump the hand sanitizer from the container beside the door and rub my hands together before I knock.

Tap, tap, tap. "Pearl, are you awake?" I push the door open and peek in, but she doesn't move.

I prop the door open, letting in enough light for me to see, but not enough to hurt her eyes, and then I plod to the window and crack open the darkening curtain, letting in more light. When I turn around, Pearl still doesn't stir, and a sense of dread washes over me. I stare at her while I walk back to the door and flip on the light switch, giving me a better look.

Pearl, with a smile on her face, is still clutching all her family's things in her arms just the way I left her last night. Her face is pale and her lips are blue. I blink away my watery eyes and place two fingers on the inside of her cold, hard wrist, but I don't find a pulse. I knew I wouldn't. I turn my head, wipe my eyes with the back of my hand, and notice the clock on the bedside table, flashing *12:00. Huh? It was working when I put her to bed last night.*

I turn back to her and see her other hand is touching the wedding ring she wears on a thick gold necklace around her neck. The necklace is twisted, so it's crossed over in the shape of an X. I slowly reach for it with a slight tremor, but I pull my hand back before I touch it and shake my head.

"Rest in peace, Pearl," I say out loud as I cover her face with the sheet and walk out the room to call the coroner.

Pearl finally joins the rest of her family in peace. Her blood runs through no other.

Epilogue

June 13, 1919

John Hayes

I giggle while I run around the trees and hear Mama call out to me.

"John!"

I'm not ready for our game to end yet, so I dash behind another tree without answering...and then another. The deeper I go into the woods, the darker it gets.

Someone's off in the distance, beside a tree.

"John," she whispers.

"Mama?" I walk a little closer and stop. It's not Mama, but I've seen her before. She's dressed in all black. Her red eyes twinkle, and she opens her mouth, showing yellow fangs, as she gets closer and closer to me. I can't move, I can't breathe, and everything goes black. Then someone grabs my shoulders and turns me around.

I wake up, wheezing. I wipe my wet hair away from my eyes. I'm hot.

"Mama!" I try to holler, but I can't get it out. The more I breathe, the more my chest hurts. It feels like someone lit a candle inside me. I scrunch up my nose and rub my chest.

My eyes start seeing better in the dark, and I see something move in the corner of my bedroom.

"Mama?" I wheeze.

It comes closer. My eyes get big when I see it's not Mama. I see its red…red eyes and then a crusty face like a…"Mmmonstter!"

It rushes to me and plops down on my chest.

My mouth opens, and I try to breathe, but it's even harder now. I'm scared.

It picks up my hand and runs a long red fingernail slowly down my arm, sending a tingle to my spine and giving me goosebumps. "You… You are the one who has monster's blood running through your veins," it says with stinky breath.

I shake my head and wheeze again.

"You will pay, Johnny boy. You will pay for what *they* did to me!"

I'm still shaking my head when its thick meaty claws cover my mouth and nose. I try to grab ahold of its wrist to take it off me, but my hand goes right through it.

My eyes get blurry.

I can't see.

I can't breathe.

It lets me go.

"Please," I cry. "I want my mama."

Monster throws its head back and laughs, loud, and it puts its claws around my neck and chokes me with force.

My throat is crushed, and I can't breathe at all. Tears soak my face. *Please,* I mouth before everything turns black.

August 5, 1919

William

"William," I hear the whisper in my ear.

I yawn and rub the crusty sleep away from my eyes with my knuckles as I sit up. "Mama?" I look around, but ain't nobody here.

I crawl out of bed and walk into Mama's room. She's still sleeping, so I nudge her shoulder. "Mama, wake up. I'm thirsty." I shake her harder, but she don't move. I lean down in her face and whisper, "Mama," but she still don't move.

"William," I hear again.

I turn around, but nobody's there. I scratch my head. *Who's calling me?*

I go into the kitchen, pull the stool out from under the sink, and step on it. Then I pick up a glass from the drainer, hold it under the spout, and pump the water until the glass is half full, and then I take a swig.

"William."

I turn my head toward the back door, take another swig, and wipe my mouth with my arm. I put the glass in the sink, hop off the stool, and push it back under the sink before I walk to the back door and peek out the screen at nothing.

"William."

I walk out and hear laughing, so I follow it.

"John?" I scratch my head when I get to the pond. "What are you doin' here?"

"Swimmin', silly," John says before going under the water and standing again.

"I thought you was sleepin' in the dirt." I step closer. "I don't understand."

"I was dirty, and now I'm gettin' clean. Come on in." He splashes.

I shake my head and take a step back. "Mama's sleepin'."

"It's okay, William. I'm here to protect you, like always."

"Who's that?" I point to the person dressed in black behind him.

I can't see who it is, but it looks like a girl.

He doesn't look back at her. "That's just a friend. Come in, William. It feels nice on this hot day. Come play with me," he begs. "I've missed you."

"I've missed you, too." I take a step closer to the water, and then another and another, until my feet are wet. I look at my bare feet at the water's edge. My toes dig into the mud, feeling squishy, and wiggle back out.

"Come on, William, further!" John sounds like he getting mad at me. "Come to me, it ain't deep here. See?" He stands, touching the bottom. The water's at his waist, it's not deep at all. "I brought you somethin'." He pulls his hand out of his pocket and holds out his palm.

"What is it?" I stretch my neck and stand on my tippy toes. My breath catches in my throat.

"Don't you want your marble back?"

I nod and nod and nod while I hold out my hand. "Yes."

He don't move. "Well, come and get it. It's yours."

I look back at the house—I wish Mama was here. I look back at John, who ain't moved.

"It's okay, William. Come on." He still holds out his hand with my marble in it.

Without thinking no more, I walk closer to John until the water is to my chin.

He looks at his friend, and she nods with a smile that scares me. He turns back to me with the same smile. "We shouldn't even be here. We should've never even been born," he says in a mean voice that ain't his, and then I'm pulled under.

I squirm, fighting my way to get back above the water, but something is holding me.

John stares at me above the dirty water, still holding the marble and smiling that scary smile.

I'm holding my breath, but I'm running out of air and my chest burns. *Please, John, please help me!* I can't hold my breath no longer. I open my mouth and take a deep breath in, and then everything turns black.

August 11, 1919

Pierce

I burned that witch's house to the ground. I did it! And I'd do it again to keep my Pearl safe. I can't let nothing happen to her. When Pearl told me Hazel has been cursing our family all summer, that she caused my son's deaths, I was fit to be tied. I'm glad she suffered—she deserved it!

When Pearl was bathing me, I caught a glimpse of Hazel outside the barn, but then she was gone. My mind was playing tricks on me, because she was gone, dead.

Now I'm wandering around in circles in the field, which I've done all night. The sun came up hours ago, but I can't leave the field to check on Pearl. I've tried—but for some reason, I keep ending up right back here, walking in circles.

"John, William, Jacob. John, William, Jacob. John, William, Jacob," I repeat over and over. "John, William, Jacob." I walk in circles over and over again tapping my fingers to my forehead until it hurts. My head feels like it's gonna explode. "John, William, Jacob… Pearl. I can't lose you too, Pearl. Please be safe. John, Wi—"

"Pierce!"

My heart skips a beat. I stop, look up, and smile. "My Pearl, my sweet Pearl. She's come for me." A great sense of calm washes over me. She looks like an angel; she *is* my angel.

Someone—Hazel—comes up behind her. But that can't be, Hazel's dead. But it is her!

My eyes widen and I take a step, but I ram into something. I can't see it. It's invisible.

Hazel grows until she's towering over Pearl with outstretched arms. "You should've never married into this evil *bitch's* bloodline!" Hazel yells from behind her and opens her mouth. Yellow fangs extend from it, almost touching the top of Pearl's head.

She's gonna eat her!

I beat on the invisible wall with my fists. "Pearl!" I scream and bang harder, with all my might, and see Pearl's eyes widen. She grabs her dress skirt in both hands and takes off toward me. I step back and trip over something, falling to the ground. When I look at what I tripped over, my breath catches in my throat and my jaw drops...and my heart stops.

It's me. I'm lying on the ground with my eyes and mouth opened, clutching my chest.

Not breathing.

"No, no, no!" I shake my head and look back at my Pearl rushing toward me, frantically screaming my name.

"I love you," I say as she slowly fades into the darkness.

January 18, 1941

Angela

Mama and Lillian are having a tea party with Dolly and Grace in the backyard, under my favorite tree, and they didn't invite me. Humph. That's not nice!

Someone's with them. I've never seen her before. She's dressed in black, and she looks really old and mean. Her face has a bunch of lines in them, like Mrs. Martha had, but a lot more. And her hair is gray and stringy like the moss from my tree. She scares me, but all she's doing is sitting in a chair and sipping tea.

I try to push open the back door, but it won't open. Mama must've locked it, so I couldn't play with them. I'm sad, and I cry.

The woman in black turns her head toward me. "Why are you crying, Angela?" She smirks.

Mama and Lillian sip their tea without looking at me or the mean woman.

I stick my bottom lip out and cross my arms over my chest. "I want to play. I'm lonely," I grumble.

"You can't play. You're not invited, because your mama doesn't love you anymore. She locked you up in that hospital to get rid of you."

I shake my head. "No, you're wrong, I'm sick. Mama does love me."

She stands and picks up a sharp knife lying on the table. It shines in the sun when she raises it above her head and plunges it into the side of Lillian's neck.

I scream.

Blood sprays out from her neck like a sprinkler and coats the grass around them.

Mama doesn't look at the mean woman or Lillian as she calmly takes another sip of her tea.

The woman removes the knife, and Lillian drops to the ground like a bag of turnips. The woman smiles at me and licks the blade clean before stabbing Mama in the heart without looking at her.

My hands go to the sides of my head. "Mama!" I cry out.

The woman's eyes never leave mine, and she beams the whole time, like she's playing a naughty game. She removes the knife from Mama's chest and throws her on the ground, next to Lillian. A pool of blood forms underneath them both.

"Now it doesn't matter, does it? They're gone, Angela—gone, gone, gone, and you're all alone in this big, bad world."

Still crying, I cover my ears with my hands and close my eyes, shaking my head back and forth, back and forth. "No, they're not. No, they're not."

"Angela," she says with a wicked laugh.

I feel her in front of me. "No, they're not. No, they're not," I continue to chant with my eyes closed, still shaking my head.

"Angela," she says calmly. "I could've had a little girl like you"—she strokes my hair—"with brown hair…and blue eyes."

I stop shaking my head, open my eyes, and slowly look up into her black, devious eyes, with their red slits down the middle. Everything around us is dark. It's just me and her here, wherever here is.

She narrows her eyes, barely showing the red slits. "But he ruined that for me. So you must die like all the rest of them!" she screams in my face.

My eyes widen and I gasp, opening my mouth.

She opens her own, and I see all the air being sucked out of my mouth and into hers.

My eyes pop open and I open my mouth, looking for air.

I can't breathe.

I heave, trying to draw in a breath, but there's no air.

I can't breathe.

I look at the floor and see the tube that was in my side is pulled out and lying on the floor.

I can't breathe. I can't breathe. I clutch my chest as it burns.

I look back up at the ceiling and heave one more time—fighting one last time—for breath before everything turns black.

April 4, 1969

Lillian

I glance at my watch and bite my lip when I hear the front door open and close. *He isn't supposed to be home this early.* I fold the shirt in my hand and put it in Meredith's suitcase.

When I turn around, I jump back and cover my racing heart with my hand. "You scared me."

Robert stands with his hands above the doorframe and a blank expression on his face. He looks over my shoulder at the opened suitcase on Meredith's bed. "Going somewhere?" He lifts a brow. "Where's Meredith?"

"She's with your mom for the night. Robert, we need to talk."

He pushes off the frame and saunters into the room. He touches the clothes folded in the suitcase and glances into her half-empty closet and the opened, empty drawers in her dresser. Without saying a word, he turns and walks past me out the door to our bedroom, with me following close behind him.

"Robert—"

He pauses in the doorway, making me come to an abrupt stop before crashing into him. Then he turns, narrowing his eyes at me and strolls toward the stairs.

I see my suitcases on the bed before I turn and follow him. My hand runs along the smooth, winding banister as I watch the back of his head bounce with every step. "Robert, I want to talk to you."

In the dining room, he takes the crystal whiskey decanter from the liquor cabinet and reaches for a small shot glass. He hesitates over the glass, moves his hand to the right, and grabs a larger crystal tumbler. "About what, Lil?" he asks, his voice hard, and he walks past me again and back up the stairs, quicker than he came down.

"About us," I say, chasing after him.

When I get to the bedroom, he's already sitting on the bed. His suit jacket lies beside him, and he's shrugging off his tie gallingly. He tosses it on top of his jacket and reaches for the whiskey.

My suitcase is pushed back, almost hanging off the other side of the bed. I tighten my lips and cross my arms over my chest. "Robert, I want a divorce."

He closes his eyes for a brief moment before taking the top of the decanter off and pouring a large glass of whiskey. He takes a swig, grimaces, and sucks air through his teeth. "I've had one hell of a day." His elbows drop to his knees, and he hangs his head as he stares at the crystal in his hand. "I lost a little girl on the operating table," he says, sounding defeated, and swirls the amber liquid in the glass. "So, today is not a good day for nonsense."

"I'm sorry, Robert. I'm sorry you've had a bad day, I really am, but this has been a long time coming."

He runs his empty hand through his hair and looks at me with tired eyes. "I know I've been working a lot. You need more attention, I know. I've been thinking about cutting back on my hours."

"No, that's not it, Robert." I look up at the ceiling and blow a breath out before I look back at his supplicating eyes. "I just want out." My eyes drop to the dark-brown shag carpet. "I don't love you anymore," I whisper.

He slams the glass on the nightstand, shattering it.

I jump.

He quickly stands and grabs my arms. "I'm sorry, Lil," he says sincerely and rubs his thumbs on my arms. "Listen, we can work through this. We can do some counseling or—"

"I…I've had an affair," I stammer.

He freezes and his face pales. I take a step back, out of his grip, and find the necklace Xavier gave me this morning hidden under my shirt. I rub it between two fingers and Robert's eyes land on it, as if mesmerized by it. After a few seconds, he shakes his head and his intense eyes blaze into mine.

"I didn't mean for it to happen."

"Who is it?" he asks in a calm voice, but his neck veins throb.

I shake my head. "It doesn't matter. I want out of this marriage."

He glances over his shoulder and hustles to the bed, picks up my purse and dumps the contents on the bed.

My diary falls out.

My eyes widen. "Robert! No!" I rush to him, but he throws an arm out, making me crash into it.

He picks up the diary. "Did you write about him?" He turns to me with glossy eyes. "Do you love him?" He blinks and a tear falls down his cheek.

My lips quiver when I look at his forlorn face and my hand goes around the X on my neck, clutching it tightly.

His eyes drop once again to my hand. He drops the diary on the bed and slowly closes the distance between us, not blinking, not moving his head, as if in a daze, and reaches for my necklace.

I reluctantly let go.

He snatches it off my neck and tosses it behind him, and I watch it land behind the nightstand.

My nostrils flare and my breathing becomes erratic. Robert has his back to me now and is digging around in his nightstand drawer. When he turns back around, his eyes are as black as coal, and they have red slits in the center of them.

I gasp and my mouth gapes as I look into his monstrous eyes. Then the gun comes into view when he slowly raises it to my forehead with a steady hand. All the blood rushes from my body. I've never been so petrified. I shake, and my eyes swell with tears. "Robert, please don't do this." I hold my hands up in surrender. "You don't want to do this."

His lips curl in disgust. "You're a *whore*," he says, in an unrecognizable raspy and malevolent voice that's not his own. "You're just like *them*."

I can feel the bite of the cold metal when he presses the barrel harder into my forehead. "Wh-who?" Tears spill from my eyes, running my mascara and burning my eyes.

"They took everything"—he jabs the gun—"I've ever loved away from me!" he yells, spitting in my face.

My heart pummels my chest. "P-please! I'm sorry!" I tremble and shake my head. "I don't…I don't want to die."

Robert's pupils dilate, and the red glows. "They didn't either," he whispers deeply, scowling.

A loud *pop* is the last thing I hear before everything turns to darkness.

June 22, 2001

Meredith

"Why did we have to leave Nana in such a hurry?" Sara takes a bite of her shrimp and grits.

I tip my head back and drink the last of my Chardonnay, savoring the refreshing acidity, and hold up the empty glass to the waiter. I lick my lips and smile at Sara, who is staring at me with a raised brow. "What?" I say, lifting my shoulders.

"*Why* did we have to leave Nana in such a hurry today?" she repeats.

"Oh, baby, she's senile. Those stories aren't real." I smirk. "People her age like to make up things to scare little girls. Don't believe a word she says."

"I like her. She's nice."

I roll my eyes and take the full glass of wine from the waiter.

"Anything else?" he asks.

I raise my glass to him. "No, I'm good." I smile before breathing in the apple-and-pear aroma and taking a sip.

"Yes, ma'am." He nods and leaves.

"Can we go back?" Sara asks.

"No, baby," I say firmly before I take another sip.

"Why not? I liked her story, and I want to hear the rest."

I cock my head to the side and narrow my eyes. "That story didn't scare you?"

"No. I liked it, and I liked her. I want to go back and see her."

I let out an exasperated sigh. "No," I repeat. "Check, please." I wave at the waiter while I dig through my purse and pull the credit card out.

"But you haven't even touched your food," Sara says.

"Not hungry."

"Will there be anything else? Dessert? A to-go box?" the waiter asks, eyeing the untouched plate of Chicken Oscar in front of me. "Was something wrong with your meal?"

"Nope. Everything was great." I salute him with my wine. "Just the check."

"Yes, ma'am." He lays the black folder on the table. "I'll take it when you're ready." He turns and takes a step.

"I'm readyyy." I slip the gold card in the clear plastic slot inside without looking at the bill and hand it back to him.

"Yes, ma'am." He takes the folder and ambles away.

"Please. I want to hear the rest of her story," Sara says.

"I don't want to talk about this any further." I point to her plate. "Finish your dinner so we can go."

She crosses her arms over her chest and slouches back in her chair with a *humph* in defiance.

"Fine, have it your way, but we're not going back." I drink the rest of my wine when I see the waiter sauntering back toward our table.

"Take your time and have a great evening," the waiter says as he places the black folder back in front of me.

"Thank you, I intend to." I sign the receipt and abruptly stand, bumping the poor boy and almost knocking him down. "Oh, I'm sorry." I reach out to grab him but he steps back, bows, and staggers away. "Okay, then," I mumble to myself and grab my purse, throw the card in, and sling it over my shoulder. "I need to use the restroom. Stay here, I'll be right back," I say to Sara and march down the narrow hall.

When I get inside the restroom, I lock the door, make my way to the sink, and throw my purse on the counter. "What a day." I look at myself in the mirror. "Time for a little pick-me-up, Meredith, you deserve it," I say to myself and dig through my purse until I find the little vial of heaven. I hold it up and grin before I carefully unscrew the lid like it's the shiniest, most fragile Christmas present under the tree, and dip my pinky fingernail inside. When I fish out a small amount of powder, I hold it under my nostril and sniff. It burns, so I quickly buff the stinging from my nose and wipe underneath. I close my eyes and take a deep breath, already relaxing and feeling better, much better.

When I open my eyes and lift my chin to look in the mirror, my face blurs, so I grab a paper towel from the holder and wipe the mirror. When it clears, I gasp and recoil, dropping the towel in the sink. Deep wrinkles line my face. My gray, stringy hair is clumped on top of my head. And my eyes...my eyes are black and cut with red down the center.

I hold the vial in front of my face, gawking at it for a moment, before shaking my head and tossing it back in my purse. I rub my tired eyes and look back in the mirror, but the reflection hasn't changed. I'm still hideous with those inhuman eyes. Without taking my eyes away from the mirror or blinking, I grip the X-shaped knob on the faucet and turn it, freeing the water. The cuts in my eyes expand, making them glow red.

My cracked lips twist. "You think you're something, don't you?" I say in a deep, venomous voice I don't recognize while I gaze at myself. "Getting drunk on that devil's water, just like them. It's no wonder—you've got his blood, that monster's blood. But not for long. You're the last...you, that little girl of yours, and..." I smile, showing tawny, rotten crooked teeth.

Bang. Bang. Bang. "Ma'am, are you all right in there?"

I shake my head and blink back tears from a stare.

Bang. Bang. Bang. "Ma'am?"

"I'm coming," I say, irritation in my voice, as I turn off the water and shove my purse under my arm. I take one more look in the mirror, running a finger along my smooth skin and a hand down my shiny brown locks, before I walk out the door and past the questioning eyes of both Sara and the waiter.

"Come on, let's go," I say to Sara, not waiting to see if she's following.

Sara stomps to the car with her arms crossed over her chest and pouting lips.

"Stop sulking, Sara. She's old anyway, she'll probably die soon." I start the engine when she closes her door.

She narrows her eyes. "That's mean."

"It's true." I buckle my seatbelt. "Seatbelt," I tell her and watch her pull the belt over her chest and lock it into place without a word. "Good girl. Now, let's go home. It's been a long, crazy day, and I'm tired," I say and pull out of the parking lot onto the two-lane road.

June 22, 2001

Sara

Silence fills the air.

Neither of us speaks for a good ten minutes until we approach the railroad tracks, and I notice the X railroad crossing sign as the flashing red lights appear.

The car inches forward and I turn to mom. "Mom, what are you doing?"

The car passes the sign and thumps when the tires cross over the railroad ties, and it stops.

"We are the last," she says slowly, staring straight ahead as if she were in a trance.

"Mom?" My mouth hangs open.

She pushes the gear shift up, putting us in park, and turns the key, shutting off the engine.

The muffled rumbling of the shunting train gets louder and louder.

"Mom, go," I say, my voice raising and cracking.

"It's time to end this," she says calmly, staring straight ahead. "Their deaths are almost avenged."

Wooo-wooo!

"What? Who?" My breathing increases. I press the release button on the seatbelt, but it won't unlock. I look out my window at the big round light coming toward us…fast. My heart beats faster and faster as the train gets closer and closer. I tremble, and I frantically push the button over and over again.

"Sara."

I look into her glowing red eyes and gasp.

"One more." She grins.

Wooooo-wooooo!

The train's brakes screech, and the wind howls.

My head whips toward the window, and my eyes bulge. I scream.

Boom. Crunch.

Darkness.

June 23, 2001

12:00 a.m.

Pearl

Beautiful flowers surround me as I stand in the middle of a field. I look up and twirl around and around while dandelions fall from the bright blue sky, covering the ground. I'm so happy, so peaceful. Off in the distance, children run toward me at full speed. Jacob, John, William, Angela, Lillian, Meredith, and Sara are all sprinting toward me with their arms outstretched. I fall to my knees, throw my arms out wide, and engulf each one of them.

"We missed you," they all say.

I kiss them all, one by one. "Oh, babies, I've missed you, every one of you."

"Save a kiss for me," a deep voice I haven't heard in years comes from behind me.

I quickly get to my feet and turn around. My Pierce is standing with his hands in the pockets of his khakis, his white dress shirt rolled up at the elbows, and a big grin stretched across his face. Wow—he's more handsome than I remember.

I leap into his arms, making him grab ahold of my waist, and we fall to the ground. He laughs. It's one of the things I've missed hearing the most. I grab his head with both hands, and I give his face a hundred kisses.

"I've. Missed. You. So. Much," I say between kisses, tears clouding my vision.

"And I've missed you. I love you, Pearl. Always have."

I smile joyously through the tears. "I love you too. I've never stopped."

All the kids gather around us. This feels good—this is home.

"Welcome home, Pearl," Pierce says as he rolls me over onto my back and gives me a long, passionate kiss.

"Pearl."

I don't open my eyes before grumbling, "Go away, I'm sleeping."

"Pearl," says the deep and unnerving voice.

A chill sweeps over me, and I shiver. I clutch my family's possessions closer and tighter. My eyes flicker open, and I turn my head. The clock sitting on my bedside table flashes *12:00*, and there's a slight movement in the corner.

"Who's there?" I croak with a sleepy voice and lift my head.

"Oh, you know good and well who it is." The voice comes closer.

The taste of death in my mouth produces the biggest smile I've had in years.

"Why are you smiling? Aren't you afraid?" She sounds surprised.

"I'm not afraid of you. I've never been afraid of you." I laugh with a cough, covering my mouth with my hand when phlegm comes up, but I'm able to swallow it back down with a grimace.

"You're lying," she says and her eyes turn red. "Aren't you curious why I'm here, Pearl, after all these years?"

"Oh, no. I know why you're here." I lie back and close my eyes. *I've suffered long enough.* "It's my time." I smile again.

The mattress dents beside me, and my nose scrunches at the strong flesh-burning odor lingering around her.

"And you're happy about that?"

I open my eyes and meet her stare, the red glow is gone. "If my time is up, it means my blood runs through no other. Am I right?"

"Yes." She nods with a wicked smile, showing brown stained teeth I remember all too well. She looks different than the last time I saw her, but the evil in her eyes is still there. Her gray hair isn't in its usual neat bun, but is past her shoulders in a chaotic mess. The dry, crusty wrinkles on her face have taken over and won. She looks older and scarier and meaner than ever.

A frown drenches my face, and I pray Meredith's and Sara's death was quick and painless. "Well, I'm not happy Meredith and that sweet daughter of hers is gone, but it was their fate from the start, wasn't it? Like all the others who came before and after I crossed the X."

She nods again.

"But I am happy I'll finally get to see Pierce, my children, and the rest of my family. I've waited a long time. I'm ready for this to end."

"Oh, really?" she asks, her voice rising. "Maybe I should let you live a little longer."

Oh, God, no. My heart beats faster. "Are Meredith and Sara really gone?"

"They are," she says nonchalantly.

"Then it's my time—it's what you said." I'm begging her to end this, and I'm not proud of it.

"True, true. Do you want to know what happened to them?"

"No, it doesn't matter. But you were behind it all, weren't you?" I ask with fire in my eyes, and on my tongue.

She throws her head back and laughs with the most malicious laugh I've ever heard. I reach up to cover my ears, but the laughter stops, silencing the room. "Every last thing, yes. I was behind it all," she says as her grin reaches her eyes.

"How?"

"Ah, your husband, your *handsome* husband, had great intuition, you know. He told you I was a witch, and he was right. But this was not the life I chose." Her eyelids droop and the corners of her mouth fall. Her face turns from evil to a terrible grief right before my eyes. "I was married and happy one time, like you were, and living in Charleston." She looks off into the distance, like she's watching the scene play out in front of her. "We had a little boy, Jeremiah, and another child on the way when the Civil War broke out. Some drunken Yankee soldiers stumbled into our house in the middle of the night looking for more of that devil's water." Her cracked lip curls up in distaste. "When they couldn't find any, they took Jeremiah from my arms and slit his throat." She slides her finger across her neck. "We couldn't stop them. I tried to look away, but they held us down and made us witness the slaughter of our precious boy.

"One of the soldiers slipped his finger inside Jeremiah's throat, taking his time rooting around, and then bringing it back out, drenched in blood. He held it up and watched as the blood dripped down his blue sleeve before he kneeled and marked an X on the floor with the blood. 'Put him here boys, so he'll have a good view,' he said. I can still hear him and his blue-belly friends laugh. Every day I hear the vicious laughter, as if it were ingrained inside my ear.

"Another soldier threw my husband on the X, made him kneel, and held a knife to his throat. Blood trickled from my husband's neck as the knife pierced his skin. He made my husband watch while the others took turns raping me and beating me, and then they left me for dead. I thought I was, too. When I woke, my husband's badly beaten body was unrecognizable. His head was barely attached to his body, hanging unnaturally." She shakes her head. "There was so much blood—too much. The only color other than red was the whites of my husband's vacant eyes staring at me."

She looks at her wrinkled hands and frowns while she scratches the red nail, but the red doesn't come off. "I was weak, on my deathbed, a death which I welcomed. A woman, Anne, was tending to me. I had already lost the baby by then—so much blood, blood everywhere. She gave me a drink, a potion, healing me, but it changed me. It turned me into this...*thing*." She bares her teeth. "She took the blood from the X on the floor and wiped it on my fingernail. 'This is how you'll find him,' she told me. I didn't understand at the time. I tried to scrape it off with no luck, even pulled my nail off once, but it grew back red. It reminded me every day of what those men did to me. I didn't age anymore after that day. You see, I was cursed, too. My heart was broken and with each passing day, I became maddened with anger until nothing but hatred filled my heart. I wanted to die— but more importantly, I wanted revenge."

Her gaze snaps back to me. "By the time I was well enough to seek it, those Yankee bastards were gone." She turns and spits on the floor. "I left Charleston"—she slowly turns her head, cutting me with the red slits in her black eyes—"and something beckoned me to Walterboro. The moment you crossed my X, I *sensed* it."

My heartbeat quickens. "Sensed what?"

"*Him*." She grins. "The one who killed my little boy and drew that X. I could finally get my revenge."

I shake my head. "What? I don't understand."

She purses her lips. "Think, you stupid, stupid girl. Where did you come from?"

I look at Pierce's flannel shirt clutched in my hand and remember the first day I saw him wearing it, the day of the auction. The same day, Daddy told me about his mama, and it comes to me like a bolt of lightning. I gasp and look back at the evil woman grinning at me.

"Your *daddy* had the blood of *that* man running through him."

"No, that's impossible," I whisper, but I'm only trying to convince myself, because deep down, I know it's true. My grandmother was raped when she was fourteen by some Yankees…the *same* Yankees. Daddy was the result. I have one of those awful men's blood in me! I blink frantically, holding back the tears. I cover my mouth with my hand when it fills with saliva. I swallow quickly, taking in a few deep breaths.

"Doing so many spells and getting inside your dreams in such a short amount of time was taking a toll on my body. I know you noticed my aging appearance."

I look back at her with narrow eyes. "You could've just killed yourself if you wanted to die," I hiss, the fire back in my voice.

"It's not that simple. Witches can't take their own lives, it's impossible. I've tried many times. Believe me, I tried." She pauses. "No, only doing black magic saps a witch's essences. That's the only way to grow old and die. It slowly snuffs out our light until it's finally gone." She blows on the tips of her fingers like she's snuffing out her light, or maybe she's snuffing out mine.

"I was aging fast. If your *handsome* husband wouldn't have burned me alive in my house, I would've died gracefully of old age within a matter of days and your curse would've been lifted. But since he took matters into his own hands, he helped seal your fate along with the rest of your bloodline."

"I shouldn't have told him," I say through gritted teeth.

"You *didn't* have a choice."

"What do you mean?"

She picks up my necklace, studying my ring. "You were a good wife, wanting to tell him about me all those times, but you couldn't…and then you could," she says and drops the ring back onto my chest with a smirk.

I look away. "You put a spell on me," I say, comprehending, and tighten my lips before looking at her again. "Did you have anything to do with Angela's rape?"

A sly grin approaches her cheeks. "Well, that simple-minded girl needed to produce a child, and it sure didn't look like she was gonna do it by herself."

"Who was it?"

She looks up at the ceiling and taps her chin with her red fingernail. "That man next door, what was his name?"

My eyes widen. "Jack? Jack hurt my baby?"

"No...no. The other one. The boy's father. The lawyer."

"Josh's dad? David Hall?" I ask.

"Yes, that was him. He was a sly one, wasn't he?"

The heat rises under my saggy skin, and I see red. "You are still the more evil one," I spit. "You did more damage than good. At least we got Lillian out of David's sins."

She looks at me with one brow up. "Is there anything else you want to know?"

"What will happen to you?"

"Never you mind about me. I may be around, but you won't. A promise is a promise. Your bloodline is no more, so neither are you. Are you ready?"

"Yes. I've been ready."

"Then say goodbye, Pearl."

She grabs my necklace and twists it so it's choking me, cutting off the air I breathe. The red twinkles in her eyes get brighter and brighter while her demonic smile, showing her ochre, corroded teeth, gets bigger and bigger.

Instead of panicking, I welcome death. So, I lie back, close my eyes, and smile. "Goodbye, Hazel. I hope you rot in Hell," I say as I take my last breath.

Acknowledgements

I would like to thank the people who without their contributions and support, this book would not have been written.

My editor, Jake Logsdon, for helping me make this a better book.

Emily Eric for designing my book cover and for being so patient with me.

Martha Hayes for your invaluable assistance. You were never too busy to answer the numerous questions I threw at you.

My readers, Sherri Golos, Angela Dial, Matthew Scura, Julie Winn, Brett Ballard, and Iaan Wiltshire for your time and comments.

Doris McMillan and Sheron Smith for the stories about our family and believing in this book from the start.

And finally, the four extraordinary people who are my heart. Erik, Tyler, Lindsey, and Michael for your love and support.